GHOSTLY
GAME

TITLES BY CHRISTINE FEEHAN

THE GHOSTWALKER NOVELS

GHOSTLY GAME	SPIDER GAME	DEADLY GAME
PHANTOM GAME	VIPER GAME	CONSPIRACY GAME
LIGHTNING GAME	SAMURAI GAME	NIGHT GAME
LETHAL GAME	RUTHLESS GAME	MIND GAME
TOXIC GAME	STREET GAME	SHADOW GAME
COVERT GAME	MURDER GAME	
POWER GAME	PREDATORY GAME	

THE DRAKE SISTERS NOVELS

HIDDEN CURRENTS	SAFE HARBOR	OCEANS OF FIRE
TURBULENT SEA	DANGEROUS TIDES	

THE LEOPARD NOVELS

LEOPARD'S SCAR	LEOPARD'S FURY	WILD FIRE
LEOPARD'S RAGE	WILD CAT	BURNING WILD
LEOPARD'S WRATH	CAT'S LAIR	WILD RAIN
LEOPARD'S RUN	LEOPARD'S PREY	
LEOPARD'S BLOOD	SAVAGE NATURE	

THE SEA HAVEN/SISTERS OF THE HEART NOVELS

BOUND TOGETHER	EARTH BOUND	SPIRIT BOUND
FIRE BOUND	AIR BOUND	WATER BOUND

THE SHADOW RIDERS NOVELS

SHADOW FIRE	SHADOW WARRIOR	SHADOW RIDER
SHADOW STORM	SHADOW KEEPER	
SHADOW FLIGHT	SHADOW REAPER	

THE TORPEDO INK NOVELS

RECOVERY ROAD

SAVAGE ROAD

ANNIHILATION ROAD

RECKLESS ROAD

DESOLATION ROAD

VENDETTA ROAD

VENGEANCE ROAD

JUDGMENT ROAD

THE CARPATHIAN NOVELS

DARK WHISPER	DARK LYCAN	DARK DESTINY
DARK TAROT	DARK STORM	DARK MELODY
DARK SONG	DARK PREDATOR	DARK SYMPHONY
DARK ILLUSION	DARK PERIL	DARK GUARDIAN
DARK SENTINEL	DARK SLAYER	DARK LEGEND
DARK LEGACY	DARK CURSE	DARK FIRE
DARK CAROUSEL	DARK HUNGER	DARK CHALLENGE
DARK PROMISES	DARK POSSESSION	DARK MAGIC
DARK GHOST	DARK CELEBRATION	DARK GOLD
DARK BLOOD	DARK DEMON	DARK DESIRE
DARK WOLF	DARK SECRET	DARK PRINCE

ANTHOLOGIES

EDGE OF DARKNESS
(with Maggie Shayne and Lori Herter)

DARKEST AT DAWN
(includes Dark Hunger *and* Dark Secret*)*

SEA STORM
(includes Magic in the Wind *and* Oceans of Fire*)*

FEVER
(includes The Awakening *and* Wild Rain*)*

FANTASY
(with Emma Holly, Sabrina Jeffries, and Elda Minger)

LOVER BEWARE
(with Fiona Brand, Katherine Sutcliffe, and Eileen Wilks)

HOT BLOODED
(with Maggie Shayne, Emma Holly, and Angela Knight)

SPECIALS

DARK CRIME
THE AWAKENING
DARK HUNGER
MAGIC IN THE WIND

RED ON THE RIVER
MURDER AT SUNRISE LAKE

GHOSTLY GAME

CHRISTINE FEEHAN

BERKLEY
NEW YORK

BERKLEY
An imprint of Penguin Random House LLC
penguinrandomhouse.com

Copyright © 2023 by Christine Feehan
Penguin Random House supports copyright. Copyright fuels creativity, encourages diverse
voices, promotes free speech, and creates a vibrant culture. Thank you for buying an authorized
edition of this book and for complying with copyright laws by not reproducing, scanning, or
distributing any part of it in any form without permission. You are supporting writers and
allowing Penguin Random House to continue to publish books for every reader.

BERKLEY and the BERKLEY & B colophon are registered trademarks of
Penguin Random House LLC.

Library of Congress Cataloging-in-Publication Data

Names: Feehan, Christine, author.
Title: Ghostly game / Christine Feehan.
Description: New York : Berkley, [2023] | Series: A Ghostwalker Novel
Identifiers: LCCN 2022049271 (print) | LCCN 2022049272 (ebook) |
ISBN 9780593638682 (hardcover) | ISBN 9780593638699 (ebook)
Classification: LCC PS3606.E36 G56 2023 (print) |
LCC PS3606.E36 (ebook) | DDC 813/.6—dc23
LC record available at https://lccn.loc.gov/2022049271
LC ebook record available at https://lccn.loc.gov/2022049272

Printed in the United States of America
1   3   5   7   9   10   8   6   4   2

Book design by Kelly Lipovich

For Joel Diehl.
Thank you for being such a wonderful friend.

FOR MY READERS

Be sure to go to ChristineFeehan.com/members/ to sign up for my private book announcement list and download the free ebook of *Dark Desserts*. Join my community and get firsthand news, enter the book discussions, ask your questions and chat with me. Please feel free to email me at Christine@ChristineFeehan.com. I would love to hear from you.

ACKNOWLEDGMENTS

Thank you to Susan Barnes and Diane Trudeau; I would never have been able to write this book under such circumstances without you. Sheila English, for the research needed so quickly. Thank you, Clint, for providing me with information I needed to ensure I was getting the detective details correct. Any mistakes are definitely mine. Brian Feehan, for making certain he was there every day to set up the pages I needed to write in order to hit the deadline. Karen Rose, for always being there when I needed a sounding board. Denise, for handling all the details of every aspect of my life that was so crazy. Thank you all so very much!

THE GHOSTWALKER
SYMBOL DETAILS

SIGNIFIES

shadow

SIGNIFIES

protection against evil forces

SIGNIFIES

the Greek letter psi, which is used by parapsychology researchers to signify ESP or other psychic abilities

SIGNIFIES

qualities of a knight—loyalty, generosity, courage and honor

SIGNIFIES

shadow knights who protect against evil forces using psychic powers, courage and honor

nox noctis est nostri

THE GHOSTWALKER CREED

We are the GhostWalkers, we live in the shadows
The sea, the earth, and the air are our domain
No fallen comrade will be left behind
We are loyalty and honor bound
We are invisible to our enemies
and we destroy them where we find them
We believe in justice and we protect our country
and those unable to protect themselves
What goes unseen, unheard and unknown are GhostWalkers
There is honor in the shadows and it is us
We move in complete silence whether in jungle or desert
We walk among our enemy unseen and unheard
Striking without sound and scatter to the winds
before they have knowledge of our existence
We gather information and wait with endless patience
for that perfect moment to deliver swift justice
We are both merciful and merciless
We are relentless and implacable in our resolve
We are the GhostWalkers and the night is ours

GHOSTLY
GAME

1

Sometimes things just go south, and there isn't a damn thing you can do about it." Gideon "Eagle" Carpenter eased his body back slowly until he was entirely supine, linked his fingers behind his head and stared up at the stars.

This was San Francisco. Viewing stars wasn't always easy because fog liked to creep in at night, at least where he was located. He was on the roof of the four-story, wedge-shaped original warehouse made of red bricks that rose like a monstrosity to stand out among all the cool newer concrete and steel warehouses surrounding it. Considering that the building was the only one on the street to survive the 1906 earthquake and fires and was still standing, despite the city condemning it and threatening to demolish it several times, Gideon thought that what others considered an eyesore was worth saving. So he'd saved it. Mostly for this—the rooftop. He'd used every penny of his share of the money and then some to see to it that the best of the best ensured the old building would withstand anything thrown at it for the next hundred years.

"Yeah, Gideon," he repeated aloud. "Shit happens. You roll with it. You don't let it get to you. You come here, high in the sky, and you get rid of it."

Because shit did happen in his life far too often. It had been happening since the day he was born, and he was damn sure it would continue to do so until the day he died. He'd created the mantra, found the highest place possible wherever he was, repeated that shit over and over until he made himself let the clouds take it all away. They had to take it away. Sometimes, like tonight, when his churning gut was in knots and the devil was riding him hard, he had to call on the universe to shoulder his shit.

A whisper of movement had him dropping his hands slowly to his sides, the fingers on one hand wrapping around the butt of one of his favorite weapons. He could shoot the wings off a fly in the dead of night if he had to. His other hand settled around the hilt of his knife. Up close and personal wasn't necessarily his first choice, but he had skills, and when push came to shove, he could use them. Few knew the code to open the hidden stairs to the rooftop, but he wasn't taking any chances. He was a careful man. That had been ingrained in him, long before he'd taken to living on the streets and a ragtag family of sorts had been formed by several throwaway kids—of which he'd been one.

He waited in silence, air moving evenly through his lungs. The trapdoor opened carefully. No one emerged.

"Gideon? You going to take my head off?"

The voice was soft, with the merest hint of an accent even those with great hearing couldn't detect. Javier Enderman. One of his brothers from the street. Family. One of his brothers from the service. One he'd live and die for. Gideon hadn't expected him, but he should have.

"I'm considering it. I'd have to get up to do it, and I'm not liking the idea of moving, so I think you're safe enough."

Javier pushed the trapdoor open all the way and climbed onto the roof. He was all muscle, but with his lithe build, it was impossible to tell. He looked young; impossible to guess his age. In their business, it was a decided advantage. Thick black hair fell onto his forehead, spilled over his ears and curled around the back of his neck. He had black, black eyes that appeared to look right through a man to uncover every secret. Once he stepped into a shadow, it was nearly impossible to find him if he didn't want to be found. Gideon considered him the most dangerous member of their team.

Javier barely made a whisper of sound as he crossed the roof to take a seat a few feet from Gideon. He added energy drinks to the cooler and three Ziploc bags of what appeared to be fresh spinach chips to the lock box that was never locked beside Gideon.

Gideon raised an eyebrow. "Where the hell did you get those?" There was reverence in his voice—awe, even—because fresh spinach chips, the real deal out of the oven, deserved awe.

"Swiped them. Stole them. Lifted them. It was a sweet little heist too. Right out from under Rose's nose. In her kitchen. Know how much you love them, and I've got to keep my skills sharp, so we both win."

"Rose will cut you into little pieces if she catches you stealing her spinach chips. They take forever to make," Gideon said.

Javier shrugged. "You want me to take them back, I'll do it."

"Hell no." Gideon burst out laughing. "She's not going to kill me; she'll go after you. And then there's Kane. You lift a finger to defend yourself when his cute little lethal wife, Rose, is cutting off your balls, Kane will beat you to a bloody pulp."

Kane had been one of the original street kids, one of those idiotic enough—as all of them were—to follow Mack McKinley into the service and then into specialized training and straight to the classified psychic GhostWalker program.

"Fortunately, she won't find out," Javier said. "You're perfectly safe with your spinach chips. Eat them in peace. I had a little help. Her son happened to start fussing, distracting her when she was putting all her fresh chips in the Ziploc bags. There were so many all over the counter she couldn't possibly know three bags went missing. Even if she counted them, the piles had fallen over." He flashed another grin at Gideon. "No one makes that many fresh chips all at the same time. Kane is addicted just the way you are. She spoils him."

That little grin Javier gave him made him wonder about Rose's son suddenly getting fussy. Kids liked Javier. All of them. Rose and Kane's son, Sebastian, was all kinds of talented. He might be a baby, but he was already exhibiting signs of psychic gifts. It wouldn't surprise Gideon if Javier had a way of communicating with the little ones recently born to various GhostWalkers. He didn't ask.

Silence fell. Gideon liked silence. What he didn't like was the reason Javier was there and what was coming next, but he couldn't think of a way to stop it, so he just remained still.

Javier shoved both hands through his hair. "Hate that you took a slew of bullets that were mine, brother."

"They were anyone's. I was just in the way."

Both knew that wasn't the truth. Javier had been out of his mind. They had all been. Gideon had been. They hadn't been prepared for what they'd seen. Innocent women and children, civilians who should have been safe in their homes. Going to school. To work. Just living their everyday lives. Mowed down. Raped. Murdered. Hacked to pieces. Dead bodies lying in the streets, like so much garbage. Left as bait for any soldiers to find, mines under their bodies.

It wasn't as if they weren't experienced and hadn't seen the worst. They were urban fighters. Good at what they did. Ghosts sent in to retrieve prisoners, slipping in unseen and getting out without anyone ever spotting them. Right in the middle of a city. Right in the middle of the enemy's home. They'd seen it all, been through it. Been taken prisoner. Tortured. They'd been shot. More than once, the plane they were in had been shot down. They were experienced, but this—seeing infants and children and women, innocents in schools and homes—this was too much for all of them.

Javier had lost it. They all had, but Javier had lost his mind. He was entitled. The sight was a trigger from his childhood buried deep, but his reaction had endangered the entire team. Gideon had taken out six of the enemy to keep them from killing Javier. But Javier hadn't stood down. He had charged with no cover, no backup, right into the heart of the enemy. Gideon, looking through his scope into Javier's eyes, had been able to see he was gone—no longer thinking. He'd shut down completely. Gideon calmly took out two more who would have killed his brother, and then he made the decision to go after Javier, protecting him the way he always had.

Gideon didn't want those memories brought here, not to his rooftop. Not when they were still burned behind his eyes. The smell in his nostrils. Even the coppery taste of blood lingered in his mouth. The pain of bullets tearing into his flesh and through his insides was far too fresh. Those memories were already too close. He hadn't had the chance to put them away.

"Wasn't the bullets, Gideon. I was out of my mind. Just like when I was a kid. You came for me." Javier dropped his head into his hands and rubbed at his temples. "You fuckin' came for me again."

Gideon regarded him in silence for a long while, letting the breeze from the ocean cool the stench of vile gore from his mind. This rooftop was his sanctuary, his one place of peace—his *only* peace—and it was so fleeting. He wanted that same peace for Javier, but he knew Javier had yet to find his path.

Gideon sighed. "Javier."

Javier shook his head and then looked directly at Gideon with his black, fathomless eyes, two dark pits of relentless agony. "Am I a psychopath? Tell me the fucking truth, brother. Should I put a bullet in my head? You've pulled me back more than once. What if you couldn't get me back? What if I just stayed in that state? I would have killed everyone. All of them. Every single fucking one of them."

"Don't you think every single one of us would have killed them, Javier? You weren't feeling anything different than the rest of us. Those intense emotions were triggered by the needless slaughter of infants, of children, of young and old women. What we saw was so wrong, and we weren't prepared. We walked blindly into that nightmare without considering it would be there. Our minds weren't in the right frame to accept it. You weren't the only one struggling to keep it together and not take out the entire unit of . . ." He broke off for a moment, searching for a word to describe who would do such a thing.

"They aren't soldiers. They aren't even mercenaries. *Butchers.* Something is wrong with them." Gideon tried not to see the images of the babies and toddlers strewn in the streets and playgrounds— *hacked* to pieces. Not shot, *hacked.* What kind of men did that? "Mack says we'll find them. If he says that, you know we will. We'll do it right, brother. As for you being a psychopath, Whitney put that shit in your head. He's the fucking psychopath, not you. We volunteered to have our psychic abilities enhanced in order to better serve our country. Dr. Peter Whitney thought he was a god. Hell, he still thinks it."

Gideon breathed deep to push other images crowding in away. "Javier, think about it with a clear head. You were reacting to what you saw. What we all saw. You weren't the one chopping up children. You would never do such a thing for any reason. And before you object and talk to me about children with guns and bombs, I'll remind you there's a difference between saving the life of a brother with a single well-placed bullet and chopping up a child for some kind of sick amusement."

Gideon prayed there was. He had so many real sins on his soul. Too many. Javier was his brother from the streets and from his unit. "Don't let Whitney do that to you. He fucked us up by giving us animal and reptile DNA, or whatever the hell he decided he wanted to play around with. We were already jacked up enough and didn't need his added aggressive DNA, but we had no say in that. Worse, he didn't tell us. He just let us discover what he'd done. We're still discovering it."

Gideon felt the burn of Javier's black eyes. They could appear like two dark holes in that handsome face. Flames could flicker there. Right now, there was intensity as only Javier could give him. Sometimes Javier looked at him as if Gideon were leading the way to water after being lost in the desert for a long, long time. Gideon wanted to tell him he was no hero. He sure as hell wasn't the man to look up to. He was lost himself.

"I tell Whitney to go fuck himself every day, Javier. He isn't going to win. Not ever. He isn't going to know one thing about any gifts or curses I have. He won't ever take a child from one of the women we protect here in our compound. He isn't going to prevent me from living whatever kind of life I choose to live. I choose to serve my country because that's my choice. When Mack decides he's had enough, I'll most likely bow out as well. We've always stood together. We're family. We always will be. Stop thinking you're on the outside looking in. Here's a little news flash for you, brother. Every single one of us feels that way. Whitney made sure of that. For all that, knowing that, I refuse to allow him to take my family from me."

Gideon didn't like talking. He never had. But this was Javier, and Javier was important, and he was one fucked-up brother. He needed help. He wouldn't go to Mack because he was afraid Mack would decide to force him to stop working with their team. It was Gideon or no one. Gideon didn't want Javier eating a bullet. Just the fact that he'd mentioned the idea made Gideon very aware that Javier had contemplated it. So that meant talking until Javier could get off his rooftop before discovering that Gideon was in worse mental shape than he was.

"You with me on this, brother? Because I need you to be. I need you to know Whitney's the psychopath and you're just fucked up like the rest of us."

Javier held his eyes for a long time. Gideon didn't so much as blink. He had eagle in him. Harpy Eagle. He could hold that gaze until the cows came home.

Finally, Javier nodded slowly. "I'm with you, Gideon. Tell me what Doc says about the bullet holes."

"Says I don't see action for a while, which is fine by me. Needed a vacation and I'm taking it."

"That isn't what I meant. You do know I have computer skills."

Gideon flicked him a quick, forbidding glance. Pure steel.

Javier gave him a faint grin. "I get it. Don't eat your spinach chips all in one sitting. You might actually get an ounce of fat on you." He stood up with his usual fluid grace and made his way to the trapdoor. He stood there, his back to Gideon, looking up at the stars while the clouds drifted across the sky.

"Don't know why you saved my ass when I was a kid or even how you found me, brother, but I know I can always count on you. I just need to say thanks, and you need to let me."

Gideon wasn't entirely mobile. He couldn't surge to his feet and wrap the kid up in a hug, not that Javier would have gone for it. More than likely, he'd shove a knife in Gideon's ribs. They really were a fucked-up lot, the entire urban team. Poor Mack. He was stuck with them.

Gideon had excellent hearing, and he caught the whisper of emotion in Javier's voice—sentiment his brother didn't often let slip. That got to him whether he wanted it to or not.

"I hear you, Javier." Gideon gave his brother what he needed to hear, and he was sincere. He watched Javier nod, although he didn't turn around. He just disappeared into the abyss that was the dark hole where the opening to the stairs led into his home. The trapdoor closed.

Gideon stared at it for a long minute before he allowed his body to begin to relax again. He hurt like a mother—everywhere. They'd given him pain pills, but he wasn't taking them. Now he was going to have to start putting himself in a meditative state once more. To do that, he was going to have to clear his mind. To do *that*, he was going to have to face those images all over again. He pressed the heel of his hand to his pounding forehead. He didn't want to go there again.

Javier thought he was the only one who wanted to rip those sick bastards into little pieces? What did he think happened to the men who murdered Javier's family? Did he ever wonder how Gideon had gotten to him before those butchers had finished hacking into him when he'd been just a little boy? Probably not. That was a nightmare Javier relived in his dreams but couldn't examine in the light of day.

A groan escaped. Not one of regret. How could he ever regret saving Javier's life? Despite the kid believing Whitney's armchair assessment of him, Javier was invaluable and had saved countless lives. That wasn't even counting the times he'd saved team members' lives. The groan was for the images of their recent mission along with those of the past, pouring into his mind when he'd fought so hard to get rid of them. It wasn't easy to force himself to breathe in and out and allow his mind to accept the horrors it had lived through, but he did it.

He built his lake in his mind, the deep, fathomless water a turquoise, the shores wide. Overhead, the skies were blue, and the clouds were light and drifted on a cool breeze. The images, when they came, tumbled into the lake and were carried away from him. He let them go, giving them up to the deep water.

A sound penetrated his concentrated breathing, that steady rhythm that brought images into the pool in his mind and allowed the ripples to carry them away. Laughter, sounding like beautifully tuned chimes skipping over water, didn't belong in his carefully built setting. Those chimes were faint and far away, but they invaded and sent the images away faster than any meditation he'd ever done. Each individual note blew up an effigy of one of his memories. The explosion over the lake appeared as multicolored fireworks.

As far as Gideon was concerned, there was only one thing for him to do, and he did it. The psychic talent he used he'd been born with. Since Whitney had enhanced all psychic talents whether he'd known what they were or not, Gideon had discovered it was stronger than ever. He closed his eyes, blocking out everything but the sound of that far-off laughter. Even after the notes had faded away, he still had the direction, and he had the exact pitch and rhythm he was looking for. He was ready for the sound to repeat itself, and it would. He was already casting his lure, sending it out into the night like a fishing line in the direction of that enticing laugh.

Minutes crept by. Gideon would have much preferred to be on the hunt in person, but his body wasn't in any kind of shape. He would have to rely on his considerable skills with his talent—using an invisible line with an anchor to find his prey, much like a spider might. He'd been honing this one since he was a child. It didn't always work. Sometimes, whoever he sought was too far away, but this was worth the try. Minutes turned to a quarter of an hour. He was patient. He'd learned patience a long, long time ago. On the half-hour mark, it occurred to him he hadn't been visited once by his past.

He opened a bag of the contraband spinach chips Javier had brought him, popped the top off a can of beer and allowed himself to indulge. Beer and chips. Not everyday fare for him. He ate the chips slowly, savored the salty seasoning on them and then washed them down with beer.

Another fifteen minutes. A whisper. Far off. A barely there thread of sound. He knew it was that same laughter. The same pitch. His hearing was acute and he was not mistaken. Those little chimes, not quite as loud this time, but he had homed in on them. Feminine for certain. Taking his time, Gideon carefully attached his thread, an anchor, much like a spider might, casting it into the air, right off the roof, sending it back along that same path to find the owner of that laughter.

Now it was another waiting game. This one wouldn't be quite as long. Gideon changed position carefully. Moving hurt. Still, with this new intrigue, he didn't feel it quite so much.

He felt the bump as the anchor attached itself to something solid. He found himself smiling. He was in San Francisco, and it was night. He didn't need the Harpy Eagle or any of the large raptors for this purpose. He wanted a small bird no one would notice. The field sparrow was prevalent across Northern California. A beautiful little bird with a gray head and rust-colored crown. Small, very slender, with a pink bill and white eye-ring; the long tail was forked.

The little sparrow was reputed to be largely monogamous, and yet they sometimes had a secret, sneaking out and singing to attract another lady. Often that lady had her own male, who seemed to turn a blind ear to the new upstart singing to entice the female out of the nest to go meet with him.

Gideon sang softly, a very short whispered song to entice a

female to him. The answer came immediately, as he knew it would. He'd made friends with the female, and she was nesting in the bushes he'd planted, which now grew thick on the wall farthest from him.

She came to him in little stops and starts. It wasn't difficult to tie her to him and send her out to investigate for him. He needed eyes and information. The little sparrow wouldn't be noticed, and if she was, no one would ever equate her with spying. That had always been his advantage. Because even as a child, he was so stoic that no one ever thought his imagination would enable him to envision calling birds to him and making them his allies.

His little sparrow flew down three long blocks on the same side of the street to land on a windowsill and peer in. The bar was noisy, packed and popular. It wasn't one of the bars the local fishermen gathered in after coming back to the harbor. This was new, with a frenetic dance floor, mood lights and a young, hip crowd. When the bar had opened, no one thought it would do very well, but the locals hadn't counted on the draw of the harbor and old-world San Francisco culture.

The bar was just far enough away that his team didn't have a lock on the building yet. They could tap into the cameras easily enough, and Jaimie—Mack's wife—or Javier could lock into the security system inside the bar. Javier might just be doing him a payback much sooner than either of them thought, because somewhere inside that building, with all those civilians drinking and laughing and hooking up, there was one woman whose laughter had the ability to erase—even if for a few minutes—the utter darkness of his past.

~

Laurel "Rory" Chappel lifted a hand to her fellow coworkers as she wound her way through the narrow maze that should have been a wide hallway leading to the back employee entrance. She was tired. More than tired. Exhausted. She was a night owl—awake all night and asleep during the day, except she hadn't been sleeping much.

She was a rolling stone, a nomad, a woman who liked to travel and see what was around the next corner. She'd been drawn to the harbor, a strong compulsion that had brought her there to check it out. She loved the water, the feel of the fog and spray on her skin. The newer buildings, farther down from the actual working harbor, were clean and inviting. She needed clean. The bar, fortunately, didn't allow smoking, so she was free to work there.

She had skills when it came to bartending, so the moment she hit San Francisco, she had researched the best-paying and most popular bars. Then she went to each district and walked around, immersing herself in the neighborhood to see if anything appealed to her. She always waited for something to click so she knew she was supposed to be there. She had instantly clicked with the harbor.

It was nice to be outside in the night air. She wasn't someone who enjoyed being indoors, or at least in cramped spaces. The bar she worked behind was ideal for her. Long and slightly curved, it went nearly the length of the room, giving plenty of space for each bartender to have his or her own workstation. Behind the bar there was room to maneuver, so when it was extremely busy, the bartenders didn't run into each other if they did have to step out of their own work area.

Rory thought she'd found an ideal situation. Her apartment was fairly new, in a building three stories high, and she was able to choose from several apartments. There was a waiting list for the first floor, but no one had requested the third-floor apartments. Each had a stairway to the roof, where they had their own little section, railed off from the neighbors for privacy. She was told she could put in a garden if she wanted. What she wanted most was to sit outside on her rooftop sanctuary and breathe in the ocean after the stale air of the bar.

Her apartment building was on the opposite side of the street as the bar but down two and half blocks toward the harbor. She was fortunate that across the street from her apartment, the building facing hers was only a couple of stories versus three or four. That meant she had a fantastic view of the harbor and, farther out, the ocean from her rooftop patio.

The building had a keypad to put in a code to access it, making it a safer place to live. Rory thought it was a good idea, but the manager didn't seem to have a very good sense of safe people to rent to. She'd used the gym nearly every day since she'd signed her lease. Ordinarily, because she worked nights, she could count on any gym she used being fairly empty during the time she chose for her workout.

Unfortunately for Rory and the other women choosing to work out in the early afternoon, a few of the apartments had recently been rented to four single males who didn't appear to work. They had money, but they hung around and leered at the women as they used the various machines. They also tended to be in the laundry room at inconvenient times.

There was no doubt in Rory's mind that the four men who pretended to be no more than casual acquaintances were not only working together but running drugs and possibly other illegal things she didn't want to know about. She did her best to avoid them, just as the other women in the building did. She'd learned early that there was always a fly in the ointment with any place she lived or worked. Nothing was ever perfect, and she accepted that. It was simply life.

Rory let herself into her apartment and tossed her bag onto the nearest chair as she hurried through the open living room and dining room to the door leading to her bedroom. She kicked off her shoes and unbuttoned her white shirt until she could whip it over her head with one hand, dragging in a lungful of air as she did so. Both hands dropped to the black trousers, the standard uniform the owner preferred his bartenders to wear while they were working. She peeled them down her hips and legs to kick them off. She did what she always did the moment she got home: she stepped into the shower as quickly as possible.

One of the apartment's best features, other than her rooftop patio, was the shower with hot water. She scrubbed her skin and rinsed out her hair. Next was moisturizing her face, throwing on flannel pajamas to stay warm, wrapping her hair in a towel and rushing up the stairs to her rooftop. Her breathing machine was inside a weatherproof cabinet, and she set it up on the little table beside her favorite chair. She liked that lounge chair. No, she *loved* it. It was the most comfortable outdoor chair she'd ever come across, and she carted it around with her wherever she went.

Rory tucked her feet under her and tipped back her head to look at the stars as she gave her laboring lungs a treatment. She could normally last an entire shift with just her inhaler as long as she went straight home afterward and used her machine. She wouldn't get rashes from an allergic reaction to the cleaning chemicals she used when she closed if she got home fast and made it into the shower. The key was to shower with cool water first and make her way to hot. She had it down to a science after all the times she'd been bartending when things had gone wrong fast.

She had sensitive skin and weak lungs. There was no getting around those two things. She'd been born that way. It hardly mattered to anyone but her. She really detested using an inhaler in front of anyone, as if that made her weak; not her lungs—her. She'd been taking care of herself for years now, and doing a pretty good job too, but she had so many problems. Not just her health. She had *issues*.

Rory made a face around the mouthpiece she was using to get the medicine into her lungs. Early on, she'd realized she wasn't going to be that girl that men raced to make a life with. They didn't want someone with her precarious health and neuroses to be the mother of their children. She wanted a home, children, a family, but once she allowed herself to be realistic, and her lungs didn't get better no matter how much time she put into exercise to strengthen them, she accepted that she was always going to be alone. Hence her decision to see as much of the world as possible. She couldn't be a wife and mother, so she chose the next best thing—she was a traveler. She was a darn good traveler, and for the most part, she was happy.

She continued to stare up at the stars. The clouds had darkened slightly, but they moved with the breeze. Fingers of fog drifted across her patio. She liked the harbor at night. Lights shone on the water, and boats rocked and swayed with the tide. She had excellent hearing and very good eyesight, a trade-off for her faulty lungs. The sounds of the waves breaking against the piers and numerous fishing boats were a kind of lullaby, allowing her to relax after so many hours on her feet.

Rory had a memory that allowed her to remember names and faces better than most people. She didn't forget drinks, not even if the customer hadn't been in for a while. That was a gift that did make her a good bartender. She also had the uncanny ability to sense lies, but that didn't help in the bartending business. It only prevented her from going on dates if she considered it at all.

The medicine had finally run out, so she could shut off the machine and just enjoy her favorite spot. As she carefully wrapped up the nebulizer and made her way across the rooftop patio to the weatherproof cupboard, a small bird flew past her ear. It was so close, the tip of its wing brushed her skin. Out of the corner of her eye, she caught a glimpse of wicked talons before an owl pulled up, screeching in dismay at missing its prey. Simultaneously, she heard a *thunk* as the sparrow hit the open cupboard door and dropped to the floor right at her feet.

Rory's heart sank. She didn't like any animal hurt or killed. The owl had to eat, so she couldn't be upset at the owl. She had opened the cupboard without thinking as the sparrow approached, cutting off its escape. The little bird ran right into the door, which meant its demise—if it was dead—was on her.

She shoved the breathing machine into the cupboard and quickly closed and locked it before sinking down in a crouch. "Are you alive?" She placed one palm gently over the bird to feel the flutter of its heartbeat. A sigh of relief escaped her.

"I'm going to examine you to make sure you're just stunned. I was afraid the door broke your neck the way you flew into it." Rory sat on the floor and cuddled the bird in her palm while she gently moved two fingers over the delicate bones and feathers. "Everything seems to be okay. No broken bones. Your little beak isn't cracked or broken. Your wings are good." She rubbed gently with her two fingers on the bird's chest in an effort to stimulate it.

The beak opened and closed. One foot twitched, the three toes with the thin, curved nails moving jerkily.

"That's it, little one, come around. You need to be getting home, where you're safe. What in the world were you doing out this time of night?"

Rory breathed warm air onto the bird and then straightened to tip her head back and look up at the stars again. The mist touched her face, feeling good on her skin. She was very tired and wanted to go to sleep, but she wouldn't abandon the sparrow. She thought it best to keep the bird outside, where it could fly away the moment the creature was feeling better. In any case, since coming to San Francisco, her nightmares had been increasing.

It didn't take long for the sparrow to open its eyes and regard her silently for a moment before it turned over in her palm and stood quietly, staring at her.

"I can see you're still a little dazed," Rory whispered, afraid to move. She didn't want to frighten the sparrow after its scare with the owl. "We can just sit here for a few minutes until you're fully recovered. I can see I'm going to have to look up what kind of bird you are and why you would be out at night."

Rory was used to talking aloud to herself. The little bird righted itself, still looking at her, its dazed eyes winking open and closed. "I think the owl has moved on to find something else to eat for dinner, but you need to get back to your home and be safe." She kept her voice soothing and very low, hoping to avoid scaring the sparrow.

The bird stayed in her palm rather than jumping out. It flapped its wings several times, all the while looking at her. Rory couldn't detect fear. The sparrow seemed to be just fine standing in her palm.

After a few minutes of staring at one another, the sparrow finally hopped from Rory's hand to her thigh and then to the patio floor. It hopped around the two raised flower beds she'd planted and flew onto them as if inspecting them. Finally, after another long look at Rory, the bird took off into the night.

Rory found herself smiling as she picked up her phone and immediately looked up images of birds to see what kind of sparrow would be flying around at night and why. She was a little shocked to find out that her visitor had most likely been going to a clandestine meeting with a male sparrow who was not her mate. She was having an affair—or she had most likely flown out of her nest with the intention of meeting a male. Rory played the recordings of the male calling to the female and the female answering.

"Naughty bird. Maybe that scare with the owl and getting hit by the cupboard door will scare you straight," Rory whispered. "Who knew birds had affairs? Sheesh. What's the world coming to? That's why I know better than to go for the kind of men I find attractive."

She detested going back inside and thought about putting a bed on the roof to sleep outside, but the weather really wasn't conducive to that. Sometimes, when she first entered her apartment after being on the roof, air would be trapped in her lungs and she'd feel as if she couldn't breathe. She knew what not being able to actually take a breath was, so it was silly, but she would have to push down a panic attack.

Rory never invested in a lot of furniture. Buying furniture wasn't practical, because she couldn't haul it around with her when she moved on. In any case, she liked as much space as possible in her apartment. She looked for open floor plans, and in the places she rented, the higher the ceiling, the better.

It didn't take long to get ready and fall onto her bed. No covers. Sometimes, if she was restless, the covers would tangle around her legs and she'd wake up fighting, gasping for air, her heart beating too hard and too fast. She loathed the sensation.

She closed her eyes and pulled air into her lungs. Slow and steady. She was such a wreck. So many silly issues. She knew she wasn't the only person in the world with health issues that had kept her from running marathons. She also wasn't the only one having full-blown panic attacks that had more than once landed her in the emergency room, certain she was having a heart attack when she wasn't.

Rory always assessed her situation at night, before she fell asleep. On a scale of one to ten, where was she? Happiness? She was a solid seven, creeping toward an eight. She liked where she'd landed this time, and she was making friends. Good friends. She liked several coworkers at the bar where she worked, and she liked her boss. She'd made friends with five women at the apartment building she really enjoyed, and that had never happened before.

She'd been in San Francisco five months already. Normally, she'd be thinking about moving on, but she might actually stay here awhile. She liked her job, and it was close to her apartment. Most days, even when it rained, she could walk to work. She had a parking spot allocated to her with her apartment, something coveted in the city, so most of the time she kept her car there and used public transportation if she couldn't walk. Yes, this was one of the best places she'd landed. Satisfied that she was in a good space, she closed her eyes.

2

Rory avoided the elevator as often as possible, choosing stairs to help keep her lungs as healthy as possible. She had missed the afternoon workout with the circle of women friends she'd made since moving in. That was a sacred time to her, because she didn't really have friendships, not the kind most people did. Making and keeping friends was difficult because she was a tumbleweed.

She liked the five ladies she'd met, and she had instantly clicked with them, which had never happened before anywhere she'd ever lived. She was cautious, but she had forced herself to be open to exploring the friendships. Four had already been friends before she moved in. The fifth moved in about the same time she did. The women were smart, funny and had good instincts.

Lydia Sawyer was a single mother to Ellen, a three-year-old girl. She was employed by a software company and was fortunate she could work mostly from home. Rory thought she was a fantastic mother and a dedicated worker. She could troubleshoot any software problems the company's clients had from her home computer.

That gave her the freedom to raise her daughter without the added burden of paying for childcare, an ideal situation because she was determined to make it on her own.

Janice DeWitt was the oldest among them. At just forty, she owned a janitorial business. Her husband had left her, cleaning out their accounts in order to keep his younger mistress happy. Janice started the janitorial service, and to her shock, it took off. She worked nights and oversaw three employees.

Pam Williams was putting herself through law school. She worked for Janice at night and studied and attended school during the day. It was easy to admire her. No matter how late she worked, she put in the time to study, determined to make her dream come true.

Cindy Atler had gotten married young to her childhood sweetheart, Matthew, and had two boys: Moses, four, and Isiah, six. Her husband had been killed fighting a fire two years earlier, and she'd been struggling ever since. She had money, but emotionally she needed to put distance between herself and her family. They meant well, but she had to stand on her own two feet and raise her sons the way she saw fit. She loved her parents but felt they were smothering her and taking over parenting duties. She told Rory and the others that she thought her husband would be disappointed in her if she continued to allow her parents to take over, so she'd moved.

Sally Hudson was tall and beautiful, turning heads when she walked down the street or into a room. Perpetually cheerful, she owned a dog grooming service, driving a large van to the homes of her customers. She loved what she did, and her business was a huge success. She'd started out as a dog trainer and then became a vet tech, but she had always dreamed of owning her own business. She had saved until she could put a down payment on the dog grooming van. It wasn't long before she was so busy that she had to turn away clients. She had moved in at the same time Rory had.

All five women were waiting in the lounge, a room near the lobby where residents could take visitors if they didn't want to bring them into their apartments. Mostly, the women used the small lounge when they got together for coffee and sorted their mail. It was a ritual they had created to touch base with one another and keep up with what was happening. The women sat sorting through junk mail, tossing it into bags to get rid of it while they visited.

Rory didn't get a lot of mail other than bills and junk mail, so she put hers in a canvas tote she had, waited until the mail piled up, and then took it to the office at the bar and used the shredder. The other ladies laughed at her for shredding junk mail, but she'd always done it everywhere she went and was a little obsessive about it. She checked her mailbox, pulled out the stack of mostly throw-away letters and rushed into the lounge.

"You're late," Cindy said, greeting her, holding out a tall to-go mug. "Your coffee."

"I think I love you," Rory said, taking the mug. "I didn't have time to make coffee, so this is going to be my first cup. I can't believe I fell asleep and stayed that way."

Cindy laughed. "I don't remember what sleep is. I don't think I've slept the entire night for the last five years."

Lydia fake-frowned, her hands stilling in midair over the stack of envelopes in front of her. "Isn't Isiah six? Are you saying you still get up with him at night? Ellen is three, and I was holding out hope that in a few months she wouldn't be getting into my bed at night."

"Honestly," Cindy admitted, "I get up to check on Isiah and Moses. I can't help myself. That first year with Isiah, Matthew took turns with me."

"You'll be checking on those kids when they're teens," Janice warned. "Only they'll be crawling out windows to go to parties."

Rory found herself laughing as she sorted through the mail, tossing the junk into the canvas tote to be shredded when she had a full bag. It was relaxing and fun to be part of the group even if she didn't contribute very much in the way of entertainment. There were times when she had funny stories of her customers to tell, but for the most part, she enjoyed listening, and the other women were used to her staying quiet.

She had plenty to talk about if she was put on the spot. She'd traveled so much and was happy to tell her friends about the various places she'd lived in. She just loved hearing them talk about their lives. She loved the camaraderie of being with the five women. In truth, she found she was enjoying San Francisco more than any other place she'd lived.

"I much prefer animals," Sally announced. "I have no worries at three in the morning that a toddler or a teenager could be climbing out the window."

"With your looks," Pam said, "the teens might be climbing in your window."

Rory laughed with the others at the horrified expression on Sally's face.

"Don't say that. Don't even think it. I was lucky to fall into this group of cool women, but most detest me on sight. If they thought their son crawled into my house via window, I'd be arrested immediately."

Janice nodded. "Sadly, Sally's right. Women should be all about the sisterhood, but some get jealous of good looks and, Sally, hon, you are one good-looking lady."

They all nodded in agreement.

Sally blushed. "Not any better-looking than the rest of you. In fact, the other day I had to make a trip to the laundry room, and

Harvey, the one always wearing the blue suit, was down there with Jarrod, the one who likes cowboy boots."

Everyone looked up, shock on their faces. Rory tossed two bills on the coffee table in front of her. "Sally, you know better than to go down there alone. Those men may live in this building, but they aren't to be trusted for a minute."

"I know, but there are cameras down there. They wouldn't try anything when they know it's all being recorded," Sally pointed out.

"That doesn't mean anything," Lydia said. "Cameras can be jammed."

"Or ripped out," Janice added. "You can't go alone where those men might be meeting and talking about things they don't want overheard."

Rory had to agree with the others. She studied Sally's face. It was clear she hadn't thought she could possibly be in any real danger. "Before I interrupted you, Sally, what were you going to say? Did they say something to you?"

"Jarrod called us all hot and asked if we took applications from other hot women to join us." Sally made a face. "He said he hoped so, because they liked watching us work out, and if we weren't all good-looking, it wouldn't be nearly as fun."

"What an asshole," Janice said. "We're not objects for them to ogle for their amusement."

"What a jerk. It shouldn't matter what we look like or how we dress," Pam said. "They aren't the most attractive men on the block, but they sure think they are."

"Harvey told him to shut up," Sally said.

"Why do you think they pretend they don't know each other?" Cindy asked. "It's silly. We see them together often. They live in the same apartment building. Who cares if they're friends?"

"If it isn't Jarrod with Harvey, it's Dustin with Ret," Pam declared. "Sometimes all four of them are together."

Lydia rolled her eyes. "If you catch them together, they act like teenagers caught sneaking out to a party, pretending they don't know each other and hurrying out of the room. It's the silliest thing I've ever seen."

"Whatever they're into is illegal," Rory announced, and then wished she'd kept her mouth shut. The others knew it already. They didn't need her to tell them that.

The women nodded and sipped their coffee and once again looked at their mail. A loud pop, pop, pop had Janice leaping to her feet.

"What was that?" Pam asked.

"That's gunfire," Rory said. "We need to get out of here."

More pops even closer had them all on their feet.

The side door to the lounge opened and a man staggered in. His chest and thigh were bloody. Two of the women screamed. Lydia scooped up Ellen from the floor and ran with her toward the back exit, following Janice, Pam and Sally. Cindy followed close behind. Rory followed the others toward the back door, away from the sounds. She dropped back to keep her body between Lydia and the stranger just in case, pausing by the door.

She'd never seen him before, but she couldn't leave the man to just bleed out. Even as she took a step toward him, the side door burst open so hard, it hit the stopper and swung back. A gun went off several times and the stranger returned fire.

"Get out of here!" the stranger shouted at her.

Rory backed out of the room, reluctant to leave him, but whoever was on the other side of the door was shooting into the lounge and didn't seem to be directing their aim fully at the man dragging himself toward the exit that would take him outside the apartment building. Cindy grabbed Rory's arm and pulled her completely out of the lounge and slammed the door. That door led into a hall, and the women ran toward the back entrance, where the gardens were.

They ran through the gardens toward the sidewalk, phones out, calling 911.

Cindy's grip was implacable when Rory tried to stop. "You can't go back into a building where there's an active shooter."

Lydia looked horrified. "Rory, what are you thinking?"

"I'm thinking that man needed help. I just left him in there. He could bleed to death."

"He was going out the other door," Janice pointed out. "It wouldn't have done him any good if you had gotten shot as well."

"Did you see who shot him?" Sally asked. "Was it one of the four clowns?"

"I didn't see anyone," Rory admitted. "The door banged open and someone started firing, but they were hidden from me." She looked at Cindy. "Did you have a better angle? Was it one of the four men we suspect are up to no good? Jarrod? Harvey? Dustin? Ret?"

"I couldn't see anything. I thought maybe one of them was shot," Cindy said. She looked at the others. "Did any of you see anything?"

Sirens were growing louder. The other women shook their heads. Janice answered for all of them. "We ran. As soon as I could, I called 911. I didn't know what was going on, but I wasn't sticking around to find out."

"It sounded like hundreds of bullets were fired," Sally added. "I've never been so scared. I just wanted out of there."

It seemed to Rory that the next hours were endless. She needed to get ready for work, but the police needed statements from them. She didn't mind giving them a statement, but she really didn't have much to say. Unfortunately, the stranger, whom she had never seen before, had collapsed and died just outside the apartment building.

The police insisted on using a gunshot residue kit to check each of their hands to ensure that none of the women had fired a weapon.

Rory couldn't blame them for being so thorough when she learned that the victim was named Peter Ramsey, and he was a detective in the police department.

Rory was careful not to speculate or tell the police officer questioning her that she was certain there were four men doing something very illegal in the neighborhood, because she had no idea what they were doing or any proof other than her suspicion. If they were selling drugs, that was a far cry from killing a detective. The other women must have felt the same, because no one else mentioned them either.

She was already running late by the time the police allowed her to rush upstairs and change. She'd texted her boss that she'd be driving rather than doing her customary walking, so no one could take her designated parking spot. Parking was always at a premium, and most of the time, she allowed others working at the bar to use her spot. She didn't take the time to give herself a breathing treatment but used her inhaler. She even used the elevator rather than the stairs.

"We have to get our mail," Lydia stated very loudly to someone Rory couldn't see.

Rory had forgotten they were sorting mail. She did have two bills that had come in. Paper bills rather than online. Then there was the junk mail in her bag. She went to stand by Lydia.

"My bills are in the lounge as well," she added, and pointed to her tote and the two envelopes on the end table. "Maybe you could just grab our mail for us?"

The officer nodded. "The lounge will be released soon. Forensics is still processing and will be for a while. But I can ask them if I can get the mail for you."

He returned with their envelopes and bags. Rory shouldered hers, hugged Lydia, waved at the cop and hurried out to her car. After tossing the bag of junk mail into the trunk, she made her way to the bar, sending up a silent prayer she wouldn't forget to bring in the two bills she'd placed on the passenger seat when she came home that night.

The moment she entered the bar, Lani, one of the female bartenders who had covered her station, began whispering to her about two customers who were extremely hot. One had come in several times, always sitting at one of the tables in the shadows, never at the bar. Always in Rory's section. Now, apparently, he was back with a friend.

"Dana's waitressing, and she's been flirting outrageously," Lani said, ending her report.

Dana rarely went home alone, and she garnered more tips than any other waitress. Rory snuck a quick look at the two men at the table facing the bar. Her breath left her lungs in a rush. The newcomer was the most attractive man she'd ever seen in her life. She spent most of her time as a bartender, so she saw a lot of men, and this man was mesmerizing and charismatic, and she hadn't even heard him speak.

Fortunately, it was extremely busy, requiring her to work fast and hard. She went on automatic pilot, although she remained aware of him in the room. She couldn't help being aware each time Dana approached the table and asked if the two men needed a refill. She thought the waitress did so a little more often than necessary.

Rory couldn't look directly at the man sitting at a table facing her station. He never came up to the bar to get drinks. She heard the gorgeous man call his companion Javier. Javier called her fantasy man Gideon. It wasn't as if Gideon was handsome in the accepted sense of the word—he was all rough edges. He had hawklike features. Sharp and angular and *intense*. Sadly, he was ripped. That meant he was physically fit and wouldn't do for her. Not at all. She couldn't afford to fall for someone and have them destroy her when they walked away.

Dana went running every single day. She probably made sure that Gideon and Javier saw her very toned abs and rock-hard glutes. And thighs. Rory sighed. She had to face it. She was never going to have Dana's perfect body no matter how hard she worked out in the gym. Worse, Dana was actually nice. Really nice. She shared her tips. She offered to babysit for Trudi, the only single mom working at the bar. She took crap shifts for others if they needed help. It wasn't like you could hate on her because she was good-looking and had a killer body. If Rory expressed interest in Gideon, not only would she quit flirting with him, but she'd also try to get information about him for Rory. That was how nice Dana was.

Dana and Lani were two of the biggest reasons Rory loved working at the bar. Trudi was the third. The bar itself and her boss also factored into her reasons for deciding to stay in San Francisco for a longer time than she usually stayed anywhere. Between work and the friendships she was building at the apartments, she felt she had a good situation for the first time since she'd begun her life as a nomad, and she wasn't going to allow it to be ruined by what happened at the apartments.

❧

"I'm not getting the GhostWalker vibe off her," Gideon said, his eyes on the woman talking to one of her many male customers.

It didn't matter that her hair was piled on her head in a sloppy knot that was falling out tendril by wayward tendril; it was obvious she had masses of hair, and it was dark cherry red. The real deal. Cherry red. He'd never seen that color of hair on anyone before. Every time she moved under a light, it blazed into vibrant life. It was difficult to keep his eyes off her.

She had those eyes. A deep green. Emerald? Jade? No, emerald for certain. Her eyes sparkled when she talked to her customers.

She looked directly at them even when she was mixing drinks, her rhythm never faltering. Sometimes she would laugh softly, the sound musical, turning heads no matter how low it was in the noise of the crowded bar.

"You've been here several times over the last couple of weeks, Javier." Gideon made it a statement. It would be difficult to get anything past Javier.

Gideon had held out as long as he could. The doctor hadn't given him permission to come see Rory in person, but he couldn't resist the compulsion any longer. Javier wasn't happy about it, but he'd come along to ensure that Gideon didn't tear open any wounds. In other words, Gideon thought a little ironically, babysitting.

"I've watched her closely," Javier admitted. "I can't see any indication that she's a GhostWalker, other than she has extraordinary reflexes. Her bartending skills are amazing. She's fast and can handle multiple orders. She doesn't seem to forget faces or names. On the other hand, I've followed her home every night, and she doesn't run or exhibit any kind of behaviors or skills a GhostWalker might under cover of darkness. She walks, Gideon. Even if there's a threat to her, which, on more than one occasion, I shut down."

Gideon didn't like that. The bartender everyone called Rory was a very attractive woman, although she didn't seem to notice that she was. She didn't flirt with her customers so much as genuinely try to connect in a friendly, positive way. If a man asked her out, she gave him a grin but refused gently.

Gideon liked the sprinkling of freckles across her nose and her generous mouth. It would be easy to fixate on both. "You did a background search on her?" Javier was a genius with computers. Gideon knew Javier had. He'd read the report multiple times and committed it to memory. He hoped Javier had updated it.

"Not much to find. She moves around a lot. Lost her parents early. Put herself through bartending school and uses that to earn her way. She doesn't stay in one place very long. She goes to a state, travels within that state for a little while and moves on to the next one."

"Anyone following her?"

"Not that I can find."

Gideon slid his fingers around the neck of the beer bottle and rolled it back and forth. "I'm really drawn to her, Javier, more than any woman I've ever been around. The chemistry for me is off the charts. That doesn't happen. Not like this. Not just with the sound of her voice. Her laughter. Now, watching other men around her, my attraction to her could be a little on the dangerous side, and you know I'm really not that man."

Javier studied him, one eyebrow arched.

"Not over a woman," Gideon clarified. "How can I trust it? You know Whitney pairs us. Would he pair someone who isn't a Ghost-Walker just to experiment?"

Javier shrugged. "I wouldn't put it past the bastard to do anything, but what would it matter even if he did pair the two of you? Look at Kane and Rose. They're happy together. Whitney didn't make that happen. He might be able to make you attractive to each other, but he can't manipulate your emotions."

"And if she's a plant?"

Again, Javier shrugged. "Then she's an enemy, Gideon, and I'll kill her. Whitney doesn't get to have spies in our home."

Every cell in Gideon's body instantly rejected Javier's casual threat. "Not happening, brother. I wouldn't be able to let you do it," he admitted. "That's another black mark to put in the column against her."

Javier tapped his beer bottle to the neck of the one Gideon was drinking. "If you don't stop staring at her, we're going to get kicked out of here." There was amusement in his voice, something extremely rare for Javier.

Ordinarily, Gideon would have been pleased to hear Javier's laughter, even at his expense, but not when it came to Rory.

"Full name again." He made it an order.

"Gideon, it's not like you don't have the memory of an elephant. I've told you three times, and you read the report I gave you. Laurel Chappel. Everyone calls her Rory. She has a few health problems. A fairly severe case of asthma. Or it appears as if it's asthma. One doctor took an X-ray of her lungs and he suspected a fungus, but she was gone before he could biopsy and find out for certain what he was looking at. She is careful and keeps up with her prescriptions for her breathing treatments, but she doesn't go to the doctor as often as she should. She also has allergies." Speculation crept into his voice.

Gideon turned his piercing gaze on his friend. "What are you thinking?"

Javier frowned and shook his head as if trying to clear away his thoughts. "I don't know, Gideon. The lung thing. It just feels off to me. It's interesting that most of the doctors she went to in all these clinics just diagnosed her with asthma or went along with that diagnosis and gave her the nebulizer and whatever medicines would help her breathe better, but they didn't bother to really check to see what the underlying problem was. Not until that one doctor did. He was very thorough. She had already planned to move, and by the time her test results came in, she was gone."

"Was that a coincidence, or did she leave because she didn't want to know?"

"I think she left before she got the news," Javier said. "But that's a guess. She doesn't seem like the type of woman who dodges bad news. She seems like she faces everything thrown at her head-on."

Gideon liked Javier's assessment of Rory. Javier was astute when it came to people. He had a gift when it came to knowing what a person was like within a very short time of being around them.

Because Gideon was so drawn to Rory, Javier had taken it upon himself, while Gideon was healing from the gunshot wounds, to find out everything he could about the bartender.

"You like her," Gideon stated.

"I don't like anyone outside our family," Javier denied. "To me, everyone else is a potential threat. She doesn't add up the way she should, and you're really into her, so she's really a threat."

Gideon continued to look at him with hooded, watchful eyes until Javier sighed.

The younger man said something ugly under his breath and then capitulated. "All right, then. I do kind of admire her. She's pretty cool in a lot of ways. I tried to find Whitney's stamp on her somewhere, but I couldn't. I got close to her on several occasions, and I didn't get the GhostWalker vibe coming off her . . . but . . ." He broke off.

Gideon turned his attention back to the woman behind the bar. There wasn't anything he didn't like about her. He was attracted to the entire package. That hair of hers shining under the lights fascinated him. He found himself watching the way she was with the male customers. She wasn't a woman leading men on. She was friendly but not too friendly. She wasn't looking for extra tips. She talked to them and laughed at their jokes. She remembered their names and their drinks. To her, she was doing her job. To them, she was making them feel special.

Gideon sighed. She was gentle when she turned down advances. Sometimes he wasn't certain she recognized when a man made an actual pass at her. She was too busy moving on to the next customer, but she could so easily acquire men fixating on her.

"You haven't seen evidence of a stalker or stalkers?"

Javier shook his head. "If she has one—and honestly, I'd be shocked if she doesn't have at least one—he's good at hiding. I did nose around a little because I was worried, but other than the two times a couple of drunks tried to follow her home, I didn't find anyone watching her."

"That's a miracle." Gideon sent him a wry smile. "I guess we can be considered stalkers. You're worse than me. You've been following her for a couple of weeks."

Javier grinned at him. "I never thought of myself that way."

"You're creepy," Gideon proclaimed. "Ask Rose. She'll tell you."

"Only because she suspects I stole the spinach chips. I'll tell you what's creepy. There were so many bags of those things, and she knew a few were missing. That's creepy. Eating them in the first place is creepy. Something is wrong with you if you want to put those green leaves in your mouth and eat them, but I'm willing to look past that because you're my brother. It goes all kinds of wrong when you know how many Ziploc bags you have strewn all over your counters. There had to be close to fifty or more. That's not right, Gideon."

Gideon couldn't help but laugh at Javier's pained expression. "Do you have any idea how difficult it is to make spinach chips? Rose made them from scratch. It takes a lot of time, and she's on her feet. She does it because her man loves them, not because she enjoys making them. Naturally, she's going to know how many bags she has of them."

"That woman holds a grudge."

"Her spinach chips are good."

"You didn't confess you had the contraband," Javier pointed out.

"I wasn't taking a knife to the ribs. I had enough wounds to recover from, and I wanted to meet Rory."

"You aren't exactly charming," Javier said. "She's shot down every single man who asked her out so far. I don't just mean tonight. That includes the other thousand I'm sure made their try over the last month. What makes you think you're going to do any better? You don't have the best track record."

"I do all right."

"You *did* all right back in the day when you wanted to spend a couple of hours with a woman. You could pick one up in record time, but you're out of practice. I doubt you know how to do more than stammer."

"At least I don't scare them off by glowering until they think I'm an assassin."

"I *am* an assassin."

Gideon tried to swallow a drink of beer, but it had gotten warm. He put the bottle down, making a face. "You're not supposed to let anyone know, in case that part escaped your notice. Try not to look like a killer."

"I don't intimidate Rose."

"That's because you stole her spinach chips," Gideon explained patiently.

The waitress approached the table and set a beer in front of Gideon. "Ice-cold. Compliments of our bartender." She picked up his warm bottle. "She doesn't like anyone drinking warm beer."

Gideon's gaze jumped to Rory's. Those emerald eyes met his. He felt a jolt through his entire body like a white-hot bolt of lightning. His vision focused completely, using the piercing gaze of the eagle, and it was easy enough to see the sweep of her long dark lashes and the smattering of freckles spread across the bridge of her nose. He gave her a smile and lifted the bottle, mouthing, "Thank you."

She inclined her head, which caused the overhead light to shine on the mass of curly dark cherry–colored hair pulled up into that messy knot. Instantly his body reacted with an unfamiliar tightening that was far more than an ache. Then another customer claimed her attention. She'd noticed him in a roomful of people. That gave him some satisfaction. It also had his warning system going off big-time.

"She doesn't go home with anyone, and she doesn't allow any-one to go home with her," Gideon mused aloud. "I have to do something different, something to intrigue her enough that she might take a chance on me."

"She'll take a chance on you," Javier said. "You're the only per-son in the bar she sent an ice-cold beer to. Notice mine is still warm. I don't think she knows I'm alive."

Gideon appreciated the cold beer even more because Rory had sent it to him. "Women fall all over you, Javier. It's just as well she didn't notice you, and I don't have to shoot you when we leave."

Javier laughed. "You've got it bad."

"Look at her." It wasn't just about her looks. If that was all it was, Gideon could have passed on her, even with the incredible chemistry. The draw was the woman. Her laughter. The way she treated others. Everything Javier had reported about her. What his little sparrow spy had shared.

"I'm looking at you, Gideon. I don't need to look at her."

"Help me figure out how to hook her. She's leery."

"Half the battle is getting her attention. You've managed to do that," Javier pointed out. "She won't let you go to her apartment. She won't want to go to your place. Not at first. That will freak her out if you ask her. She's going to want to feel like she's safe." Javier looked Gideon over. "You don't look safe, bro. In fact, if I was a woman, I wouldn't ever be alone in the dark with you."

Gideon gave him the finger, making sure to keep it along the neck of the beer bottle away from the bartender. Javier was having way too much fun at his expense.

"Maybe we should have the women befriend her. They could come to the bar and talk about what a great guy you are."

"Fuck you, Javier. You know they'd be worse and more invasive than your investigations." Which was true. Jaimie, Rose and Rhi-anna were fiercely protective of the men in GhostWalker Team

Three. Jaimie and Rhianna had grown up on the streets with them, and Rose had married into the team. Gideon wasn't about to unleash those women on Rory.

"I'll figure it out." If he was going to win his lady, he was going to have to do it on his own.

He heard a soft sound emerge, the perfect replica of a field sparrow, the little female singing her song. Looking up, Rory was singing the notes as she made several drinks at once.

Gideon looked down at the ice-cold beer she'd sent to his table and responded by sending back the notes of the male field sparrow. The song was short and to the point, asking the little female if she wanted to meet him later.

She sang the notes again as she worked, and he answered her a second time. Startled, Rory looked up, her eyes meeting his. A small smile lit her face. Her nod was nearly imperceptible. But he didn't miss it.

3

Gideon had to be the most fascinating man Rory had ever met. She had no idea what compelled her to agree to meet with him after the bar closed, and truthfully, right up until the moment she stepped out the back door and saw him waiting for her, she considered calling it off. She opened her mouth to tell him she'd thought better of it, but a thousand butterflies took flight in her stomach, and not a single sound emerged.

He stood draped against a column in the parking lot, looking so much a part of the night, she could barely make him out, and there were lights scattered throughout the lot. He had dark hair with a few streaks of silver in it. She knew his eyes were blue because she'd secretly studied him in the bar. At night they appeared darker, but then if the light caught his gaze just right, he'd have an odd glow, much like an animal that could see in the dark.

He straightened to his full height, and she realized he towered over her. That might have intimidated her, but she realized immediately that he had covered a slight wince. Not an outward one. There was no change of expression, but somehow she read more of him than she expected, as if they were connected.

When he'd left the bar after last call, she'd noticed he'd been cautious when standing and that his friend had hovered. Again, Gideon hadn't shown annoyance, but she'd *felt* that he hadn't wanted his friend to call attention to him.

Rory smiled at him. "I'm Laurel Chappel. My friends call me Rory."

"Gideon Carpenter. Thanks for taking a chance on meeting with me. Especially so late." He nodded his head toward her apartment building. "I thought we could talk in the Koi Garden. I'm not sure why they named it the Koi Garden when the koi were eaten the first month they were ever put in the pond and never restocked, but the name remains."

The garden was situated right next to her apartment building, but she'd never gone into it. She'd always intended to. It looked peaceful and inviting, but when she had a day off, she nearly always went to Golden Gate Park and hiked around.

"I'd like that. I've always wanted to go inside and look around."

She was a little shocked she could manage to speak. Up close, he took her breath away. He really was a gorgeous man. Fit. He moved with fluid grace, although she did have that strange sensation that it wasn't as easy for him as he made it look.

They walked together down the sidewalk, Rory setting a slow pace, thankful she had thought to use her inhaler before she left the bar. As she continued along the sidewalk, Gideon suddenly halted and indicated a narrower pathway that cut between two buildings.

"Don't you walk this way? It cuts your time in half." He frowned and rubbed the bridge of his nose. "I'm sorry. Of course, you wouldn't. It isn't as well lit. I'm used to not worrying about my safety. That was a really ridiculous question to ask you."

Rory could tell he was genuinely upset with himself that he'd made the inquiry. She peered into the narrow pathway between the buildings. It wasn't a dirt alleyway. Normally, she felt confident that she could defend herself against any attacks, but danger clung to Gideon like a second skin. The feeling of threat wasn't directed toward her; in fact, she felt safe with him. Safe wasn't something she was used to feeling.

"I haven't explored much around the apartments yet. I intended to, but I've been working extra hours for Brad. Brad Fitzpatrick is my boss. He's a really good man, and he's been trying to get his business off the ground."

Rory took a deep breath and decided to take another leap of faith. She had no idea why she had such a strong compulsion to meet him after work when she didn't date and was never attracted to any of the men who asked her out. Or why she would risk walking home alone with him. Or why she would ever agree to walk down a narrow pathway between buildings in the dark, which was the epitome of stupidity, but she was going to do it.

"You're safe with me, Rory," Gideon said. "Do you want to text your family or one of your friends and let them know who you're with and what we're doing? Take my picture and send it to them. If you don't want to bother them this late, you can send it to your boss. You know he's still up."

Gideon was *such* a good man. Who offered to let their just-getting-to-know-each-other date do something like that? He knew she was nervous and he'd made the offer. "You really don't mind?"

"I think it's a smart idea."

She did too. She took his photograph. He didn't smile, but then she could see he wasn't given to smiles. It didn't matter. She thought he was hot as hell anyway. She group-texted her five friends that she was out with Gideon Carpenter, taking a shortcut from the bar to the Koi Garden, where they were going to be getting to know one another.

"Thank you, Gideon. I should have thought of that." She had relied on herself for so long, she never considered letting anyone else know where she was or who she was with.

Gideon took her hand and stepped ahead of her onto the path between the two buildings. The moment his much larger hand enveloped hers, her heart went crazy, and she concentrated on slowing her heartbeat. She felt like a silly teenager. The moment her heart lurched so insanely, her breathing followed, getting out of control.

Rory did her best to block out everything around her and tried to get a natural rhythm going, breathing in and out. *Please don't wheeze. Please don't wheeze.*

Something had happened to Gideon. She knew he'd been injured, maybe a major car accident, but he had volunteered to walk her to the Koi Garden, and he was maintaining despite his injury. The last thing she wanted was for Gideon to see that she couldn't walk two blocks without a problem. She detested that she would look weak next to him.

In her next breath, she was angry with herself for caring that it mattered to her. She didn't have low self-esteem—at least not most of the time. She thought of herself as a confident woman until it came to her lung issues and sometimes her size, and only when she considered being around someone like Gideon. She was fit, but there was a voice in her head telling her she would never be good enough.

Gideon stopped in front of the double iron gates of the Koi Garden. "Rory, do you have an inhaler with you?"

She cursed inwardly and refused to look up at him as she fished in her jacket pocket for it. Naturally he would hear her struggling to breathe.

He waited for her to use it before he opened the gates. She went through before embarrassment had her turning around. She refused to be a coward. If he didn't make an excuse to end their first meeting, neither would she.

"There's a pavilion over here, so even if the wind comes up, we'll be protected," he said. "The chairs are comfortable. I have a blanket in my backpack for you to use so you won't get cold."

Gideon pulled out a chair and took the one opposite her. She noticed his chair was at an angle so he could see the entrance as well as both sides of the garden. It was only behind him that he didn't have a good view of. He placed the blanket in front of her as well as two bottles of water.

"I have asthma," Rory blurted. "It's fairly severe. No running for me."

"I'm impressed you work so fast at the bar the way you do. You must make an effort to stay fit despite having asthma."

She heard the genuine admiration in his voice.

"I've always been lucky when it came to physical abilities. Good reflexes, that sort of thing, but I've got friends who have to work their asses off to stay in shape. I respect them because I know how difficult it is for them. We're not all born with the same gifts or challenges." Gideon spoke matter-of-factly as he casually reached for the water bottle in front of her and loosened the cap before opening his own. "How did you learn to duplicate the song of the female field sparrow so perfectly? That was truly amazing."

She laughed; she couldn't help it. He sounded impressed. Who knew such a silly thing would impress a gorgeous man with muscles all over the place? "I love music. I hear music in everything, meaning traffic, buildings, birds, especially the birds. I've traveled quite a bit and like to write songs, so I'm always listening wherever I go."

"That little piece is very specific. Not too many people notice it," Gideon said, persisting. "Field sparrows are common, but until recently, scientists weren't certain what those little notes meant."

She laughed again. "The other night, a little female sparrow came flying onto my rooftop, with an owl determined to make her a meal. I accidentally bashed her with my cupboard door. I knew she shouldn't have been out of her nest at night, so once she flew off, I looked up field sparrows and, much to my shock, learned about them having affairs. I couldn't resist hearing the song of a female calling or answering just so I would recognize the notes. Then I did the same with the male sparrow."

"After the sparrow was chased by the owl and hit your cupboard door, you said she was fine? Are you certain?" There was concern in his voice.

His concern caused a melting sensation in her heart. She nodded. "Yes. She flew off. How did you know the notes to sing back to me?"

For the first time, Gideon looked a little sheepish. One hand swept through his thick wavy hair, making his already unruly hair even worse. He sent her a boyish grin that didn't quite reach his eyes. She wanted to reach out and push his hair off his forehead, not because it wasn't attractive but because it was too tempting. The pull toward him was very strong.

"I've been all over the world, and I study birds. They're fascinating to me. Everything about them, from the way they build their nests to the way they care for their young. They're all so different. Some are monogamous. Some are not. Some go back to the same site year after year."

As he spoke, his voice became more animated. It was all Rory could do to keep from smiling. Gideon's features remained an expressionless mask for the most part, but his eyes and voice changed. His eyes were beautiful. She had noticed a silver ring around the dark blue color of his eyes, but when he spoke of the various birds, the color lightened, and the silver ring seemed to thin. His voice, although still low and gentle, definitely became more dynamic.

"It's amazing that you can reproduce bird songs after listening to them when you're writing music."

"I traveled to South America, and my guide took me to a section where there was a nest of a Harpy Eagle about ninety feet high up in a kapok tree. I felt very privileged to have even seen one. I know they're very difficult to spot," Rory said. "He also told me that, for the most part, the Harpy Eagles are silent. But I camped close to their tree, and I listened. I found they make a variety of sounds. To me, each note was unique and beautiful. With the background of the wind moving through the canopy, when I heard the sound, I immediately felt music and lyrics."

Gideon flashed her another grin. This one was again very brief, but it lit his eyes. "I've been to the South American rain forest multiple times looking for the Harpy Eagle. Beautiful bird. Nothing like it in the world. Those talons, large like a grizzly's. They mate for life. Did you know that?"

His voice was mesmerizing. She leaned her chin into the heel of her hand, feeling she could listen to him all night. The sound of his voice was pitched low, a velvet-soft blend that seemed to stroke over her senses until every nerve ending was singing. She'd never had a reaction to another human being the way she did to him. Spending time in his company was both exhilarating and frightening. At the same time, it was addicting. The more time she spent with him, the more she wanted to be with him.

"The guide mentioned those things to me, along with the fact that the Harpy Eagle was considered the most dangerous of all raptors. He said it's actually so powerful that it could puncture a man's skull with ease."

Gideon nodded. "They're no joke, yet you camped close to their nest. After what he told you, you weren't afraid?"

Rory tried not to look at his long fingers wrapped around the bottle of water. He had big hands. The Harpy Eagle had five-inch talons, comparable to the five-inch claws of a grizzly bear. There was tremendous danger and power in the raptor. She could see power and danger running through Gideon. It was strange to think those things when he was so soft-spoken and gentle.

"I wasn't afraid in the least. I stayed a distance from the nest. It wasn't as if I was going to climb ninety feet into the air and try to see their little chick. It was thrilling to share their space and hear them. I saw them bringing a howler monkey to the nest once. But I was there for their music."

"I like that you heard music in them."

His eyes were on her, his blue gaze intense, causing the invasion of butterflies all over again. The silver rings around the blue intrigued her. He had beautiful eyes, and he focused completely on her, making her feel as if she were the only woman in the world.

"I hear music in everything and everybody." She was proud of herself for managing not to stutter when he was looking at her so intently.

"What do you hear in me?"

Her heart jerked. Her stomach did a slow somersault. She hadn't been expecting that question. She should have. He seemed interested in everything. She pressed her lips together nervously. If she said the wrong thing and he was upset with what she heard, she might lose this connection before she had a chance to even explore it. She could always say they hadn't spent enough time together, and she needed longer, but she didn't like lying.

"Rory, you aren't going to hurt my feelings. I'm interested in your artistic impressions of me, but if you feel that's too personal for you to share, I'll understand. The last thing I want to do is make you uncomfortable."

His voice was very gentle, so gentle tears burned behind her eyes. No one had ever spoken to her like that—as if she mattered. As if how she was feeling mattered. She had lived her life alone for so long she didn't know how to react to kindness or caring.

"The last thing I want to do is offend you." She did her best to keep her voice from trembling. When she opened herself to her surroundings to listen for music, the notes came to her easily. With Gideon, it was a blend of notes just like the impressions she had gotten of him. She had already placed the notes of the Harpy Eagle into his song. A hawk. A Great Gray Owl. Strangely, all predatory raptors and a wolf. She found the wolf note in him fascinating. All animals with a protective side.

She hummed each note softly, blending one into the next, ending on the wolf's howl, calling his family to him. She lifted her lashes. "There's more. Quite a bit of a blending, but those are the more prominent ones I hear in you. If I were going to create a song, I would start there."

She was *so* going to write a song about him. Never, not in a million years, would she ever show it to him or anyone else, because it would be her first love song, but she was writing it. She was already hearing it in her mind. She wasn't certain she'd be able to sleep until she at least started the music. Thank heavens she had a fresh supply of notebooks stashed in her room.

"You're amazing. Honestly, Rory, that was one of the most extraordinary assessments of my character I've ever heard, and you did it in just a short time after meeting me."

Rory felt color slipping up her neck into her cheeks. He sounded sincere. His gaze continued with that intense focus, the blue of his eyes deepening and the ring of silver brightening so that it appeared to be a true silver and not an anomaly.

She forced a smile. It had been terrifying to give a true rendition of what she actually heard when she listened to her artist's soul. "I thought it was beautiful, but that didn't mean you would. I'm glad you weren't offended. I hear a blend of sounds with you. Power. Danger. Kindness. Protection. The notes move in and out. Usually there are street notes blending with people." She heard them faintly with him, but she didn't get that it was the biggest part of him.

She heard other notes she wasn't going to mention. The sound of bullets. Those were prominent in the music surrounding him. She wanted to take that out when she was alone and assess the sound of it. Combat? A war he had fought in? That discussion could take place at a different time, when they knew one another better.

His smile took her breath. It wasn't much of a smile. It didn't really reach his eyes, but it did curve his lips. He had chiseled lips. She had a strange need to rub her finger along his bottom lip, but then she wanted to do the same with his angular jaw and the rest of his sharply carved features. She felt it was important to learn every feature, commit him to memory with the pads of her fingers, as if she could imprint him on her soul. He was already there through the music, but she still wanted that physical touch.

"The sun is coming up, Rory, and you need to sleep," Gideon said. "I'd like to see you again." He stood up.

She noticed he did so slowly, under the pretense of screwing the caps on the water bottles and shoving them into his backpack. There was definitely something wrong. She folded the blanket and handed it to him. He stuffed it inside the pack and shouldered it before walking with her back to the street.

"I've got to work for the next three nights. We're slammed. Brad, my boss, wasn't expecting business to pick up so fast. That means all the bartenders are pulling extra shifts." She'd taken more hours because she didn't really have much of a life outside of work.

No family to go home to. Now she regretted that she hadn't taken a night or two off when she could have.

"When's your next day off?"

"In three days."

"I know a restaurant right on the wharf. It's a little hole in the wall. It's between your apartment building and my home."

She hesitated. She really wanted to say yes, but there were times when someone called in sick, and Brad really relied on her.

"What is it?"

They were right in front of her apartment building. She punched in the security code. "I want to go, and I'm going to say yes, I'll go, but if my boss has a problem, he'll call me. I'm always the backup."

"I understand, Rory. The man is getting his business up and running, and you're his best bartender. That was evident when I was there. It's natural he relies on you, although he should give you a night off. Even if your boss called you in last minute, I think you'd be able to make it. If not, no worries. We'll reschedule."

He was so nice. He didn't seem upset that she had to work. She was hearing even more musical notes surrounding him, and she liked every one of them.

"I'll need your cell number," he said before she stepped inside. "And I'll give you mine."

She had never given her number to any man other than her boss. Rory had to control her breathing when she sent her number to him and accepted his. Once the lobby doors closed and locked, she watched as he turned away and began to walk down the street. A dark SUV pulled to the curb alongside him just as she started to turn away.

Javier jumped out of the passenger seat, stripped the backpack from Gideon and tossed it onto the back seat. She couldn't see the driver. He helped Gideon into the front seat. There was a brief exchange between the two. At one point when he was helping Gideon into the vehicle, he had his arm around Gideon and looked as if he were partially lifting him. It could have been her imagination. Gideon couldn't possibly have been that injured. He hadn't shown signs of any real pain. She would have heard it in his music. Or felt it. Still, it worried her. She turned and went up to her apartment to write.

～

"Good grief, Rory," Sally said, fanning herself. "That man is the hottest thing *ever*. Does he have a brother? I really need to hang out in your bar."

"He looks a little intimidating to me," Cindy said. "I was glad you sent the photograph and told us where the two of you were going. That was so smart, Rory. If more women did that when they went on their internet dates, there might be far fewer disappearances."

"I wish I could say I was the intelligent one," Rory confessed. "I was too busy staring at his muscles. He's got them everywhere. If he moves, his muscles move. But it isn't just his body. He's fascinating when he talks. He's soft-spoken and kind. He was the one who suggested I take his photograph and send it to a friend, along with his name and where we were going to be, so I would feel safe. I liked everything about him."

"He probably expected you to say no, you didn't need to do that," Pam said. "Most women wouldn't. They would be embarrassed, and most men would know they wouldn't follow through."

"Had I acted like such a ninny, I'm certain he would have insisted," Rory said staunchly. She *was* certain.

"Where does he work?" Lydia asked. She reached down to sort

through a box of large crayons and gave the red one to Ellen so she could color the big pony in the book she had on the table.

Rory frowned. "Honestly, I didn't ask him. I should have, I guess. Sheesh."

Why hadn't she asked him what he did for a living? That was a logical question. She hadn't asked him about his injury either. That made no sense. After watching the SUV pick him up and the way Javier treated him, she was a little worried.

Gideon was physically fit. More than physically fit. He was a man who looked like he could handle himself in any situation. If she saw him on the street in the distance, she might think he was a professional athlete. Up close, she would guess he was a man in a job far more serious, far more dangerous, although she couldn't imagine what, not after speaking with him. He was very gentle and kind.

"If you don't even know where he works, what in the world did you talk about?" Lydia asked. "I was worried, so I got up every hour to check to see if you texted that you were home, which you had not."

Color crept up Rory's neck into her face, something that didn't happen that often. "I'm sorry. I should have texted that I was fine. He's so fascinating. Even his voice is sexy." She pressed one hand to her hot cheek, feeling silly. "I've never, not one single time in my entire life that I can remember, felt this way about a man. I really like him."

"I think we get that, Rory," Cindy said. "I'm happy for you. We just want him to be a really good man before you go all in."

"There are a lot of *not* nice ones," Pam said.

"Tell us what you did," Sally said.

"We talked about places he'd traveled that we both have in common. He really liked that I write songs by listening to birds as well as the different surroundings I'm in when I'm writing. I could tell that he really understood and wasn't just trying to placate me."

"How could you tell?" Pam asked. "Men can be very deceiving when they want something, Rory."

Rory looked around at her friends, feeling a glow of happiness. They were being protective of her. She felt that vibe. They weren't being mean or trying to put her off Gideon. They wanted her to be cautious. They understood she wasn't naturally trusting, because they'd been around her these last few months and had observed her. This was what it was like to have friends. She felt protective of them, and they returned those feelings. They wanted her to continue to be cautious now that she'd found someone she was attracted to, and they were right. She had to be careful.

"I know this sounds kind of crazy, but working at a bar for as long as I have and being around so many customers telling me whoppers, I've learned to get a good feel for the difference between lies and truth. I hear it. Gideon doesn't give much away with facial expressions. His eyes warm up, but he's stoic. I can *feel* the truth versus a lie. I might be wrong, because I want him to be the real deal."

"Give it time," Lydia advised. "You aren't committing to anything by seeing him."

"We're slammed at work, and I told him that. It isn't like I can go on dates with him for the next few days. It's work at night and sleep during the day. I'm not comfortable enough yet to meet him at his place or to have him come to mine. He was very sweet about it. He said he'd walk me back to the apartment, and when I had a day off, we could go to an early dinner. He knows a restaurant on the wharf that's close. He didn't push or act upset at all."

Pam raised an eyebrow. "A little too good to be true?"

"*Pam.*" Cindy hissed a reprimand. "We don't know that. Let's give the man a chance. There are decent men in the world. My husband was a good man. Gideon might be as well. Besides, we need to talk to her about the other thing that happened today." She glanced down at Ellen, who was coloring. Cindy made all kinds of hand gestures pointing toward the child.

Rory raised her eyebrows and sipped at her coffee. The circle of women instantly sobered. "What's up?"

"The police were back today," Cindy said, "but it thankfully didn't have anything to do with us." Again, she glanced at Ellen. "Someone who lived in one of the apartments on the main floor um . . . took his . . . um . . ." She broke off.

Lydia took up the narrative. "S-U-I-C-I-D-E," she said, spelling out the word. "It was Dustin Bartlet. Fortunately, it had nothing to do with us, and no one came to question us. None of us live on the main floor."

"It was weird that so many cops were here," Pam pointed out.

"I do feel bad about all the awful things I thought about him," Cindy said. "I could have been nicer. He just seemed like he was always leering. Was he? Did we imagine it?"

"Once in a while, it occurred to me," Rory ventured, "that the four of them—Harvey, Ret, Dustin and Jarrod—didn't want to get caught talking together, so they said idiotic things to get us to go away." Now she felt guilty too.

"I guess you never know how someone is really feeling," Sally said. "As many times as they made comments, none of them ever made a real pass, at least not at me."

The other women shook their heads.

They hadn't at Rory. None of them had come to the bar. The men knew the women gathered in the lounge, and they had never joined them. There had been opportunities for any of them to harass the women individually, but they hadn't taken them. She should have asked herself why.

She took another sip of coffee. "I'm a bartender. It's my job to read people. I failed that one epically."

"Rory, what he did isn't on you," Cindy said. "We didn't know him that well. Just enough to say hi and hurry out of the room. That was about it."

Because she hadn't bothered to take the time, but then during her travels she rarely, if ever, had. It was these women and the ones at her place of work who had changed everything for her. Changed her. Opened her up to new possibilities. To Gideon. And yet even with him, a man she was interested in, she hadn't asked about his injury. She'd been closed off for so long, she'd forgotten how to talk to people.

"Where's Janice?" Rory asked, concerned that she wasn't with them.

Pam looked around and lowered her voice even more. "A friend of hers called and said it was important she meet him regarding the D-E-A-T-H here. She should be back any minute."

"For a safe apartment building, things are a little dicey here right now," Sally said.

"I've lived here nearly two years," Pam said. "It's always been quiet here. In fact, if you don't count the fabulous four creepers—rest in peace, Dustin; and they're really more annoying than anything else—then it was quiet until the detective was shot."

"Do you think someone from our building had something to do with it, or an outsider?" Lydia asked.

"That's a good question," Cindy said. "One would think it would have to be someone residing on the ground floor or someone able to get in and out the lobby doors."

"That could be anyone. The deliverymen have a way in," Pam pointed out.

Janice rushed in looking disheveled and a little pale, Rory thought. She took her usual chair beside Pam and looked around at her friends, twice opening her mouth to speak and then closing it when she glanced down at Ellen.

"Should I take Ellen upstairs to our apartment?" Lydia asked.

Ellen glanced up, proof that she was paying attention to the conversation.

Janice took a deep breath. "Give me a minute. I'm not even being dramatic. I swear." Janice was rarely given to dramatics. "It might be best, Lydia. I can fill you in after I tell the others."

"I'll go up and watch her," Cindy promised.

Lydia immediately rose, lifted Ellen into her arms and took the elevator up to the second floor.

Rory looked expectantly at Janice.

"I'm telling all of you this in absolute confidence. You have to give me your word this won't go any further. My friend risked his job to warn me." Janice waited for each of them to verbally give them their vow of silence.

Rory could see she meant business.

"Dustin didn't commit suicide," Janice whispered. "He was shot. Tortured. And then hung. Someone murdered him. No one is supposed to know. My friend wanted me to be on the alert. He said not to go anywhere alone."

A chill went down Rory's spine. They stared at each other in shock. "Could he be mistaken, Janice?"

Janice shook her head. "He risked his job to warn me. He examined Dustin's body. You can't tell anyone. I mean it. The gunshot wasn't to kill him, only to subdue him. Whoever tortured him took their time and inflicted a tremendous amount of pain and damage before hanging him. Go in pairs everywhere."

Cindy took a deep breath. "This is crazy. Why didn't the police warn us?"

"I have no idea. They didn't tell anyone. They let everyone believe his death was a suicide."

"I moved here with the boys believing they would be safe. First the detective was murdered, now this. I need to rethink our living arrangements."

"Cindy," Janice wailed.

"I'm not telling anyone," Cindy said. "I'm just going to start thinking about where I can move with the boys that's safer."

Rory couldn't blame her. If she had children, she'd think about it too.

4

Gideon could barely take his gaze from the vibrant color of Rory's hair. They were seated at one of the outdoor tables on the wharf at a restaurant only the locals frequented. The sun spotlighted all that dark cherry, now shining so bright it was nearly blinding him.

"You have beautiful hair." He blurted it out and then flashed her a grin, shaking his head at his own stupidity. "I suppose you get told that a lot."

Rory's long lashes lifted. Now that he was so close to her in daylight, he could see that her lashes were dark, but they were dark cherry, just like her hair. Gorgeous. Everything about her was beautiful. He felt the impact of her green eyes.

"Actually, no. You're the first, so thank you."

She was telling the truth. He could hear lies. No one had ever given her a compliment on her hair? What was wrong with the men she dated?

"I don't date much, so I'm awkward, and I don't want to mess this up," Gideon said.

She smiled at him, and that smile was genuine. "I don't have much experience in the world of dating, so I probably won't notice if you're awkward. I moved here recently and had never even heard of this restaurant. It does have the best view of the harbor. You were right." She'd asked some of her friends, and only Janice and Pam knew of it, but they hadn't eaten there.

"It sits just high enough above the water that you can see the waves rolling in. It doesn't matter if the fog is hanging out at sea or the sun is out; the view is outstanding. And wait until you have the food. No one does clam chowder the way they do. Everything on their menu is fresh and very good."

Rory picked up the menu and bent her head, so the sun once more turned her hair into a fiery glow. "You know what I do for a living. What do you do?"

"I'm employed by the government in a security capacity. At the moment, I'm off for a while. I had quite a bit of vacation and sick time coming to me, and the boss was insistent I take it."

She glanced up at him, amusement in her eyes. "Are you a workaholic?"

He shrugged, flashing another grin her way. "I live alone. Don't even have a cat. I'm not that good of a cook. I do have a great roof-top though."

Those green eyes studied his expression, and then she laughed. "You're definitely a workaholic. Good excuses though. I especially like the one that you're not a good cook."

"I can cook," he clarified. "I'm just not great at it. And who wants to cook for one person? I wouldn't mind showing off my skills for you, which admittedly aren't much, if we get that far. Cooking for two is far more fun than one. You any good in that department?"

"I watch the cooking channel, if that counts."

The amusement in her voice sent heat streaking through his veins. Before he could reply, the waiter was there to take their orders. She was all about the soup and shrimp. She was also ready to try the house bread. He was willing to share that with her and gave his order as well. As the waiter walked away, he was shocked to see two members of his team take a seat at a table behind Rory.

Gideon knew it wasn't a coincidence that Brian Hutton and Ethan Meyers had come to the restaurant. They weren't following him. That meant something serious had to be communicated to Gideon.

"It has to count as much as my abilities do," Gideon conceded. "You said you moved here recently. Where is your family?"

"I lost my parents a long time ago, and I don't have any other family, so I decided to see as much of the United States as I could. Well, at least the parts that interested me. I don't like the heat, so I tend to stay away from places that get really hot. I visit during the good weather. I wanted to see New Orleans, so I went during the cooler weeks."

"That makes sense." He took a quick scan of the table behind her. Brian signed, keeping his hands close to his chest. It was their private street code. Rory had been followed from her apartment building.

Gideon's gut tightened into knots. Javier had assured him just a few days before, when they'd been in the bar, that she didn't have a stalker. Now, in broad daylight, she'd been followed? He took care to keep his features clear of the alarm he felt. The man had been careful to stay a block or so back from her and in the shadows.

"What about you? Does your family live here in San Francisco?" she asked.

"It's difficult to explain my family. The simple answer is yes. I grew up a street kid. No real home. The kids I hung out with eventually became my family. We ended up sticking together. Just up the street from where you work is a huge warehouse. Jaimie, a woman I grew up with and consider my sister, is a computer genius. The man you saw me with in the bar, Javier, he is too. Nothing gets by them. That warehouse is home to Jaimie and Mack and Rose and Kane, as well as the computers that allow us to do our work. Our family is still together, only now we work together."

"That's fascinating," Rory said. "Are there more of you?"

He nodded. "Quite a few more. We get in each other's business. Kane and Rose have a son now. We all take turns spoiling him. Rose acts tough, but she isn't. She's a marshmallow inside and doesn't mind us giving Sebastian attention. She's good about sharing him with us."

"Your voice goes soft when you talk about Sebastian," Rory said.

Gideon noted that *her* voice sounded soft. He liked that. Her green eyes certainly looked at him with approval.

"Why security?"

He should have been expecting that question. "We didn't always feel safe on the streets. It wasn't safe. We had to learn to protect ourselves and each other. It was a natural progression to protect others."

Rory glanced toward the rolling waves, and Gideon took the opportunity to tap on his shoulder in code to Brian and Ethan. *Where is the man following Rory now?*

"That makes sense. Do you like living here?"

"San Francisco? The harbor? Yes. Jaimie found the place first. She was renovating the warehouse, and we all thought it was a great idea. I found a building that had survived the 1906 earthquake and fires but needed so much work it was condemned. It was four stories high, and the rooftop was so unbelievably cool, like a giant eagle's nest. I had to find a way to save it. The building was an odd shape, built of brick. Everyone wanted to demolish it but me. I had to have it, which I suppose was silly, but I've never been sorry."

He followed her right into the restaurant, Ethan coded.

"I know exactly what building you're talking about. It's beautiful now. You saved it from being torn down after all." There was admiration in Rory's voice. She reached out and brushed her fingertips over the back of his hand. "Saving that building wasn't silly at all."

His entire body reacted to that featherlight touch. He felt it like a hot streak of lightning rushing straight to his groin.

"*I* didn't save it. I brought in a couple of experts who knew what they were doing to make sure it could withstand earthquakes and anything else thrown at it. Then Jaimie found a couple of other experts to design the outside to look the way it did back when it was first built, but with up-to-date seismic codes that we know are going to hold up when the earthquakes hit. I need open spaces, so inside, I wanted the spaces to flow into one another. In all honesty, I don't spend much time on the lower floors. A service comes in to clean them once a week. I live mainly on the top floor and rooftop."

"I'm not going to lie. I might have to keep seeing you just to see inside that building and go out on the rooftop. I rented a top-floor apartment just to get a rooftop patio," Rory admitted.

Gideon couldn't help exchanging a smile with her. "Some people have a problem with heights."

"I never have. I don't like to be inside very much," she said. "When I was a little girl, I was trapped in an attic, and it was very stuffy. There were no windows and there was so much dust. I couldn't get out." She hesitated for a moment and then shrugged. "You may as well know now, I have the worst lungs. You know I have asthma, but it's really bad. I can barely breathe sometimes and need to use a breathing machine to give myself treatments. I thought I was going to die in that attic, and ever since, I can't stand closed-in places."

Her green eyes stared right into his, defiantly waiting for him to pass judgment on her. She expected him to think less of her because she wouldn't be able to keep up with a physically fit man. That much was written all over her face. She hadn't wanted to use her inhaler in front of him when he'd walked her home from the bar. That hadn't made sense to him.

"How terrible for a child to be trapped like that, especially one already having breathing problems. I don't have the excuse of breathing problems, and I have trouble with claustrophobia. I can control it, but it takes an extreme amount of concentration and discipline."

Her gaze didn't leave his, not even when the waiter placed their food in front of them. He cursed himself silently for giving too much away. She was waiting for more. If he gave her more, that could lead to even more, and just about everything about his adult life was classified now. He couldn't share that with her. He wanted her in his life. He wanted to hook her deep, draw her in. Keep her. Again, that red flag went up because the connection between them, the chemistry, was growing stronger and stronger, but he chose to ignore the warning.

Gideon sighed. "I told you, I grew up on the streets. I didn't have the best childhood. Things happened when I was a kid." How best to blend the past and present? He said it fast. "I joined the military. Got my school paid for. When I served, I was taken prisoner. Tortured. Kept in a box and buried to my neck. Bad things happened. Luckily, I had my family. They came for me."

Her eyes instantly went liquid. Her lashes fluttered and went down, concealing her reaction. "How terrible. I didn't mean to bring up such a bad memory, Gideon."

"It isn't one I ever forget, Rory." He indicated her soup with his fork. "We're getting to know one another. These are things we're going to run into. My past isn't always pleasant. Getting accidentally locked in attics and nearly dying isn't either."

"You're very fit."

"I do security work. It's in my best interest to be able to move fast when needed."

"I'm never going to be able to run."

He could hear the warning in her voice. He arched an eyebrow at her. "My woman isn't required to do security work with me, which means she never has to run if she doesn't want to. In fact, I'm one of those overprotective men who prefers to know she's safe bartending and having fun with her friends while I'm on assignment."

That earned him a smile. Not a huge one, but still a smile. He could tell she was into him. He didn't know why she would be, but he'd take it. He'd take anything he could get from her. The chemistry between them was intense. He wasn't the only one feeling it. The heat flared strong.

He'd managed to brush his fingers against hers twice, and both times, every nerve ending in his body jolted alive. Little sparks of electricity crackled between them. Each time they did, her vivid green gaze would jump to his and a hint of color would steal into her cheeks. Her breathing changed, and those lashes of hers fluttered irresistibly.

He wasn't going to make any mistakes with her. She was leery, feeling her way with him, expecting him to reject her. He didn't understand how a woman as beautiful and intelligent as she obviously was could possibly expect rejection from men.

"I hate to break it to you, but bartending isn't always the safest profession." There was a teasing note now.

He gave her a real Gideon growl. "I saw that for myself the other night when half the men in the bar were hitting on you. I worried that you might have stalkers." He gave her a little frown. "You don't have stalkers, do you?"

"Not that I know of. When I say bartending isn't the safest profession, it's more because fights break out. Or sometimes we spot jerks putting something in a woman's drink—or even a man's drink—and we intervene. That's always risky. We try to be discreet, but if we're found out, the consequences can be ugly."

"Have those things happened?"

She nodded. "This is *great* food. How come I didn't know about this place?"

She clearly wanted to change the subject. Gideon debated and then allowed her to get away with it. He looked around the restaurant, keeping it casual. He spotted the man watching Rory right away. He was dressed in a suit and was sitting at one of the smaller tables for two situated against the far wall of the patio in the shade. He was in the darker shadows, but Gideon took in every detail of his appearance and filed it away.

The man was close to forty, or maybe he'd already crossed that mark. He was fit, rough looking. Nervous but trying not to show it. Looking around, not just fixating on Rory. He didn't have his phone out, taking pictures. He just sat in the shadows, watching her. Watching Gideon. Studying him. Looking around as if he might be in danger.

Was it possible the man was watching over Rory? Shadowing her for a reason other than stalking her for his own purposes? He seemed more interested in the people around him and those coming onto the patio rather than Rory. He waited until Rory was studying the rolling sea again and the antics of the seagulls before he signaled to Brian and Ethan the various possibilities.

Using telepathy was easier and safer than code, but not everyone on their team was able to have the natural pathways without a strong bridge. Gideon was a strong telepath, but practicing code was something they did to keep sharp, so they could use the form of communication out in the open anywhere and never be seen.

"I imagine it looks like a hole-in-the-wall outside. You barely notice it when you walk past it," he said aloud. "Living here, I started noticing the locals hit it hard for lunches and dinners. I just followed them." He flashed another grin. "When you're a man and you're hungry, you tend to do that kind of thing."

She looked back at him and sent him another small smile, reaching for the bread. He pushed the butter closer to her, and she didn't hesitate to slather the salted garlic butter onto the warm slice of freshly made bread. He liked that about her too. She ate real food and enjoyed it. He liked watching her enjoy eating.

The wind tugged at her hair as if trying to pull at those dark cherry strands she'd insisted on taming. She'd gathered her hair into a knot and then twisted it, tried her best to flatten it with two decorative combs against her scalp at the back of her head so that only the top of the knot showed the waves of cherry red shining in the sun. The more the tendrils escaped, the more he found he liked it.

"I'm going to have to bring my friends here," Rory said. "Cindy was just telling me the other day that she couldn't find anywhere close with decent food the boys would eat. She's a single mom with two children. She would love this restaurant, and it could be a place she could occasionally bring the kids when she was too tired to cook. It isn't that far from the apartments either. Thank you so much, Gideon."

He'd been concerned that she might expect him to bring her to a nicer place, an expensive place, but she hadn't batted an eyelash when he'd brought her to what appeared to be a dive from the outside. She'd looked up at him with that killer smile that had the potential for giving him a heart attack and had gone right on in with him.

"How bad were you injured on the last mission—or whatever you want to call it—you went on before you took your leave?"

She asked the question quietly, almost casually. She pushed food around on her plate, but her green eyes were steady on his face. He didn't want to start off their relationship by lying to her.

"Was in the wrong place at the wrong time. Got tagged in a couple of places." He moved to ease his body and realized he'd probably done so a couple of times, just as he'd done in the bar and when they talked together in the Koi Garden. He gave her a self-deprecating smile. "I told you I wasn't good at this. Give me a little time. I'll get better at it. You weren't supposed to notice. I'm not healed yet. Everything's tight. I would normally hole up on my rooftop, but I wasn't taking the chance that someone else was going to swoop in behind my back and steal you out from under me."

She laughed. He loved that sound, could listen to it for the rest of his life. "Because so many men are rushing to take me out that you had to worry. In all honesty, Gideon, I'm glad you came in when you did and asked me out. But you didn't answer my question, as sweet as that is. I'm persistent when I want to know something. 'Tagged in a couple of places' tells me nothing at all."

"I suppose it doesn't." Deliberately, he looked around the room as if on a covert mission. He lowered his voice, so she had to bend her head to his. "This is our first official date. You come out with me again, I can give you that information; otherwise, it's classified, and I can get into a lot of trouble divulging that to you."

She burst out laughing again, just as he knew she would. "You are so full of bullshit. But since I really want to know and I want to see your rooftop, I'm committing to another date."

"On my rooftop?"

She hesitated the slightest bit, but he was aware of it. She nodded her head. "I'll bring a picnic."

"Would you prefer to bring someone with you rather than coming alone? It's a big step coming alone to my place on a second date," Gideon said, giving her an out.

"Technically, it can be considered our third date. And since you gave me the idea in the first place, I'll just send pictures and the address to all my friends. If you're a nutjob, they'll all know you were the last one to see me."

"I can live with that." He took another slice of bread. "How many friends do you have?"

She laughed again, and Gideon found himself laughing with her. He'd never felt so relaxed in his life. He wanted to know everything there was to know about her. Everything. The expressions chasing across her face, what each meant. The little shifts in her moods, what those signaled. Why she didn't have the confidence she should in herself. Why she moved around so much. He wanted to unlock every mystery for himself. He wanted her to stay.

~

The women were waiting for Rory in the lounge, all five of them. Her friends. They were eager to hear every word. She could see the hope on their faces that Gideon really was a good man. The minute they saw her face, all five of theirs lit up. Janice's and Pam's expressions held more caution than the others, but they still looked happy.

"He continues to be awesome," Rory announced as she threw herself into the chair opposite Lydia. "He couldn't have been better. I looked for flaws, really looked for them, but he was so nice, in fact even nicer than he was the first time."

"Are you going to see him again?" Sally asked, handing her a coffee. "I'm coming to the bar. If you can meet men like him there, I'm totally going to hang out with you."

"I'm definitely going to see him again," Rory said. "As for meeting men like him at the bar, I think he's a fluke, entirely one of a kind." The smile faded. "Having said that, I'm not certain I *should* see him again."

Cindy scowled at her. "Why in the world would you even hesitate, Rory? You're clearly attracted to him. You say he's nice. What's wrong with him that you'd worry you shouldn't see him?"

"I knew it." Janice jumped on her hesitation. "He doesn't work, does he?"

"Probably a total con artist," Pam concluded.

"Are your alarm bells ringing like crazy?" Lydia asked.

Rory shook her head, feeling guiltier than ever. "No, he has a good job, and my alarm bells aren't ringing, but his should be. I can tell he's looking for a relationship, not a one-night stand. He wants something permanent."

"And?" Cindy prompted.

"Isn't that a good thing?" Sally asked.

Rory shook her head. "I move around all the time. I don't think I've been in the same place for longer than four months, maybe five at the most." She'd considered staying longer, but she hadn't yet found somewhere she wanted to stay that long. This might be her first. She'd been here past that five-month mark already, something unheard-of for her. She should have been restless, but she found herself wanting to stay.

"It wouldn't be fair to lead him to believe we could have a long-term relationship when I know I'm going to pick up and move."

There was a short silence while the others thought about what she'd said.

It was Janice who responded. "Why do you have to move around, Rory? Why do you feel it's so necessary?"

The question hit her hard, a punch that landed in her stomach and even made her hunch. She hadn't allowed those doors to creak open. She'd just kept moving, never looking back. She didn't want to look back now. The nightmares were getting worse. She didn't seem to be able to outrun them.

"After I lost everyone, I decided to visit the places that intrigued me and see as much of the country as I could take in," she admitted. "Once I made that decision to map out the places I wanted to go, I just kept moving forward and never really stopped."

"But you could stop if you really wanted to," Sally said, drawing her feet under her and reaching for her coffee. "Here. With all of us. You could stay, couldn't you, Rory?"

"You have a good job," Lydia pointed out. "And you like all the people you work with."

"With the exception of Harvey, Ret and Jarrod, everyone living in the apartment building is nice," Pam said. "Well," she qualified, "the ones we've met."

"And Harvey, Ret and Jarrod haven't actually done anything to us," Sally was quick to point out.

Janice rolled her eyes. "Sally, you always have to be so nice. I don't think you ever see bad traits in anyone."

Sally ducked her head, but not before Rory caught a glimpse of pain in her eyes. Rory hastened to take the spotlight off her. "That's why we all love you so much, Sally. Me, I'm always looking for the worst in people, so I find it. That was what was so shocking about Gideon. He looks rough and tough. He isn't handsome in the accepted sense of the word, but I'm not in the least attracted to pretty boys."

"What do you mean, rough and tough?" Pam asked, suspicion in her voice.

Rory shrugged. "Meaning lots of muscle. Tattoos. Scars. His hair is thick and unruly. He doesn't really try to tame it, just pulls it back out of his way. The color is dark but streaked with silver. I thought that was unusual because he can't be more than middle thirties; at least, he doesn't look older than that. He has a mustache but trimmed. No beard but lots of dark scruff on his jaw. He has beautiful eyes. I mean gorgeous. At the same time . . ." She broke off, unsure how to put her feelings into words.

Gideon did have beautiful eyes. So blue. They could be blue like the sky. Or arctic blue like an icy glacier. Or what? Deadly. A piercing predator dark blue with a silver ring around the color. When that happened, he didn't blink at all, and he looked as if he could see right through skin and bones into the very heart of you, where he could rip out every organ if he desired to do so. She didn't want to say that. Nor did she want to say there was a part of her that reacted to that part of him.

"His eyes," Cindy prompted. She looked around the room, sighed and stood up. "My little hooligans were supposed to stay right here or in the library next to us with the door open. Do you see the door open? Because I don't."

Lydia stood up as well. Her daughter was looking through a picture book right next to her on the sofa, but having a child, she knew the anxiety it caused when children were out of sight. Rory and the others immediately got up to help look for them. Cindy's sons made an art of disappearing in the apartment building. They especially loved to hide in the laundry room. There were many intriguing places in the basement for the boys to slip into where adults couldn't fit. They knew better than to leave the building, and so far, they had obeyed that mandate.

They had always played, running around every level of the

building, until the women had gotten the word that Dustin had been murdered. Now the apartment building was no longer a place for the boys to call a jungle gym. They had strict instructions to stay within sight.

Cindy pushed open the door to the hallway and called out for her sons. She had the mom voice down pat.

Isiah, her oldest, came running halfway up the hall. He looked pale, every freckle standing out. "Mom. You need to come now. Hurry."

He waved his arms at her, his eyes bright, but he didn't look happy. In fact, Rory thought he looked scared. Cindy must have thought so too because she began to run.

"What's wrong, Isiah? Where's your brother? Where's Moses?" There was a hitch in her voice.

"That's what I'm trying to tell you. Moses wanted to slide down the garbage chute. We do it all the time, but he couldn't. He got stuck because Ret was sliding down it before him, and he got stuck and it isn't nice. MoMo is crying and I couldn't reach him to get him back out."

Rory's heart dropped, and hard knots formed in her stomach. That didn't sound good at all. She didn't want to think about Ret. He wouldn't slide down the garbage chute on his own. If Moses had landed on top of him and had gotten stuck, that meant Ret was dead. Dustin was dead. If Ret was dead and no one had seen Harvey or Jarrod since the cop had been killed, what did that mean? Her stomach lurched at the idea.

"Ret wouldn't play in a garbage chute," Janice whispered as they hurried after Cindy, who ran up the stairs, following her son.

"Moses shouldn't be sitting on top of a dead man," Lydia hissed, Ellen on her hip, her head turned away from the little girl so she couldn't see. "He's too sensitive. He'll have nightmares for the rest of his life."

Little Moses was only four. He was a firecracker, bright and funny, but very sensitive. He followed his brother's lead. Wherever Isiah went, Moses went. What Isiah did, Moses did. But Rory knew the two boys had very different personalities.

"Who will have nightmares?" Ellen whispered into her mother's ear.

Lydia hushed her.

Rory's mind had to solve puzzles. That was just the way she was. Now she knew she would be turning the pieces she had over and over in her head until she had more and she could fit them together and make them work, but nothing added up. A detective murdered in their apartment building. Dustin murdered. Now Ret in the garbage chute. Someone had to have put him there. No one had seen Jarrod or Harvey since the detective had been murdered. Were they dead as well?

They rounded the corner of the hall, and Cindy came to an abrupt halt, forcing those behind her to halt as well. Rory caught at Cindy's shoulders as she rocked back. Isiah had run right up to the garbage chute. He'd propped the door open with a stick. There was a chair directly in front of it the boys had dragged from the little alcove about twenty feet away, where a small visiting area had been set up.

Cindy walked slowly up to the chute and peered down. "Moses. I'm here, baby. Mommy's here now. I'll get you out."

Rory heard a little sob, and then it stopped, as if Moses had jammed his fist into his mouth.

"I need a flashlight to see how best to get to him," Cindy said. Her voice shook, but she kept it together. That was Cindy. She had the boys, and she didn't lose it when she had to be strong for them.

"I've got one on my keychain." Rory passed her the keys. "It's pretty bright, so tell Moses to close his eyes." She could use the light against an attacker by flashing it in his eyes to temporarily blind him. It wasn't like she was the fastest runner in town, so she had to have other devices that would work for her if she was attacked.

"Mom," Isiah said, tugging on Cindy's leggings. "Ret's there. I could see his head. There's a plastic bag around it, and his mouth is open wide and so are his eyes. I told Moses not to look at him. I told him to stare up at the door. I tried to reach him to pull him back up, but I couldn't get to him."

"You did the right thing coming to get me. Moses, you need to close your eyes and keep them closed," Cindy called down to her son. "I'm using Auntie Rory's flashlight and it's superbright. She says it could blind you. Close your eyes very tight while I look down and see how far you are. I want to know if I can just reach down and pull you up."

"You're too short, Mom," Isiah announced. "Auntie Jan maybe could do it, or Auntie Pam, but not you."

Cindy ignored Isiah's proclamation. "Are you ready, Moses? Do you have your eyes closed? I'm going to shine the light on you."

"Yes." The answer was shaky.

Rory wrapped her arm around Cindy and stepped up with her to the edge of the garbage chute. The first thing she saw was little Moses with his face upturned toward them, his shock of sun-bleached hair and his hands over his eyes. Then she saw Ret's face in the plastic bag, his mouth open as he died gasping for air and his eyes wide open in shock. It was an ugly sight, one Moses and Isiah should never have seen.

Moses was sitting right on top of the head, as it was turned sideways. Ret's shoulders were wedged in the garbage chute, wrapped in plastic as well. Rory could just barely make that out. Cindy started shaking so much that her entire body sagged. The light went all over the place. Rory caught the keychain before it bounced down the chute. She helped Cindy to sit to one side of the opening. Isiah rushed to his mother and burst into tears as he circled her neck with his arms and buried his face in her neck.

"Janice, do you think you can reach him?" Rory asked. Janice had peered into the chute as well.

Janice nodded grimly. "Pam stepped out and called the police. They'll be here soon. We want Moses out of the chute and both boys in their apartment with their mother by the time the cops get here."

Rory took a breath and let it out. "That's good. Little Moses can't handle much more."

"I'm coming for you, Moses," Janice called down to the boy. "You don't have to do anything but reach your arms up very, very high when I tell you to. Otherwise, hold really still until you hear me tell you to reach up. Can you do that for Auntie Jan?"

"Yes," Moses's shaky voice answered. He sounded even quieter than he had the first time.

Rory could barely hear him. She was suddenly afraid for him. She didn't know that much about children, but she did know trauma could wreak havoc on victims. If Moses became so traumatized that he couldn't deal with the reality of the situation, it would be much more difficult getting him out of the chute.

"Hold the light to the side so I can still see down into the chute, but keep it out of his eyes."

Janice climbed onto the chair, positioning herself directly over the middle of the garbage chute, and leaned in. Pam had returned, and she quickly anchored her ankles. Rory held the light aloft and to one side, making certain that Janice could see the little boy but the bright light wouldn't hurt their eyes.

"All right, Moses, reach up for me. Stretch as far as your arms can go. Don't try to stand up," Janice instructed. "Let me catch your wrists, and I'll pull you up and out of there."

For a moment, Moses sat very still, almost as if he didn't hear Janice or he was too terrified to obey. Then his little arms began to rise slowly into the air. Rory's breath caught in her throat as Janice strained to reach him. It looked as if she might tumble into the chute, but Pam refused to allow her to fall, holding her firmly. Cindy added her strength to Pam's, both women anchoring Janice as she stretched toward the little boy.

Rory willed Janice's efforts to be successful. The woman took her time, murmuring softly to the child, letting him know she was close. Then her fingers managed to wrap around the boy's little wrists. Rory wanted to cheer, but she kept silent, not even telling Cindy that Janice had the child. He still had to be pulled out.

Rory glanced over to Sally and Lydia. They had to help Janice out of the chute. Pam and Cindy didn't dare let go of her. She might end up headfirst inside the garbage chute right on top of Ret and Moses. Sally and Lydia didn't need a verbal command. One circled Janice's hips and the other her waist, and they began to slowly pull her back out of the chute while Rory kept the light steady.

Janice finally emerged, and then Moses did. Cindy gave a small, inarticulate cry and gathered the little boy into her arms, holding him tightly against her, paying no attention to grime or smell.

"Get the boys to your apartment," Rory advised. "The cops will be here any minute. You don't want them talking to the kids, especially Moses."

Cindy nodded, reached down for Isiah's hand and hurried away.

5

Rory recognized three of the four detectives who came in to talk to her and her friends. Detective John Westlake had been the partner of Peter Ramsey, the detective who had been killed. Westlake had been grim-faced and abrupt to the point of rudeness, but she hadn't blamed him. He was visibly upset and had left the room several times to go outside, where she'd observed him with his head down and his hand over his eyes.

Westlake was a man of about forty, very fit, with shrewd blue-gray eyes and dark closely cropped hair. Although he wore a wedding ring, he clearly was a breast man, because his gaze dropped to Rory's chest often when he questioned her. He didn't ogle her the way some men did, but it was still disconcerting. She worked out every day, but that didn't mean she was thin by any stretch of the imagination. She had breasts and she had hips and a butt. She wasn't huge, but she wasn't the accepted slim model figure one supposedly aspired to be.

Detective Warren Larrsen was a bit younger, perhaps thirty-five, with a headful of dark chestnut hair, dark brown eyes, a trim mustache and no wedding ring. He was very pleasant and often said things to reduce the tension. He didn't look at any of the women's breasts, but he did look at Lydia out of the corner of his eye when he thought no one noticed. Rory was a bartender. She noticed everything. The detective was very interested in Lydia, although he was careful not to let the other detectives see.

Detective Leo Carver was the oldest, a man pushing fifty or already there. He was married, as evidenced by the ring he wore. He also wore glasses and seemed kind when he asked questions of them, especially when he was asking after Westlake snapped something harshly. It was difficult not to like him.

Detective Miles Abbott was quiet, allowing the others to ask the questions, standing back, observing more than anything else. He was a thoughtful man of about forty-five, clean shaven, sandy-colored hair. His shrewd cop eyes seemed to notice everything and everyone. Of all the detectives, Rory thought Abbott was the one who appeared to take in every reaction and gesture of everyone in the room.

Rory was uneasy in their presence. She didn't like questions. She didn't like anyone prying into her life. She moved around, and it was clear these cops already knew that she did. The fact that she moved continually appeared to be a red flag to them, although she couldn't understand why. They kept coming back to that fact. Westlake played bad cop, and Carver or Larrsen would play good cop, soothing her ruffled feathers when Westlake would demand to know why she picked up and left a perfectly good job to move to a new location.

The other women stayed close even when they were told they could leave. Lydia scowled at the detectives, and twice Janice had to stop her from snapping at them when they pointedly questioned Rory.

"When was the last time you saw Harvey Matters and Jarrod Flawson?" Westlake barked at her.

Rory considered giving him a smart-mouthed answer, saying both were hiding out in her closet, but she didn't think any of the detectives had a sense of humor, with the exception of Larrsen. He might still have retained his ability to laugh.

"I think it was the day before the detective was shot. They came into the gym when I was working out."

"What did they say?"

"I left without speaking to them. We aren't friends."

"Why aren't you friends?" Carver asked.

Rory shrugged. "I don't know them. I work nights and tend to stay to myself unless I'm around . . ." She broke off to gesture at the women in the room.

"Have you seen either man in the bar where you work?" Westlake asked. His gaze once more dropped to her breasts.

Rory was uncomfortable enough that she looked around for a blanket or throw to cover up with. She wasn't wearing anything revealing, but he made her feel sleazy.

"Recently? As in the last couple of days, or ever?"

"In the last couple of days," Westlake snapped. "I think we've made it abundantly clear we're looking for them."

She let her breath out slowly. "No, I haven't seen either one of them in the bar recently. I think I've been very cooperative, even though you've been a complete asshole. I'm done here. I'll call my boss. He has plenty of lawyers and no doubt will loan one to me." She pulled out her cell phone. "I'll meet with you at the precinct if you have more questions. Let me know what time you want me there."

She stood up, suddenly furious with all of them. "Your good-cop-bad-cop routine sucks. We had a bad scare finding Moses in the garbage chute. And then discovering Ret Carnes with a plastic bag over his head was traumatizing. None of us have ever experienced anything like that. You are supposed to be the good guys, but instead of making us feel better and helping us understand what's going on where we live, you're making us feel like shit."

"I'm sorry you feel that way, Miss Chappel," Detective Carver said. "That wasn't our intention. These men are persons of interest in the murder of a police detective."

"Harvey Matters and Jarrod Flawson could be in danger," Detective Abbott said. "You can see how important it is for us to find them." He jerked his chin toward the door, and the other three detectives made their way out. "Please accept our apologies." He gave Rory a little salute and followed the other detectives out.

"I can't believe you said those things to them, Rory," Sally said. "I was afraid they'd arrest you right on the spot."

"For what? Calling them out? Speaking the truth? They were being assholes." Rory wrapped her arms around her middle. "Did you see little Moses? He was drooling. His face was slack even when Cindy took him from Janice. I think she's going to have to take him to the hospital."

"Cindy did," Janice confirmed. "She took both boys. I was glad she took them, even if Moses didn't need to go. That way the police couldn't question them even if they wanted to. Once the doctor sees Moses, he's not going to give anyone permission to talk to the kid without the psych doc right there." There was satisfaction in her voice.

"Moses can't tell them anything anyway," Rory said. "What would he be able to say? But you saw them. I don't care that Detective Abbott apologized. He didn't sound all that sincere to me. They would rip those little boys to shreds."

"I agree," Lydia said. "Well, maybe not Detective Larrsen. He didn't seem nearly as aggressive and mean as the others. He kept interrupting them and frowning at that awful Detective Westlake."

"We should try to remember Detective Ramsey, the man who was shot to death practically right in front of him, was his longtime partner," Sally reminded gently. "Westlake had to go home and tell that man's family he was killed."

Pam sighed. "I know Ramsey was his partner, but he doesn't have to be so nasty."

"And did you see the way he kept looking at Rory's ta-tas?" Janice was indignant. "He had a wedding ring on his finger and was staring at her boobs."

"She does have amazing boobs," Lydia pointed out. "I'm a little jealous."

Rory burst out laughing and then sobered, looking at her watch. "I've got to put together a picnic basket and forget all about Ret's face wrapped up in a plastic bag and those detectives yanking my chain. I have a date with Gideon, and I've already blown it. I'm late. I'm supposed to put a picnic basket together and meet him. I even cooked earlier. I should have been there fifteen minutes ago. I'll have to text him and tell him I can't make it."

For some reason she wanted to cry. She never cried.

"Oh no." Lydia jumped up, reaching down to gather her sleeping daughter into her arms. "Go shower. Text him. Tell him you'll explain everything when you get there, and then do it, Rory. Don't make this worse by not going. If he's really into you, he's not going to mind waiting another half hour while you get ready."

Rory's stomach dropped. She pressed her hand hard into the roller coaster to quiet it. "You think?" She looked around at her friends.

They nodded.

Her hand shook when she texted Gideon. She didn't want him to tell her that he didn't want to see her again. She couldn't text him when the detectives had been interrogating her. It had felt like an interrogation, not simply asking questions. They'd been abrupt with everyone, but she felt like they'd been especially nasty with her.

She waited for Gideon's reply to her simple I'm sorry I'm late. Unexpected holdup. If you still want me to come, it will be another half hour before I can get there. Will explain when I see you. She hadn't taken a chance on saying anything else.

Rory waited. Her friends waited with her. All eyes were on her phone. The answer came fast, proving Gideon had been waiting for a text from her. She didn't know if fast was good or bad, but she took a deep breath and looked down.

Will be waiting on roof. You have the code to get in. Looking forward to seeing you.

She couldn't understand the joy that blossomed through her, but she knew it was in her eyes when she looked at her friends. "He's waiting for me."

"Then go get ready," Lydia urged. "Do you need us to throw together food?"

"I've got that covered, but thank you," Rory said, rushing for the elevator.

Gideon, she's on the move, Javier reported. *She's being followed again. Same man. He's staying way back. He's not the only one watching her. Two cops. Undercover, dumb enough to think no one's going to make them. I spotted them going into her building earlier with two other cops.*

Gideon moved across the roof to the street side of his building, staying in the shadows of recesses he'd had built into the thick railings. It didn't take him long to spot Rory. She was beautiful, totally feminine, moving with her natural grace around the few people on the sidewalk. She had her head up, and she wore a long skirt that flowed over her hips to her ankles. A sweater buttoned down the front clung to her breasts and ended at her midsection, drawing attention to the fact that she had a small waist. Her hair cascaded down her back in a riot of curls and waves.

Gideon pressed his palm over his heart and forced his gaze from her. He was looking to find the man following her. It didn't take long to spot him. It was definitely the same man who had been in the restaurant. He was about a block and a half behind her, staying in the shadows, keeping to the doors and alcoves, his gaze on the two undercover cops more than on Rory.

The two detectives—Javier had identified them as John Westlake and Leo Carver—were watching Rory as she walked from her apartment to his building. Gideon didn't like the idea of anyone spying on her, not even the cops. He was aware a body had been removed from her apartment complex. Since it had become apparent to other members of Gideon's unit that Rory was important to him, they had set up surveillance on the complex. Javier had made it his mission to keep Rory under his eagle eye once they realized someone was following her.

Gideon could see Javier talking and laughing with a group of teens. He stood right next to the cop car, obscuring the detectives' vision of Rory as she stopped at Gideon's building and put the code in to unlock the door. Gideon couldn't help smiling as Westlake shoved open the passenger door and leapt out onto the street in an attempt to see around the group of teenagers who had stopped in the wrong place. With much more dignity, Carver got out onto the sidewalk. Rory had already disappeared into the building.

Cursing, Westlake shoved through the crowd of teenagers and hurried up the sidewalk to try to catch up with Rory. He seemed to forget he wasn't wearing a badge or a uniform or driving an official vehicle. Led by Javier, the teens flipped him off and shouted curses at him. Carver got back into the car, leaving Westlake to stomp back on his own, muttering curses back at the teens and flinging himself into the car, glowering at his partner. Carver drove away.

Gideon found himself grinning. He knew Javier would follow the man stalking Rory. Gideon could enjoy himself with the woman he'd been looking forward to seeing all day. He looked around his rooftop to make certain he had everything ready for her. Two comfortable chairs close to the firepit, which was already lit, the flames burning low. His night flowers were in bloom, looking beautiful, the blossoms turning their petals up toward the moon. Even the weather had cooperated, giving them a relatively clear night so the stars could be seen.

The trapdoor opened slowly. Gideon knew he should help, but he found himself frozen, unable to move a muscle, watching Rory's face come into his line of vision. She was really here in his home, on his rooftop, meeting him. He'd never been open to relationships at all. In fact, he knew he was a very closed-off person. He had been since he'd been that boy who was homeless with the other street kids. He'd seen too much, had been betrayed too many times. To be in any kind of a relationship, one had to have trust. He had lost that ability far too many years ago.

His first sight of her face and that hair of hers, with the moonlight shining down on her, robbed him of his ability to breathe. There was no air left in his lungs. He knew he was staring, but he couldn't stop. "You're so damn beautiful, Red," he whispered. The wind brushed across his face, and he hoped it carried his silly words away from her and all they admitted about the way he felt.

Her lips tipped upward, and if she could have gotten any more beautiful, she managed it. Her smile lit her entire face. The green in her eyes became even more vivid, deepened into a brighter emerald.

Gideon forced himself to break free of his frozen state and

hurried to help her off the staircase and onto the roof. He took the basket from her but didn't let go of her arm.

She tilted her head to look up at him. "Thank you for being understanding. I was hoping you'd wait for me."

"I would have waited all night to see you, Rory." He couldn't help the sincerity in his voice, although he was afraid he was going to creep her out with his intensity.

She gave him another smile, and it eased the knots that had gathered in his belly. He really wasn't good at this. He'd watched Kane with Rose and Mack with Jaimie, but there wasn't a lot to guide him into the newness of a relationship. Mack had known Jaimie from childhood, and Kane had a history with Rose before the others had ever known her.

He hadn't learned a thing from observing the couples together, other than that they didn't seem to be able to keep their hands off each other, and the men were extremely protective of the women. That seemed to exasperate the women. Gideon understood Kane and Mack. He felt protective toward Rory already. As far as keeping his hands off her, the chemistry was explosive, and he didn't dare get too close and test it until she knew he wasn't about having a one-night stand with her or just using her and then walking away.

He took the picnic basket from her. "Food is always appreciated, Red, but you didn't have to go to the trouble, especially when something clearly happened to make you late."

Gideon led the way to the area he'd set up for the picnic. He'd made certain the space was surrounded by his plants to make it more intimate, although the rooftop was extremely private. This area had the best view of the harbor and out to sea. The plants gave them some protection from the wind.

"This is so beautiful, Gideon." She spun in a slow circle. "I'm on the third floor. Having a view from the fourth floor really makes a difference."

"I have a throw blanket for you just in case it gets cold."

"I'm sure the firepit will keep me warm enough, but that was very thoughtful," Rory said. She took the chair closest to the planters and held out her hands to the fire. "You wouldn't believe what's been happening at my apartment complex recently."

She told him about the police detective, Peter Ramsey, being shot and killed that first day he'd come to her bar when she'd been late. She disclosed that Dustin Bartlet, a man living in the apartment building, had been found dead a couple of days later. She finished by filling him in on what happened that day.

"You're telling me a cop was killed there the other day, along with a man you knew, and now another man's body has been discovered?" He didn't let on that he had all that information already.

Rory nodded, her green eyes fixed solemnly on his. "Yep. Ret was in the garbage chute, wrapped in plastic like a mummy. Someone had killed him by putting a plastic bag over his head. It was really disgusting. When the detective was shot, my friends and I were in the lounge. We like to meet for coffee and visit when we can. It was our day to sort junk mail. The next thing we know, we hear the guns going off, and the cop staggers in with blood all over him."

"You didn't tell me any of this," Gideon pointed out.

"Well, no," she conceded. "I thought it was over. I didn't know they were going to find Ret in the garbage chute. Poor little Moses is traumatized for life. He was playing with his brother, sliding down the chute, which they were not supposed to be doing, and Moses got stuck on top of Ret's head."

Gideon sighed. "Red, your life is crazier than mine."

Her eyebrows went up. "Red? You keep calling me Red."

"Your hair. Dark cherry–colored. I can't help but think of you as Red." He flashed a smile he hoped didn't make him look like more of an ass than he already felt like.

He was discovering he wasn't the kind of man who courted a woman. He was more the caveman type, like Javier. If he could, he'd just keep his little redheaded woman safe in his home and persuade her he was the right choice for her—somehow.

"You're frowning."

He wasn't. He knew he wasn't. Inside maybe, but not on the outside. "You're not supposed to be able to read my mind."

Her laughter slipped out. Those bright notes that sounded too much like sunshine when nothing in his life had ever made him feel the way she did. It wasn't even the chemistry arcing between them like electricity—so much he expected to see white sparks snapping off their skin whenever they were too close. It was the things about her that he'd learned while watching her from a distance. From reading the reports Javier had given to him. The generous way she interacted with others. She was real.

Gideon had no idea how or why she managed to take away his demons, but she did. "It's probably best if you can't read minds." It slipped out before he could stop the words from tumbling out of his mouth. *Hell.*

Her eyebrow went up. She had a hint of red in her eyebrows. Staring at them was much safer than staring at her lips.

"What is going on in your mind that I shouldn't know about?"

Gideon turned fully toward her, drawn by a source outside himself that was much more powerful than he could control. He shook his head. "I didn't lure you up here to scare you. I've never been so attracted to a woman in my life. I didn't expect the kind of chemistry we have between us. I'm hoping it isn't all on my side."

Her emerald eyes drifted over his face inch by slow inch. He swore he could hear his heart drumming out a beat louder than the pounding sea. A slow demure smile curved her full lips, drawing his attention right back to her mouth. "I don't believe it is all on your side, Gideon."

He let his breath out, the relief tremendous. She was honest and she hadn't taken the least offense. He reached for the cooler in an effort to distract himself from his need to kiss her. "Beer? A soft drink? Water? Flavored water?"

"Water sounds good to me." She opened the picnic basket. "I hope you're hungry."

"I waited to eat, so yes, I'm very hungry."

He loosened the cap on the bottle of water and held it out to her rather than putting it on the table between them. Mostly it was an excuse to touch her. He wanted to feel her skin again. The pads of his fingers slid over her wrist when she took the bottle. Once again, he felt electrical charges snapping between them.

"What did you bring?" He slid his index finger back and forth along her inner wrist. He knew he shouldn't, but the sensation created between her satin skin and the snapping electrical flashes was too hot to resist. Heat poured through his veins, and he felt the answering fire in hers, as if the connection between them was growing stronger.

She didn't pull away. "Traditional picnic fare. Fried chicken and potato salad, but then I went off the rails and made spring rolls and shrimp fried rice. I thought it would be fun to try a couple of different dishes, and you seemed open to new possibilities."

He liked that she thought he would be adventurous enough to try something different. "I do like to try new foods. When I travel for work, I make it a point to try the local dishes." He had to release her, and he did so reluctantly.

"Do you do your own gardening?"

"For the most part. Gardening is soothing to me. Everything up here is designed around making this a peaceful retreat." That along with protecting him if he had to defend his team from enemy fire.

"I do the same thing with my much smaller rooftop patio." She made up a plate of food and passed it to him with a fork and napkin. "Your rooftop is huge and has all sorts of cool recesses built into it. Were they already there?"

He hesitated. It was a natural question. "I tried to stay as close to the original blueprints as possible on the outside of the building, but not up here. I designed most of this myself." He could see miles out to sea, all over the harbor, blocks on either side of the road. It was a sniper's dream, and if drones or helicopters were put in the air, he had so many places to hide, it would be impossible to see him.

"I've never quite understood what makes a person decide to put roots down in one place," Rory said, curiosity in her voice. "Or what causes them to choose that place."

Her green eyes met his intently but then slid away from his gaze. To give himself time to assess the situation properly, he took a bite of the potato salad. "This is outstanding," he declared after chewing it properly and taking a second bite, just to be sure that he was right about it. "Yep, fantastic."

He studied her averted face. "It's perfectly all right that you enjoy seeing new places. I see them when I'm working. I'm certain traveling to various places for work satisfies my need to see new horizons. Do you think traveling is something you want to do, or something you're compelled to do?"

Rory's eyebrows drew together. The elegant lines had those same hints of dark cherry red when the lights fell across her face directly. He had to keep himself from leaning into her and brushing kisses over those winged brows. He even liked the way she contemplated his questions. She was thoughtful, not answering immediately.

"I don't have family. Nothing to tie me to one place. I guess I thought it would be good to see all the places I would want to while I could, before I settled down to have a family. I suppose it's become a habit. I'm used to being alone now. It gets difficult to be in the company of too many people for too long."

"And yet you bartend," he pointed out. "The chicken is delicious."

"Thank you. I found that recipe online a few years ago and then experimented a little bit until I got it exactly the way I wanted it." She flashed him a little smile that turned her green eyes to a dark emerald. "I do like to bartend, and the bar puts a barrier between me and everyone else. Even when it gets crowded, I feel safe. Or safer, I suppose, is what I should say."

Taking his time, he thought that over as he ate the fried chicken. She had put that in a peculiar way. When it got crowded, she felt safe. Or safer. Why did she need to feel safe? Why was she continually moving? He was beginning to revisit the idea that she might be running from someone. But if she was, it didn't make sense that she used the same name everywhere she went and that she grew comfortable with the people around her. She was relaxed and didn't appear to be paranoid about her security. That didn't go with someone on the run.

Rory still felt like a GhostWalker to him. He had no idea why. She didn't act like one in the least. She didn't have a GhostWalker tattoo that he could see on her. She didn't appear to have any unique special skills, although he suspected she was extremely good at her job due to a psychic ability, but many people had psychic gifts they weren't aware of.

Gideon was around GhostWalkers every day. He knew them. The energy that surrounded them. They controlled that energy to a point, but everyone gave off energy. It was simply a matter of being alive. At times, like now, when she was restful, Rory gave off that low energy the GhostWalkers did, so low one was barely aware of their existence. They could be in the same room and no one would notice them. An enemy would walk right past them. It happened all the time.

"The bar makes you feel safe," he echoed casually. "Safe from what?"

Her long lashes fluttered. He had to ease his legs out in front of him to give himself a little relief. He wasn't cold in the least, but he thought it was a good idea to snag one of the throw blankets he'd set out to hide his reaction to her. That was becoming a big problem. A huge problem, he corrected himself. And a very uncomfortable one. He'd never had that before either. It was one he had to get on top of before she noticed and got scared.

"That's a good question. You seem to ask very good questions. I'm sure I had great answers at one point, but over the last year or two, I've forgotten. I just don't feel safe, but I don't know why. I think it's my inability to breathe. I can't run if I need to. When I'm walking home from work or I'm at work or really anywhere, and someone confronts me, I feel extremely vulnerable."

He was a strong man. Exceptionally strong. And fast. Since Whitney had performed his experiments, faster than human beings had ever thought possible. He'd had enough time to start taking those newer talents for granted. He worked on controlling them and learning to use them to the best of his ability, and that meant pushing his limits every day. There was no way he could put himself in Rory's shoes.

She couldn't physically get away from a confrontation. He hadn't considered what that would feel like. She was short, and men would loom over her. If they deliberately wanted to intimidate her, they knew they easily could. He despised that for her. He could see why she would always want a barrier between her and a crowd.

"I've taken self-defense classes and I can handle some weapons, but the truth is, I don't have staying power." She stopped abruptly and pressed her fingers over her lips, her eyes going wide. "I suppose I shouldn't admit that to you. You're really a stranger to me. I don't know why you don't feel like a stranger when you really are. This is so bizarre."

"You don't feel like a stranger to me either," he admitted. "Since I don't know the first thing about relationships, I can't call it bizarre. For all I know, when a man finds the right woman, they just click, and they aren't strangers at all."

She shook her head. "It isn't like that."

"You said you don't know anything about relationships either, so you can't say for certain." He held out his plate. "More of everything, please."

Rory gave him one of her smiles. "You ate all that while you were talking. How did you manage?"

"It's a practiced art. Street kid, remember? You eat what you can, when you can. Then most of the family joined the military with me, and I had to fight for my food all over again. Now they're with me here, and when one of the women cooks, it's every man for himself. I know exactly how fast those men can eat, especially when they try to distract you by talking."

Her laughter washed over him like a bright warm wave. "I see. You really are like one big family. I imagine if you wanted seconds, you would have to eat fairly fast."

"Not fairly." He took the plate from her. "Just plain fast. Manners go out the window if it's fantastic food. We try to pretend we're civilized later, but during the actual dinner, it's every man for himself."

He couldn't help teasing her just to watch her eyes light up.

"I'm a big man, Rory. The time to worry about coming up here alone with me was before you did it, not now. Telling me you run out of steam fast is going to put you at a disadvantage even if you had ten weapons on you."

She shrugged, not looking too upset. "I told you I felt abnormally comfortable around you. I'm just going with it. Besides, you might start worrying about me. Did you ever once consider I might be a black widow?"

He'd been in the process of taking a drink from the bottle of beer he'd just opened. He nearly spit it down the front of him, mainly because his mind kept circling back, wondering if it was possible she was a GhostWalker. If she was, that meant Whitney most likely sent her out to spy on them.

"There's that. I hadn't considered that possibility. I suppose I should have. Are you?" he asked solemnly. He heard lies. If she answered verbally, he should be able to hear one way or another what she was there for. He sent a silent prayer to the universe that she wasn't there to screw with him.

"No. You said you worked in security. People who work in security companies aren't typically wealthy, Gideon. I think black widows usually go after wealthy targets. It didn't occur to me you might have money when you came into the bar. Men with the kind of money to own a building like this one wear a certain type of clothing and act with a kind of entitlement you don't. I suspect your company owns this building, not you. At least I hope your company does, because I wouldn't know what to do or even say if you owned it."

Every word she said was the absolute honest truth; at least he heard the truth. He let out a sigh of relief. She didn't ask him for confirmation, probably because she didn't want to embarrass him. He ate the potato salad and washed it down with beer. She had such a compassionate nature. He was allowing her to believe things about him that weren't true, but it was safer for her. At least until he had her completely hooked.

Her long lashes kept sweeping down, an alluring temptation that was becoming much harder to resist. He set the beer bottle down and turned fully to her, reaching to remove her water bottle. The moment his fingers brushed against her skin, he felt the familiar shocking sizzle of electricity rush through his bloodstream.

"Gideon." She whispered his name, her eyes going wide. She gave a cautionary shake of her head.

He felt the sound of her voice combine with sparks of electricity to streak through his veins and spread through his body. Gideon slid one hand into the thick silk of her untamed cherry-red hair. He'd been a little desperate to feel it, and he wasn't in the least disappointed. He closed his fist around the wild waves and curls, tipping her head back slightly and holding her still.

"This might not be such a good idea." She regarded him steadily under the veil of her thick reddish lashes.

"It's the only sane idea," he countered, because it was. The *only* way he could take another breath. Think another thought. Survive the next minute.

"I'm not going to be good at this," she warned.

He urged her closer to him, just enough that her upper body rested against his. He felt the softness of her breasts against the heavy muscles of his chest. Her heartbeat accelerated. His clenched hard. He had to suppress a groan. Up close, her eyes were larger and even more gorgeous than he had first realized, surrounded by those long cherry-tipped lashes. The dusting of golden freckles and her full lips were temptation itself.

He slid the pad of his thumb over the soft curve of her bottom lip. So soft, like velvet. His gut clenched. His heart jerked in his chest. He knew if he kissed her, she would own him, but then she already did. He was tied to her in a way he didn't understand, but every minute in her company only deepened that connection. He'd never had a reaction like this to anyone—this recognition. The awakening of his body and mind. Every nerve ending coming alive.

The scorching flames leaping from cell to cell, spreading through him. Through her. Consuming them both. He knew it was both.

"Gideon." This time she moaned his name. An ache, her lips moving erotically against his thumb. "We could be in trouble."

"I don't think we have a choice, Red." He stroked caresses along the curve of her bottom lip. *He* didn't have a choice, not when her tongue touched his skin, a sinful temptation that sent heat swirling into a fierce fist in the pit of his stomach.

His fingers tightened in her thick hair, and he lowered his mouth to hers. He was a rough man. He'd never known tenderness in his life. He was gentle with her. Tender even. He coaxed her with small kisses, nibbling at the corners of her mouth, tugging at her lower lip, nipping gently. Using his tongue along the seam of her lips. Tasting a hint of wild Spanish lavender.

Gideon nipped a little harder, a little more aggressively, at her lower lip, and she gasped, allowing him to take advantage. He slid his tongue into the scorching heat of her mouth, claiming her, tying them together irrevocably. She was pure fire, the flames roaring through him, branding him. He forced himself to hang on to control. It took more effort than he ever thought possible.

Her palms slid up his biceps and then around his neck, the fingers of one hand crushing his hair at his nape while the other hand found his skin. The touch felt like she burned her brand into his skin. She was already inside him. Now she was branded on the outside of him. He had to take care that she didn't find her way into his mind as well. She was close there too. He felt her filling all the lonely places he'd had his entire life.

He lifted his head to look down at her. "I thought you said you weren't good at this."

Her lashes fluttered. Lifted. Her green gaze had gone sensual. A little dazed. Shocked even. Now she looked amused. Her lips curved into a smile. "I might have been wrong."

His heart stuttered. He brushed a kiss over her smile. "We'd better stop while we're ahead. Think of something to talk about. My brain is fried."

Rory laughed softly, the laugh that reminded him so much of perfectly pitched chimes. Dropping her arms from his neck, she sat back in her chair but touched the black ink scrolling along one of his forearms. "Beautiful artwork. Birds. I especially love the Harpy Eagle. It's gorgeous. You have quite a bit of art. Is it all various birds? From what I can see, it's mostly black ink."

"Not all. I don't really do color on my tats, so most are various shades of black. I particularly like birds. I didn't just choose my tattoos because I was drunk and I wanted to be inked. Each one means something to me." He left it at that.

"I have three tattoos," she admitted. "The one on my ankle I think is gorgeous and is my favorite. My name is Laurel, like the English laurel tree." She pulled up the hem of her skirt and showed him her bare ankle.

Gideon's breath hitched in his lungs. The tattoo was beautiful. One of the best he'd ever seen. Glossy green leaves and clusters of dark cherries coming off a tree branch. He'd seen that tattoo artist's work only once before. He knew the woman who had it on her ankle. She was Rose Cannon, who was married to Kane—a fellow GhostWalker.

6

Gideon stared down at the damning evidence for what seemed like far too long. With the precision of a sniper, he placed his plate on the table between them. He reached down and very gently lifted her ankle, placing it in his lap, smoothing his palm over the beautiful art piece.

Dr. Peter Whitney had "gifted" several of his orphan girls with a tattoo from a private artist. He had placed high-tech tracking in the petals of the flowers so small they appeared to be specks of dust. That way Whitney could track the women if they escaped.

"It's really unique, isn't it?" Rory said. There was a soft warmth in her voice. It was clear she really liked her tattoo.

Gideon glided his palm over the leaves and berries again. "It's one of the most beautiful pieces I've ever seen, Red."

He used the pads of his fingers to stroke little caresses over the artwork, using the lightest of touches. He knew what he was look-ing for. The chips had been cutting-edge. Flat. So flat Whitney had been certain they would never be discovered. They were part of the tattoo itself. Part of the intricate design.

There they were. Silently, he swore over and over. Was she a spy sent out by Whitney? If she was, why would she show him her tattoo? Why would she risk it? Whitney was aware the GhostWalkers—and the women who had escaped him—knew of the chips he'd put in them, along with the viruses. Rory's history didn't make sense if she was a spy. Javier had checked on her repeatedly. She had been to every single place he'd uncovered. She seemed to be an open book. Would Whitney have a spy waiting in the wings to put in play after a few years? Did that even make sense? Nothing about Rory made sense.

"What's the name of the tattoo artist? Where did you get it?" He ran his thumb over the incredible art one more time before releasing her ankle. "If I'm ever in the vicinity, I want to visit the shop."

She reached down and rubbed her hand over the art piece, paying particular attention to the cherries. "I can never remember his name. It's so strange because I never forget anything. I really don't. Not the slightest detail, but when I try to remember him and his shop, I can't. I've tried before when friends have asked me where I got it."

Rory sounded genuinely puzzled. "You have no idea how much that bothers me. It's a small thing, but because I use an inhaler and a nebulizer, I sometimes wonder if I don't get enough oxygen to my brain."

He couldn't help the smile that slipped out.

"Don't laugh. I'm being serious, Gideon. I don't forget things. I just don't. A customer can come into the bar where I work and talk to me about his family. He won't come in again for a month, and when he comes back, I remember his name and what he told me about his wife and children. Even his dog, if he mentioned he had a dog. I love this tattoo. How could I not remember where I got it?" There was genuine distress and puzzlement in her voice.

"I'm not laughing at you, Rory, but you aren't losing brain cells. You're intelligent. Whatever is keeping you from remembering where you got that tattoo could have a simple explanation, such as trauma. I had an experience that was extremely difficult to endure, and my mind shut down afterward. Not for all of it—that was the strange part—but afterward for small blocks of time. Even when my friends have talked to me about how we escaped, I don't remember."

He was deliberately leading her. Using trigger words. Trying to feel his way with her. She had put her bottle of water up as well. She pulled her feet onto the chair so that her knees were up, and she wrapped her arms around her legs and put her chin on top of her knees. No GhostWalker would tie his weapons up that way. She wouldn't be able to move fast. And she was looking directly into the flames of the firepit. She was agitated and struggling to comprehend why.

Gideon felt like a first-class dick. He wanted her to associate him with protection and everything safe.

"What kind of experience, Gideon?"

"I've already told you I was captured and tortured. I fought back, never said a word, never told them a thing, never gave up. My friends came for me, and that's when my mind shut down. I think it would have been a lot more helpful if it had shut down when I was going through the torture part." He gave her a half smile.

She reached out and slipped her hand into his. "I don't think anyone ever tortured me, not like that, Gideon. We talked about this. Me being in an attic and you being practically buried aren't the same thing. I don't have a real concept of torture. I think suffering blackouts after an event like that would be natural. Why would I have them?"

He slid his fingers over the soft skin of her inner wrist, sliding back and forth in a soothing caress. "That's the question, isn't it? If you don't remember, there's a reason for it. You suffered a trauma, and it's somehow connected to that tattoo."

Her palm covered the artwork. "Do you have nightmares, Gideon? About the things they did to you?"

"Yes. That's why I created this place. Up here, the nightmares can't find me. Even if I fall asleep, I usually can escape them." He answered honestly. He wasn't going to pretend she would be getting a bargain if she did choose to try to have a relationship with him. "When I'm inside, I don't sleep very well."

He kept stroking her wrist right over her pulse. Her heart rate was climbing. He bent toward her. "What is it, Red? You're safe enough up here. Just tell me."

"I have nightmares too. Often. Almost every night. They've been getting worse." She whispered it to him but broke off before she told him what her nightmares were about.

The wind tugged at them through the foliage, cool on their faces. Gideon remained silent. Waiting. Her fingers curled in his. Held tighter.

"I don't remember my childhood." The confession came out like a sin. "Nothing. Not a single thing. How can I not have a single memory of my life before my parents died? Why would I block out those years?"

She turned her head to look at him, and there was pain in her eyes. She couldn't fake that. Had Whitney taken her memories from her and sent her out into the world? Why would he do that? What would be his motivation? Gideon couldn't see past the pain in her. It was so real he ached for her.

"Do you remember your parents?" he asked, keeping his voice as soft and as gentle as he was able.

She hesitated, and then she turned away from him, but not before he caught the sheen of liquid in her eyes as she shook her head. "I don't know why I'm telling you all this when we're supposed to be having a fun time."

"We're supposed to be getting to know one another," he corrected. "I want to know everything about you." He brought her hand to his chest. "I've got things in my past that are going to be difficult to navigate. Maybe that's why we're so drawn to one another. We fit."

She turned to him, her smile back. "You always seem to say the right thing."

"I know we can work, Rory. I've searched all over the world looking for the right woman. I'm not about to give you up because there are a couple of issues."

Her laughter bubbled up. "A couple of issues? At least you didn't say *little* issues."

He found himself returning her smile. He liked that she had a sense of humor. She would need it with him. He settled back in the chair, retaining her hand against his chest with one hand and picking up his beer with the other. "So, no past history at all. You just found yourself moving around a lot. Do you know where your history came from? Did you read about yourself on the internet?"

She followed his lead, picking up her water for a sip. "I created my past. I had to have one. It was easy enough to do."

His eyebrow shot up. "Very few people have the skills to create a past, and that includes the paperwork that could pass scrutiny by experts." Two experts had gone over her past, and neither had caught that it was fake. "Do you have those kinds of skills too?"

Rory's lips tipped up. Her eyes took on an even deeper green. "I've got mad skills when it comes to paperwork. I'm good with languages too. That really helps when I'm bartending. I can look out for my customers."

He found it interesting that looking out for her customers was her first priority, and speaking several languages was useful to her in that regard. She was a GhostWalker with a need to protect others, whether she knew it or not.

"Where did your name come from?"

She gave him that little frown again, the one he was beginning to find endearing. She could make his entire body react, come alive, without even trying. He'd thought he was long dead, but somehow, she'd found a way to bring him back to life.

"I think it's my real name. But you're looking at me with the same expressionless look on your face that you get when you're frowning inside."

She leaned across the little table separating them and brushed along his jaw with the pads of her fingers. Then she moved those fingers to his lips, and his heart jumped. She rubbed back and forth as if she could erase the frown she saw in his mind. He felt each stroke moving through him like an electric arc.

He shouldn't have kissed her. The moment she touched him, his entire body remembered that kiss and what she felt like.

"Do you want the truth? I'm afraid if I tell you what I'm thinking, you'll run away so fast I won't ever see you again."

She removed her fingers, and his heart was able to slow down to a normal rhythm. Her smile turned mischievous. "I told you, I can't run. You're in luck."

"I was thinking I was dead inside, and you managed to find a way to bring me back to life. That's a hell of a responsibility to put on someone. I listen to your voice or your laughter and find myself feeling joy. I didn't remember there was joy in the world until I heard you laugh. Isn't that strange?"

He brought her knuckles to his mouth and kissed them before

once more tucking her hand close to his heart. "I know we don't know each other the way other couples do before they declare they want to be together, but I'm certain. Absolutely certain."

"Gideon." Her tone was cautionary. "It has occurred to me, and you need to consider this: Someone could have removed my memories. I've got skills most people don't."

He brought her hand under his chin and rubbed her knuckles along the bristles of his jaw. He found it interesting that she had considered that someone might have removed her memories. That would never have been a consideration to most people. Head trauma, yes, that would be a logical conclusion. Somewhere in the back of her mind, she must have a faint memory because she was genuinely worried. "Have you ever felt anyone watching you?"

She shook her head. "I checked the first few years for someone following me. Or watching. So much time has gone by now that I honestly don't think anyone's interested in me. But I still can't shake the idea that I had to have had my memories removed." Her frown came back, and she rubbed her left temple. "And that I was trained in things others haven't been."

"Are you getting a headache talking about it?"

She nodded and then shook her head. "When I try to figure it out, I get an odd sensation. Not pain exactly. Something else." She pulled her hand away from him and wrapped both arms around her middle, drawing her legs up even tighter to her body. "It's getting stronger."

Gideon didn't know whether to push her or give her a little time. He decided time was what she needed. He ran his hand down the back of her head, feeling the soft silk of her hair. "I call this place the Eagle's Nest. Just feel the peace and the way it seeps into you. Don't think about anything, Red. Just let this place do what it was created for." He kept his tone light and soothing. A brush of velvet.

Rory sent him a hesitant smile. "You're really a very special man, Gideon."

His gut clenched. Tied into a million knots. There would come a time when he would have to open up to her. Let her see all of him, not just pieces—not just the best of him—and there wasn't much in that regard. He'd lain up on this very rooftop with his rifle. That rifle was a part of him. He'd killed men. So many. Too many. Most he knew were deserving. Some, it was combat. Their side. His side. Someone above them making the call. He protected the troops. He would always do that.

He was good at what he did, and he knew it. Maybe one of the best. That didn't make it right, only real. But he was also good at hand-to-hand combat. And he had killed too many men that way as well. Those men were never a part of the nightmares, but they should have been. Perhaps if he were really as good a man as Rory thought he was, those men wouldn't have been staring at him at night, demanding to know why he had killed them. Instead, he put them aside, refusing to give them consideration after they were dead.

"That frown again, Gideon. You don't like me saying nice things about you."

"Mostly because I don't want you disappointed when you get to know the real me. You have this misguided idea of who I am. With you, I suppose I could be considered one way, but with others, I'm not so nice."

That earned him one of her smiles. It wasn't her brightest, but she gave him one that lit her eyes. "Do you walk around intimidating other people?"

He couldn't help flashing a little grin at her. "Well, yeah. That way I'm not expected to talk. And they move out of my way."

"Why in the world did you go to the bar that night?"

"To see you."

"Me?" Her eyebrow shot up, and she turned fully to him. The moon caught her hair, and it blazed into a glorious dark red shine that was beyond beautiful. "How would you even know about me?"

He laughed. "A little bird told me about you."

She studied his face. "Your friend. The one who came into the bar with you. He'd come in several times before. You call him Javier. He's come in with a couple of other men. One called Ethan. And another man named Brian. They sat at the same table. Javier likes that particular table or the one up against the wall in the darkest corner of the room. He sits there sometimes when he comes in alone. He told you about me, didn't he?"

"We've had a few discussions where you came up," Gideon said.

"Why would he think you'd be interested in me?"

"He knew. I talked about you enough times. I told you, I dreamt about you before I ever met you. He knew all about you."

Rory tilted her head back to look up at the stars. The clouds drifted across the darkened sky, threatening to obscure their perfect view. Gideon could see her delicate features. As far as he was concerned, he still had the perfect view. In profile, the woman was just as beautiful as when she was looking him straight in the eye. Those long lashes of hers had a little curl at the ends. Her eyes had gone liquid again.

"Red." He whispered the endearment. "I didn't mean to upset you. What did I say? You have to tell me so I don't fuck up again."

Her lashes swept down and then back up again. Her mouth curved up in a slight smile as she gave a little shake of her head. "You didn't eff up, Gideon. I'm beginning to think you're too good to be true. You do realize I don't have anyone at all. I can't look back and see my family. Yours may be a street family, but you have one. You chose to be part of them, and you stick with them. They stand by you. Do you know how lucky you are?"

She didn't wait for him to acknowledge that he knew. He

counted on his family. They might not be blood, but with all the blood they'd shared together, maybe they were even closer.

"I know what a miracle it is to have a man like you tell me you dreamt about me so much that your friend saw me in a bar and went back to you and told you about me. You can't imagine how that makes me feel. To have one person in this world care enough to look for me. To have his friends looking for me. I know that sounds pathetic, but it's the truth."

Rory didn't look at him when she gave him her revelation. She kept her face averted, tilted toward the sky. Her face was an oval shape. Right now, he swore he saw liquid diamonds glittering on her skin beneath her eyes.

"You know you're killing me, Rory. I'm trying to be a gentleman and not scare you, but if you're crying, I'm going to have to pick you up and put you in my lap. I have no idea what will happen after that."

A ghost of a smile tipped the corners of her mouth up. "You don't? Are you trying to absolve yourself of all responsibility?"

He sighed and swept his hand through his hair to push it back. The wind was picking up even more, managing to sneak through the shrubs. "Unfortunately, I wish I could be like that. I've always wanted to be. I tend to be the stick-in-the-mud sober driver who watches over the others when they want to cut loose. I can't help myself. In other words, I'm not the fun guy. You may as well know that right now."

Strips of hair fell across her cheek, and she shoved at that silken mass, tucking it behind one ear. That didn't do her any good, so with a little sigh of surrender, she dragged a scrunchie out of her skirt pocket and twisted her hair into a high ponytail. Once her hair was secure and out of her way, she turned her head to fully look at him again.

"No, Gideon, you're the steady man. The rock. The one everyone counts on in a bad situation." Her delicate brows drew together. "I'd bet any amount of money that you weren't captured and tortured because you were careless in some way but because you were protecting someone. You waited too long in order for them to get away. I have no idea what you were doing, but that would be my guess."

She saw too much. Her insights weren't guesses. She saw into him—into his mind—and caught glimpses of his past. He didn't see into her the way he did others. He should have. He could still discern the truth from lies, but he should have been able to see into her mind.

Her stalker hasn't left, Javier reported. *He's going all the way to the end of three blocks, but he hugs the shadows. He pays attention to the traffic. Twice, undercover cops have walked the same three blocks on either side of the street. Not the same cops that were in the first vehicle. Not Carver and Westlake.*

Gideon framed Rory's face with his much larger hands. Held her still so he could stare down into her vivid green eyes. "Be the real deal for me, Red. Don't be someone looking to harm me or my family. Come to me because you honestly see me, and I matter to you."

If it were at all possible, her green eyes softened even more. "Gideon. I want to be real for you. More than anything on this earth, I want to be real for you. I'm so afraid though. What if I'm not? You're the most wonderful man I could ever imagine meeting. If I ever stayed in one place, it would be here with you, but I'm terrified now that I could be something horrible."

No one's first thought would be that they were something horrible. They would think they'd been in an accident and had no memory of it. A brain injury. A significant event happened that traumatized them. They wouldn't consider that someone had programmed them to become something harmful to others.

"Why would you believe you may be something horrible?" He

repeated her words back to her in question form, pitching his voice low. Gentle. Soothing. Used his weapon ruthlessly. Compelling an answer.

She frowned again and rubbed her left temple just the way she had before. Her body gave a little shudder.

"What's happening right now, Rory?"

"That feeling."

"Describe it to me." Now he was the interrogator. Soft-spoken but very much in command. No one disobeyed when he used that particular tone. He reached out and took her hand, his thumb sliding along her palm in a gesture of soothing comfort. He turned her hand over so his fingers could brush caresses over her inner wrist and feel her pulse pounding there.

"It feels as if I've got another skin covering me. Like a snake. Or a lizard." She gave another shudder. "It's a sickening feeling."

She was panicking, struggling to breathe. He could hear the wheeze starting, and it was very real.

"Rory." He placed her palm on the side of his rib cage. "I want you to look at me. Only at me. Feel me breathing with you. Think only about the air moving through your lungs and my lungs. We're safe up here. Nothing can get to you."

"It's in me. On me. I can feel it."

"Breathe with me." He made that a command, using his voice to direct her. Using the sound of his own breathing. Loud. In. Out. His eyes staring into hers. Compelling her.

She followed him, settling into the rhythm, able to pull out of her panic attack, but she definitely needed her nebulizer. Once she was steady again, he was concerned she might have to leave in order to get to her medication.

"Did you bring an actual nebulizer or just an inhaler?"

"I have a small travel nebulizer with me."

"Use it, Red. We'll talk about what's worrying you after. I

meant what I said about being safe up here. If you have a second skin that needs to be shed, we'll figure it out."

She pulled out a small machine that resembled an inhaler but used her medicine in it. Gideon took the opportunity while she inhaled it to study her skin with his superior eyesight. Her skin was abnormally soft under the pads of his fingers, but his hands were rough, calloused.

He used the superior vision of the eagle, studying every square inch of exposed skin Rory had. She had a dusting of freckles along her forearms, but he couldn't detect anything that might indicate she had a second skin. He reached up to brush a caress along her left temple. He traced her entire face from her forehead to her eye with the pads of his fingers. This was where she said she always seemed to feel the strange sensation.

She removed the small nebulizer and gave him her green-eyed steady gaze. "Gideon, you're doing it again. That frown. You worry about everyone. Who takes care of you? Who looks out for you? Don't tell me your family does, because it's very clear to me that you're the one watching over them."

"Red, do I look like a man who needs others to watch over me?" It was worrisome to him that she could see that frown in his mind, and yet he couldn't see into hers no matter how hard he looked. And he was looking.

She nodded slowly, not taking her gaze from his. "Yes, I think you do. Do you think I'm programmed to hurt someone? Tell me the truth, Gideon."

"You're afraid of knowing the truth, Rory. I don't think you're ready to find out yet. When you start to get close to knowing anything, you panic and can't breathe. I don't want you to associate me with anything bad. I want you to associate me with being safe."

Gideon wanted those things to be true. He even needed them to be. He was sincere. At the same time, he was full of shit, and he knew it. He had to get to the truth of what she was and why she was there in San Francisco. She was a GhostWalker. Whitney had no doubt experimented on her just as he had so many other orphaned girls. Rory was the last woman he wanted to mislead, but he had no choice. He had to protect the others. He also had to protect her whether she knew he was helping her or not.

"The odd thing is, Gideon, I do feel safe here. I've never told anyone the things I'm telling you. I wouldn't have considered it. *You're* the one who makes me feel safe. This is the first time I've ever felt brave enough to discuss this with anyone."

The pads of his fingers slid over her temple lightly. Seeking. "You had a panic attack, Red." He kept his voice gentle, the tone sliding into intimate. "I didn't like being the cause of that." He didn't. It was necessary and it might happen again. Sadly, he was afraid it was inevitable.

"You have the frown again. Tell me what you're thinking."

There was a little demand in her tone that made him want to smile. He didn't want to push so hard that she'd leave. What would he do then? Try to stop her? That could be a disaster. "I was trying to think of ways to best help you figure this out without putting undue pressure on you. You're just really confronting the truth. You don't have to do it all at once."

Rory's smile nearly took his breath away. She put her nebulizer back in its case and then in her skirt pocket. "I can't believe how I lucked out. In my wildest dreams I never thought I'd meet a man as nice as you, Gideon. I had given up."

He wasn't a nice man. He wasn't even wholly a man anymore. He didn't know what he was. He had started out the evening thinking he was going to reel his woman in slow and easy. Court her. Hook her. Make sure she had every reason to believe in him. Every reason to stay in San Francisco and give the two of them a chance. Every reason to explore the chemistry flaring between them.

He was deceiving her. He might not be lying to her, but he was misleading her. One of the things Gideon was very good at was reading people. Rory was going to feel as if he had made a fool of her once she found out who and what he was. Eventually, she would have to be told. There would be no getting around it. She would find out about his ability to use his voice to compel her to answer him. She would consider that a weapon used against her. That wasn't even the worst. He would have no choice but to betray her. Really betray her. There was Sebastian living in the compound. There was Rose. Jaimie. He had to tell the others about Rory. Once that happened . . . His sins were rapidly piling up. How could she forgive him? Would he forgive her if the roles were reversed? No, he would not. Silently, he cursed.

This was the woman meant to be his. He knew it with every fiber of his being. It was more than possible Whitney had engineered the pairing as he had so many others, but that didn't matter to Gideon. In fact, if it was so, he welcomed it. Whitney might be able to enhance the chemistry between them—and he was quite all right with that aspect of their relationship being enhanced. Whitney couldn't force emotions between them. The man was a cold fish and didn't understand emotions. Gideon knew his feelings were already involved when it came to Rory. He'd developed them rapidly, and the more he was in her company, the stronger they became.

It was entirely possible Whitney had programmed Rory and sent her out to be an unknowing spy for him. Or worse, if she was programmed to kidnap Sebastian, Gideon couldn't allow that door to be opened.

Abruptly, he took his hands off her and reached for a cold beer. "I think I'm going to have another piece of chicken and contemplate the merits of bartending."

"You sound like Lydia. She lives at the apartment building and has a three-year-old daughter. Ellen has a disorder called selective mutism. Lydia is working with the people at UCSF Medical Center. She doesn't have the best insurance to cover the cost, and she works for a software company, troubleshooting for their customers so she can work from home. She says she thinks she would prefer bartending. She watches YouTube videos all the time and has me show her tricks and how to make various drinks. She's getting fast at some of them." She set the picnic basket between them. "It would help her make more money to pay the bills for Ellen's care. I've watched all the videos on how to work with a child who has selective mutism and have been learning how to help get little Miss Ellie to talk."

That was so like the Rory he was coming to know.

"Where's the baby's father?"

"He left Lydia the moment he found out she was pregnant. She decided to have the baby on her own. Lydia lives frugally. In fact, she rarely leaves the apartment building. Ellen has cute clothes and lots of toys, but Lydia doesn't have tons of things that I've noticed. She's not a buyer. I think she's paid a good wage. If she didn't have the medical bills, she would be fine. I could get her on part-time, and if she's not on the same shift with me, I could watch Ellen. She'd be asleep, so it wouldn't be any big deal."

There it was. An immediate offer to help someone else without reservation. That was Rory's true nature. This was killing him. He took a swallow of the beer and stared out at the gathering fog. He wasn't a bitter man. He didn't sit around and think about the shit hand life had dealt him. He didn't moan and groan and complain. He was considering changing that. He might even get drunk.

He took another bite of chicken and kept his gaze on the fog as it formed an ominous dark bank that spread across the water. "Are you looking at that?" He indicated the very gray mass with the half-eaten chicken.

111

"I am now."

"One of the reasons I like sitting on this rooftop is seeing that. It was clear five minutes ago. San Francisco weather changes in a heartbeat. Life does as well. We learn acceptance if we're going to get through it gracefully." He took another slow sip of beer.

"Is that what you do, Gideon? You accept the changes in life gracefully?"

She sounded curious. He glanced at her. She was looking at the thick fog bank. He'd diverted her attention from the strange phenomenon she'd revealed to him—the second skin. He needed a little time to puzzle it out and talk to the others about it. With all of them considering possibilities, they might come up with answers fast.

"I try. What other way is there to live large?"

"I like that." She glanced at her watch. "I can't stay out too much later, although this has been nice, especially after the horrible interrogation by the cops. I swear Detective Westlake has it in for me for some unknown reason. I realize he lost his partner, but it isn't my fault. I didn't shoot the man. I was only in the room with him for a minute. Westlake acted like I'm a suspect in his murder or something. I finally threatened to call a lawyer if he didn't stop. That's why I was so late. If he hadn't been so mean and kept at me, I would have been here on time."

"Sometimes grief can make men act like idiots," Gideon said. "I'm sorry he was ugly to you." He had the unexpected urge to visit Westlake at his home and teach him some manners, but then who was he to give anyone a lesson in etiquette? He was about to commit the biggest betrayal of them all.

He finished off the chicken and spring rolls and washed them down with beer. Everything suddenly tasted like ashes. He wanted to sit with her for the rest of the night. Just sit quietly in the dark without speaking. Breathe her into his lungs. He wasn't certain when he would ever have this chance again.

"I'm going to walk you back to your apartment, Rory," he said decisively.

"That isn't necessary. It isn't that far. I'm used to walking at night."

"I don't like you walking alone. I've got a bad feeling. I always go with my gut, so if you don't mind giving me this one, let me walk you home."

She gave him one of her smiles. "I'd like that."

7

Mack McKinley was all muscle, built solid. He had dark eyes and charcoal hair. He was the urban GhostWalker's team leader, responsible for all of them in the field and off it. He took that responsibility very seriously. The entire top floor of the enormous warehouse was the home he shared with his wife, Jaimie. She had been one of the children they'd grown up with, going to school with them at far too young of an age because of her intelligence. Mack and the others had looked out for her.

Mack didn't take his gaze from Gideon's face the entire time he explained everything he knew of Rory Chappel to the others. When he was finished talking, his gaze jumped to Javier, who gave his report, citing what he'd learned from his in-depth research on the computer.

"You're certain Whitney has paired you with her?" Mack asked.

Gideon nodded. "Absolutely. But I'd spent time with her prior to knowing all this. I watched her and studied her. I didn't have a clue she was a GhostWalker. I liked her then and I like her now for who she is."

"Is it possible she's putting on an act?" Marc Lands, one of his teammates, asked. He had lived on the streets as a child along with Gideon and Javier.

Gideon shook his head. "She'd have to be the greatest actress of all time. Javier vetted her up close several times before I met her personally. I took her out and talked with her. We were alone together, and she showed me the tattoo on her ankle. That led to the revelation that she didn't remember getting the tattoo or who the artist was, even though it was her favorite piece of artwork. I could see it really bothered her, so I pushed a little. At that point, she was rubbing her left temple. It wasn't the first time she'd done that. There was no way she could fake that. I just don't see how, Marc. And why bring it up? Why give herself away?"

"I was in the bar with her a few times," Ethan Meyers said. "Sat at the bar and talked with her. I didn't get the GhostWalker vibe from her, but I think she could repeat verbatim what any customer said to her."

"So, let's say she's telling the truth," Kane said.

He was Mack's right-hand man. Married to Rose and father to Sebastian. Admittedly, he had the most to lose. Still, just the way he put it set Gideon's teeth on edge.

"She's telling the truth." He kept his tone low, but the challenge was there.

Mack's gaze hit him hard. Gideon felt those burning eyes strike at him, but he didn't answer the summons. He kept his predator's stare on Kane.

Kane straightened slowly, his shoulders stiffening. "I meant no offense. This is a complicated issue, and it's put you in a bad position."

"I'm selling her out. That's more than a bad position. I'm doing it for Rose, Jaimie, Rhianna and Sebastian. The rest of us can take care of ourselves."

"Uh, Gideon. I'm quite capable of taking care of myself," Rhianna Bonds protested. "But I love you for including me."

Rhianna had also grown up on the streets with them. She was every bit as lethal as any of them. Gideon didn't care. None of them did. As far as they were concerned, she was their little sister and under their protection.

He pushed his hands through his hair and then forced himself to be still. Even with his family, he rarely allowed his agitation to show. "I don't want to lose her. She doesn't have anyone and hasn't had anyone. She's letting me in and I'm going behind her back. If she did that to me, I wouldn't be very forgiving. I doubt if any of you would be."

There was a small silence because, damn it all, he was right. They wouldn't be forgiving. They were a tight-knit group, and they were very careful of who they were around.

"What were you going to say, Kane?" Mack asked.

"Is it possible Whitney removed her memories? If he did, what would have been his purpose?"

"Her past is real enough," Javier said. "Meaning the various places she's worked. I've verified all of them. I can't imagine he took her memories and sent her out on the off chance he could use her to kidnap a baby. I think there must be another reason."

"You said she has bad lungs," Rhianna mused aloud. "Could it be as simple as she didn't measure up to Whitney's idea of what a GhostWalker should be, so he kicked her out?"

"He tends to end things permanently with anyone not measuring up," Mack pointed out, "especially girls or women." He turned to his wife. "Babe, would you see what you can find on her? When she disappeared. Who remembers her as a child. Who grew up with her. Anything at all. Don't say why, just make inquiries. If they ask, say you're working on something."

Jaimie nodded. "I believe she was one of the original twelve Whitney took at the same time he acquired Rose, so she would have known her. I don't know for how long. He often moved the girls around so they wouldn't bond with one another. He didn't do it at first. He didn't have any understanding of what happened when he enhanced their psychic abilities and they didn't have any filters. He had no idea of the pain he caused. Once he did understand, he didn't really care. Those first girls were all throwaways to him."

Gideon could feel the tension in the room rise. No one liked the idea that Rose and Rory had known one another as children. Was that simply another coincidence? The world was a big place. How was it that Rory had ended up not just in San Francisco but on the harbor where they had established their compound? Whitney certainly knew they lived there. It felt to Gideon as if things were getting worse by the minute.

"She would have been there when he gifted them with the tattoos," Javier pointed out. "How old were they? I assumed they were older, but we don't know that. Kane, did Rose ever say how old she was when Whitney brought in the tattoo artist?"

"She talked about the puppies they raised and how he brought in fighting dogs. They were traumatized when their puppies were killed in front of them. It was sometime after that," Kane answered.

"They couldn't have been that old when he gave them puppies," Mack said. "Rose told us Whitney wanted them to learn a lesson about survival. They had taught their dogs everything but how to fight for survival. Of course, he hadn't revealed that he would put them in a fighting ring with experienced fighting dogs when the puppies turned a year old."

"He's such a bastard," Rhianna said. "I've tried dozens of times to find him."

Gideon turned sharp eyes on her. He wasn't alone. Every man in the room looked at her.

"What the hell, Rhianna?" Javier snapped. "Without backup? What if you found him?"

"That was the plan," she said calmly. "I would have killed him."

"I've warned you countless times, Ree," Mack interrupted before Javier continued. "You gave me your word you would stop going rogue."

"I've kept my word, Mack. I was referring to the times I tried to find him *prior* to promising you I wouldn't go off alone." She flashed a little mocking grin at her street brothers. "I'm trying to learn some Mack-sense, whatever that is."

Jaimie laughed. "Mack doesn't have any sense, Rhianna. Don't let him fool you. He just pretends so all of you will think he's a wise man and you'll keep following him."

"If I wasn't so lazy, I'd strangle you, Jaimie," Mack said. "In the meantime, cancel asking anyone outside our circle any questions yet. Let's keep this to ourselves."

Gideon was grateful for that small reprieve. The minute Jaimie asked any of the other women any questions—particularly Lily Whitney-Miller, Peter Whitney's adopted daughter—they would get a visit. Lily would come immediately. She was brilliant. There was no fooling or misleading her. She was actively looking for the women she had been raised with—the ones her father had experimented on over and over. She was determined to right as many wrongs as possible.

Gideon knew Lily. Her father's guilt weighed heavily on her shoulders. She was innocent, but that didn't matter. She still felt that weight. She was aggressive in looking for solutions for the women. She shared with the GhostWalkers the money she'd inherited from an ongoing, very sizable trust. Gideon couldn't fault her for her tireless work ethic, but he didn't want or need her interference when he was desperate to save his relationship with Rory.

He had felt, for a brief moment, real happiness. He'd never had that. He'd never felt hope or a sense of looking forward to waking up. There was no anticipation. Now, there had been Rory. The brightness of her. The reality of her. He knew she was genuine, whether the others believed it or not.

"Here's an interesting idea." Paul Mangan spoke and immediately the room went silent.

Gideon could count on one hand the few times Paul had ever contributed to their free-for-all brainstorming meetings. Paul was the newest member of their team and also the youngest. He was the only nonfamily member, having been placed there by his father, Sergeant Major Theodore Griffen, who ran the team.

All of them protected him in much the same way as they tried to protect Rhianna. She tried to protect him too. He had gifts few had, and no one, especially Peter Whitney, could find out about them. Gideon could never understand why Paul didn't give his opinion more. It wasn't like they didn't know he was the smartest man in a room already filled with extremely intelligent men.

"Have her join us. Introduce her to everyone. Express your concerns. Bring them right out into the open so you're not going behind her back. Explain everything to her. Who we are. What we do. Tell her about Peter Whitney and the experiments he did on the orphan girls. Tell her she's one of them. Drop a couple of names. See if she reacts or remembers. Let me examine her."

Immediately, his suggestion was met with heads shaking in disagreement. Even Gideon, who had liked his idea up to that point, found himself reacting negatively.

"You can't take a chance, Paul."

"I can if Javier is sitting right next to her."

Every cell in Gideon's body rejected that suggestion. "Absolutely not. Even if I agreed to someone killing her, it won't be Javier. I know Rory's mine. There isn't going to be another woman for me. I've been struggling for a long time now. Having just a small taste of what my life could be like with her, the drop will be severe. It will take a long time to get over her death, let alone someone in my own family killing her. I would have a difficult time forgiving them. I might even be dangerous."

He had to be honest. He was a predator through and through. Whitney had made him that way. All of them were. They'd started out with the aggression already in them. If they hadn't had it, they wouldn't have survived on the streets. Those instincts had been honed as they'd grown, fighting for their needs and keeping human predators off them. Once Whitney had performed his experiments on them, they were exactly what he wanted: killing machines. Gideon had considered himself one long before Whitney had gotten his hands on him.

"Gideon." Javier spoke quietly. "She wouldn't feel a thing if it was me. She'd never see it coming. I would make certain she would never know."

Gideon's gut clenched and he couldn't sit. He was up and pacing until his dangerous energy filled the room to overflowing. The walls trembled.

"Not you," Gideon bit out. "It would be best if I took her away from here."

"It would be best if you trusted your family." Mack's tone was mild. "It's clear that she's yours already. A part of you. That makes her ours and affords her the protection of every one of us. She's family. We don't let go of family, no matter what Whitney has devised. *And,* just to be clear, if there is a decision to be made on when someone in our family can't be saved, it is my responsibility alone to handle that. *I* make that call and *I* take care of it—not Javier, not anyone else."

Mack met Gideon's stare unflinchingly from across the room. There was no backup in him. "Rory is your woman. That makes her family, so she will be saved. There isn't going to be any other possibility. We start with that premise. Let's all calm down and listen to Paul. His idea has merit."

Gideon took a deep breath. Mack didn't mince words and he meant what he said. He understood that Rory belonged with him. It didn't matter that they'd only been together a couple of times. Mack was aware that Gideon's mind and body recognized her. Sometimes, with GhostWalkers, that happened. For them, it was the one. The only. They didn't know if some of the changes Whitney's experiments had made in their DNA had contributed to that strange phenomenon. However it happened, they recognized that some of them became aware of their mates instinctively and the bond happened fast and irrevocably.

"What are you saying, Mack?" Kane objected. "Even if we're all right there, if Whitney programmed her as a bomb, who would be fast enough to save Paul? Or for that matter, if we were here, Rose and Sebastian?"

"I'm either part of this team, or I'm not," Paul said unexpectedly. "I go on the same missions. I see the same things all of you do, and I make sure to pull my weight, although you make that difficult for me, just as you're suggesting now. I don't like the fact that you continue to treat me like I'm an outsider simply because I didn't grow up with the rest of you. If you don't trust me, you need to say so, and I'll ask for a transfer to another unit. I'm damn tired of always being put with the women and children instead of being treated like I'm part of the team."

Gideon could hear the resolution in his voice. He might speak softly, but he meant every shocking word. The team exchanged long stunned looks. It might have taken them a little time to trust Paul when he'd first been assigned to them. He was young and didn't seem to fit into their well-oiled team, but after getting to know him, they all felt differently. They'd grown fond of him. More than that. He was family to them. How was it that he didn't feel that from them?

Gideon knew they all protected him. Paul wasn't wrong about that. They tried to shield him from the worst of what they encountered, mostly because he was very sensitive. He had to be. He was a healer. His psychic talent was one of the rarest, if not the rarest. No one spoke of it. It wasn't documented and it never could be.

"Paul, I'm not sure what you're talking about," Mack said. "You're considered a very valued member of our team. You're trusted by everyone here. It isn't that anyone doesn't want you here because they don't trust you; it's because none of us wants to risk your life."

Gideon had never seen such a stubborn look come over Paul's face. "Each of you has an expertise. Gideon's woman needs someone to see *inside* her. That's my expertise. Why would you send me away when no one else can see if she's programmed with a bomb inside her? I can see what's wrong with her lungs. I can tell you if she has a second skin or a cloaking device of some kind. It's ludicrous to have me slink away like a child and hide while all of you take the risk when you won't find out anything at all. Gideon's already questioned her. He can compel answers, and he didn't get any satisfactory ones because she doesn't know the answers."

It was the most Gideon had ever heard Paul say at one time. He was asserting himself, challenging Mack to listen to him as a professional of his talent. He was right. There was no getting around the truth of what he was saying. None of them had to like it, but they had to listen to what he said.

"It isn't just because we all have tremendous affection for you, Paul," Mack said carefully. "You've managed to gain our respect and find your place in the family. You may not like the fact that you're the youngest brother and everyone looks out for you in that regard. But your talent is needed. We guard you carefully for that as well. Those restraints, I'll admit, sometimes are a bit too tight."

"A bit?" Paul asked. But he asked with a hint of a smile. "I have to be here to examine her, Mack. And, Gideon, I believe if you're up front with her right from the beginning, full disclosure, she's going to forgive the fact that you didn't tell her right away."

Jaimie nodded. "She did have a panic attack and then a breathing problem. It would be natural not to put more on her. To wait. To want to protect her."

Gideon flicked her a quick glance. Jaimie had a way of putting things that made sense. Was it possible to convince Rory it was in her best interest to talk to his team? He'd already spoken with them without her permission. That was one thing he couldn't get around, but maybe he could find a way to make that work.

"We shouldn't use this building," Mack said. "Gideon, she's already been to your home. We can do better damage control there. Up on your rooftop. We can contain any problems Whitney may have introduced."

He was talking about bombs. Gideon knew they had to consider that possibility, but it still stung. He didn't let it show, but few things got past Mack.

"She'll be more comfortable there, Gideon. You've already told us that she's the kind of woman who worries about everyone else. Do you think, after explaining to her what we are and what you think she is, that she would come here to my home and risk Jaimie and Rose and Sebastian?"

Gideon knew Rory wouldn't. She would pack up everything she owned and leave immediately. She might anyway.

"You're right, Mack." He looked around the room at the men and women he had always counted on. They were there for him, and they would be for Rory. "I'll talk to her. She's not going to agree to more than a couple of you meeting with her."

Mack nodded. "Paul's made it clear he has to be there to read her. I'll be there. She knows Javier and she's seen Ethan. I think that's more than enough." He ignored the dark look of protest on Kane's face.

"I've always been with you, Mack," Kane said, making his protest out loud.

"I'll have Javier and Ethan with me. I'll need you with the others," Mack replied, his tone firm. "Paul and Gideon will be on Rory."

Kane clearly didn't like it, but he didn't voice any further protest.

"Let us know when you work out the details, Gideon." Mack continued, "What do we have on her stalker?"

"Harvey Otis Matters. Forty-two years old," Jaimie said. "He's a big-time arms and drug dealer. He doesn't distribute on the street. He brings the product in and sells to the dealers. You have to be a big dealer to even get close to him. By that I mean you must be able to take large amounts of product and pay for it up front. He doesn't mess around. He has partners. Or had them. Two have turned up dead. Jarrod Flawson is in the wind."

Alarms shrieked at Gideon. "The men living in Rory's apartment building? Why in hell would they be there? They have to have all kinds of money."

"And own homes and property," Rhianna chimed in.

"They do," Jaimie agreed. "Harvey has two beautiful estates. One here in California and one in Nevada. He's smart about his taxes."

"He pays taxes?" Jacob Princeton asked. He was their underwater expert. "On the money he makes from his drug deals?"

Jaimie laughed. "He has quite a few legitimate businesses, Jacob. It isn't well known that he's a huge arms and drug dealer."

"What's he doing in Rory's apartment building?" Ethan persisted.

"That's the question, isn't it?" Jaimie said, sobering. "The partners never go near one another. They don't have anything to do with one another, yet they all moved into an apartment in that building around the same time a little over two months ago. I pulled the surveillance cameras, which aren't very good, and they show nothing. The men were aware of the cameras and avoided them."

"Something had to have brought them to that building," Kane said.

"And brought the cops," Gideon said. "The detective was shot and killed there, presumably by one of those men."

"But that hasn't been determined yet," Javier pointed out.

"What does that mean, Javier?" Mack asked. "Do you believe someone else killed Ramsey?"

Javier shrugged. "I don't ever jump to conclusions when it comes to cops. I don't like them. They don't like me. Some are good. Some are bad. Who knows what happened to Ramsey? But someone killed two of Harvey's partners. Maybe it was the cops looking for revenge."

"Maybe it was Harvey," Brian Hutton suggested. "Or the other one, Jarrod Flawson."

"Could have been," Javier conceded. "But if it was, why hasn't Harvey left town? If it were me, and I did everyone in and knew the cops were hunting me, I'd get the hell out."

Gideon had to admit Javier had a good point. "Why would Harvey be following Rory around? Especially when the cops are watching her so closely."

"Yeah, and why are the cops so interested in Rory?" Javier asked.

There was a long silence as Gideon's team mulled it over, trying to figure out why Harvey would be following Rory and why the cops were just as interested.

"Gideon, we have to ask the hard questions here," Mack said. "You'll have to forgive us while we consider every possibility."

He had known the questions would be coming. He had asked them himself. He was the only one, other than Javier, who had really been close enough to Rory to read her true character. As much as he disliked Mack and the others doubting her even for a minute, he knew, since he'd considered the possibilities, they would as well. He just had to keep his protective nature under control.

"For Harvey to be such a big-time dealer, he must distribute in other cities. Rory has traveled extensively. Is it possible she works for him? If they all moved into that building and she was there as well, they could have had to meet in person for a reason. That has to be what the cops are considering."

Gideon looked Mack straight in the eye. "I would be a fool not to have thought of that, but I dismissed it immediately. Rory isn't capable of working with a drug dealer. She doesn't have the personality for it."

"I'm going to back Gideon on this one," Ethan said. "She's too much of an empath. You'll see for yourself. She'd be the type who would blame herself for the suffering around her."

Javier nodded. "I've followed her for a while now and haven't seen any evidence at all of criminal activity. She's not the type, Mack. If anything, she'd try to stop Harvey. I don't mean kill him or call the cops on him. She'd probably sit him down and do her best to talk to him logically and explain the error of his ways."

There was a low murmur of laughter. Even Gideon smiled, but not for the same reason as the others. They laughed with disbelief. He laughed because it might be true. He could just hear Rory talking to Harvey in a sweet, reasonable voice, doing her best to convince him how wrong he was. If she didn't succeed, then her temper would kick into gear, and anything could happen.

"Anyone have any other ideas why Harvey would follow her

rather than getting the hell out of town? Especially when the cops are showing such an interest in her?" Mack asked. "I imagine the cops believe she's working with him. I can't imagine they would be suspicious of any of the other women. Rory is the only one who fits the right image. She moves around. She bartends. She's perfect for working for someone like Harvey."

Gideon couldn't fault that way of thinking. Rory had told him the detectives had acted as if she were a person of interest to them.

There was another long silence. Jacob cleared his throat and sent Gideon a quick look.

"Spit it out," Gideon said.

"The woman is gorgeous. All that dark red hair. That face and her . . ." Jacob searched for an appropriate description that wouldn't get his head bitten off by Gideon. "Skin." He ignored the ripple of laughter that went through the room. "He could be interested in her and just not want to let it go."

"I appreciate your discretion, Jacob," Gideon said, his sense of humor returning. "The rest of these jokers wouldn't have had your ability to think so fast on their feet. I did observe him in the restaurant when we were there. He didn't spend that much time looking at her. If another man was sitting with the woman I was interested in, I'd be watching their every move together. He wasn't."

"That's true," Ethan agreed. "That man wasn't paying that much attention to Rory. Not like he should have been if he was crazy about her."

"We'll have to find him before the cops do," Kane said. "He's off the street again."

"Who do we have watching over Rory?" Mack asked.

"Our cameras are installed," Javier said. "We aren't taking chances that she'd spot any of us. She's got too good of a memory. Once she sees someone, she isn't going to forget that face, especially now."

Gideon had been afraid to send his little sparrow to spy. Rory was that good.

"Westlake must suspect that she's part of Harvey's ring," Jaimie said. "Otherwise, he wouldn't be keeping such a close watch on her. He was really pissed that he lost track of her on the street. He sent patrolmen looking for signs of her."

"The fact that she managed to elude him will only have him looking at her harder," Ethan pointed out.

"That's true," Rhianna agreed. "He's a hothead too. I watched him chase after her when he got out of the car. His face was red. He had his fists clenched. He was angry with teenage boys in his way. I think he would have hit them if it weren't for his partner being right there."

"The excuse of losing Ramsey only goes so far," Mack said. "We've all lost people we care about. He knows where Rory lives. He could take her down to the precinct anytime and question her if he wasn't happy with the answers she gave him. I didn't think the way he reacted made much sense. No one is making sense, and you know how I don't like anything that isn't logical." He turned his head to glare at Jaimie.

She exchanged a look with Rhianna, and they both burst out laughing, breaking the tension in the room.

Gideon didn't blame Mack. He had a point. Rory was a Ghost-Walker, yet she had no memories of being one. Gideon hadn't known she was one when most GhostWalkers recognized one another. Very wealthy criminals had taken apartments in a lower-rent neighborhood, meeting together when they never did. Those men were turning up dead. Harvey should have left San Francisco, or at least gone into hiding, but instead, he was following Rory around. Cops were being killed. No one had any idea why.

"We aren't getting anywhere," Mack reiterated. "Let's call it a night. We'll keep surveillance on Rory, and if we see Harvey, pick him up and bring him to the interrogation room. Gideon, when you feel like the time is right to have an open talk with Rory, do it. Don't wait too long. My gut says this has some urgency to it."

Gideon's gut was saying the same thing. He nodded. "Thanks, everyone. I appreciate the input."

He was up and moving before the others, waving at Jaimie and Mack, and taking the stairs when he knew he should have taken the elevator. His body was nowhere near healed. The bullets had made a few decent-sized holes in his body. Paul had saved his life. There was no getting around that fact. He wouldn't have lived without the man working one of his miracles.

Once out on the street, Gideon could breathe easier. He had never liked being cooped up. The feeling seemed to be getting worse, especially since he'd been wounded. Or was he inadvertently sharing Rory's emotions? They seemed to touch minds and then bounce off one another, pushing each other away.

As he walked along the sidewalk, he deliberately tried to connect with her. He was a strong telepath. He knew the way to her mind. He traced his way carefully, meticulously, building the images in his head. He needed to know she was safe in her apartment, locked in and asleep after working her shift.

He should have gone straight to Mack and his team once he knew Rory was a GhostWalker, but he'd waited, processing, considering what to do. Knowing whatever he did, the odds were more than good that he would lose her. Now, he worried she was in more trouble than he'd first thought. With every step he took, the feelings of urgency and fear increased. His? Hers?

Gideon made it to his building, put the security code into the panel and hurried inside. He wanted to be in the Eagle's Nest, where he could breathe. Where he could see and hear. Where he felt he had a direct line to Rory. He knew she had left work and, from the security cameras along the street, gotten home safely.

There were no sightings of Harvey, but two undercover cops had been in the bar, and two others had followed her home. She hadn't acted as though she'd spotted them. He wasn't certain he believed she hadn't.

Once he was on the rooftop, Gideon faced the building where Rory rented an apartment on the third floor. She loved her rooftop for the same reasons he did, and often fell asleep there. He wasn't certain that was a good idea. The nights in San Francisco could get cold and damp, and with her lungs being compromised, he knew it wasn't healthy for her to sleep outdoors. She had to know it as well, so why did she do it?

He closed off his mind to the worry of her health and focused solely on the connection he knew was between them. At first, he couldn't find her. He tasted her. A slow burn of need and desire. An explosion of fire and passion. She smelled of a blend of lavender and something else with a citrus undertone he couldn't quite put his finger on. A coppery taste intruded. The passion and fire gave way to fear. Fear gave way to terror.

Dark. So dark. Hard to make out the figures through the veil between them. *Shush. You have to be quiet. Be still. Absolutely still. Be part of the cliff.*

Gideon recognized Rory's voice, although she sounded like a child. A very young child. She was shaken. Her voice trembled, although she was very firm. He couldn't see her. It was more as if he were looking through her eyes. Someone was with her. Either Rory or the other person was wounded.

Shadowy figures moved past them. Close. So close he could see they were grown men and they carried automatic weapons. Gideon felt as if he could reach out and touch them.

Useless. You're utterly useless. The voice was harsh. He recognized that voice. Dr. Peter Whitney. The man from hell.

A chorus of protests, young girls' voices drowning out the next thing that abrasive and severe voice snapped before Gideon could hear it again.

Take them out, all but her. There was a long silence while Whitney's order was presumably obeyed. Then he began berating Rory again. *They could have all been killed because of your utter incompetence. If you cared enough about them to work harder, you wouldn't endanger them, but you're just too selfish and lazy.*

Despair. Guilt. Self-loathing. It was difficult to breathe, but the determination not to wheeze, not to allow the sound to be heard, was paramount in young Rory's mind. She did her best to control her inability to find air while Whitney's voice continued to insist she was worthless and she had nearly gotten everyone killed. Whitney called for the guards and told them to escort Laurel up to her room, and he told her she should stay there and come up with reasons he should keep her around.

Gideon felt the heavy weight of each one of her steps on the stairs. The airless, stuffy room, hot and miserable, filled with layers of dust, making it impossible to breathe adequately.

Hot tears tracked down Rory's face, and he felt each one. She walked to the other side of the room, where a tiny square of a boarded window let the night in.

Alarm shot through Gideon as he read the intent in the child's mind. The girl in the nightmare wiggled a board loose, something it was clear she had worked on for some time. She stepped out onto the ledge. In real time, Rory, trapped in her nightmare, stepped to the ledge of the three-story building.

Rory. Wake up. Wake up now. He called to her imperiously. Commanded it. At the same time, Gideon didn't hesitate.

Uncaring of his injured body, he leapt to the very edge of the wide concrete railing that surrounded his rooftop. Flinging his arms wide as if he might fly off, he called on every owl in the vicinity and sent them flying straight at the woman he considered his. He had to use his body as well as his mind to direct them. His heart and lungs. His entire focus. His very being so he became the owls.

Screeching, the raptors complied. Wings beating hard, they flew at Rory's face and around her body, pulling up sharply at the last minute. Gideon felt her wake, disoriented at first but gripping the railing tightly and then stepping back, panic in her mind.

8

The music seemed overly loud, and for some reason, Rory couldn't turn it down in her head the way she normally could. Noises didn't get to her because she controlled the volume in the way she mysteriously did a number of odd little things she had come to take for granted. Tonight, she had a pounding headache that just wouldn't go away, and the noise level in the bar seemed to increase with every hour she worked.

She'd always had nightmares, but lately the frequency was escalating. Waking up to the sound of Gideon's voice and owls flying at her head as she stood at the very edge of her rooftop terrified her. If she hadn't awoken, would she have fallen to her death? Yes. The answer was yes. There was no doubt in her mind. The spot over her left temple burned and hurt like hell. The strange sensation had grown into pain. The pain had worsened with each nightmare until it was like her nerves were too close to the surface.

"You okay, Rory?" Dana asked in a whisper as she collected drinks to take to her tables.

Alarmed, Rory raised an eyebrow. "Does it show?"

Dana shook her head. "No, you're talking to the customers as usual, and you're just as fast. You're just not you."

"Later," Rory said, not meaning it.

What was she going to say? What could she say? She was uneasy and didn't know why. She wasn't used to sharing her life with friends. She wanted to learn. She even wanted to settle there in San Francisco and keep the friends she was making. She wanted a family. She wanted to take a chance on Gideon, but everything was falling apart.

Dana nodded, picked up her tray and moved easily into the crowd. Rory, pouring drinks and making small talk with her customers, couldn't help looking for him. Gideon. She wanted him to come in. Two of his friends were sitting in the back, which was a good distance from her. She recognized them. Ethan and Brian were their names. Both would be considered good-looking men. Hard if you looked at their eyes. She knew few women would see past the tall, ripped bodies. She hadn't exactly seen them with Gideon, but she knew they were part of his family.

If she were being honest with herself, she didn't want to know how Gideon's eye could go from soft sky blue to arctic cold like a dense glacier. There were a couple of times he looked more like a predator than a human when she'd looked into his eyes. She'd blinked and the illusion was gone, but which was the illusion? Man? Or predator?

She read the energy of people around her fairly easily. Gideon was a dangerous man, just as Ethan and Brian were. Javier was extremely dangerous. Yet Rory felt safe with them when she hadn't felt safe in years. Why was that? And why hadn't Gideon come to see her? Where was he?

Rory realized, as the hours had gone by and he had not arrived, the tension in her had grown. She had to give that some thought.

She wasn't dependent on anyone—least of all a man. In reality, she barely knew Gideon, yet she couldn't stop thinking about him. The anxiety she was feeling wasn't just for herself but for him. Since her nightmare and hearing him call her name, more and more she was becoming certain he was in danger. She just didn't know where it was coming from.

A man with dark blond hair and brown eyes took the seat directly in front of her when a customer and his friend got up and headed to a table. The blond gave her a friendly smile. He had one lower tooth next to his molar capped in shiny gold. He looked very fit, wide shoulders encased in a tan tee stretched over heavy muscles. He had a darker-colored hoodie unzipped over the tee.

"What can I get for you?" She took one more quick scan of the bar and then another of her new customer. She gave him a bright smile.

"Old-fashioned. Johnnie Walker Black Label. Name's Scott Tinsdale. Didn't expect my bartender to look like you." Deliberately he looked at her hand. "Married? Engaged? I don't want to step on someone's toes asking you out."

"Moving a little fast, aren't you?" She laughed as she mixed his old-fashioned with simple syrup and two dashes of aromatic bitters. She didn't look at the tall ice-filled glass but kept her gaze fixed on him.

Something was very wrong. The anxiety that had been growing in her since she'd woken from her nightmare had continued to worsen. Her mind sought Gideon, but she couldn't touch him. The connection between them seemed to be broken.

"I'm a decisive kind of man. I see something I like, and I go after it," Scott declared.

"That's a good way to be," Rory said, setting his drink on a napkin in front of him. "Thank you for the compliment, but I'm in a very committed relationship."

Dana was there again, leaning on the bar, gesturing toward her. Rory hastily excused herself and went to the waitress.

"The two men at the table in the back gave me this note for you." Dana indicated Brian and Ethan. "That and a very healthy tip."

Rory opened it and read: *Something wrong?*

She pulled a pen from her pocket and wrote: *Please check on Gideon now.* She didn't care if she ended up looking like a fool. She knew something had happened to him. She didn't know what or how, but something was terribly wrong. She pressed a hand to her stomach, suddenly frightened for Gideon as she watched Dana take the folded note back to the table. Would they even take her seriously?

Both men looked up at her, and then Ethan was up and out of the bar while Brian was on his phone texting. That fast. No one asked questions; they just took her at her word. She let her breath out and did her best to turn her attention to her work.

Scott Tinsdale kept his seat at the bar, eating a few pretzels and ordering a second drink. He was very pleasant without being overly flirtatious. He talked to the man on his left side and bought him a drink. He watched the mirror quite a bit. He wasn't looking at the women in the room. He wasn't even looking at Dana. Most single men looked at Dana. Tinsdale kept his eye on Rory, but he also appeared to be watching both entrances. He was subtle about it, but he was aware of who came and went from the bar.

As the night wore on, she realized Tinsdale paid attention to anyone conversing with her. Once, she was certain he had hit the record button on his phone and laid the phone on the bar, which really made him a creeper. She was tempted to accidentally knock it off the bar while she worked, but she turned away to help several people down the bar from him. Scott Tinsdale was making her very uneasy. She had walked to the bar earlier in the day and would have to make her way home on foot.

Last call for alcohol was announced, and Tinsdale slid off the barstool. With a friendly wave, he went out the side door toward the parking lot. That meant she no longer had eyes on him. She wasn't scheduled to close. Lani was staying late with two of the waitresses, and Brutus, one of the barbacks, was cleaning.

Rory went to the back room and used her nebulizer, taking her time, inhaling the medicine while she considered her options. She had no choice but to walk back to her apartment in the dark unless she wanted to call an Uber or a cab. Leaning against the long cabinet, she did her best to clear her mind and focus on Gideon. Again, she couldn't connect with him at all. Where before she'd felt warmth when she reached out to him, there was nothing but a cold abyss. Instantly, she didn't want to go home; she wanted to go to his house to check on him. No one had contacted her to tell her he was all right. What could have happened to him?

She stood there in the break room, her heart pounding, her nightmare coming back to her. Had she brought him into it somehow? The idea was preposterous, but she'd been curious about various paranormal talents, and she'd read about them. Experiments had been done in quite a few countries. Some had centered around dreams. She'd heard his voice calling out to her.

Gideon. She whispered his name in her mind. *Please be all right. Please don't let me have done something terrible to you.*

She pulled out her phone and stared down at Gideon's name. What if she had inadvertently hurt him? She remembered waking up with owls flying all around her. She'd been standing right on the ledge of her patio. Had he been locked on to her? She should never have gone out with him. All along she'd been nervous about dating him. She'd been too attracted, the connection between them far too strong. Nothing about their relationship made sense.

They had bonded too fast. She had already begun to make plans to stay when she never stayed anywhere for long. She'd blurted out private things to him she'd never told a single soul. That wasn't like her either. Nothing about Gideon and her made sense, and yet . . . she couldn't stop thinking about him. She wanted to be with him. She was obsessed with him.

Rory glanced at her watch and then pushed the call button. Gideon's cell went directly to voice mail. She left him a text message. I'm worried about you. Was coming over to check on you. When you get this, call me back. She hesitated but decided to tell him about Tinsdale just in case. Am about to walk home from work. Strange man was in tonight and he gave off a weird vibe. I'm a little nervous. Check in with me, okay?

She felt like a complete fool. She wasn't a woman to be so anxious she had to ask a man for protection. She wasn't clingy. Yet she was becoming that woman. Shoving her phone into her pocket, she stomped out of the break room to the back door. Mostly, she had to know he was alive and well, even if he didn't want to see her anymore, which, truthfully, would be best for him.

Habits were ingrained in Rory. Even as she stepped out the door of the bar, she automatically scanned the parking lot and then the street for signs of danger. Finding nothing out of the ordinary, relief rushed through her, making her feel a little weak. Shouldering her small backpack, she walked briskly toward the apartments, grateful it was only a couple of blocks from where she worked.

Rory kept her pace the same as always. She didn't want to run out of oxygen, and that happened if she pushed her limits. Once she couldn't breathe adequately, she couldn't think. In an emergency, she needed to be able to use her brain. Already, the fog had blanketed the streets. The damp air gave her lungs a problem. That was the one bad thing about living in the area. She might love it, but her lungs didn't love the fog.

The biggest problem she had wasn't being worried about her own safety; it was trying to keep her mind from straying to Gideon.

As she walked toward the harbor, the feeling of uneasiness grew stronger. Without conscious thought, she continually reached out to Gideon, anxious to know if he was alive and well. She had nearly decided to bypass her apartment building and see if she could get him to answer his door when the feeling of immediate danger rushed over her.

She took a deep breath, drawing in air. Was the danger to her? To Gideon? The warning signals were alarmingly strong. She was too far from Gideon. She spun around, facing back the way she'd come. The danger seemed to be emanating from that direction. The fog had crept completely in, leaving the streets gray and damp, making it difficult to see very far. She had excellent hearing. The fog could muffle sound, but not from her. She tended to be able to hear whether that heavy mist had rolled in or not. It was one of the reasons she never worried about walking home at night.

Listening, she heard muffled movement in the street. Not a car. Footsteps. Hurrying. Not running but coming at her fast. There was no time to make it to her apartment building. She was right at the crosswalk, so there was no building to shelter against and blend in. Her heart rate increased before she had a chance to keep it under control.

Instantly, there was a faint stirring in her mind. *Red? Are you in danger?*

Gideon sounded very far away. His voice was thin. Thready. The moment he spoke to her, there was someone else protesting, pulling him away from her. She detected the presence but didn't recognize the person, and she knew Gideon wasn't alone. The distraction allowed her assailant to reach her before she'd prepared an adequate defense.

Scott Tinsdale caught her wrist as she stepped to one side to put herself off the sidewalk and onto the lawn of the closest building's landscaping. She let him have her wrist, but she brought her arm up, closing her fist as if prepared to fight. Shifting her weight to the balls of her feet, she kept her legs shoulder-width apart, knees light.

"Tinsdale." She feigned surprise. "Let go of me. What do you want?" Pushing outrage into her voice, she kept her tone a little shocked and frightened, twisting her wrist and pulling experimentally to see what he'd do. She wasn't surprised when he automatically tightened his grip.

"I just want to talk to you. I need you to deliver a message for me."

"You could have asked me in the bar."

"Someone could have overheard. It's important no one hears."

"If no one can hear the message, it's the kind of thing that can get someone in trouble. I don't want any part of it." Rory began working the moves she needed to break away from him over and over in her mind. She was certain she could get him to release her wrist, but trying to break his kneecap was risky. She only had one shot at it. If she missed, he'd be on her too fast and she'd never get away. Not to mention, he'd be royally pissed.

"We don't have anyone else, so it's on you." He tucked an envelope into the pocket of her jacket. "I suggest you keep that sealed. He'll know if you opened it. Give it to Harvey when he comes to you."

"Harvey? The Harvey who the cops already think I'm working for? They're following me everywhere I go and asking me all kinds of bullshit questions I can't answer. I don't want any part of this. Take it back." She reached into her jacket with her free hand.

"Leave it. You don't want us coming after you. We're just asking you to deliver the message to him. That's all. No one is asking anything else of you. Just give him that when he sees you next. You don't have to look for him; he'll find you. Just carry it on you and when he comes to you, hand it over. That's not a lot to ask."

"It is if it involves me in anything criminal," Rory protested. "Westlake thinks Harvey killed his partners. He's not going to let up until he finds Harvey. I don't want to get caught up in that."

"Westlake is dirty. You can't trust him."

Rory went still inside, trying to read whether Tinsdale was lying or not. It was difficult to get the answer when the situation was so tense. Was Harvey trying to frame her? That was a possibility too.

"Let go of her now, or you're a dead man." Javier's voice came out of the fog. It was low and intense, and there was no mistaking he meant business.

Tinsdale released her instantly. "Remember what I said," he hissed, then turned away from her and walked into the street, away from the sound of Javier's voice.

There was a brief silence that made her aware Javier hadn't traveled alone. She was certain Tinsdale would be followed. Javier came out of the fog like a silent specter. He made no sound at all. He'd always carried an air of menace around him, but now, in the early morning hours, surrounded by fog, he seemed deadlier than ever. She couldn't help shivering.

"Did he hurt you?"

"No. Do you know if Gideon is okay? He didn't come into the bar tonight. I texted him and I called too. I left him a message. It just doesn't seem like him not to answer." She didn't bother to keep the worry out of her voice.

"You're shivering. Let's get out of the cold."

She was beginning to struggle to breathe properly. She detested showing weakness in front of Gideon's friends. She knew it shouldn't reflect on him that she was his choice of a partner, but somehow it was ingrained in her that it did. It was insane how invested she was already in Gideon, when she'd only just met him. She felt as if they'd been together forever. As if no one else would ever fit with her.

Rory indicated the direction of her apartment building. "Thank you for coming when you did. I live right up the street." She began walking in that direction, trying not to wheeze. Every breath she took seemed to be getting more difficult.

Javier didn't even brush against her, but as he paced along beside her, he offered her something. She took it without thinking, only to find it was her own inhaler. He'd taken it from the inside pocket of her jacket, which seemed impossible.

"Have a lot of practice picking pockets?" She used the inhaler. What was the point of pretending she didn't need it?

"Yep. Stayed alive that way as a kid. That was how we ate," Javier revealed. "Stole money and shit. I got really good at it. I was much smaller than Gideon and the others, and looked even younger than I was. They provided a distraction, and I went in and cleared out the tourists' pockets or purses."

He said it matter-of-factly, as if his childhood were normal. It instantly conjured up images of hungry little children with no homes or loving parents. Her heart hurt for them.

She waited to speak until she was certain she could breathe normally again. "Well, the practice certainly paid off. You're good."

Javier flashed her a grin. It was quick and cocky, but it was genuine and transformed his youthful, stoic features from looking deadly to handsome.

"I take it you grew up with Gideon. He told me he grew up on the streets and you're very good friends with him."

Javier nodded. "That's true. More like brothers. We've always looked out for one another."

There was a distinct warning in his voice that would have ordinarily made her smile. She loved that for Gideon. Unfortunately, with him out of her reach and her wondering if she'd done something in her nightmare to harm him, she thought that warning was aimed directly at her.

"Tell me what's wrong with Gideon, Javier."

They were at the front of the apartment building. She stood at the entrance, turning her back on the door to face him. Javier reached around her and punched in the code to open the door. She twisted around, shocked. He took her elbow and escorted her inside, straight to the small lounge she preferred to go to with her friends. It was far warmer there. Javier indicated a chair and Rory sank into it.

"You seem to know your way around this apartment building." She made it a statement.

Javier shrugged. "What happened this evening before you went to work? I thought you didn't work tonight."

"I wasn't on the schedule. It wasn't my regular shift, but how would you know that? Why would you even know that?" A shiver of awareness went through her. Something was very wrong. Javier had shown up at precisely the right time, intervening when she needed help. He knew the code to get into her apartment building. He knew her shifts at work.

"Gideon knew you weren't supposed to work. He keeps track so he can make sure you get home safely, or he can take you out."

That seemed reasonable enough, but it wasn't the entire truth. Rory studied him. He sat across from her, looking totally relaxed. She supposed he was, but at the same time, she thought he might be a snake, coiled and ready to strike if she gave a wrong answer. Javier might look casual sitting in the chair, but he gave off the most dangerous vibes she'd ever been around. Frankly, he terrified her. It occurred to her that he was capable of killing the cop. Or Dustin and Ret. She much preferred the honesty of Detective Westlake showing her his utter distaste of her, or Tinsdale delivering his veiled threat.

"You aren't telling me how Gideon is doing," she said, persisting. She needed the information, and then she was going to politely excuse herself, go to her room, pack and drive away fast.

The cops hadn't yet told her not to leave town, but she was afraid that was coming. She would have to get out before that happened. Tinsdale and Harvey had their own agenda that she didn't want any part of, and she was horribly afraid she would harm Gideon. If she stayed any longer, she would get so attached to him she wouldn't be able to leave. She feared it might already be too late. She felt she was that connected to him. That obsessive over him.

"We're getting there. The doc could use information. We need to know what happened tonight."

Her heart clenched hard in her chest. Her lungs seized. For a moment, there was no getting air. There was no thinking. There it was. The worst. She had done something to him. "How bad is it?" The whisper came out strangled, the words trying to make their way through the huge lump in her throat.

"Tell me what happened tonight." Javier was firm.

She choked back the need to yell at him to just tell her what she needed so desperately to know. He wasn't going to give her the information. "My boss, Brad Fitzpatrick, called me. One of the bartenders said they could only work a half shift tonight. He was looking for someone to come in late. I said I would do it for him. I needed to sleep before going to work, so I went to my rooftop patio. It's very peaceful there."

She stopped abruptly. What could she say that didn't sound crazy? And she didn't know him. She didn't want to tell him her personal business.

"Keep going."

Rory shook her head. "Then I fell asleep and had a nightmare. I get them often."

Instantly, Javier looked alert, as if having a nightmare weren't an everyday occurrence many people had. "A nightmare?"

She shrugged, trying to look casual. "Yes. Don't you ever have nightmares? I thought most people did."

He ignored her comment. "Was Gideon in your nightmare?"

"No, not at all."

His dark eyebrows drew together for a moment. "What was your nightmare about?"

"Childhood things. Scary childhood things. Nothing to do with Gideon at all." But he was obviously hurt, and a doctor was trying to help him. "In the dream, the girl stood on the ledge of this horrible house. I heard Gideon's voice telling me to wake up. Then owls were flying all around me, and I did wake up. I was standing on the ledge of my rooftop, and the owls drove me back onto the floor of the patio. Gideon wasn't with me, and he wasn't in the dream. I did hear his voice though. At least I think I did. I think it was real."

Javier had pulled out his phone and was texting with lightning speed.

Rory pressed her finger to the place over her left eye that always felt strange, that hurt like hell, that felt as if her skin were ripping apart. "He did wake me up, didn't he?" She didn't care that she sounded defeated. She would have to leave.

"Yeah, babe, he woke you up." He glanced down at his phone. "He's going to be fine. He just tore open a couple of places the doc had been watching. That's on him, not you." He sighed. "And maybe more on me."

"Why would it be on you?"

"He took several bullets meant for me. He's saved my life on more than one occasion. Gideon's a good man, Rory. And off-the-charts protective. You didn't do this to him. He makes his own choices, just like we all do. He sent me here tonight. He knew you were in trouble, and he's going to ask me who that man was and what he wanted."

She was afraid he would ask, and she didn't know what to tell him. She definitely didn't want to involve Gideon in that mess.

"The last thing he needs is to worry about anything to do with that man or his associates."

Javier's entire demeanor changed. "If you are Gideon's woman, he will worry about every aspect of your life. *Every* aspect. That's who he is. If you can't accept that, you can't accept him. I understand you wanting to protect him, Rory—"

"Needing," she interrupted. "I need to protect him as well. He looks out for everyone, Javier. I can't help who I am. I need to look after him."

"Look after him all you want. It will be good for him. I want that for him. His entire family wants that for him. But you have to allow him to protect you as well. He'll go insane if you hold things back from him."

Rory could hear her heart beating too loud. There were so many things she didn't know about herself. Things that could possibly hurt Gideon. She would never share that with Javier. That was for Gideon alone. No one else. She could barely face knowing she might have something dangerous in her past that could harm others, let alone tell others. It had taken a tremendous amount of courage just to tell Gideon.

"He came into the bar tonight and asked me out. I told him I was seeing someone, and he backed off right away, but he stayed the rest of my shift. I noticed he didn't flirt with any of the women in the bar, not even Dana, and she's gorgeous. He paid a lot of attention to the doors and any conversations I had with the customers."

"You'd never met him before?"

"I'd never even seen him before."

"You're certain?"

She wasn't going to tell him she remembered faces and conversations. He didn't need to know too much about her. She wanted to see Gideon again before she made the decision to leave or not. Already she was going back and forth. It was pathetic.

"I'm very certain. I didn't have to close, so I stalled a little before I left, just to make certain he wasn't waiting outside, and then I started home. I don't think he would have caught me off guard, but I was so worried about Gideon that I didn't pick up on the danger until he was there. Mostly, he just wanted to talk to me."

"About?"

"A man living in the same apartment building. His name is Harvey Matters. The crazy thing is, I don't even know Harvey except to say hello. He hung out in the gym sometimes when my friends and I were working out. Or in the laundry room when we were doing our laundry. He was always with other men. He didn't really say much to any of us, and never to me in particular. The odd thing about it is the cops think I have something to do with Harvey as well."

Javier was silent, but his gaze was intense, piercing even, like twin laser beams. She felt his scrutiny, as if he were analyzing every word of her statement, looking for a lie. She wasn't lying. She didn't understand why everyone thought she had a connection to Harvey. She was beginning to think she was going insane. Maybe she didn't remember her relationship with Harvey, just like she didn't remember her parents.

"What did he want to know about Harvey?" Javier asked.

"He wanted me to give Harvey a message the next time I saw him. I explained I had no reason to see him. I told him Harvey was wanted by the police. It didn't seem to matter."

"What was the message?"

"He didn't give me a verbal message for Harvey. And you came and interrupted us."

Again, Javier studied her. "Did you get the feeling he was an associate of Harvey's?"

She nodded slowly. "Yes, I did. I tried to make it clear I didn't want anything to do with Harvey or him. It didn't seem to matter what I wanted. He scared me," she admitted. She wanted to add, *Not half as much as you do.*

"Did he give you something to give to Harvey?"

She remained silent, looking at him. She would only tell Gideon. She only trusted Gideon.

Javier sighed. "I'm trying to help you. I know it's difficult to trust anyone, Rory, especially if you've been alone for a long time. Gideon's my brother. I would do anything for him. I'm just trying to help you out while he's recovering."

"If you know how hard it is to trust, then you'll have to let this go. It took a lot to go out with Gideon. I don't do that sort of thing. You don't have to believe me, but I don't. He's different. And very hard to resist. You may be afraid for him, but I'm terrified that I let down my guard and trusted him. I let him in. If he isn't the man he says he is, I'll have no one and nothing. He has all of you. That may not be a big deal to you, but I feel pretty vulnerable. Trust is fragile, Javier, as you should well know."

Javier leaned toward her. "Gideon is one of the best men I know, Rory, if not the best. He's a good man. He's all in with you. All in. One hundred percent. He'd be here instead of me if he wasn't hurt tonight."

"Why haven't those wounds healed properly?"

Javier sat back and for the first time looked upset. "He should have died. He almost did. It was my fault." He shook his head and shoved both hands through his hair in agitation. "We were on an assignment, and we knew we were going to see some bad shit. It was just that we didn't know it was going to be like that. I have leftover triggers from childhood. We all do. It isn't an excuse, although Gideon says it is. In any case, I blacked out. I just went after the people who did that shit to the kids. Hacked them to pieces and left them lying on the ground like garbage."

Rory heard the raw pain in his voice. She wanted to stop him, knowing he saw the images in his mind. He was probably never going to get them out. Gideon had seen them as well.

"I must have gone right out in the open where a dozen men were firing at me. Gideon threw his body in front of mine. He took me down, protecting me with his own body until the others drove them off."

Javier's eyes had gone liquid. His voice rasped as he looked down at his feet. "We barely managed to get Gideon to a safe enough place for the docs to work on him. We were lucky enough to have two surgeons with us; otherwise, he wouldn't have stood a chance. He's tough, and we have the best when it comes to doctors."

He sat up straight, looking as if the past few moments hadn't occurred. Flashing her a small grin, he shrugged. "Gideon doesn't like staying put. He's a man of action. Now that he's got you, he'll have a reason to want to be home."

She wasn't so sure about Gideon having her, but for one second, she allowed herself to bask in the idea of it. "Thank you for coming to my rescue, Javier. I really appreciate it. Please ask Gideon to let me know when he's strong enough for visitors, and I'll come by to see him."

She stood up, determined to send him on his way. She also rounded the chair. She didn't want him to pretend he wanted to hug her. At least she knew Javier was human now, but she also knew he wasn't the hugging type. He was the type to pickpocket though, and she had the envelope she was going to tell Gideon about but wasn't going to let Javier take from her. If Harvey showed up looking for it and she had to tell him it was stolen from her because she'd told someone about it, he'd probably kill her.

Javier flashed another grin. She noted none of the most recent smiles actually reached his eyes. He was back to being his dangerous self. "I'll wait down here until you're inside your room and safe. You can text me when you're there."

"I don't have your number."

"I'll give it to you." He proceeded to do so.

She gave him a little wave and took the elevator. At least she knew Gideon was going to be fine. She had no idea he'd been hurt so bad. He'd downplayed the seriousness of his wounds. She should have known. *Gideon.* She whispered his name. *What am I going to do with you?*

Unlocking the door to her apartment, she texted Javier that she was safe and he was off duty.

9

Someone got into my things too," Janice announced. "While I was at work last night. They trashed my apartment. I called the cops, and they still haven't shown up. I went to spend the night in Pam's apartment after taking detailed pictures, but her place had been broken into as well. They hit three of our apartments last night. Rory's, Pam's and mine."

"They got mine too," Cindy said, her voice stiff. "I spent the night at my parents'. I took the boys to visit with them. It's a long way, so I always stay over. Everything was destroyed. I found the mess this morning when I came home. I called the police as well."

"I did too," Pam said.

Rory took a sip of her coffee. She hadn't gone to bed. She wasn't about to wake up Sally or Lydia in the middle of the night and ask for a place to sleep, so she'd stayed in the sitting room. She'd been afraid to close her eyes. "I called in a report too. Only Sally and Lydia were spared, probably because the two of you were home last night."

"What?" Lydia demanded. "This was supposed to be one of the safer apartment buildings. I hope you complain to the owners. And why didn't the police send someone? They got here fast enough to interrogate all of us when they found Ret in the garbage chute."

Rory couldn't help laughing at the outrage in Lydia's voice. It was the first thing she'd found to laugh about since the confrontation with Scott Tinsdale three days earlier. She hadn't heard from Gideon, but Ethan and Brian had been in the bar the night before. She knew Javier had followed her, presumably to keep her safe. She was fairly certain the same two undercover cops had been in the bar two nights in a row.

The women sat in the lounge they preferred. This time, it was Sally who had provided Rory with her coffee, since she was always the last one to join them. She slept later than the other women. Lydia had Ellen with her, but Cindy's boys were with her parents.

Rory didn't even have junk mail to sort through. Not one single piece. That made her feel sad and a little apart from everyone else. The others didn't ever comment on her lack of mail, but she knew they noticed.

"Could you tell if anything was taken?" Rory asked. "Because nothing was taken from me that I could tell, not that I had much in the first place, other than my guitar and my notebooks with my music. Most of those were torn, but I can salvage them."

"That's what was crazy," Janice said. "I don't really have anything of value I keep there, other than my artwork. Anything else is kept at the bank. My drawers were pulled out, emptied onto the floor and smashed. The bed was stripped, the mattress torn apart. Every chair had its stuffing pulled out. Whoever was there was looking for something and thought it was inside my furniture."

"That's crazy," Sally confirmed. "Did you buy all your furniture at the same place? Could someone have hidden something inside the furniture, and then they came looking for it?"

"No, I bought different pieces from various shops," Janice said. "I have no idea what anyone could have been looking for."

"You do own a janitorial service. You find things in offices," Lydia ventured. "Maybe someone lost something important."

"If I find anything in an office, it's left there in the lost and found, and I leave a note for the office manager," Janice said. "That note is copied to me and others so that my butt and my employees' are covered."

"That's not it, then," Sally said.

"It was the same at my place," Pam said. "We both went through Janice's apartment, trying not to touch anything, but we didn't find anything missing. Then we went through mine. We couldn't tell why anyone destroyed everything. We just took pictures and called the cops."

"Maybe that yummy detective will show up, Lydia," Sally said. "The nice one."

Lydia looked steadily into her coffee cup. "I'm sure I have no idea who you're talking about."

"He was the only nice one," Sally said. "You know the one; you blushed every single time you looked at him."

"I most certainly did *not*," Lydia denied.

The women laughed.

Rory had to join them. She nodded with the others. "You did, babe. You blushed. Turned as red as a tomato. But it was cute, and he was into you."

Lydia put both hands over her face. "Did he notice?"

"He was blushing too," Sally said. "We all noticed that. He kept trying to look like he wasn't staring at you. If he asks you out, I'm babysitting, so don't use Ellen as an excuse."

"I'll babysit too," Rory offered.

"Me too," Pam said. "Janice will give me the night off."

"I will?" Janice asked.

"Yes," Pam said firmly, glaring at her boss. "You absolutely will."

Even Lydia laughed.

"There you have it, Lydia," Janice said. "When good employees rebel, you can't do anything but go out with the devil in order to make certain she gets her chance to babysit."

"Throw me under the bus to get your time with Ellen," Lydia said. "I'm not too worried that he's going to ask me."

"He's going to ask you," Pam assured.

"He could be married," Lydia objected.

"He's not married," they all said at once.

Lydia shook her head again. "There are a million women he could ask out. Women without children."

"It's the age of enlightenment," Sally pointed out. "You can go to the police station with a plate of those fabulous cookies you make and talk to him about the break-ins and how we're all so nervous. That should do it. During the conversation, find out if he's single, if that worries you. Then just ask him out."

Lydia looked as if she might faint. "I'm not going to the police station to ask him out. Oh my God. You all have lost your minds."

Rory couldn't help but laugh with the others again. "Lydia, we're teasing you. We know you're not going to the police station with a plate of cookies, although your cookies would have most of the cops coming around making certain no one is breaking into our apartments and trashing them."

Everyone nodded.

"Yours are the best," Janice confirmed. "We wouldn't have to worry if we started bribing the cops to take shifts guarding the place."

Rory noticed that Cindy laughed with them, but she seemed

introspective. Now she had a strange look on her face. "What do you think about all of us looking for a different apartment building together? This one doesn't feel safe anymore. It *clearly* isn't safe anymore."

There was instant silence. Rory didn't want to move. The building was close to work. Close to Gideon. Very convenient for her. If she was leaving it, she should be going away for good. This was probably the best time for her to go. Her furniture was gone. Her things were gone. Her nebulizer was still intact, but even that had been flung on the rooftop floor.

She could understand why Cindy would want to take her boys and find another place to live. The children were traumatized by finding a dead man in the garbage chute. There had been a policeman killed in a shootout in the apartment building. Another man had been found dead in his apartment. Now four of their places had been broken into. Their homes had gone from feeling safe to feeling scary dangerous. If she had children, she would consider moving too.

Lydia wrapped her arms around Ellen and pulled her into her lap. The little girl had been coloring quietly, and she appeared startled, but she didn't squirm. She just looked up at her mother as if Lydia did this often.

"Honestly, I can't afford to move, Cindy. It would be first and last month's rent and a cleaning deposit. I signed a lease here. Even if I could eventually break it, that would take time and probably going to court to do it. I'm just not up to that. I'll admit all this scares me, but I'm barely getting by. That's why I've been trying to learn bartending. I thought maybe I could earn extra income to help offset some of the bills."

Cindy nodded. "I understand. It was just a thought. I love this complex and all of you, but I can't keep my sons here when things like this keep happening. It isn't fair to them. I do have the resources to leave. My family would lose their minds if they knew everything going on here. Thankfully, they tend to be above paying attention to what goes on with us mere mortals. All the boys' things were trashed. Their beds and toys were broken. They would have been devastated if they had seen the damage."

"I thought about moving the moment I saw my apartment was trashed," Janice said. "I have renter's insurance, but it was frightening to know someone has been inside my home. Then I got mad. I'm not going to let the owners of these apartments get away with false advertising. They told us we would be safe here. We were charged more money to live here. I'm expecting them to keep their word. I've already drafted a letter to them and hope all of you sign it. I'm going around to the other tenants as well to try to get them to sign it."

Pam nodded. "I can't afford to move either, Cindy. I don't want to see you go. Would you be willing to wait long enough to see if the owners are willing to do something about our safety?"

Cindy pushed both hands through her hair. "I don't know. I've got the boys seeing a doctor next week. Let me talk to him first before I make any decisions. They're staying with my parents at the moment, and after the cops okay it, I'm having cleaners come and get everything out of the apartment. I want it put right before they're back. I must do what's right for them. If the doctor thinks it's best to get them away from here, we'll move. He might say they need to face the reality of what happened to them."

The door opened, and Rory couldn't help but look at Lydia. Maybe all of them did. The man striding into the room with such confidence was Detective Warren Larrsen. He wore a dark gray suit that fit his wide shoulders. His chestnut hair gleamed under the lights and his dark eyes immediately sought out Lydia, confirming the collective opinions of the women that he was interested in her.

"Ladies. I'm looking for Janice DeWitt."

Janice reluctantly held up her hand. "That would be me."

"I'm Detective Larrsen. We met the other day under unfortunate circumstances. It seems we're destined to do the same again."

"Would you care for coffee?" Sally asked.

"Thanks, I could really use a cup." He indicated a small table a short distance from the others. "We could talk over there before I take a look at your apartment."

"We have cookies too," Sally offered. "Lydia made them, and no one can bake the way she does."

Larrsen sent Lydia a dazzling smile. It was so gorgeous that even Rory had to admit it made him attractive as all get out. "I have to admit, I have a weakness for cookies. I'll have to try them to see if they're as good as your friends say."

Lydia groaned and turned a cute blushing shade of rose. "Don't listen to them. They always say that, and it isn't true."

When he smiled, Rory noted Larrsen had a hint of an intriguing dimple. "I'm going to see for myself, Ms. Sawyer."

Rory nudged Lydia. Detective Larrsen remembered Lydia's name.

"I'll talk to Ms. DeWitt first and then Pam Williams." Detective Larrsen looked around at the women in the room until he settled on Pam. She nodded, lifting her hand. He gave her a brief smile. "Ms. Atler?" He clearly knew who Cindy Atler was. Her husband had been a firefighter who had died fighting a fire. She came from an extremely wealthy and powerful family. Detective Larrsen must have found it strange that she was living in the same apartments and was friends with them. *Good* friends with them. "I'll interview you after Ms. Williams. And, Ms. Chappel, if you don't mind waiting, I'll take you last."

Rory sighed. "Sure, no problem."

He clearly heard the hint of defensiveness she didn't bother to keep from her voice. The other women were no longer looking at Warren Larrsen as if he were their knight in shining armor. He had suddenly become the enemy.

"I left you for last because my notes indicate you said this was your day off. Both Ms. DeWitt and Ms. Williams work tonight, and I didn't want to make them late. Ms. Atler had indicated that she wanted to be able to start clearing the apartment for her sons as soon as possible. If you need to be somewhere sooner . . ."

"No, it's fine." Rory waved Janice toward the table the detective had first indicated they use for the interview to give their statements. She felt guilty for lumping Larrsen in with Westlake when Larrsen had treated her with kindness. "I didn't mean to sound grumpy. I didn't sleep last night. I should have gone to a hotel, but I was too tired to make the effort. I just came down here with a couple of blankets."

"Rory," Lydia protested. "You should have stayed with me."

"I wasn't about to wake you up."

"You're always helping me. How many times have you bailed me out when I needed someone to watch Ellen? Or when I needed extra money? You've been teaching me how to mix drinks. I want to be able to help you."

"My bed is smashed, and my mattress is torn to shreds. I'll be happy to sleep on your couch, at least for tonight," Rory teased.

She was aware of Larrsen paying close attention to the exchange as he scooped up cookies, put them on one of the little paper plates Lydia had provided and carried them over to the table where Janice had set his coffee.

"After I take each of your statements, I'll need to see the apartments, take pictures and dust for fingerprints. Then you can have your places back," Larrsen assured them.

"Maybe Cindy should go first so she can get started right away on getting her place ready for the kids," Janice said.

"No." Cindy shook her head. "They'll be with their grandparents long enough for me to get everything done, but thanks, Janice."

Rory's phone vibrated, and she pulled it from her pocket and glanced down. Her heart jumped and then accelerated. Gideon. At last. She was foolish enough to run the pad of her finger over the text on the screen, her pulse reacting to the sight of seeing what he'd written.

Red, everything all right? I'm doing better. Any chance you can drop by today? Javier said you're taking extra shifts. Hoping you didn't tonight, and you can spend time with me.

She wanted to sag with relief. He was doing better and wanted to see her. Thankfully she hadn't taken an extra shift, although she was exhausted and she should sleep. What did that matter when she had the chance to see Gideon? She could assess the damage done to him for herself. If she thought he was up to it, she could share the message Scott Tinsdale had given her for Harvey, and she'd tell him about the break-ins at the apartment building.

No extra shift this evening. Would be happy to come by. What time would be best?

"You've got that dreamy look on your face, Rory," Sally accused. "Gideon is texting you, isn't he?"

Rory couldn't help laughing. She felt joy at the prospect of seeing him. Just knowing he was alive and well made her slightly giddy. "Yep. And I don't even care if you tease me about him." She touched her hair. "I must look a mess. I *feel* a mess."

"You can use my shower," Lydia offered immediately. "Do you have clean clothes?"

Rory made a face. "I threw clothes into the washing machine a little while ago. The alarm hasn't gone off yet. I'll shove them in the dryer when it does."

Come now if possible.

That made her even happier. He was as eager to see her as she was to see him. She loved that. A part of her was a little afraid he wouldn't still be quite as interested. She didn't want to be a clingy, needy girlfriend. *Girlfriend?* She'd never been anyone's girlfriend. She'd never let herself trust anyone to get that close to her.

I can't make it for a couple of hours, but if you're hungry, I can bring us takeout when I come.

"I'll take a shower as soon as I transfer my clothes to the dryer," Rory announced to the others. "That way, I'll cut down on the time it will be before I can get over to see him."

None of your homemade dinners?

Alas, without kitchen. It's takeout or nothing. She added laughing emojis in the hopes that he would think she was teasing him.

It took him longer than normal to get back to her. At once, an uneasy feeling crept in. Maybe she shouldn't have teased him. Gideon was uncannily perceptive, especially when it came to her.

Is everything okay? Javier mentioned you had a run-in with someone the other night.

She was right. He was much too discerning when it came to her. The alarm on her watch went off. "My clothes are ready, and I've got to claim the dryer before someone else tosses my clothes from the washing machine and all the dryers are taken."

"It would be a war if that happened," Pam declared. "No one's ever done that to me. Has it happened to you, Rory?"

"Not here. At another place I lived, there was a woman who did it on a regular basis. She would stop washing machines and take other people's clothing out so she could use the quarters they'd already put in the machines. Someone took all her clothes out of the dryers when they were nearly dry and put them back in the washing machines and then put all kinds of money in the machines. She was so angry. She kept trying to find out who did it." Rory grinned at them. "She never did."

"Didn't they have cameras?" Lydia asked.

"Yep. She even demanded security check the footage, but it was the strangest thing. No one was on there, just white snow. She claimed it was a conspiracy and wanted to sue the owner of the apartment building." Rory stood up and stretched. She was stiff from trying to sleep on the couch. "You really don't mind if I use your shower, Lydia?"

"Nope. Here. Take the spare key to my apartment. That way, if you come in late tonight, you'll still be able to get in." Lydia tried winking, but she wasn't very good at it.

Ellen held out her arms. Rory took the key and then turned around. "You want a piggyback ride, Miss Ellie May Rider?"

Ellen giggled and nodded her head.

"If you want to ride the horsey, you have to answer yes or no," she persisted.

Ellen ducked her head against her mother. "Yes."

Rory's heart fluttered. More and more, Ellen was talking to her and the others when they implemented the tools they were given.

"I'm headed down to the laundry room. I'll be galloping down the stairs. You'll have to hold on tight."

Lydia lifted Ellen onto Rory's back, and the child wrapped her arms around Rory's neck and clamped her knees against her ribs. Ellen giggled again and then let out a loud whoop, presumably to get Rory to gallop toward the door. She did so, making Ellen squeal with joy. Lydia started to trail after them, but Sally caught her arm.

"You stay here. She can't always be with you. Remember, we talked about this. You don't want her to have separation anxiety on top of everything else. I'll go with them. Let Rory and me look after her. We'll be right back up."

"I think *I* have separation anxiety," Lydia confessed.

Cindy had risen to her feet, and she put her arm around Lydia.

"Rory and Sally have this. We've all been watching the videos on selective mutism and the tools for working with Ellen to help her to talk to us. You have to let us help you, Lydia. We want to help."

Rory didn't wait to see if Lydia was going to hang back this time. The moment Sally opened the door, she galloped through, doing her best to sound like a horse as she approached the stairs, hitting them with her shoes, clattering loudly on each tread. Sally added to the noise with her own feet, in an effort to sound more like they could be part of a herd.

Rory coughed twice on the way down the stairs because the little hands were so tight around her neck. She didn't stop though. Her phone continued to vibrate in her pocket. She realized she should have answered Gideon before she offered to give Ellen a piggyback ride.

Lydia had explained that she had also suffered from selective mutism as a child, although no one had put a name to what she had. She simply was so severely shy that she didn't speak to anyone, not even most relatives. Later, she had anxiety attacks. Lydia didn't want that for her daughter, and she was doing her best to get Ellen the tools to deal with her social anxiety. Her friends wanted to give her whatever she needed to help.

Rory set Ellen on one of the machines that was vibrating. Ellen laughed and clapped her hands. Sally stood close, wrapping one arm around her waist to ensure that the little girl didn't fall. They watched as Rory transferred the clothes from the washing machine to the dryer. Several of the washing machines were being used but only two of the dryers.

She pulled her phone out and glanced down. Gideon was worried.

I detest that I can't come myself. Should I send Javier?

When she hadn't answered him right away, he had waited approximately two minutes and sent another text.

He said you were uneasy around him. Ethan is free.

Gideon was such a good man. He was so worried about her. He was the one injured, and yet because he couldn't get to her, he was going to send one of his friends to check on her.

She texted him back. I'm sorry I worried you. I'm washing clothes and playing with a friend's little girl. All is well. When I'm finished with chores, I will come to you with food. Let me know what you're in the mood for.

She hoped by mentioning Ellen, he would relax.

There was a brief silence. Normally, Gideon texted lightning fast. He also had a tendency to touch her mind. It was always light, but he took advantage of the connection between them. He hadn't done that, not since he'd awakened from whatever dark place he'd been. She suspected he'd been put into a medically induced coma by a doctor. It was the only explanation she could think of that would have taken him so far from her. Had that broken their mental connection—made it so they no longer could touch one another telepathically?

I'll call in an order to the restaurant in the harbor. The Salty Dog. It will be waiting. An hour?

She'd told him two hours. She still had to shower, dress, fold her laundry and interview with Larrsen.

Seriously need two hours to get everything done. Will hurry. If I get it all done before then, I'll text you.

She did her best to sound matter-of-fact. She could tell he was uneasy, but she didn't know why. She shouldn't have tried to tease him about not having a kitchen. She wasn't good at texting. Until she'd made friends with the women at her apartment building and Lani and Dana at work, she rarely texted anyone other than a boss for work. It was no wonder she didn't know how to make him laugh.

He gave her a thumbs-up. She really wanted to see him sooner, but she wasn't going looking as if she'd spent the night on a couch.

"Come on, little Miss Ellie May Rider, you need to get back on your trusty steed." She galloped around the room and deliberately looked as if she were bucking and rearing. "If you *dare*." She made her voice menacing and then whinnied loudly.

Ellen squealed again and held out her arms to Sally as Rory continued to trot around the room like a crazy person. "I *dare*," Ellen insisted. "I dare. I dare," she repeated, her voice pitched higher with excitement.

Rory and Sally exchanged a look of triumph. Ellen had spoken to them on a couple of occasions, but it was only a word or two and never with the animation she was displaying now. Sally lifted her from the washing machine and placed her on Rory's back. Rory reared up like a wild stallion, making all the appropriate horse noises.

Ellen laughed and clamped her knees tightly around Rory's ribs. They raced up the stairs as fast as Rory could go, her lungs burning for air. She could hear wheezing each time she tried to make her stallion trumpet. Ellen didn't seem to mind the strange noise that interfered with Rory's best horse sounds. Once in the lounge, Sally hastily removed the child from Rory's back, allowing her to collapse on the floor.

She pulled out her inhaler and took a deep breath of the medicine. Ellen sank down next to her, wrapped her arms around her neck and hugged her.

Alarmed, Lydia sat down beside her. "Can you breathe?"

Rory nodded.

"You have to stop doing that."

Rory took the inhaler away from her mouth. "She loves it and she talked to us, Lydia." She whispered it, trying not to cry. "Ellen, you love to play horsey with Auntie Rory and Auntie Sally, don't you?"

Ellen transferred her hug from Rory to Lydia, nodding enthusiastically. "I love playing horsey, Mommy," she confided in an overly loud whisper. "Auntie Rory is the *best* horsey."

"She is, isn't she, Princess Bo Peep?" Lydia asked.

Ellen laughed and squirmed away from Lydia's teasing kisses. "I'm not Bo Peep. I'm Ellie May *Rider*," she declared, rolling around on the carpet between her mother and Rory.

"You are?" Lydia asked as if shocked. "Let me see. Sally, come look. Does she look like Princess Bo Peep or Ellie May Rider to you?"

Rory managed to sit up gingerly and draw air into her lungs. She glanced toward the table where Detective Larrsen was now taking Pam's statement. It looked as if they were finishing up. He had his eyes fixed on Lydia and Ellen. Then he raised his gaze to her and smiled. He did have a very nice smile. Rory couldn't help but smile back.

She stood up. "If I promise to hurry, do I have enough time to shower? I have somewhere I need to be this evening."

"By all means. I'm going to be taking photographs and dusting for prints," he replied. "I'm also going to check the footage in the security cameras. I've got plenty to do."

Cindy stood. "I promise to talk slow when I give my statement, Rory. Take your time."

"I'll fold your laundry for you and bring up your clothes," Sally volunteered. "I set my alarm, so don't worry about anyone taking over the machines. I can bring them to Lydia's apartment, and you can choose which outfit you want to wear tonight."

Rory looked around at the friends she'd made. It was hard to blink back tears. "Thank you. All of you. It means a lot that you'd help me."

"You've certainly helped every one of us multiple times," Janice pointed out. "We know you like Gideon, and we don't want you to be late for your date. Go take your shower."

"The hair dryer is under the sink," Lydia said. "Do you want help with your hair?"

"No, but . . ." She broke off, glancing at the detective. She really did detest showing weakness, but he'd already seen her on the floor wheezing, using her inhaler. "I did put my nebulizer just inside the cabinet where all the magazines are kept. Would one of you mind getting it out for me? It's in a cloth bag right on top. It's a little heavy."

If Sally was going to fold her laundry and bring it to her at Lydia's, she would have time to give herself a treatment before she went to Gideon's. She could leave her machine at Lydia's, knowing it would be safe there until she got back.

"I'll get it for you," Pam volunteered. "Get moving."

"It's nice to see that you're all such good friends," Larrsen said, holding out his hand to Lydia to help her up so she wouldn't have to let go of Ellen.

Rory couldn't help smiling as Lydia took his hand and allowed him to pull her to her feet. Ellen buried her face in Lydia's neck. That didn't seem to bother him at all. He just smiled down at Lydia.

"The cookies are the best I've ever eaten. Seconds seem appropriate under the circumstances."

"What circumstances are those?" Lydia asked.

She tried to sound challenging, but Rory thought she sounded breathless. She wondered if she sounded like that when she talked to Gideon.

"I came down on the side of Miss Ellie May Rider, and I was right. That should earn me cookies."

Ellen turned her head sideways, and for one moment, her little white teeth flashed at the detective, and then she buried her face again in her mother's neck.

"If that little smile she just gave him is anything to go by, I think Miss Ellie May concurs," Rory said, wanting Lydia to know Ellen wasn't above succumbing to the detective's charm.

"What do you think, Princess? Did his vote earn him more cookies? He is working hard, and he did say they were the best cookies he's ever had. That was truly a nice thing to say. What do you think? Should I say yes?" Lydia feathered a series of light kisses over the side of her daughter's face and neck.

Ellen nodded vigorously even as she giggled and squirmed. She was obviously ticklish around her ear and neck, and her mom was hitting every sensitive spot.

"Thank you, Miss Ellie May Rider," Detective Larrsen said in a very solemn tone as he scooped more cookies onto his plate and returned to the table to join Cindy.

"Well done," Cindy approved.

Rory found herself smiling all the way to Lydia's apartment. For the first time in her life, she had amazing friends.

10

The front door to Gideon's home opened into a huge space with a high ceiling. The walls angled inward the way the building did, but that in no way took away from the large open area his living room provided. Gideon was waiting for Rory on a couch made of black leather. It was wide and long with a high back. There were several throws on it, each one a different shade of gray. Before, she hadn't really looked at how the house itself was painted or decorated, but she found the colors rather soothing. Mostly, she looked at Gideon.

There was a distinct gray cast under his tough features, but his blue eyes lit up the moment she entered his home. The fact that he wasn't on his rooftop told Rory more than anything else that he was really injured.

Rory was totally unprepared for the way the sight of him would drive the strength from her legs, leaving her so weak she could barely stand. She clutched the bags from the restaurant, just drinking him in. Inhaling his scent. Feeling she might faint. "I was worried about you."

"Why are you standing over there?" He crooked his finger at her. "It would be nice if you were right here." He indicated the spot beside him on the sofa.

"I like looking at you." She couldn't move. She couldn't do anything but stare at him, grateful he was alive.

"You could look at me while sitting next to me." He patted the spot beside him on the wide couch.

Rory gripped the bags of food tighter. "You really scared me, Gideon." She tried not to sound accusatory. "I couldn't reach you. I didn't know if you were alive or dead until Javier finally talked to me." She didn't bother to try to keep the pain from her voice because it would have been impossible. At that moment, it didn't even matter to her how much of her feelings she was giving away. She'd been so confused on whether to stay or go. Having been terrified she'd lost him, and now seeing him, she knew he was too important.

"I'm sorry, Red. I didn't have time to tell one of my brothers to reassure you."

"I thought I hurt you. Maybe killed you when I found out you really had awakened me from my dream." For one terrible moment she felt herself choke. Her lungs burned. Her throat felt raw. She had to fight past the gut-wrenching pain at the thought of losing him. "I believed I pulled you into my nightmare, and somehow, I might have harmed you. I've read about things like that happening. I know they do happen."

She felt weak just looking at him now that she could see he was alive. Her knees felt like jelly. She leaned against the wall, clutching the takeout bags. All along, she'd felt a strong compulsion to come to San Francisco. Specifically, she'd been drawn to the wharf.

For the first time, she'd found a place of work where she'd met people she liked enough to want to stay. She'd found friends at her apartment building who tempted her to stay. Looking at Gideon, she knew he had been the one to draw her here. It was the intense connection between them.

Gideon was a magnet she couldn't resist, and she'd felt his need, his call, the intensity of their chemistry and connection, not just physical but far deeper. She had been lonely all along, and suddenly, there he was, offering her everything she'd ever wanted. She just hadn't realized the bounty had been coming from him.

"You didn't do anything to me. What happened was all me."

She studied his face. Those sharp angles and planes. His features might be a bit gray beneath his skin, but he still looked as dangerous as ever. She thought he might never lose that feature even as he grew older.

"Come here, sweetheart." His tone was soft. Compelling. "I need you next to me. I didn't like worrying about you any more than you liked worrying about me."

She could see that was true. Taking a deep breath, Rory went to him, settled on the leather couch right beside him. The moment she sank down, his heat seemed to envelop her. His scent. She wanted to throw herself into his arms, but she was afraid of hurting him.

Gideon took the two bags of food from her and put them on the end table. Turning to her, he framed her face and very slowly bent his head to hers, giving her every chance to pull away. She watched him coming toward her. Those icy blue eyes that were no longer ice but had gone deep blue. Filled with emotions she didn't know how to read. He had silver rings around the blue. Dark, thick lashes.

Then his lips brushed hers, and a million butterflies took flight in her stomach. He tilted her head up, and she parted her lips when his tongue slid across the seam, seeking entrance. She tasted him.

Gideon. His touch was gentle. Lips just brushing back and forth. He transferred his hold to her nape, one large palm curling around her neck possessively while the other fit along the back of her head.

The pressure was slow and steady as he drew her closer to him. She would have stayed a distance away, not because she didn't want to be as close as possible but because she didn't know where he was injured, and Javier had indicated that he could have died. There was no resisting. She should have, but the temptation was too great. She wanted his kisses. She needed them.

Her heart accelerated. Pounded. Her breasts ached. Her nipples hardened into tight peaks. Her stomach somersaulted. She clutched at his shoulders, digging her fingers into the hard muscles there, her only anchor when his teeth tugged at her lower lip with exquisite gentleness. Her sex clenched, panties going damp. Gideon might be at death's door, but he was lethal.

He kissed the corners of her mouth, his tongue teasing at the seam and then along her bottom lip again. He placed a velvet caress along her upper lip and then, without warning, bit down harder on her lower lip, his teeth sinking in and holding to tug until she gave a little gasp. At once, his tongue slid over the little sting, soothing and caressing.

His lips coaxed hers and she opened to him. His fist bunched in her hair, tightened in her scalp as his tongue swept in. Just like that, she belonged to him all over again. He was pure fire pouring into her. Ruling her. Hot bright flames showered down around her like rain. They came together in a storm of such intensity that it felt like a crown fire raging out of control. The hunger kept building rather than abating as they fed one another more and more explosive fuel. The blaze roared hotter than ever.

Rory couldn't stand the weight of her clothes and wanted them gone. She needed to touch his skin, not the fabric of his shirt, and she found the hem so she could slide her palm under it. The moment she did, she encountered a long piece of gauze. She pulled her hand back and let out a small sound of anxiety.

"Gideon." She whispered his name as she leaned against the hand in her hair.

"Red," he whispered against her lips.

The name he called her felt like a flame.

"We have to stop."

"Why?" He pressed his forehead tight against hers. "I've been waiting a lifetime since the last time we kissed. I never want to stop."

"If your doctor was here, he'd throw me out."

"He'd have to get through me to do it."

"I think we can be a little patient. Besides, I was afraid we were going to set your house on fire." She pulled back to look around her. "It's a nice house. I never really looked at it before. I wanted to go to the rooftop and just hurried up the stairs, but this is beautiful. You told me about renovating the outside structure, but you didn't talk about the inside much."

Rory was talking too fast, the way she did when she was nervous, trying to distract herself. It was difficult to force herself to let go of him, but she managed. "Are you hungry? The restaurant gave us napkins and utensils if you're fine with just eating out of the takeout boxes."

"That's fine, Red." There was definite amusement in his voice. "I'm hungry and I don't eat off fancy plates."

"Do you have fancy plates?" She caught up the bags from the restaurant and sorted the boxes and utensils, hoping everything was still warm enough.

"As a matter of fact, I do. Rose, Jaimie and Rhianna went shopping for the plates and silverware. They sent me so many pictures I was ready to shoot all three of them." He laughed, remembering the photographs coming into his phone one after another. The three women were clearly having fun. Too much and at his expense. He had threatened to shoot them, but sadly, they weren't in the least afraid of him.

Rory's laughter sounded even better than he remembered. "I love that for you. Your friends must be very fun women."

"They're more like siblings and they're pains in my ass. Jaimie is married to Mack, and Rose is married to Kane. We all grew up together. Rhianna grew up with us as well. She's younger and always wants to be Miss Independent. I suppose she's as capable of taking care of herself as the rest of us, but none of us like to think so."

"Because she's female?" Javier had said that Gideon was very protective, and if she was going to be with him, she would have to accept that trait in him.

"Yes." Gideon opened a container of soup. "She was very young. So was Jaimie. We all fell into the habit of looking after them, and I guess we never got out of it."

Rory thought the prawns were excellent. The restaurant had surrounded the boxes of food with heat packs. She thought Gideon might have asked them to do that for him. She doubted it was a standard practice, but maybe he got takeout from them all the time.

"Javier said you were super protective. That it was part of your character. I have the feeling that you aren't the only one. He seemed protective—at least of you."

"He is of the women too."

Rory nodded. She had her mouth full of ginger noodles and couldn't reply. Javier was extremely protective of Gideon, to the point that she felt intimidated by him.

Gideon paused in the act of bringing a forkful of fish to his mouth. He studied her expression over it. "Did Javier say something to you that was upsetting?"

"Why would you think that? I just pointed out that he was protective. *I* feel protective of you as well. He doesn't have a corner on that particular trait."

He took the bite of fish, his piercing blue eyes never leaving her face as he chewed. Rory felt the butterflies taking wing again, but this time for entirely different reasons. He seemed to see right through her. He wasn't buying her misdirection. Those blue eyes had gone arctic chill. The silver around the blue had widened until the ring bled into the blue, giving his eyes the appearance of bluish mercury.

The color of his eyes fascinated her. The human aspect was nearly gone. He didn't blink and appeared nearly hawkish. Not the color so much but the difference in his appearance. It was eerie and a little scary.

"You didn't really answer my question. What did Javier say or do to upset you, Rory?"

She realized he rarely called her Rory. His voice might be compelling and even commanding at times, but the tone was low and gentle. Now he used a different tone, one she hadn't heard before. Raspy. Husky. His voice still had that sexy component that got to her, but his tone had a ruthless quality to it.

"Do you realize you can sound very intimidating, Gideon?"

He didn't so much as blink. "So I've been told numerous times. You're stalling. Tell me what he did or said, please." He put his fork down and rested his palm on her thigh.

Her heart jumped. His touch was light, but it was impossible to ignore it. "Javier is just . . ." She broke off, searching for an adequate description. "Javier. He's a very scary man. I think you already know that. One minute he's protecting me, and the next he's warning me that I'd better not do anything to hurt you. Then he's being sweet and disclosing that he's got major pickpocketing skills and how he got them."

For the first time, Gideon looked surprised. "Javier told you he was skilled at picking pockets? How did that subject come up?"

"I needed my inhaler and wasn't going to use it in front of him. He took it out of my pocket without my knowledge and handed it to me. I didn't even feel him brush up against me. He told me about living on the streets when he was a child and how the rest of you would provide a distraction and he'd steal wallets and jewelry."

"I don't think he's ever told anyone else anything about his childhood. Javier doesn't talk to anyone he considers an outsider."

A little part of her liked that Javier had accepted her into his circle, although she wasn't naive enough to think he *really* accepted her. He watched her like a hawk. He was Gideon's family, and the moment something went wrong, or Javier perceived it as wrong, he would turn on her in a second.

"I really love that you have family, Gideon. Maybe it started out rough for you, and even, at times, they are a pain in the ass, but they have your back, and that must feel good."

He didn't take his penetrating gaze from her face. "Yeah, Red. I'll admit to you, as long as none of them are around to hear me say it, it does feel good. Although, when they're around, they can drive me crazy. I'm used to spending a certain amount of my time alone, and they can be a lot when they're all together. They like to give me a hard time."

She couldn't help giving him a teasing smile. "I can't imagine why."

He raised an eyebrow. "Any insight would be welcome."

"You give off the tough-guy-loner vibe. You have no expression on your face, and you look dangerous and badass. One can't help but tease you."

His eyes went dark blue, the silver once more thin rings. She was more than fascinated. It was impossible to look away, especially when amusement had crept in, adding a gleaming brilliant sapphire color to his eyes. "Does that mean I can expect the same kind of sass from you?"

She pretended to weigh the idea while she ate another delicious prawn. Slowly she nodded. "I do believe you'll have to put up with a lot of teasing on my end just to see if I can get that look off your face."

Gideon concentrated on eating the soup while he considered her reply. "I see," he finally replied. "The others I have to put up with. You, I can think up interesting responses to various tactical situations. I'm good at that. It's one of the things I'm known for."

A hot, sexy thrill slid down her spine. His voice indicated all kinds of intimate, sinful things she might not have ever heard of.

"Such as?" she prompted.

"If I tell you ahead of time, you'll be prepared. That won't be helpful to me, will it?"

The teasing note in his voice made her shiver inside. She'd never had this kind of fun before. "I'll look forward to your tactical solutions and come up with a few countermoves of my own."

"I'm always up for a good challenge."

"I noticed. Particularly when it comes to food. How can you eat like you do and stay so fit?"

He laughed. "I don't feel very fit right at the moment."

She put her hand on his lower abdomen. It was impossible to feel the bandage through his shirt. "Are you in pain? You don't show it, so it's easy to forget."

He shrugged. "I've learned to ignore it for the most part. I don't take painkillers. I use ice and meditation."

"What did your doctor say in terms of how long it's going to take before you're really out of danger?"

"I *am* out of danger."

"Gideon." She didn't believe him. He might be looking at her with his wide blue eyes, but he was lying through his white teeth.

He gave her a boyish grin that completely transformed his features, lending him a mischievous look for a brief moment. She wanted to see that expression often.

"You're really not a very good liar," she reprimanded. "What's going on?"

He gave an exaggerated sigh. "I despise talking about my health. There's one wound that's being stubborn and keeps opening and bleeding. Since it's internal and no one can see when the damn thing rips open, I lose a lot of blood before I know something is wrong. Doc has been working to strengthen it."

That didn't sound right. Stitches. Gluing. What the heck? She frowned at him. "I don't think I quite understand. You must have had surgery. Didn't the surgeon repair the wound then? And repair it a second time when it ripped open? What do you mean, 'strengthen it'?"

He set the containers of food aside and picked up his drink. "Red, does it matter? I barely understand why it isn't healing. The bullet nicked something vital apparently. That has to regrow, and it isn't doing it fast enough. I'm too active. I don't feel like I've been active. I feel like I lie around doing nothing and have been for over a month. I even asked him if there was something artificial they could shove in me to replace whatever isn't working, but he said no."

Her heart squeezed hard in her chest. "You really could have died, Gideon. There was a reason Javier acted protective over you."

"Every time I go to work, there's a chance I could die, Red," he pointed out. "Every time you go to work, there's a chance you could. Walking down the street or getting into a car. You can't live your life in fear. If you do, you're not living. You're just existing. You've got one life, sweetheart. Live it. You get knocked down, stand back up. Keep going and enjoy the ride."

"Is that what you do?"

"I tried. I wanted to enjoy it. I was looking for you. Every damn day, I went out there hoping to find you. Now that I finally found you, I intend to enjoy the ride with you. Good or bad, we'll find our way together."

She couldn't help the way her reaction to his declaration touched her lonely soul. Each moment spent in his company seemed to weave them tighter together. Part of her thought they could have been together in another life. That was how well she felt she knew him. She believed they were meant to be together. Rory knew she should question her acceptance of how readily she trusted him, but she no longer cared to.

"Kissing has to be out until your doctor gives you permission," she said firmly, knowing that would definitely get a rise out of him.

"Permission from my doctor to kiss you?" His voice sounded raspier than ever.

She did her best not to smile. "Written. In a note with his letterhead so I know you didn't forge it. I'm certain you're capable of forging notes."

"You want me to ask my doctor to write a note on his letterhead giving me permission to kiss you?"

Now there was a distinct threat in his voice. Sheer menace. She was really doing her best not to laugh because he looked and sounded so outraged.

"Like I'm a schoolkid." He practically growled it.

"Well, yes. Because you tend to ignore the doctor's advice just the way a schoolkid would." She was playing with fire but it was fun. She needed fun and so did Gideon.

He took the food containers from her hands and set them alongside the empty ones on the end table, leaving her feeling a little defenseless.

She put up her hands, palms out, and leaned back away from him. "You behave yourself."

One long arm reached for her, his palm curling around the nape of her neck. "Kissing you is mandatory. I don't need my doctor's permission. In fact, kissing is the one thing guaranteed to make me better much faster."

"It is?" She widened her eyes, trying to look as if she were skeptical instead of wanting to kiss him until they both burned up in the fire.

"Yes, Red, it is. I need to kiss you. I need to do more than just kiss you."

Now she couldn't breathe. She needed to do more than just kiss him, but they could be in real trouble if they did more. "Gideon." She poured caution into his name even as she allowed him to draw her closer.

"I'll show restraint. I have discipline. You'll see."

"I'm not sure I do," she admitted. "Javier is really mean, and he scares me."

"He's afraid of me."

"He isn't afraid of anyone," she corrected.

He gave her his bad-boy roguish smile. "He will be if he starts interfering with my time with my woman."

He kept applying steady pressure on the nape of her neck. Gentle. Firm. Sure. She found herself scooting up against him. That didn't seem close enough for him.

"Gideon," she cautioned.

"Red. Sit in my lap."

She shook her head and placed one hand on his lower abdomen. "No, we're going to be very careful."

"Straddle my thighs. There's nothing wrong with my thighs."

His voice was pure temptation, and she was weak when it came to him. The pressure on the nape of her neck was relentless. She found herself held captive by the burning intensity of his eyes. There was such a mixture of affection and pure sensual lust, it robbed her of her ability to think clearly.

Rory found herself obeying his command and straddling his thighs. The moment she did, his hands found her hips, and he pulled her tight against him, aligning their bodies much more intimately. Before she had a chance to protest, he gripped her hair with one fist, pulled her head back and took her mouth.

He'd always been gentle. This was a complete takeover. Ruthless. Predatory. Merciless. His teeth caught her lower lip and bit down hard enough for her to gasp, and his tongue slid into the heat of her mouth. There was an instant explosion, as if he had lit a match and set off a stick of dynamite. He poured fire down her throat.

Flames rushed through her veins. There were no smoldering embers bursting into flames. The fire was already out of control, burning hot and wild. She could have sworn a volcano exploded and molten lava ran through her body, branding his name on every bone and organ along the way to pool wicked and sinful, low and hot, between her legs.

One of his hands moved to the little pearl buttons on her blouse. His mouth never stopped dominating hers, turning rougher. More insistent. She gave herself up to that fire, letting it take her until she was boneless and pliant in his arms. His fingers were on her right breast, stroking, kneading, tugging on her nipple until she cried out in need, rocking her hips against him.

The moment she did, a semblance of sanity returned, and she pulled back, tearing herself out of his arms and scrambling off his lap. Her blouse was open. How he'd managed to undo every button was going to remain a mystery. She could barely catch her breath.

"You're a menace," she accused, returning her blouse to order.

"Come back to me. We were just getting started."

"We're finished, Gideon." She didn't want to be finished, and she was extremely happy that he didn't want to be finished either. "I mean it."

Rory had to put distance between them, or they were going to have sex on the couch, and he would start bleeding internally again. "I have to find your kitchen and put the rest of the food in your fridge. And I need to locate a bathroom."

He stood up immediately and held out his hand to her. "I'll show you the kitchen and bathroom. I should have given you a tour."

She noticed he did so without the fluid, smooth way she associated with him. "You don't have to do that. Should you be moving around?" Rory felt shaky, every nerve ending still alive. He couldn't get near her. He really couldn't. Maybe he was already cooling down, but she didn't trust herself yet. "And I'm not taking your hand."

"Red. Helping you up isn't going to rip open my wound." Now there was male amusement in his voice, and it was creeping into the blue of his eyes.

"I'm not worried that helping me up will tear open your wound. It's tearing off your clothes and leaping on you, wrapping my legs around you and doing bad things to you that you need to worry about. We both need to worry about," she corrected. Talking too much again. Making a fool of herself again. "Just step back and stop grinning." She couldn't breathe, and she was going to have a panic attack. The room was already beginning to spin a little.

"I'm in danger?"

"*Yes*. At least pretend you're afraid. That would be helpful." She crossed her arms over her chest to keep from the temptation of taking his hand.

The color of Gideon's eyes deepened to that nearly royal blue and softened to velvet. No man should have eyes like his. It wasn't fair. And how could one man's eyes change color the way his did so often? "A woman could fall in love with you so easily."

Had she blurted that out loud? What was wrong with her? He'd just kissed her and he'd made her lose her mind. "I should go home."

"You should stay here. Use your inhaler. I'll take the food to the kitchen. One of the many bathrooms is straight across from you. Right there." He indicated a door with one long finger. "I'll bring you a bottle of cold water. Take a breath, sweetheart. I love everything you're saying to me. I've said the same to you."

Gideon leaned down and brushed her forehead with a kiss, gathered up the food containers and sauntered across the room.

Rory watched him go before she went to his guest bathroom. It was spacious with black and gray tiles. She used her travel nebulizer, thankful she'd brought it with her. Why in the world did she blurt out everything she was thinking to Gideon? She'd always been so careful to keep her own counsel. For years she hadn't talked to anyone about what she was thinking or feeling, but now she couldn't keep her mouth closed. If she thought it, she said it to him.

She stared at herself in the mirror, taking her time. She was getting in deeper every moment she spent with Gideon. It was now or never. If she didn't run while she could, break away and get out of San Francisco, she might never leave. Every indication told her to go.

What about her worry that she could harm him? She didn't know about her past. It was a complete blank to her. There was that nagging worry that something was terribly off, and she might have some terrible secret hidden inside her that could harm someone. But it had never happened in all the years she'd traveled around. Never once had she done anything to hurt anyone. She was alone so much and had such a vivid imagination that she easily thought up reasons to fill in her past. It was ludicrous to think that she would hurt Gideon.

It was just another excuse she gave herself to leave, because she made so many. She was insane to stay. Everything was happening too fast between the two of them. She had no reason to trust

Gideon, and yet she did. She was jumping in with both feet, and it made no sense.

Free-falling. Euphoric. She'd never been like this. She'd never had this. Goose bumps ran down her arms, and she held them out in front of her before wrapping them around her. She felt as if she'd always been alone and fearful. Of what, she didn't know. With Gideon, everything was different. She had him to talk to. To laugh with. To kiss. To want to be intimate with.

Did she want to give that up because she was afraid she might get hurt? Just because their connection was happening too fast and she didn't understand it? She didn't know what a relationship was, but Gideon was worth sticking around for and finding out. In any case, she knew with absolute certainty that she wouldn't feel the same with another man.

Rory took a deep breath while she washed her hands. She was going to stay. She had finally found a place she liked, with people she enjoyed being around. Most of all, there was Gideon. She wanted to be with him. She was going to put her faith in him and see their relationship through. She wanted him to be right—that they could make it through good and bad together. She wanted him more than she wanted her own life.

Gideon sat on the leather couch, waiting, and his gaze locked on her immediately. His eyes were piercing, like that of an eagle. Rory had the feeling he could see right through her and knew she'd been struggling to decide if she should stay or make a run for it. His smile was warm enough to turn her heart over.

"Are you going to come sit by me?"

"Maybe it would be better if I sat across from you, where it's safer."

She didn't sit down. She felt too scared. Too restless. She'd made a big decision, and she had a lot of things she needed to tell him. About Tinsdale and the envelope he'd given to her for Harvey. She was a little afraid of what he might think when she told him about the two men using her as a go-between. He would be upset with her for not telling Javier the night he'd walked her home that she had the message in her pocket, but as far as she was concerned, that was only between Gideon and her.

Gideon patted the spot next to him on the couch. "You're wandering around instead of sitting beside me, Red. That tells me instead of being relaxed the way you should be, you're nervous."

He was far too good at reading her. "Some things happened over the last couple of days that I want to tell you about." She shoved her hands into her pockets and felt the envelope Scott Tinsdale had given her for Harvey Matters. For some unexplained reason, it felt like a burning coal. That didn't bode so well.

"I feel ridiculous talking to you about it when you've been so ill. This is probably one of those things Javier would disapprove of me bothering you with."

Something dark crossed his hard features, and just for one moment, his eyes went that crystalline bluish-silver. "Javier doesn't dictate what goes on in our relationship, Rory. I want you to tell me when anything bothers you. You give that to me. We talked about this. This is your safe place. *I'm* that safe person for you."

Rory pressed her lips together, still hesitating. "Who is your safe person, Gideon? You nearly died for Javier. He said it wasn't the first time. I don't understand what happened the other night when you tore those wounds open, but I know it had something to do with me and my nightmare. I think you sent those birds to wake me up."

That sounded ridiculous, but looking at him with his strange, focused, raptor-like stare, she could imagine him ruling birds of prey. But then, she had a very vivid imagination.

"I heard you call out to me," she confessed. "In my dream, I heard you call my name. That's what woke me. I was standing on the very edge of the ledge, and I was surrounded by owls. They were flying at me, and I jumped back to the patio. Had I not awakened, I would have fallen three stories."

"It isn't a good idea for you to sleep outside, Rory. Not when you're having nightmares."

"No, you're right. But you sent those birds to me, and that contributed to tearing open those wounds." She made it a statement and watched to see if she could read his expression. It didn't change at all.

"Red, come sit down next to me, where you feel safe, and tell me what's been going on."

His voice dropped into that soft velvety lure she'd heard him use that was so difficult to resist. She realized she *wanted* to go to him. She wanted to tell him everything. She'd come to him needing to see him, to know he was alive and well, but once she was there, the feeling had been growing in her all along that she wanted to tell him about Tinsdale and her apartment being broken into. She'd been reluctant to tell Javier, but it felt entirely different with Gideon.

Rory crossed the distance to that long couch and sank down beside him, turning so she was facing him. She drew her legs up and pulled one of the lighter throws over her. She even ignored the fact that Gideon didn't answer her about whether he was responsible for sending the owls to her. She hadn't really expected him to answer the question, but she had hoped he would.

There were so many things she wanted to know about him. His childhood. His teenage years. What he did now. They had time to learn about one another if she was just courageous enough.

11

don't even know where to start. Nothing makes sense to me. It doesn't to my friends either. We talked about it. All of us. Well, I didn't tell them everything." Rory knew she was rambling again. Talking too fast. Not making sense.

Gideon didn't interrupt her. He allowed her to find her way. She took a deep breath and let it out. "You know there was a detective killed at my apartment building. His name was Peter Ramsey. There were four men living at the apartments who acted like they didn't know one another, but they did. My friends and I would see them together in the workout room or the laundry room. We thought it was silly that they would pretend to be strangers."

Rory rubbed her hands on her thighs. She had to start somewhere, and she needed to give him a picture of what it was like at the apartments. "We saw them every day, but we didn't interact with them other than to say hello. None of us were comfortable being alone with them. In any case, a couple of days after the detective was killed, Dustin Bartlet, one of the men, turned up dead in his apartment. We thought suicide."

"You sound as if you're questioning the suicide verdict."

She hesitated. "I can't speak about that, not even to you. But it might not have been."

"Red. Who would I tell? Do you think this place is bugged?"

Rory sighed. "It's one thing to tell you my secrets, but I'm uncomfortable telling you any of my friends' secrets. It isn't necessary, and it has nothing to do with what I'm telling you."

"Go ahead, sweetheart. We'll talk about relationships and what the expectation for ours is to be later," he said.

She hesitated. She was doing the best she could. She thought it was very reasonable not to break a friend's confidence. Janice hadn't given the name of her friend, but she'd made it clear that if anyone found out she'd been given the information, her friend could be fired. She asked they not repeat it.

"The point is, I think Dustin was murdered. Then Ret was murdered, and his body was in the garbage chute. That leaves Harvey Matters and Jarrod Flawson alive, and both have disappeared. No one knows where they are. The police seem to be looking for Harvey and Jarrod. A few nights ago, when you were hurt, I took an extra shift at the bar to help out. A man came in and introduced himself as Scott Tinsdale. At first, he hit on me and acted like he wanted to take me out. I told him I was with someone."

Gideon looked pleased. "I'm happy to hear that."

"A couple of your friends were in the bar that same night. I was really worried about you because I couldn't feel you when I reached out to you. At first, I wasn't paying as much attention as I might have been to the man. Eventually, I started noticing that he wasn't looking at any of the other women. He watched the exits. He paid attention to my conversations to the point I was sure he was trying to record them. He made me very uneasy."

"Why didn't you reach out to one of my friends?"

"I don't know them. I did ask them to check on you."

"Yes, and you most likely saved my life," he conceded. "The bleeding was slow but steady. Thank you for reaching out to them. I know that made you uncomfortable."

"I didn't mind since it was on your behalf."

"But not on your own? Even for your own safety?"

She didn't have a way to tell him why. She was uneasy around strangers. She knew they would have insisted on walking her home, and she would have been just as awkward with them as she was with Tinsdale. She preferred to rely on herself.

"I didn't have to close that night, so when I was certain Tinsdale had left, I started home. The fog was thick, and I was extremely worried about you. In fact, I was thinking more about you than about him and where he might be. I should have been more alert. The closer I got to home, the more uneasy I felt, and I thought it was because of you. Then he came out of the fog, and I realized my radar had been going off, and I'd put my warning system down to the wrong thing."

That envelope in the inside pocket of her jacket was so hot that she swore she felt it burning her skin right through the material of her blouse. What if she was doing the wrong thing, and telling Gideon would get him killed?

"Don't stop now, Red. I can see it on your face that you're hesitating again. You're afraid for me. What did he do? Did he want you to do something for him? Did he threaten you in some way? Who is he?"

"He's an associate of Harvey's. That's my best guess. I don't know for certain. He told me he wanted me to give Harvey a message. I told him I didn't know Harvey, I wouldn't be seeing him, and I didn't know how to contact him. Nothing I said mattered to him. He was adamant that if I didn't do it, there would be consequences, and I wouldn't like them."

"So, he did threaten you."

She nodded.

"Javier showed up. I knew you were in trouble. I sent him to you. Doc wasn't happy with me, but I wouldn't go under until I knew you were safe. You didn't tell Javier much."

"Javier isn't you."

"Did Tinsdale give you a message?"

She nodded again. "It wasn't a verbal one. He gave me a sealed envelope and told me to always carry it on me. He said if Harvey showed up, to give it to him."

Gideon wore his impenetrable expression, that strange crystalline silver-blue color taking over his eyes as his gaze fixed on hers. "You have this message on you now?"

"Yes. I'm afraid to leave it anywhere. I have the feeling Harvey is going to show up for the message and I'd better have it for him. The cops are around all the time. I know they think I have something to do with Harvey. When they question my friends, they don't ask them pointed questions, but they do me. Especially questions about all the places I've traveled and why I move around so much. I don't even know what Harvey does, but clearly, they think I work for him in some capacity. If they think I'm delivering messages to him, they'll never believe anything I say. And maybe Tinsdale is setting me up, but for what, I have no idea."

"You haven't touched the envelope with your bare fingers, have you?"

"Of course not."

"I'd like you to show it to me, but when you give it to me, don't touch it with your bare fingers. Use a glove or your shirt."

"It's sealed."

"It isn't hard to open a sealed envelope and reclose it without damaging it, but I suspect you already know that. Did you open it?"

She shook her head. "I didn't want to know what was in it."

"Harvey Matters is a major crime lord, for lack of a better description, Rory. He's one of the biggest players when it comes to selling arms and bringing in product. He doesn't live in apartment buildings. He owns large estates. He's very wealthy. Scott Tinsdale is one of his top lieutenants."

Her heart began to accelerate. "How would you possibly know that?"

"I told you, sweetheart, I'm in the security business. We're sent out to other countries to prevent shipments from entering this country as well as tracking them if they do manage to get in. We've run into his people on multiple occasions. He's never come out into the open before. Never once. Certainly not near any of his partners, and both Ret Carnes and Dustin Bartlet were longtime partners of Harvey's. Jarrod Flawson is as well. You don't want any part of those men."

Rory sat back against the dark leather and looked up at the hard angles and planes of his face. "Why would they be living at the apartments where I live?" The envelope was really burning a hole through her pocket. She didn't want anything to do with it, but now, more than ever, she was terrified that if she didn't do what Tinsdale ordered her to do, he'd kill her.

"I have no idea."

"Harvey's going to come for this message, isn't he?" She kept her gaze fixed on him.

"My best guess would be yes."

She pulled a pair of thin suede gloves from her pocket and put them on before extracting the envelope. She put it carefully on the leather couch between them. He stood without preamble, holding out his hand for her glove. Using the edge of one of the gloves, he picked up the envelope and walked over to the bar. He put the envelope in a plastic bag and then into the freezer.

"What else did Tinsdale have to say, Red?" Gideon asked, glancing at his watch.

"Javier ran him off, and then we walked back to the apartments." She moistened her suddenly dry lips. "We talked downstairs for a little while, and then he waited until I went upstairs."

"Why do I have the feeling there's more?"

"There is, but not about Tinsdale. At least I don't think he had anything to do with it." She pushed a hand through her hair, feeling nervous. "When I got home from work last night, someone had broken into my apartment."

Gideon whirled around to face her. She knew immediately that she was in trouble. His usual expressionless mask was gone, and in its place was pure fury.

"What did you just say?"

She swallowed down panic and the need to step back. She had followed him partway across the room to see what he was doing with the message Tinsdale had given her. Now she wanted to be on the other side of the couch.

"You have excellent hearing, Gideon."

"Maybe I couldn't believe my ears. Why wouldn't you call immediately?"

"I hadn't heard from you. I knew something terrible had happened and knew you would contact me when you could."

"You have Javier's number." A hint of menace crept into his tone.

"I don't know him," she defended. "I know you. I trust you. I don't tell other people my business. I knew I would have to make a police report, but I wanted to talk to you. I went through the apartment to see if anything was taken, but I couldn't find anything. I was careful to touch only my guitar, clothes and music."

"You went through the apartment alone?" He was sounding more upset by the moment.

"Gideon, stop. I'm used to handling everything on my own. I went downstairs and stayed in the lounge where I meet with my friends. It turned out that three other apartments were also broken into that night. Janice's, Pam's and Cindy's. All are friends of mine. We hang out together. Janice and Pam, like me, were working that night. Cindy had taken her two boys to her parents, and she spent the night there. Our apartments were unoccupied, so someone had a field day trashing them."

"Was anything taken from any of the apartments?"

"Not that we could tell. Not that we had anything of real value for them to take. Cindy might have, but the rest of us, no."

"It isn't safe for you to stay there, Rory. You should stay here."

She shook her head. "That's not safe for you. You know it isn't, Gideon. We wouldn't keep our hands off each other."

"There are several bedrooms."

"That wouldn't matter. Maybe we'd be good for a day or two, but then we wouldn't. I can stay with Lydia. She has a little girl, and I think it makes her feel safer with me there."

Gideon shook his head and glanced at his watch again. "If Harvey and Tinsdale are looking to use you as a go-between, it isn't going to be safer for your friend Lydia and her daughter to have you there. We'll see what the message has to say, and you can decide then."

She wasn't taking a chance with his life, no matter what he said. She'd sleep at a motel. She just needed a bed. She could change locations every night if she had to.

"Javier would have gone through your apartment before you stepped inside to make certain no one was there."

Rory tilted her head but met his gaze squarely. "You have to remember, Gideon. Javier is your family. You trust him. He's a stranger to me. I don't trust him. I'm not willing to share my life or my secrets with him. I can barely open up to you. You're the first person I've talked to about anything in years—if ever. It isn't easy. You can't push me or expect me to include others because you know them. *I* don't know them. I don't feel the same way about them that you do. I have to talk myself into staying here and not running quite often, because I'm terrified. You have no idea how difficult this is for me. Just trusting you. Putting my faith in you is the hardest thing I've done in a long, long time—if ever. If I've misplaced my trust, it would shatter me, and I know that. I just hope you're real."

It was the first time she'd ever seen Gideon look uncomfortable. He pushed both hands through his dark hair, leaving it looking rumpled and more unruly than ever. Shadows entered his eyes.

"Rory." There was an ache in his voice.

Her gut clenched. A small little warning. A red flag. Her head went up, and she carefully searched his face, feature by feature. Something in his eyes. Something in those dark shadows. Wary. Worried. Gideon was always confident. Inside, where she caught glimpses, he was frowning where he wasn't on the outside. What was it? She had never been able to read him fully, but there had been images. Now there was a brick wall. Solid. Thick. Just that frown. That concern. That worry.

She didn't ask the way she normally would have. Something was off. He hadn't reassured her. That was what felt off. He should have reassured her. He wasn't lying about Harvey Matters. She could hear lies, and everything he said sounded true. Like the cops, did he believe she was part of the criminal circle Harvey ran? It didn't seem likely that he would have known to target her and get her to fall for him.

She pressed her fingers to the spot that sometimes ached and felt strange near her left temple. It always made her feel as if her skin was loose and wanted to slip off. Now it was just plain painful.

"You're getting that strange feeling again, aren't you?"

She put her hand down quickly, nodding. Gideon was observant. She wasn't certain what triggered the reaction. Her uneasiness? Gideon looked genuinely concerned. His eyes had lost that shadow and had gone to the soft, gentle affection that seemed to be real.

"Do you work tomorrow night at the bar?"

"Yes. I'm back to my regular shifts."

She watched him take the plastic bag from the small bar freezer and open it carefully. Sitting on a barstool, he pulled on plastic gloves he got from under a shelf. While the glue was frozen, he used a knife to pull the flap up. Very carefully, he extracted the single card partway, took a picture of it and replaced it. He resealed the envelope using a sponge to reactivate the glue.

"Leave it out for a few minutes just to make certain the glue is going to hold. If it does, you can put it back in your jacket and leave it. If not, we'll apply a thin layer to ensure it stays. It should be fine though."

She came closer and looked over his shoulder to see the screenshot on his phone. "It's in code."

"I'll run it through our computer."

At once, her lungs began to burn. Her heart began to pound. He couldn't do that. "No. Absolutely not, Gideon. That could get me killed. If you do that, anyone with access to your computers will see it too. Can't you just find a way to do it yourself?"

Gideon sighed and waved her back toward the couch. "Sweetheart, we need to do some talking. I don't think you really understand what it is I do, and you need to. There are things in my past that you need to know that concern you."

"Maybe you should send that screenshot to me and permanently delete it from your phone before we start this talk. At the end of it, I can send it back to you." Rory had no idea why she made the challenge to him, but she suddenly felt very threatened.

His dark brows drew together. "What's wrong, Red?"

"I don't know. Something. You tell me. Suddenly, I just feel something is wrong." Her phone vibrated, she looked down, and the screenshot was there. Gideon held up his phone and the image disappeared.

Rory breathed a sigh of relief. "Thank you."

He wrapped his hand around hers and tugged until she went back to the sofa with him. "I want to talk to you and hopefully make everything clearer for you. And I want you to know about me, about who and what I am and what I do."

Rory wanted to know everything about him. She'd talked a lot about herself. Too much. He hadn't talked much about himself. She knew more about him from Javier than from him. She sat beside him, just as she'd done before, turning to face him, pulling up her legs onto the cushions beneath her skirt, the way she did to feel comfortable.

There was still that little nagging doubt in her gut, a worrisome flag she ignored because she wanted this to go well. She wasn't the best at relationship talks, so she was going to keep her mouth shut as much as possible and let him do the talking. She hoped to find out about his childhood and his career.

"Do you remember when we talked about tattoos a few nights ago, and you showed me yours? I have one on my arm." He pulled his shirt off and turned his shoulder toward her. "All of my brothers and sisters wear this symbol on them."

Rory looked at his biceps. He had two tattoos. She knew the significance of the top one instantly, but she didn't know why. The spot above her temple gave off the weird sensation so strong that she wanted to gag. She pressed her finger to it hard in an effort to keep from getting sick. She had to look away. The moment she did, he pulled his shirt back on.

"You can see them."

"I'm not blind."

"Do you recall ever hearing the term 'GhostWalker'?"

"No. I'm not really much for watching television, Gideon. I don't know where you're going with this."

"You know you have some psychic abilities, right? You know I do. That's part of the connection we have. I have a way with birds."

"You did send the owls to wake me up." She pounced on that. She had known.

"That's how you know when something is wrong with me, and I know something is wrong with you. That's part of the reason we bonded so quickly. We have strong psychic chemistry as well as physical and emotional."

"That makes sense." She believed in psychic gifts. Some people had them stronger than others, and some people worked at developing theirs. She had deliberately tried, mostly because she had so much time on her hands being alone so much.

"Have you ever heard of a man named Dr. Peter Whitney?"

He spoke quietly. Gently. His eyes were focused, intense, his gaze never leaving hers. She felt as if he held her captive, refusing to allow her to look away from him. He held one of her hands, his thumb sliding back and forth over her inner wrist right over her suddenly pounding pulse.

The name felt like a punch to her midsection, hard and mean. She hunched, trying to absorb the shock of pain. The spot above her temple wiggled and spasmed, desperate to slip off. The combination made her dizzy. It was difficult to breathe, and black spots began to appear in front of her eyes.

"Rory. Keep looking at me."

She heard him calling her name from a distance, but he sounded very far away.

"Rory, breathe with me. Follow my lungs."

She heard that. She felt the movement. In. Out. She was making a fool of herself again. He'd said a name. She couldn't even remember who he had said. Someone. Was he important? Had he asked her more than once? She drew air into her lungs and kept breathing, trying to remember.

"Who is he?" She gasped out the question. "Don't say his name."

"He's a man who took young girls, infants and toddlers from orphanages and performed experiments on them. He's still doing it. He's committed so many terrible atrocities, and yet he has a coalition of people in the government protecting him. So far, he hasn't been found."

"Why would anyone want to protect him when he's experimenting on children? That's criminal."

"Yes, it is."

"Do you hunt this man?"

"We've fought his guards and his soldiers at times, but he's always gotten away."

Rory found herself rocking back and forth. "I don't want to talk about him anymore. I thought we were going to talk about you, Gideon. What does he have to do with you? Did he take you away from your home when you were a boy? I wanted to know about your childhood."

Beads of sweat formed on her forehead. She pulled her hand away from his and wiped at them. With her other hand, she formed a fist and pressed it tightly into her stomach, where a knot had formed. "How is this conversation in any way me getting to know you? You know quite a lot about me, but I don't really know much at all about you. You're the big mystery man."

"He didn't take boys to do his experiments on, just girls," Gideon said. "No, I actually was someone you wouldn't have wanted to know when I was growing up. I was bigger than some of the other kids. Mack had a home, and he would let us into his basement at night when it was freezing. He was smart. Always way ahead in school, and he was popular. He tended to collect those of us without parents."

Rory waited when Gideon fell silent. He had said more about Mack than he had about himself. She'd learned he was bigger than some of the other kids and that he was someone she wouldn't have wanted to know. That was it. "Gideon, you aren't sharing much about yourself or your life. You don't have to. I don't know how we're going to get to know one another if we don't talk, but I get it. I don't remember my past, and yours wasn't that pleasant." She glanced at her watch. "It's late. I should probably go."

He put a restraining hand on her knee before she could uncurl. "Not yet, Red. I really do want to sort through some things. It's necessary. I just don't know how to get us there."

What had he had to do to survive? Was that what he was finding difficult to tell her? He was so reluctant to tell her about his past. He didn't want to tell her the slightest detail. Not about when he was a child or a teen, and not about his life with his security company.

"I'm trying to let you off the hook, Gideon. If you're some kind of assassin, you don't have to tell me. I'll just slip away quietly, and we'll call it a night."

She tried to make a joke of it, but neither of them laughed. She hoped she hadn't hit too close to the mark. If someone told her Javier was an assassin, it wouldn't shock her. There were moments when Gideon looked menacing enough that she might believe it of him, except that most of the time, he was just too kind and gentle.

"I just need to get some things out into the open, Rory. We have some concerns, and we want to put them behind us so we can get on with our relationship."

"Concerns? Now I'm really confused. For some reason, I thought you were going to talk to me about your childhood and teenage years. Maybe about your work. I talked to you about the things that bothered me about my past. I told you things I've never told anyone. I opened up to you. You know things about me, but I really don't know anything at all about you. Now you're talking about concerns. What concerns do you have, Gideon? Concerns about me? About us?"

That knot in her gut was pulling tighter. The flag was getting stronger. She had a bad taste in her mouth. He reached for her hand, but she refused to let him take it.

"Just answer the question. What concerns do you have? You didn't seem to have any before. You were sure about us. You said so over and over."

"I'm still sure about us. I know we belong together. That hasn't changed," he assured. "Don't sound afraid. There's nothing to be afraid of."

"Then why aren't you telling me whatever it is you want to say?"

"What I have to say involves the person you don't want me to talk about. It's necessary to include him in the backstory, or nothing makes any sense."

Rory pressed the pad of her finger to the spot above her temple. It wasn't fair to Gideon that a random name she couldn't remember was a trigger for her. If something in his background had to do with that horrid criminal, and Gideon felt it was important enough that she should know, she knew she was strong enough to listen. After all, he had lived through it.

She nodded her head. "All right, then. Tell me what he did to you. Whatever he did, Gideon, it's okay. We can deal."

He dropped his palm onto her thigh. "It isn't just me. He has many victims, both men and women. But he started with girls. Orphans. He bought them. Because he bought them, he believed he had the right to do whatever he wanted to them. Some he gave cancer to. He raised them in small, isolated groups. Aside from the psychic experiments, he raised them as soldiers—disciplined, learning hand-to-hand combat, weapons, languages, every skill possible—and then he would send them out to perform for him. He would threaten those left behind in case those in the field tried to run off."

He was watching her very closely. She hadn't allowed him to take her hand, so he wrapped his palm around her ankle. She was sure it was to give her comfort. She needed it, when she really thought she should be the one giving it to him. He was clearly uneasy telling this to her. She didn't understand yet how the story related to his past, but he was bound to get there, and she wasn't going to interrupt him again.

"If he thought any of those girls didn't measure up, he all but tortured them to force them to do better in his eyes. For instance, if he determined they weren't running fast enough because their lungs weren't functioning properly, he might lock them in a hot, stuffy attic with no air in retaliation."

She froze, staring at him as if he might be a cobra about to strike her. That was what it suddenly felt like. "Are you talking about you, Gideon? Or me? This doesn't sound like you're talking about your background."

"You told me you didn't remember your parents and you were worried because you always remember everything." He pushed the hem of her skirt up enough to expose the artwork on her ankle. "You showed this to me. I've seen artwork like this before on an-other woman. She was taken from an orphanage and experimented on by that same man."

Rory tried to pull her ankle away from Gideon, but he refused to let her go. A shackle made of his fingers went completely around her ankle. His hold was gentle but firm.

"No one but a GhostWalker can see the tattoos on my shoulder, Red. You saw them, and I have no doubt you understood what they mean."

She did. She didn't want to admit that to him. She knew the top emblem symbols represented "Shadow knights who protect against evil forces using psychic powers, courage and honor." She didn't know why she would be able to see a tattoo that no one else could see or know its meaning.

"I don't need to talk about me, Gideon, or my past. I don't want to know about it. I'm not ready yet. I barely was able to talk about it to you. I did think about whether I could harm you before I decided to stay with you and try a relationship, but then I realized in all the years of not knowing my past, even when I had nightmares and was worried, never once have I harmed anyone. I was using that as another excuse to leave. That's what I do, find excuses to move on. I didn't want to let myself do that with you."

"Whitney is after any children the women who escaped have, Rory. There's a woman living quite close who escaped. One you knew when you lived in that military compound. She has a child he wants."

The moment Gideon said Whitney's name, the same unexplained reaction on the spot above her temple occurred. This time, the feeling was accompanied by a strange crackling noise in her ears, as if her skin were too dry and peeling away. She looked down, half expecting to see fractures everywhere, but her skin appeared as smooth as ever.

"Gideon, please let go of my ankle. I don't understand where all of this is leading, but it's making me feel sick. We aren't getting to know one another better. This isn't about your background or what you do now. This is what you think might have happened to me in my past. I just told you I'm not ready to face it yet. When I am, I'll let you know. Right now, I think it's best if I go."

Rory did her best to be very firm. This conversation wasn't getting them anywhere. She wasn't so sure about relationships and even Gideon. So much for feeling safe and having his understanding. She'd come to him feeling so hopeful, and now she just felt lost and alone all over again. She pressed her fist deeper into that knot in her stomach.

Gideon released her ankle immediately. "Sweetheart, just take a minute and think about this. I know it's scary, but I'm right here with you. I can get you through this. We can face your past together, get through it, and then it will be over. You'll know once and for all what happened to you and if you're a threat to anyone. You're a GhostWalker. I know you are. Everyone's willing to help you. They'll be able to ensure no one gets hurt and see what's going on inside you that's blocking your memories and maybe even what he did to your lungs."

Everything in her stilled. She heard the clock on the wall ticking. Her heart beating. The taste in her mouth was bitter. Then ashes. She heard that crackling noise again, only this time it wasn't her skin. She felt cold. Ice-cold. Wrapping her arms around her body, she rubbed her hands up and down the goose bumps.

"Everyone?" she repeated, her tone very, very quiet. "You told other people the things I told you in absolute confidence?"

12

Rory didn't look away from Gideon's silvery-blue, very focused stare, not for one moment. He looked every inch the predatory hunter. She had seen that look on many occasions; now she took heed.

"You told me this was a safe place, Gideon. You told me you were safe. I don't know how many times you reiterated that to me. Over and over. You even said it to me tonight. You used your gifts. Your voice is compelling. I knew that, but I didn't mind because I felt you were safe. I felt this place was. But all along, you were lying to me. It wasn't safe to tell you things I'd never shared with another human being."

"Red." There was an ache in his voice—that one that had given her the first flag of alarm. Regret. Worry.

She shook her head. Ice entered her veins and moved to surround her heart. She'd never felt so cold in her life. "Don't, Gideon. There's no taking this back. No way to explain how you could tell me you wanted me to be yours, to make a life with me and then betray me. And what you did is betrayal. You didn't talk to me first. You just went to however many strangers and told them everything I told you. It's been hell for me living like this, and yet you had no problem spilling all the details to your friends. I hope you managed to entertain them."

"Rory, you can't believe it was like that."

She stood up, and when he did as well, she glided away from him toward the door. "Here's what we're going to do. I'm going to block you from my phone. Your friends won't call or text me either, and they're going to stay away from me. If they don't, I'll call the police and file harassment charges. As soon as possible, I'll be moving on. I don't know when that will be because I have other things I'm dealing with. That isn't your business, and you stay out of it. I don't want to see you again. Or hear from you again. Not ever."

"Rory, what's happened to you isn't going to stop. I can help you. The things I said to you weren't lies. I didn't handle this right, maybe that's true, but Whitney is still around, and he's dangerous."

"You don't have to worry that I'm dangerous to you or your friends. I won't be around."

"Damn it, Red. I meant every single thing I said to you. You can hear lies. You know I mean what I said to you. We're meant to be together. Don't do this, Rory. Stay with me."

She did not deign to answer him. There was nothing to say. The crackling was far louder as the ice covered her heart, and it shattered into a million pieces. Head high, she walked out without looking back. She knew how to be alone better than she knew how to be with someone.

The fog had covered the night in a thick gray blanket of mist. She wanted to disappear into that mist and become part of it just for a little while so she could cry in peace, and no one would know.

Gideon followed her outside. "Sweetheart, please just listen to reason. You're surrounded by danger. Harvey Matters and his crew. Whitney. We have no idea if the cops are dirty. You need someone on your side. I know I handled this all wrong, but I did it trying to help you."

She couldn't stop herself from swinging around to face him. "Did you, Gideon? Did you tell them because you were trying to help me? Or were you afraid for that woman and her child? Did you tell them because you thought that terrible man sent me to do something horrible to all of you? I dare you to tell me the truth. Look me in the eye and tell me the truth. Say it out loud so I can hear."

She'd been reasoning out why he would tell his friends. What would be his motives? She'd concluded that he thought she was a threat to all of them.

Gideon didn't stop until he stood right in front of her. "Rory, Whitney builds traps."

"It's an easy enough question, Gideon."

"No, it isn't. Once you remember, you'll understand what I'm saying about him. At least let me help you get your memories back."

"I find it very interesting how you manage to avoid answering any question you're certain I won't like the answer to. Your motivation in telling your friends wasn't to help me at all, Gideon. Had it been, you would have consulted me first. There is no chance of a relationship between two people when there is no trust. You proved to me that there is no safety with you. No trust with you."

"That isn't true."

"You proved to me it is the truth. You have your friends and family, and they come first in your life. That's fine. The next woman you find, I suggest you don't lie to her like you did me. I'm not a threat to any of you. If that horrid man you're so afraid of sent me or programmed me, he didn't do a very good job of it. I meant what

I said about calling the police and filing charges. I want to be left alone. There's no reason for any of you to come near me."

It hurt just to look at him, and she turned away, no longer able to be near him.

"I have to make sure you get back to your apartment safely." There was despair in his voice.

She didn't answer. She wasn't going to worry about his wounds. That was on him—choices that he made for himself. Then he was gone and Javier was pacing behind her. She should have known. His friends and family would never allow Gideon to put himself in danger any more than he had allowed them to be in danger from her.

Javier was silent for nearly a block. "Rory, Gideon was worried you might take what he did the wrong way. He was trying to get you help."

She sighed. "I'm not discussing this with you. I'm staying away from you people, and I want you to stay away from me. I mean it. I'll leave the city as soon as I can."

"What about Gideon? I thought you cared about him."

As much as she wanted to stay silent, she was so upset that she couldn't help snapping at him. "You don't have a relationship with someone who breaks trust with you, Javier. You of all people know that. You would never, under any circumstances, trust that person again. Over and over, he told me I was safe with him. He assured me anything I told him was safe with him. That wasn't the truth. He didn't tell you my most intimate secrets to save me. He told all of you to save you."

She knew he couldn't deny the truth any more than Gideon could have. She didn't try to hide the pain in her voice or on her face. She didn't even dab at the tears filling her eyes. They didn't spill over, and she turned her head straight to face toward the apartments.

"Look, this all appears bad. Really bad. I know it does. We can't talk about things that go on in our lives, and that makes it hard for Gideon to share the things he wants to with you about himself. He'll be able to when you get past this."

She had to hand it to Javier. He hung in there and kept trying when she knew instinctively he wasn't a man to bother. He was the type to just walk away.

"I appreciate you trying to fix things for your friend, Javier, but there isn't going to be a resolution for this. You already know it, so please just let it go. My apartment building is right there. I can cross the street on my own and get inside."

"The last time didn't end so well. You went up to your place alone last night, and it was trashed. I'll just go in with you. Where are you sleeping?"

"Lydia's apartment. I have her key."

"Just so you know, I'll be escorting you all the way inside. Hopefully, her kid is a sound sleeper. I'm not taking any chances this time."

She didn't reply. There wasn't much she could say, not when she had to admit she was just a little nervous going into the building. They walked the rest of the way in silence. Javier opened doors and rode the elevator in silence to the second floor. Lydia's apartment was quiet, and he went in first, signaling her to wait. When he returned, he just nodded and sauntered away. She felt oddly grateful that he didn't prolong his goodbyes. She didn't want to continue the argument. There was nothing more to say.

Rory found herself taking another shower, trying to scrub Gideon's touch from her skin and lips. She wished she could scrub his memory from her mind and forget him the way she had her parents. She found herself sobbing. She had never broken down completely like this. She cried like a baby, weeping with abandon until it hurt.

He had done this to her. Gideon. No, she had done this to herself. She had always believed in taking responsibility for her own actions, and she had let herself trust him. All along, there had been warning flags. She saw them. Felt them. She'd even talked to herself about them. Still, she'd chosen to ignore them.

She should have known better. She should have left when everything had begun to go south. So many warning signs along the way. She liked her friends too much. Her job. And him. Gideon. Why had she connected so fast with him? Fallen so hard? She was so lonely. That was the only reason. She had unbelievable chemistry with him. Chemistry could happen with any number of men. She just hadn't been open to it. When she moved, she would have to explore that possibility. Not a relationship. Just sex. Just fun. Just someone to share a little time with so she wasn't quite so lonely and wouldn't fall into any more traps.

Rory took her time drying off. Her skin hurt. Her muscles. Her heart hurt. She couldn't remember aching inside and out like this. She'd packed most of her clothes and recovered ninety percent of her things from her apartment. Once she put in her notice and met her obligations, she could leave. It would be wrenching to leave the friends she'd made at the apartment building, but it would be so much better for her to know she would never have to run into Gideon or any of his friends. And it would kill her to see Gideon with another woman. She wouldn't be able to face that. She was crying all over again. An endless faucet. At least no one was awake to witness her foolish breakdown.

There was no way to fall asleep. She just stared at the ceiling. Most of the time, she couldn't see it because she was still crying. All that did was give her a headache. In the end, she dressed in jeans and a T-shirt, wrote a note to Lydia, grabbed her car keys and jacket, and headed to Golden Gate Park. She needed to walk somewhere quiet away from the wharf with no chance of running into Gideon's friends.

Golden Gate Park was a getaway she'd found almost immediately when she'd first arrived in San Francisco. She needed wide open spaces, and the park had over a thousand acres of lakes and meadows to explore. She liked to walk and often chose to investigate the various trails, taking photos of the shrubs, flowers and wildlife, particularly the birds she came across.

The park was open twenty-four hours and free to the public. There were popular attractions that cost admission, but Rory avoided people for the most part. She wanted to be out in nature, and the park had never-ending trails for her to take to the lakes.

On the drive to Golden Gate Park, Rory did her best to stop crying, but it wasn't easy. Once she'd started, she couldn't seem to turn the faucet off. She didn't want to get into an accident because she had finally cried and now couldn't stop.

She might have eventually gotten to a place where she would have been able to allow Gideon to talk to his friends about her past in order to know why she couldn't remember. He could be right, and she had been bought from an orphanage. Every time that man's name was mentioned, she got that terrible sensation above her left eye. That had to mean something.

Rory parked her car in her normal spot. Dawn was breaking. There were runners and people walking their dogs, so she wasn't alone, but she wasn't taking chances. She took weapons with her. She knew she could look like someone easy enough to assault. That wasn't the case. A time or two, it had been tried, and no one had been successful. She wasn't in a very good mood, so she hoped no one was foolish enough to try.

She chose one of the wider, more well-traveled paths to start on. It was beautiful and quiet, and the peace of her surroundings began to slowly push aside the wild grief and pain of betrayal. She wanted to think more clearly about the things Gideon had said, not focus on his betrayal.

Dr. Peter Whitney. Deliberately she made herself think the name. The moment she did, her body had that same visceral reaction, violently rejecting even the thought of the man. That spot above her temple gave off that strange sensation that made her feel sick. So sick she even stumbled. She refused to give into it. She was alone and walking along a beautiful path toward the lake. There was a slight breeze tugging at her hair. She'd swept it up into a high ponytail to get the thick mass off her neck. Touches of mist kissed her face. She breathed deep, drawing in the morning air.

Whitney wasn't going to defeat her. Gideon wasn't going to defeat her. She would figure out what was going on with her without help. She'd been alone for so long and she was used to relying on herself. It was better this way. She just had to go over the things Gideon had told her and determine if what he said was fact or fiction. Just because she didn't like hearing it didn't mean it wasn't the truth.

All right, so Gideon had said Whitney had taken female infants and toddlers from orphanages. That would explain why she didn't remember parents. If Gideon was correct about where she came from, she didn't have parents. Once more, she deliberately thought in terms of Whitney's name. Focused on it. Tried to put an image with the name, but the sickness increased without any visual on the man.

Breathing deep, Rory forced her mind to go blank as she walked along the trail, breathing deep again. She could only take that horrible feeling of her skin trying to peel away for so long. She concentrated on allowing the serenity of her surroundings to bring her peace again. It wasn't easy, although she was used to taking walks out in nature to calm her mind. It was just that now that she was determined to solve the mystery of her past, her brain kept looping back to the things Gideon had revealed.

GhostWalkers. That term wasn't familiar to her. The two tattoos on his shoulder weren't familiar, were they? How could she see them when he claimed no one else could? And what of the tattoo on her ankle he said another woman he knew had? How could all that be true when she knew nothing about it? A small moan of despair escaped. She detested that he'd betrayed her confidence to his friends. If he'd just given her a little time to process the information, they could have worked it out together. She would have gotten there eventually.

And what about Gideon? Why didn't he want to tell her anything about himself? What was that all about? Why didn't he give her anything about himself? If he had, she would have been more willing to listen to him. No, wait. She *had* been listening to him. Until she found out he'd told his friends everything she'd told him in confidence.

Now she was crying again. She cursed Gideon under her breath, grateful she was alone. How would she ever explain to her friends that she couldn't stop crying? Lydia was close to taking a chance on accepting a date with Detective Larrsen, who appeared to be a good man. The last thing Rory wanted to do was mess up that situation.

Dabbing at her tears and cursing Gideon more, she considered the things he'd told her about Whitney's punishments. His way of making the girls feel bad about themselves. Training them to be military assets. She couldn't run. Her lungs were terrible. Had she been experimented on? Could Whitney have done something to make her lungs the way they were? Did she have asthma, or was it something he had done to her?

Was she beginning to believe the story Gideon had told her? That she was one of those orphaned girls Whitney had taken? If that was true, was she a threat to the people around her? Her lungs burned for air, and she had to stop and find her inhaler. She had a terrible feeling the things Gideon told her were true.

Rory had always loved the tattoo on her ankle. She often rubbed the berries and leaves when she sat in the evenings after work, just relaxing. Now the tattoo felt like a brand of evil, marking her as something deadly to others. She even wondered if she should be around her friends at the apartment. Was she a danger to Lydia and Ellen and the others?

A headache was rapidly developing. Along with it, her warning system was signaling there might be danger coming her way. She couldn't tell which direction it was coming from. Her gut feeling was weak, but she wasn't ignoring it. She'd done that too many times with Gideon, and look where that had gotten her.

Rory pulled a very small knife from the inside of her jacket. The blade was no more than two inches, but it was incredibly sharp. Wrapping her fist around the handle, she flattened the blade out of sight along her wrist and continued to walk along the trail, all senses scanning for trouble.

She had acute hearing. The sound of birds filled the air, calling back and forth to one another. Some wooed partners. Some were angrily running others away from nests and eggs or the best feeding spots. Others sang merrily in the early morning hour. Squirrels raced up and down trees. Lizards skittered under leaves and vegetation on the ground.

She paced herself a little slower and stayed to the middle of the trail. How would it work if Whitney had programmed her to hurt others? She had moved from place to place bartending. Never once had she even considered hurting another individual, not unless they tried to assault her; then she did defend herself. But she'd never considered staying in a city. She'd never believed she could be in a relationship with anyone. Was that part of the programming? Would finding another GhostWalker somehow activate the program? Seek out and destroy?

Another light moan escaped. She pressed her free hand to her head, where the ache was becoming much more pronounced. Damn Gideon anyway. She would have been better off never knowing any of this. She wouldn't worry about hurting her friends. If she hadn't met him, if he hadn't lied to her and told her he wanted to be with her, she wouldn't have to worry she might have a bomb in her head.

What was the point in telling her he wanted a relationship? Why not just talk to her up front about his concerns? That would have been the right thing to do instead of pretending she meant something to him. He wanted to have sex with her. His body couldn't lie. The chemistry between them was crazy hot.

Her warning radar blared loudly at her. She gripped the handle of the small knife in her palm with the blade lying along her wrist, out of sight. Keeping her arm swinging along her thigh as she walked, Rory kept her head up, looking around. Danger was definitely close. At least someone was close; whether they meant her harm remained to be seen.

Harvey Matters stepped out of the brush ahead of her, one hand up as if in surrender. "Don't mean to startle you, Rory. Just want to talk."

She halted abruptly, keeping a safe distance between them. "The feeling isn't mutual." Plunging her hand into her inside pocket, she came up with the envelope Scott Tinsdale had given her. She held it out to him, keeping a distance, making him take the step forward. Her knife hand was held loosely ready. She was confident he couldn't see she was armed.

He took the envelope and stepped back. "Thank you."

"Don't ever use me again. I won't deliver any more messages. I mean it. I'll tear it up. You tell your associate that. I'm leaving San Francisco as soon as my two-week notice is up. I don't want anything to do with you or your people."

He tilted his head to one side, studying her face. "I heard about the break-ins at the apartments."

"I thought you might be behind that." She knew she didn't sound accusing, only wary. She didn't want to make him angry. She was alone on the trail, and as far as she knew, no one was close by. She didn't want to have to kill him, but she would if she had no other choice.

He shook his head. "No. I don't know who did it or why."

He looked and sounded sincere enough that she believed him despite everything Gideon had told her about him.

"They didn't take anything from any of us, and they didn't bother to make it look like a robbery."

"That's what's worrisome." He even sounded worried. "I didn't kill that cop. They're trying to pin his death on me. I'm hearing rumors that they're trying to say it was my gun. I didn't have a gun. And I didn't kill Ret or Dustin. They were my friends and had been for years. Jarrod is missing. If he were alive, I would know it, but he hasn't contacted me or any of our trusted allies."

"Is it possible Jarrod killed Ramsey, Dustin and Ret, and is trying to frame you? He could have been the one to break into our apartments. He would have known which ones we occupied."

Harvey scratched the bridge of his nose. "I've known Jarrod since we were kids."

That wasn't an answer. People betrayed friends. Lovers. They broke hearts. Grief nearly overwhelmed her.

"Why were you at the apartments, Harvey?"

She shouldn't ask. She had no business asking. It was stupid. She'd just told him she wanted nothing to do with him, but she asked anyway. What was the old saying? Curiosity killed the cat? If what Gideon told her about him was the truth, it made no sense that Harvey would be in the lower-rent apartments. He supposedly owned estates worth millions.

"Someone's been methodically killing key people in our organizations. We never meet in person, and we thought if we did meet somewhere no one would ever consider we would go, we could figure it out. We didn't want to use phones or email. Nothing traceable. Nowhere we could be overheard."

"Were you able to figure out who was killing off your people?"

"Not who was doing the killing. But we began to suspect who was providing the information where our people were going to be so they could be killed. Movement was always a closely guarded secret, and few people knew."

"Someone close had to betray all of you."

He rubbed the bridge of his nose. "Usually a woman. Someone close. Someone you love and trust." He looked sad. "That's why I told the others not to take that chance. Not to fall. Betrayal is the worst pill to swallow."

To her horror, for one terrible moment, tears burned and shimmered in her eyes. She swallowed the lump in her throat and nodded. "Sadly, I do have to agree, although I'll say men are just as capable of betrayal as women. Don't put your trust in them either."

There was a long silence. Harvey turned away from her to look out over the flowers lining both sides of the path before he spoke again. "That man is an idiot for letting someone like you go."

"I'm not such a prize, but thank you, Harvey. You know who betrayed all of you?"

"Jarrod had a woman living with him. Met her a few years ago and fell hard. She was in it for his money, but he couldn't see it. She cheated on him with a cop. Ret, Dustin and I had her tailed after we started losing our key people and had narrowed our suspects. Unfortunately, Jarrod wouldn't believe us. I think he confronted her."

Rory's heart stuttered. "Please tell me she wasn't seeing Ramsey."

Harvey shook his head. "Not Ramsey. We didn't know who she was seeing. Ramsey was a good cop."

Rory had the distinct impression that Harvey might have been working with Ramsey to uncover who had been murdering the key people in his organization. Would a criminal do that? Could he do that and not incriminate himself?

"Can't you just ask her? Did Jarrod ask her?"

"She's dead. And no, Jarrod didn't kill her. We believe her lover did."

Icy fingers trailed down her spine. Harvey was telling her the woman's cop lover had murdered her. "Don't take this the wrong way, but I don't want the cops or anyone else to see us talking together. The police already suspect I work for you."

"No one knows you're here. My men ran interference to keep you from being followed. The cops are a little thin to keep twenty-four-hour surveillance on you. Carver and Westlake are usually the ones to follow you, but they're busy a lot of the time. They have two friends, retired cops now, Bill Morris and Jerome Michigan, who take turns keeping an eye on you for them when they can't. None of them can stay on you all the time. Most of the time it's your man's friends. They're harder to spot. We tried investigating them, but they're ghosts. That means they're government. Or CIA. Or worse."

"He's not my man anymore. I told you, I'm leaving. I'm putting in my notice tonight, and once I work that out, I'll be gone. Why did you tell me all this?"

"Because I think you're being set up right along with me. Everything is pointing in that direction. You're the logical choice. The more knowledge you have, the better the chance you have of protecting yourself. I'm worried about you and your friends staying at the apartments. Particularly the two with the kids. I know you don't like me or what I do, Rory, but sometimes you need a safe place to go. I'm going to give you a key and a number. That's it. If you and the women and kids need to get away and hide somewhere, just call the number, get into a car and start driving north. You'll get instructions on where a safe house is. My people will run interference. The house will be stocked with everything you need for a couple of weeks. Think of it as a vacation."

"If I'm not with them, can my friends still use the house?" She did her best to keep the challenge from her voice.

"Of course."

"Thank you, Harvey. I don't know why you'd help us, but I appreciate it." She didn't trust him any more than she trusted Gideon, but she took the key and card with the single phone number on it. Everything was so uncertain, she had no idea what might happen.

"I was the one who chose those apartments. It didn't occur to me that any of this would happen, but it did. It's my mess and I need to clean it up."

He was right. It was his mess, but at the same time, someone was framing him if he was telling the truth. She wasn't so sure her lie detector wasn't faulty after her encounters with Gideon, but Harvey appeared sincere. People weren't all bad or all good.

She pressed her fingers to her temple where the headache had fully formed from all the crying. At no time did she reveal the knife she held. She had learned not to trust years earlier, and Gideon had only reinforced that lesson.

"Harvey, were you ever married? In a relationship?" She should keep her mouth shut, let him go. He was a stranger, and she had no one to ask questions of. She wanted answers.

"I've never married. Too many women made it easy for me to find another one."

She frowned. "I don't know what that means."

He gave her a half smile, one that didn't reach his eyes, very reminiscent of Gideon. "You wouldn't know what that means, Rory, because you aren't the kind of woman to go after a man for his money. If you decide on a man, you're going to be loyal to him, and you'll be with him for all the right reasons."

"What if I don't know what the right reasons are?"

"Rory, you aren't the one at fault."

"You don't know that. I don't know the first thing about relationships. I've never been in one. I've never seen one that worked. I never even wanted to be in one until I was with Gideon. I fell so hard and fast for him, it was crazy. I didn't even think. I didn't have time to think. It was the dumbest thing I ever did."

"Not that *you* ever did. That he ever did," Harvey corrected. "When a man is in his twenties, and he acts the fool, he can be forgiven because he doesn't know better. But by the time he's that man's age, he should know a good thing when he has it. He should have been treating you with love and concern. Watching over you. Putting you first. That's a relationship. And that's his failing, not yours."

"I don't even know why I'm asking you these questions, Harvey."

"I'm not a good man, and I'm lonely for a reason. You're a good woman, and you don't deserve to be lonely. That doesn't mean you aren't. We just happen to be in the same place at a bad time for both of us."

Rory knew he was right, and she couldn't tempt fate any longer. Someone was bound to come along the trail soon. In any case, Harvey had said his men had run interference to keep Gideon's people from following her car, but she wouldn't put it past Javier to have her vehicle bugged. For all she knew, Gideon might even have put a tracking device on her phone. She was going to look the second Harvey was gone. She should have considered that right away. She'd been too upset to reason everything out.

"You'd better go before someone comes along and sees us together," she told him. "But thank you for talking to me."

"Keep that card with the number on it for emergencies. If you call it, someone will answer and help you." Harvey lifted a hand, turned away from her and walked up the trail leading toward the lake.

Rory watched him go until he disappeared around a bend. She turned back toward the parking lot, sliding the knife back into the small sheath inside her jacket. She had a long walk and a lot to think about.

Taking out her phone, she permanently deleted the screenshot of the message Gideon had taken that Tinsdale had sent to Harvey. Maybe she should have told Harvey about unsealing the message and how Gideon had taken a screenshot. She didn't know if he had duplicated the message before he had deleted it or sent it to someone else. He could have. She didn't trust him anymore. But she wasn't taking any chances with Harvey going from being nice to pulling out a gun and shooting her.

She took her time walking back, turning over the things Gideon had told her about GhostWalkers. She realized her nightmares fit with everything he'd said. Or maybe he'd taken her nightmares into account so she would have reason to recognize pieces of what he told her. As much as she wanted that to be the truth, in her gut, she knew it wasn't.

By the time she reached her car, she'd concluded that Gideon had been telling her the truth, and she most likely had been bought by Dr. Peter Whitney from an orphanage to be experimented on. What that meant in terms of what she was now, she had no idea, but she wasn't going to take any chances with anyone's life. She was the same person she'd always been before she came to San Francisco. She was intelligent. Self-reliant. She could manage even with the new knowledge she had. It was frightening to think that Whitney— and she kept repeating the name in the hopes she'd stop having such a visceral reaction to it—planted something in her that might harm others.

She drove back to the apartment building and parked in her usual spot. Each tenant had a parking place specifically for them. She was grateful no one had taken hers, which was sometimes the case. She didn't want to drive around the parking garage looking for a new parking place. She was exhausted. Part of her problem was she needed to use her regular nebulizer. It was in Lydia's apartment.

The moment she entered, Lydia jumped up, ran to her, threw her arms around her and hugged her tight. "I was worried."

"Didn't you get my note?"

"Yes. But you didn't sleep all night. Something clearly went wrong. You didn't stay at Gideon's, and you didn't stay here. You should have woken me up, Rory."

"You have a three-year-old and you work long hours, Lydia."

"That doesn't matter. You matter more to me than sleep. Seriously, Rory, tell me what you need right now."

"My nebulizer first. I can barely breathe. It's in the guest room by the bed."

"You sit down and I'll get it for you." Lydia rushed off.

Rory sank into one of the two nice chairs Lydia had in her living room. Ellen was playing with her dolls on the floor, and she immediately crawled up on Rory's lap and pressed a kiss onto her cheek. Rory kissed her back.

"Good morning, Miss Ellie May Rider."

"Morning."

Rory's heart melted. That was the first time Ellen had spoken without an elaborate go-between. She kissed her several more times, making her squeal the way her momma did, grateful she'd made such good friends. Gideon might have made her feel broken and shattered, but friends went a long way to comfort her.

13

Gideon stood on the very edge of his rooftop, facing the bar. "There's no recovery from this one, Javier. I sold her out and she called me on it. I told her she could tell me anything and she'd be safe. I meant it too. I had no idea she was a GhostWalker. I knew she was afraid of a relationship, but I didn't have a clue why. I wanted her to know she was safe with me."

"I heard the resolve in her voice," Javier confirmed.

"I can't blame her. Everything she said was true. I didn't tell any of you the things she said to me in confidence to save her. I told them to you to save you."

"Gideon. You had no choice."

"There's always another choice. I should have thought it through. Taken a couple more days. I could have kept her away from all of you and then talked it over with her."

"You know better."

"She's in trouble, Javier. I know she is. I can feel it. She's cut herself off from me, but I can still feel the danger to her, and that means it's growing, getting worse. It's bad. I don't know where it's coming from. She won't let me in."

"She doesn't know all of us."

Gideon turned to look at Javier over his shoulder. "Rory isn't going to be so easy to fool now. She'll be looking. And now she'll think about the things I told her, and she'll be afraid she might harm someone. That's going to be uppermost in her mind. I didn't blow my chance with the only woman I'll ever want to be with so Whitney can run his program on one of you."

"You're not killing yourself over this, Gideon. Sending out your spies to watch over her is too dangerous for you."

Gideon turned back to look at the building several blocks down where the bar was located. With his superior eyesight and hearing, he could see the strobing colored lights and hear the music and conversations flowing. He zeroed in on Rory's voice immediately. She wasn't laughing the way she normally did. She talked with customers. He was certain no one would notice the difference in her voice but him.

He'd hurt her. No, it was far worse than that. He'd devastated her. She'd cut all ties with him—blocked him from communicating with her. Blocked him from being able to touch her mind. He was a very strong telepath, and when it came to Rory, he had developed an even stronger connection than he normally would have with others. When Rory was concentrating on her work, she forgot to keep the shields in her mind strong, and he caught glimpses of images of what she was thinking or doing. None of it was good. Not when it came to him.

"I'm not leaving her unprotected, Javier. I did this to us. She's alone because of me. Something or someone is after her. If I hadn't betrayed her, she'd be safe with me right now."

"I can agree with that, Gideon. But you tearing open that wound and bleeding to death isn't going to save her life. Watch and listen, fine. Give me some time to figure this out. You know I'm going to help whether you give me the okay or not."

Gideon glanced over his shoulder again, his piercing eyes ringed with silver, never a good sign. "She knows what you look like, Javier," he repeated.

"She'll never see me. And in case you're wondering, I like her. I'm not just doing this for you. Whether Whitney programmed her or not, she's a good person and she deserves better than she got."

"She has no idea about her past. Whitney was very successful in erasing it. She isn't a part of whatever plan he's conceived."

Javier nodded. "I'm very aware of that. Don't send your spies, Gideon. Let me work on this. You keep watch yourself. She's safe while she's working. It's been a couple of days. She's staying with Lydia. Her friends are keeping close to her."

"She gave her notice to her boss."

"Yeah."

"He was upset. Tried to talk her out of leaving. She was adamant that she has to go." Gideon turned back to look at the bar. "When she goes, I have this really bad feeling I won't be able to stop myself from following her."

"We'll cross that bridge when we come to it." Javier glanced at his watch. "I've got to handle something. I'm going to keep an eye on her though. She's not going to just be hanging out there alone. Don't do anything stupid, Gideon."

Javier made his way down the stairs and back out onto the street. Rhianna was draped in her usual sexy fashion against the wall outside Gideon's home. She couldn't help the way she looked, with her thick curly black hair and incredibly blue eyes. Every movement she made was enticing and sexy. Beside her was Ethan Meyers. He was Gideon's friend, a very hard man to spot in the shadows.

"How is he?" Rhianna asked.

Javier knew Gideon better than any of the others in their close-knit family of GhostWalkers, and by the concern in Rhianna's voice, she was aware of it.

"Not good. We're going to lose him if we don't find a way to fix this."

They fell into step with him as he started toward the warehouse Mack and Kane called home. "Can you talk to her?" Ethan asked.

"I tried the night she walked out on Gideon. The thing is, he did betray her. He told her she was safe with him. Everything she told him was in confidence. If a woman said those things to me and then turned around and told all her friends everything I said to her, I wouldn't forgive her. In fact, I'd probably slit her throat."

"That isn't good," Ethan said.

"No, it's not," Javier said. "And he couldn't tell her anything about himself or what we do. To make matters worse, she realized he told us for our sakes and not for hers. He was looking out for us, not her. It wasn't like he was trying to save her from Whitney. He was trying to save us. So that betrayal went even deeper."

Ethan swore under his breath. "How do we make this right?"

Javier glanced at Rhianna. She shook her head. "That kind of betrayal had to devastate her. If she found it hard to trust in the first place . . ." She trailed off.

"We all know what having trust issues is like," Ethan said.

They stopped in front of the three-story warehouse that Jaimie, Mack's wife, had found first and begun to renovate into a home for herself. When the others found her, Mack had moved in and never moved back out. Now the place was completely finished, with Kane Cannon; his wife, Rose; and their son, Sebastian, residing on the first floor. The second floor was where the GhostWalker team met and planned their missions. Jaimie and Javier had computers set up on another part of the same floor. The entire top floor was home to Mack and Jaimie.

The three made their way to the second floor, where the rest of their GhostWalker family was waiting for them.

"It's bad," Javier announced without preamble. "We're going to lose him if we don't do something. He'll take matters into his own hands; in fact, he's planning to do just that."

Mack sighed. "I'll talk to her."

"What can you tell her that Gideon couldn't? We're classified. Until we know she isn't a threat, you can't tell her anything. You can't say he told us to protect her, because she's intelligent and she already figured out he told us because he was worried Whitney may have sent her after Sebastian. Or to harm us in some way."

He knew he sounded belligerent when Rhianna put a hand on his arm. Her touch was very light, but it was a reminder of who he was talking to. He knew none of this mess was Mack's fault. It just was—a mess. And this was Gideon.

"She doesn't know most of us," Kane said. "Paul's idea can still work. We go to the bar. One or two at a time, not sitting at her station, not paying attention to her. Paul can sit at the bar with Mack and get close enough to her to examine her. Is that feasible, Paul?"

"That could be difficult. If she's moving around and there are quite a few people close by, it wouldn't be easy," Paul said. "I'm not a miracle worker."

"We could go during her slowest time," Mack said. "I could engage her in conversation. Talk about my wife."

"If you made one misstep with her, she would know. She's looking for us now," Javier pointed out.

"We're GhostWalkers," Mack said. "If we don't want to be seen, no one sees us. We hide in plain sight."

"But not from each other," Jaimie reminded him. "Don't be so arrogant. She's a GhostWalker too. She may not remember, but she has all the instincts, doesn't she?"

"I didn't think so," Javier said. "At least not at first. I followed her home from the bar a couple of times she was followed. I took care of it because she didn't seem to notice. Now, I don't know. Her lungs are shit. That's for real. She couldn't outrun anyone if she tried to. I don't know how she is at self-defense, because I've never seen her in action."

"She seems like a decent person," Ethan said.

"You know I don't like being around many people outside of"— Javier circled the group with his finger—"but Rory can be included in those I'm fond of now. She's genuinely a good person. I spent a couple of weeks watching her before Gideon ever approached her. I didn't want her hurting Gideon. I like her, and that's saying something."

"I knew Rory as Laurel when we were children growing up," Rose volunteered. "Whitney despised her because she had trouble breathing. She had an amazing memory, and she was good with languages. She had skills when it came to weapons and hand-to-hand combat. That didn't matter, because she didn't have what Whitney called 'staying power.' He wanted her to run for hours. She couldn't run. And she couldn't hit the times he demanded of her. He made them impossible. The more she failed, the worse her punishments were."

"What does that mean?" Ethan asked.

"He would make it so she really couldn't breathe. He'd force her to wear a mask over her mouth and nose, and then send her out to run in the heat. He'd have two of his soldiers chase her. They weren't kidding around either."

"Meaning?" Marc Lands asked as he poured himself a cup of coffee.

"They would kill her if they could."

The team members looked at one another with horror on their faces. "How old was she?"

Rose shrugged. "He started that kind of thing with a few of the girls when they were very young. Around seven or eight. The ones he didn't like and thought were expendable. He believed she was useless and wanted to teach us all a lesson. None of us knew what that lesson was supposed to be."

"But she survived," Mack said.

Rose nodded. "She always came back. The soldiers didn't. It was always hours later."

"Did you ever ask her how she did it?" Kane asked. His hand slid up to Rose's neck. He cradled his son's little bottom in the crook of his other arm. Sebastian was listening intently, as if he understood every word being said.

Rose shook her head. "We were careful not to ask those kinds of questions of each other. We didn't want Whitney to know any of our psychic abilities. By the time we were five, we understood he would use anything against us. We even tried to pretend we weren't close, because he would use friendships against us. He tricked us all the time. We were young and wanted to believe him."

"Do you know what happened to her?"

"He rotated girls in and out of the facilities." She rested her head against Kane's arm. "I was about ten when Whitney gave us all puppies to take care of. Each of us got one. We were so happy. We had the responsibility of looking after them and training them ourselves. Laurel and a couple of the other girls were younger, but they still took care of their puppies. When the dogs were a year old, he took us all to the arena. He had fighting dogs brought in, and one by one, he put our puppies in with them. In front of us they were killed. He blamed us and told us we didn't prepare them. We didn't teach them survival skills."

Rose pressed trembling fingers to her mouth. "You can't imagine how horrible it was. Laurel couldn't breathe. I remember she tried to get into the ring with those terrible animals to stop them, but one of the guards stopped her. I think Whitney would have let her. I think he hoped the dogs would turn on her. She fell to the floor and went into convulsions. There was a doctor there and he went to her. She was carried out. Whitney called her a disgrace. He said she wasn't strong enough to be a soldier and never would be. He always talked about her like that."

"If you were ten," Mack said, "and she's younger than you, she had to have been seven or eight."

Rose nodded. "After that, he sent her on mission after mission. She was forced to sleep in an attic. It was horribly stuffy and dirty. We tried to go up there to clean it, but he had guards to keep her from getting out or us from getting in. After every assignment, he would force her to go into that place."

"When did he give you the tattoos?" Rhianna asked.

"It was just a couple of weeks after he killed our puppies. None of us would cooperate with him. I think he thought he needed to do something that would turn everything around, and it did. We were all young enough to want to have a parent. He was all we had. Each one of us had artwork that was beautiful and specially designed just for us. We were very excited. Laurel loved her tattoo, but she wasn't like a couple of the girls. She didn't trust him. I don't know if he had expected she would fall for his gift and fawn all over him, but when she didn't, he went back to sending her out on as many assignments as possible. Then one day, she just wasn't with us anymore. He never said where she went. Whether she was alive or dead."

"Did Whitney act upset, as if she had escaped him? Or did you think he sent her away to another facility?" Mack asked.

Rose sat up straighter, obviously trying to remember. "It was a long time ago. He detested so many of us. None of us ever pleased him. He'd sent her out on a mission with two of us, and everything went wrong. We were trying to get away and Ivy was wounded. It

CHRISTINE FEEHAN

was clear we couldn't outrun the men following us. The terrain was sandy. The air was dry. There were these formations like dunes but made of rock, dirt, sand and grass. One had a bit of a hollowed-out area. Not much. You could see it plain as day, even though it was night."

Sebastian, as if knowing his mother was reliving a bad experience, reached out with his little baby fingers and touched her face. She immediately took his hand and kissed it.

"I'm fine, honey," she reassured him. "This happened when I was a little girl." She took another deep breath. "Laurel indicated the ground swelling and told us to press tight against the wall of dirt and not to move or make a sound. Just to trust her. She was wheezing bad and trying not to cough. Then she went silent. I did what she said. To this day, I don't know why. I thought it was crazy. Anyone should have been able to see us. We were right out in the open. She put her body in front of ours, especially in front of Ivy's. The next thing I knew, I was looking through what appeared to be a gray veil. That's the best way I could describe it."

"A gray veil?" Javier echoed.

She nodded. "The men following us came running straight at us. They were so close we could have reached out and touched them. They were carrying semiautomatics and cursing up a storm because we'd stolen the plans to the underground fortress and tunnel system that had just been completed. Nearly everyone who'd worked in the tunnels or on the fortress had been killed, at least according to Whitney. My guess is those guards were going to die for letting us get away with the plans. Those blueprints were kept in a vault under high security."

"The blueprints should have been burned," Mack said.

"It was a maze down there. I think Angelo Perez, the man who had it built, was afraid he might get lost," Rose replied. "In any case, the guards didn't spot us even when they looked right at us.

It was so weird. Ivy was bleeding, but they didn't see the bloodstains. Laurel was no longer coughing or wheezing, and even our normal breathing was muffled to the point I couldn't hear it."

There was silence in the room filled with GhostWalkers. All of them were used to the various psychic gifts the others had, but Rose was describing something a child of seven or eight had done to protect others under extreme circumstances.

"Laurel—Rory—shielded you from your pursuers?" Mack wanted clarification. Astonishment and maybe even awe showed in his tone. "At that young of an age?"

"She had to have, Mack," Rose said. "How else weren't we seen? Those men were right on top of us. They would have caught us. There was no way we would have gotten away from them. It cost her though. We stayed hidden for hours. They came back over and over, searching most of the night. When we were finally able to step away from the wall, she collapsed, gasping for breath and coughing. She was far worse off than Ivy."

"I take it Whitney wasn't pleased with her."

"We couldn't tell him what she did for us. No one ever told him anything. He was terrible to her. He said the worst things, even told her she was better off dead. That we'd be better off if she were dead. He had her dragged to the attic when she desperately needed a treatment for her lungs. We wanted to go to her and tell her we would have died if she hadn't been with us, but we couldn't get to her. We never saw her again after that. She disappeared. Ivy and I talked it over. We thought maybe she died in the attic because she couldn't breathe." There was sorrow in her voice.

"I'm sorry, Rose. That must have been very difficult for you," Javier said. "For all of you. Whitney deserves a very special place in hell for everything he's done."

"I wish I could tell you more, but I have no idea what really happened to her," Rose admitted.

"There's no doubt that she's a GhostWalker," Mack said. "We still don't know if Whitney took her to another facility and programmed her and then sent her here to try to take Sebastian from us. Or to harm one of us."

"Mack," Jaimie protested. "I investigated her background. She's traveled all over the state for the last few years. It seems unlikely that she would have waited this long to approach us if she meant us harm."

"Unless her background is entirely fabricated, Jaimie," Kane pointed out. "You know that's possible."

"True, but it would be unlikely anyone would be good enough to hide the fact that they contrived their background from me. I'm very thorough and so is Javier. We both investigated her separately. I can't imagine that we would be fooled." She looked to Javier.

He shook his head. "She traveled to each of those places and worked at the various bars. I'd bet my life on it."

"That's it, then. Gideon is family. Rory is his choice. His woman. That makes her family. This is for him," Mack said. "No one has to help. It's strictly volunteer. We don't know how much of a threat Rory represents. I'm going to go in with Paul and see if he can tell whether she's been programmed in any capacity. Hopefully not with a bomb. That's my greatest fear."

Jaimie raised an eyebrow. "I didn't even think of that. I guess I was wondering how you were going to tell if Whitney had ordered her to make a try for Sebastian. How would you determine that?"

All eyes turned to Paul.

"Hopefully, I'll know when I look at her. I'm very interested in examining her lungs and bronchial system. Even if she had asthma to begin with, Whitney clearly made her situation worse. I'll try to find out everything I can."

"I can go with Paul, Mack," Lucas Atherton spoke up. He had

the good looks of a model and was considered charming. "I can talk with the best of them."

"I already told all of you, this is my team and I'm responsible. If there is a problem, I make the decisions. I'm with Paul. We'll see how things go."

"Jaimie, make a schedule for the next couple of weeks for us," Kane suggested. "That way we aren't overrunning the bar. See if you can get Rory's shifts at her work so we know when she's on."

"That won't be a problem," Jaimie agreed. "And I'll be taking a shift as well."

"Anyone who wants to help look out for Rory, put your name on the roster," Mack added. "We need to make sure the camera feeds in the apartments are working, as well as the ones we added on the street. We want eyes on her."

"Gideon has a bad feeling," Javier said. "He said he's sure she's in danger. Gideon has never been wrong about his feelings." He stood up. "I'd better get back to him before he does something crazy, like try to send his spies to her. Paul, you want to come with me?"

"I'm probably not his favorite person right now."

"You will be when you tell him you're going to the bar to try to make sure she's healthy."

"Don't bet on it. I'm the one who had the brilliant idea to be honest with her," Paul reminded him.

"You were right," Rhianna said. "There was no other way to handle it. It would have been ten times worse if Gideon had lied to her about telling us."

Javier ignored the byplay between them, suddenly anxious to get back to Gideon. As a rule, Gideon was one of the most patient of all the team members. He could always be counted on to put things into perspective. But ever since he'd been shot so many times and the wound wasn't healing as fast as Gideon thought it should, he'd been acting differently.

Javier knew Gideon had almost died. No one, not even Paul or Marc, had expected him to live, and Paul was a brilliant psychic surgeon. Marc was an incredible medic. Had Paul not been in the field with them, Gideon wouldn't have had a chance. Even now, Javier could tell Paul worried. Whatever he had done to save Gideon, no other surgeon could have done. Paul was aware the repair was still fragile. He didn't want Gideon moving around the way his patient was doing. That made Javier nervous, and Javier wasn't the type to get nervous.

Gideon was still standing in the same spot facing the bar where Javier had left him. He didn't turn around when Rhianna, Paul and Javier joined him.

"I felt a threat to her entering the bar just a few minutes ago," he announced to the others.

"How close?" Rhianna asked.

Gideon tapped his fingers against his chest over his heart. "He's a distance away from her, still close to the door. I'm losing him in the crowd."

No one would ever question Gideon's assessment of a threat. He was right too many times. If he said there was an enemy close, they took it as gospel.

"I'm leaving now," Rhianna said. "I'll sit at one of the back tables with Jaimie. If I spot anyone who looks like a threat, I'll let you know. If you can dial him in, you let me know."

"Mack and I will sit at the bar, and I'll see if I can get a sense of whether Whitney has done anything to make Rory a threat to Sebastian or even to herself," Paul added.

"Is it a good idea for Jaimie and Mack to be in the bar at the same time without appearing to be together?" Gideon asked. He still didn't take his gaze from the building several blocks down.

"They give off fairly heavy energy when they're in the same room. She's sensitive to energy."

Rhianna bit down on her lower lip. "I hadn't thought of that. You're right. I'll text her that we should take second day. We'll send in Jacob and Lucas. She's never seen either of them. I'll let them know they need to go in now and expect to hear from you if you spot any threat getting close to her."

Paul was already moving toward the trapdoor, and Javier shadowed him.

"Can you tell if the threat is from Whitney?" Javier asked.

"I have no way of knowing where it's coming from, only that someone entered the bar and their attention is centered on Rory, and not in a good way."

Gideon focused completely on the building in the distance. It wasn't an easy thing to do. It took a great deal of concentration and was very draining. He was weaker than he wanted to admit to himself, let alone the others. He'd always been extremely strong, both physically and mentally, as well as psychically.

As much as he despised Peter Whitney and his experiments, the man had increased his abilities to aid his family a thousand percent psychically. The unexpected additions of animal and raptor DNA had been difficult to adjust to. Once he was able to get most of the predatory instincts under some semblance of control, he could concentrate on the more useful aspects of his new, unwanted genetic makeup. Even those traits helped to guard his family, although there were multiple downsides to them.

He hadn't considered that he would find a woman he would want to spend his life with. That meant he hadn't considered what it might mean to have children with her. Kane and Rose had clearly passed on their genetic and psychic traits to Sebastian. The child was very advanced for his age already, both physically and psychically. He displayed the skills found in a much older child. He was coordinated and had fast reflexes. He already seemed to have a feeling for danger.

Gideon pressed his fist closer against his heart to focus his thoughts on Rory. When she was very busy, she couldn't keep her mind blocked against him. Once he had a clear path to her, more and more he was becoming adept at pushing his way into that narrow conduit that took him into her mind, where he could catch glimpses of what was happening around her. What she was thinking. What she was feeling. He shared the pain he'd caused her. The devastation she felt.

The intensity of her loneliness matched his. She had wanted their relationship every bit as much as he had. She had cared for him. She still did. That was one of the worst things he faced each time he touched her mind—knowing she was well on her way to developing strong feelings for him. It hadn't been all about the intense chemistry. Their bond had been emotional.

Whitney may have influenced them sexually, but he hadn't created the emotional connection between them. They'd begun to build a foundation. Part of that had been because Gideon's wounds had prevented him from acting on his desire for her. He had also been very aware of her fear of trusting anyone, and he'd wanted to take it slow with her so she knew he was someone she could count on. Just thinking how he'd let Rory down disgusted him.

Gideon caught the image of faces staring at him. Eyes. Some laughing. Overbright. Streaked red. Others starkly depressed and sorrowful. Flushed faces. Mouths forming smiles. Frowns. Calling out. Heads turned toward one another or toward the front of the bar looking at Rory or another bartender.

The bar was down more than one bartender, and Rory was extremely busy. She was thinking of her customers and each order, keeping them separately in her head, coming up with the most efficient way to make several drinks at once. Prioritizing them. A waitress leaned over the bar and called out more orders. Rory didn't lose her calm or patience but became even more focused, adding them into her list of drinks to make.

Rory lined up glasses and began pouring syrups and alcohol. Gideon was amazed at how fast her mind worked. She was like a computer, generating recipes and implementing them like a machine on autopilot. Drinks that were the same were done almost as if she were simply making one drink for a single person. If other drinks had ingredients she was using, she poured those.

She had eighteen drinks made in a matter of minutes and sent out to the waitress and customers, then was on to drinks made in blenders. While those drinks were in three different blenders, she was shaking two others. All the while, she was carrying on a conversation with a couple of different people sitting at the bar.

Gideon found the way Rory's mind worked interesting. She filed away the things the customers said to her as if they were in categories. Things about families. Facts about weather or history or the city. Personal information. Flirting. If they were a repeat customer. Everything said to her was compiled and arranged unconsciously for her use. She responded instinctively, without thought, as she worked.

Gideon tried to feel around her for any threats. While Rory worked, she wasn't thinking in terms of threats, especially now. Her boss was very upset that she'd turned in her two-weeks' notice, and a part of her felt guilty for leaving him when she knew he needed her. She was an excellent bartender, and the place was very popular and growing even more so.

Gideon didn't believe the bar, her friends or anyone else needed Rory as much as he did. He was drowning. He hadn't known how much until she had come into his life. He'd known things were bad with him. They'd gotten so much worse since he'd been shot. She'd filled all those lonely places and given him laughter. Someone to share life with. Someone to make his life worth living, because he hadn't been doing a very good job of it.

He felt the moment Mack and Paul found their way to Rory's section of the bar. It hadn't been easy to make their way through the dense crowd. With only a couple of bartenders, the customers had realized fairly quickly that she was extremely fast at making drinks for them. Gideon already knew there was no way Paul was going to be successful at reading Rory. She was moving too fast, and they could stand between those customers seated on the barstools for only so long. Others would want to order drinks and expect Mack and Paul to move out of the way once they'd been served.

Mack ordered for both men, engaging with Rory, his voice low, the noise of the crowd nearly swallowing the sound. Gideon should have told him that wouldn't work to buy them more time with her. She had acute hearing, just as Gideon did.

Paul leaned into the bar, his gaze moving over Rory, hands reaching, palms outward, looking as if he were trying to get to the napkin dispenser. Rory bent slightly toward him as she pushed the napkins closer. At the same time, she gave an icy beer to a man behind him.

Gideon felt Paul's frustration as he tried to read beneath the surface in the very short time he could before they had to move. She had already stepped back to make the drinks Mack had ordered.

Gideon knew it wasn't going to work. Paul was being jostled, and there was no way to give him a calm enough space to perform his precise psychic skill. Gideon appreciated that the youngest and newest member of their team had tried for him though. He appreciated that his adopted family would rally around when he needed them, but he feared it was far too late.

14

have mad love for you, Lydia, but go away. I didn't get to bed until four thirty this morning, and I haven't been sleeping." Rory pulled the covers over her head. "I don't care what time it is. Go away," she repeated.

"I'm sorry, hon. You need to wake up."

The combined notes of regret and urgency caused Rory to drag the covers down to her nose and force her lashes to lift just enough to focus on her friend's face. She wasn't the only one in the room. The man standing behind her was tall and grim-faced. Detective Larrsen. Her breath caught in her throat, and she grasped the covers, her first thought that something had happened to Ellen. Reason hit next. Lydia would have been hysterical.

"Gideon." She whispered his name and sat up slowly, dragging the covers with her. She wasn't wearing much. "It's Gideon. Something's happened to him." She knew the color had drained from her face. She hadn't forgiven him. She couldn't. But nothing could happen to him. She couldn't live with that. Just the thought of something happening to Gideon left her feeling sick.

As the intensity of her feelings hit, there was a stirring in her mind. Then Gideon poured in, filling every lonely, aching place she had until she didn't feel alone and apart from everyone.

Rory wrapped her arms around her middle, relief flooding her. *Red? What's wrong?*

He was there. So strong. She felt him stronger than she ever had before, as if the connection had grown between them during their separation. Or he had become more powerful. She wanted to cling to him. To stay. Never be alone again. She couldn't believe in what he was offering, no matter how enticing. No matter how much, on her side, she cared.

She closed her mind to him, regretting that she'd let him in, because now the loneliness and feelings of complete devastation were far worse than they had been before.

"No, no, honey. As far as I'm aware, Gideon's just fine," Lydia hastily reassured her, sitting on the edge of the bed and pushing back some of the hair that had escaped the braid Rory had hastily woven the night before.

"Our friends, then?" Rory was beginning to feel desperate. Why didn't they just tell her?

Once more, Lydia looked up at the detective as if asking his permission. At his nod, she took Rory's hand. "Someone beat the crap out of your car," Lydia said. "They slit all the tires and wrote graffiti all over it. It's bad, honey."

The relief was tremendous, so much so that Rory had to cover her face with the sheet. "I'm so glad it was my car and not one of you or Gideon. I was so scared when you woke me up like that." She took the sheet from her face. "There have been so many horrible things happening around here lately, I thought . . ." She trailed off.

"Get dressed," Lydia said. She stood up and left the room, with the detective following her out.

Rory closed her eyes and took several deep breaths. It was just one more thing to deal with. One at a time. She had insurance. It couldn't be that bad. She didn't have the best car in the world anyway. The car was a *thing*. Her friends were people. Gideon was Gideon.

"Get up, Laurel," she ordered aloud. "You can't hide from your problems. No one is going to help you but yourself. Stand on your own two feet." Her mantra.

Flinging the covers back, Rory placed both feet on the floor and forced herself to get up and dress. She didn't do more than splash water on her face and brush her teeth. She'd already met the man of her dreams, and he'd turned out not to be her prince. *Wouldn't you know?* She wasn't going to dress to impress, put on makeup that she really didn't know how to use anyway or try to tame her wild San Francisco foggy curls.

Lydia and Detective Larrsen were waiting in the living room for her. She noticed right away that Larrsen stood close and looked very protective of Lydia.

"Where's Ellen?" Rory asked.

"Pam and Janice are watching her," Lydia said. "They took one look at your car and immediately decided to call Detective Larrsen. They told me they'd watch Ellen so I could be with you for support."

Rory pressed her lips together. Funny, once Gideon had opened the waterworks, now the floodgates were turned on permanently. She wasn't used to kindness. Or friendship. It would be so difficult to give that up. *Gideon*. She'd lost so much when she'd lost him. The city she'd come to love. The job she enjoyed so much. These friends she'd really come to love. That had snuck up on her when she wasn't even aware.

"Don't look so sad, Rory. We'll go car shopping," Lydia promised.

"Although"—she made a little face, burst out laughing and looked up at the detective sheepishly—"I've never bought a car before. I've always taken public transportation."

"That makes sense," Detective Larrsen defended her as he led the way to the elevator. "There's very little parking in San Francisco, and if you're a native, you know how to get around with buses. There's little need to have the additional expense of a car."

Lydia leaned against the brass handrail in the elevator, her face glowing as she looked up at Larrsen. That look made Rory smile. She wanted Lydia happy. She'd struggled for a very long time, and the detective seemed to be a good man. Just because Gideon hadn't been sincere in the things he'd said to her didn't mean the cop wasn't truly interested in Lydia. How could he not be? Lydia was sweet. She was a good mother. She wasn't the clingy type. She had made it on her own without help for years.

The elevator door opened on the third floor of the parking garage, and they stepped off. Lydia seemed reluctant to view the car again and hung back a little, so Rory walked toward her parking space. Larrsen kept pace with her. She stopped when she came up on what had been her car. She just froze, unable to move.

Her hand went to her throat defensively, her breath catching there. Whoever had done such damage despised her. This was personal. Very, very personal. She just stood there staring, unable to believe the wreck had once been her car. It was barely recognizable.

Her lungs burned and it was difficult to draw in air. The parking garage spun in a curiously lazy circle. Little black dots appeared behind her eyes, and voices faded in and out. She found herself sitting abruptly on the concrete floor right in the middle of shattered glass, twisted metal and chunks of rubber. One door and part of a seat with the cushions ripped to shreds floated in and out of her line of vision.

Rory. Talk to me. Use your inhaler, baby. You need your inhaler. Where is it? Take it out and use your inhaler. You aren't breathing right.

She was hearing things. Gideon's voice. Her mind playing tricks on her. She really couldn't breathe though. She did need her inhaler; she just couldn't move her arms. They felt like lead. She couldn't lift them. She could barely look around her at all the glass from the shattered windows. The doors torn off, the trunk popped open and jagged tears in the metal as if someone had tried to tear off the trunk the way they'd ripped off the doors. All the seats had been taken out and trashed. The sides of the car had been beaten in, creating craters. The hood was ripped off and something poured all over the engine. The outside of the car was spray-painted, telling her what they were going to do to her, none of it good.

The giant letters blurred unless she really focused, but why bother? She wasn't certain why she was a bitch or a whore. Why someone was going to fuck her raw. This was pure hatred. She couldn't possibly have given anyone reason to hate her this much.

Red, I know you're upset with me, and you have every reason to be, but you have to use your inhaler. I'm coming to you. I'm on my way. If you need to call the cops, do it. I can't leave you alone when you're in trouble.

That was definitely Gideon talking in her head, not a figment of her imagination. She had to pull it together. The roaring in her ears wouldn't go away, sounding so loud it nearly drowned out his voice.

She felt a hand on the nape of her neck, pushing her head down. It should have helped, but her lungs and airway refused to open, shutting down even more. She was too close to the concrete and the dust and dirt. Her panic increased. Her heart accelerated, pounded out of control, going crazy, the pressure in her chest so severe it was painful.

Far off, she could hear voices talking, but she couldn't distinguish one from the other, and she had no clue what anyone was saying.

She became aware of being lifted. Of her palm on a chest and her inhaler pressed into her mouth.

"Breathe in, Red."

It was a command, nothing less. She heard that very distinctly. She felt the chest lift beneath her palm, and she automatically took a breath, instinctively following that same pattern. In. Out. At first, she was unaware who had her, but then his scent hit. Gideon. She was shaking so much she wouldn't have been able to hold herself upright if he hadn't been pressing her so tightly in his arms. Surrounding her with safety.

She refused to cry again. She was already a mess. He didn't need to see her as more of one. But however much she didn't want to see him, she didn't want Lydia or the detective to call an ambulance. She would be totally humiliated.

Feeling a little stronger, she made an attempt to take the inhaler herself. Her arm still wouldn't cooperate. Pins and needles began to replace the numbness, as if her body were returning to life. The roaring in her ears receded enough that she began to hear the conversations happening around her.

"I'm Detective Larrsen."

"Gideon Carpenter." Gideon kept his arms around Rory. "She has severe asthma."

"I should have known she needed her inhaler," Lydia said, a sob in her voice. "I'm sorry, Rory. I couldn't think. I just couldn't think."

"I take it you and Rory are seeing each other?"

Rory tried not to react. She knew if she objected and said she'd split up with Gideon, he'd instantly become a suspect. No way had he done this. She nodded her head, not looking at either Gideon or Lydia. She sent up a silent prayer to the universe that Lydia wouldn't contradict her.

"How did you know Rory was in trouble?" The question was asked in a mild, almost casual voice.

"I texted him when she went down," Lydia said. "Pam, Janice and I talked it over and thought Gideon should know. We were worried after we first saw the car. Rory is very independent, and we weren't sure if she would tell him, so we agreed we should. I still hesitated until she went down like that, and then I just had to."

"I see," Larrsen said. There was amusement in his voice.

Rory wasn't certain if Lydia was telling the truth or not. She sounded very honest, but then she knew Rory had broken up with Gideon. She didn't know why, and Rory hadn't told any of them. They only knew Rory had been heartbroken. Lydia was a romantic at heart, and maybe she saw this as an opportunity to get them back together.

Rory might not want suspicion to fall on Gideon, but she told herself that was because she wanted the real perpetrators to be hunted down.

"There are security cameras in the garage, right?" Gideon asked. He began to massage Rory's arms, helping to get the blood flowing much faster.

"That was the very first thing taken out. Clearly, they knew what they were doing. Every camera was destroyed coming into the parking garage. There's no recording of them driving in even on the lower levels."

"This was planned out very carefully," Gideon observed. "And it was done by more than one person."

Larrsen agreed. "Rory, did you have anything of value in your car?"

She shook her head. It was still impossible to put a coherent sentence together. Her lungs burned, but the raw ache was beginning to subside along with the terrible panic. She kept her gaze away from the wreck of her car.

"Janice said she picked up mail, registration, insurance papers and a notebook that were strewn all over the floor of the garage and shoved them in a tote bag."

"By the looks of the car, this attack was personal. Was it the same in her apartment?" Gideon asked.

Larrsen shook his head. "The break-in at the apartment didn't feel personal. My take was someone was looking for something in the furniture. None of the women bought their furniture from the same place. Nothing appeared to be taken. There was no graffiti in the apartment, like on the car. No message written."

Rory started shaking all over again when she'd just begun to get herself under control. No one had ever hated her—that she knew of. What could she have possibly done to cause someone to despise her so much? She remembered everything after her childhood. Every conversation. She didn't intentionally snub people. Or hurt their feelings. Had she ignored someone at the bar? How had she not noticed someone following her home?

"Could someone be trying to hit at you through her, Gideon?" Larrsen asked. "Do you have enemies that would do something like this to her?"

Gideon thought it over before answering. "It doesn't seem likely. Rory and I have talked at the bar where she works, but mostly after closing. It's always very late, and no one's ever around. We sit outside or just inside her apartment building in the lounge area. We did go to the Salty Dog restaurant once in public together. Sometimes we go to my place and sit on the rooftop. We keep things low-key. The point I'm making is we aren't seen in public together a lot."

"Is there a reason for that?" Larrsen asked.

Gideon shifted and pulled his wallet from his pocket. He fished a single card from it and handed it to the detective. "That would be the reason. I'm careful with her."

Larrsen studied the card a moment, nodded and handed it back to Gideon, who slid it into his wallet. "You have cameras set up in the garage?"

"Unfortunately, she rarely uses her car. We have them on the street coming to the apartments. We may have picked something up. I'll have my people go through everything we've got."

"I'd appreciate it."

Cameras? They had cameras? On her apartment building? Gideon and his people were supposed to have ceased all contact with her. She'd *threatened* him with calling the police on them. Now she was lying and telling Larrsen that Gideon was her boyfriend. She couldn't look at her car, and she couldn't look at Gideon. She couldn't inhale too deeply, or she'd drag his scent into her lungs.

She wished the earth would open up and swallow her. Was it too much to ask for an earthquake? Not a big one, just a tiny little tremor that would split the ground wide enough for her to slide right in and disappear.

What about the man you call Whitney? Rory was proud of herself for using the despicable man's name.

It isn't his style.

Obviously not him. Rory tested her legs, straightening them. They still felt like rubber, but she was gaining strength. *Could he have ordered someone to scare me?*

I don't see what the purpose would be. If he programmed you for a specific purpose and you don't have a clue what that is, why would he try to threaten you?

She didn't want to discuss Whitney or his programming with Gideon, but she didn't have anyone else. Still, she wasn't going to talk with him about it. That felt too much like forgiving him. What he'd done was betrayal at the worst.

"I'm better." She tested her voice. Shaky. She sounded scared. Not fierce. "I'm going to be fine. I really appreciate everyone's concern." There was that terrible lump in her throat coming back. She didn't feel fine. She felt lost.

Are you going to look at me?

No. I do appreciate you saving me from an embarrassing ambulance ride, but you need to leave. I don't want to see you. It hurts too much, and that's me being honest. I'm not pretending you didn't get to me, because you did. I don't know what your motivation was, Gideon. Maybe you play a lot of games with women, but I'm not someone who can deal with your level of sophisticated manipulation.

Even as she flung the accusation at him, she knew she had struck out at him to hurt him, and it was entirely unfair. She might not understand why he'd done what he had, but it hadn't been to play her. He had genuine feelings for her, and he was every bit as devastated as she was. Rory was ashamed of herself. She rarely hurt others on purpose. In fact, she didn't remember ever doing so.

Gideon didn't react right away. He sat very still, holding her on his lap, his arms surrounding her as if he could keep her safe from the maniacs who had destroyed her car. She tried to tell herself Gideon had destroyed her heart the same way, but she felt his pain. It was impossible not to, even though he wasn't trying to share it with her. His devastation came off him in waves. Swamping him. Swamping her.

I'm sorry. I was deliberately striking out at you. I know playing me wasn't your motivation. I don't understand you or why you did it, but it wasn't for that reason. I tried to hurt you back.

He ran his hand down the back of her hair. His fingers tangled in her braid for a brief moment, making her heart stutter. *I'm already hurting enough, Red. There's no need to try to make it any worse, although I deserve it.*

She hated the fact that she wanted to soothe him. She needed to get away from him. At the same time, she wanted to prolong her time with him. She was beginning to breathe much easier. The blood was flowing just fine to her legs. She really didn't have an excuse to stay in his lap other than she felt safe in his arms.

When she began to shift her weight to slide off his lap, he tightened his hold. "I'll carry you away from this glass."

"It's safety glass," she reminded.

"Nevertheless."

"You can't carry me," she practically hissed it, trying not to sound like a shrew. *You're wounded.*

Thanks for the reminder. I doubt I would remember without everyone telling me every few minutes.

It wasn't his normal voice. There wasn't sarcasm or self-pity; there was more of an edge, a bite. She was open to his mind, and she caught images of a little boy with a mop of thick black hair and too-old blue eyes staring up at her. There were dark bruises on his face. Swelling around his eyes and jaw.

Do you need another reminder, Gideon? I can get your sister out here. If you'd rather we practice on your sister instead of this dog, I'd be happy to get her for you. She's going into the whore stable anyway. Won't make me much in the way of money, but at least she isn't worthless like this old dog. Your choice.

Rory drew in her breath when Gideon slammed his mind closed to hers. The detachment was harsh and abrupt. He dropped his chin onto the top of her hair, his arms tightening around her. She didn't move when she had been prepared to slide from his lap. That small vignette was her first glimpse of anything personal from his childhood. The memory, as tiny as it was, was heartbreaking. She knew something terrible was being demanded of that young Gideon. Rory felt the need to console him. Console the child as well as the grown man.

"Are you going to be okay, Rory?" Lydia asked. "Can you

breathe now? I should have thought to find your inhaler. I thought I was good in a crisis, but I failed you epically." She'd said it twice.

"Lydia," Detective Larrsen said, his tone gentle, "there's no need to be upset with yourself. Looking at this wreck and then seeing your friend fall to the ground was terrifying. You did your best to support her. I think it would be wise for both of you to go back to the apartment and let us sort this out."

Lydia's eyes met Rory's. "Are you coming?"

"I'll be right behind you. I'm just getting my legs. Would you mind bringing my nebulizer to the lounge where we always meet?" Rory knew giving Lydia something to do would help ground her again. She'd never seen Rory have a full-blown panic attack before, and it must have been frightening.

Lydia brightened immediately and nodded. "Yes, of course."

Larrsen watched Lydia until she was safely in the elevator and it was on the way down to the second floor.

Rory took the time to look around her. A small crowd had gathered. She spotted Javier and Ethan. Javier didn't look very happy. His phone was out, and he seemed to be taking pictures of the wreck of her car from every angle he could. There were several people she recognized from the apartments. They looked horrified. Scott Tinsdale stood in the middle of the little crowd talking to another man she'd seen in the bar twice. Scott looked up and met her eyes. She couldn't help the icy-cold fear that slid down her spine.

What is it? Gideon followed her gaze.

Tinsdale had already turned away. Some of the crowd was dispersing as uniformed officers were insisting they leave. He moved with the others, unhurried.

Gideon, see the man in the gray shirt wearing the gray newsboy cap? He's maybe thirty? Jeans and expensive sneakers? He's been in the bar a couple of times. He's never talked to me. Always orders a whiskey. No ice. No frills. Never has more than two. Tinsdale talked to him briefly after I spotted him. Tinsdale may have just been standing next to him and used him to distract me by just simply talking to him.

She saw that Ethan had slipped into the crowd, most likely shadowing Tinsdale. She noted that Gideon hadn't shared with Larrsen that Tinsdale was connected to Harvey Matters, but then she hadn't either.

I passed on the message to Harvey without trying to read it, and then I deleted it permanently from my phone just in case that horrible Detective Westlake decided to question me again and insisted I show him my phone.

Once again, Gideon stroked a caress down the back of her hair before tangling his fingers in it. He stood with one easy, fluid movement before she had another chance to protest. He did so with her in his arms. His strength absolutely astounded her every time. He carried her across the parking garage to the elevator before he set her feet on the concrete floor. He didn't let go of her, keeping one arm wrapped around her waist.

Did Harvey threaten you in any way?

No. He seemed afraid for me. For all of my friends, especially Lydia and Cindy with the kids. He didn't like that he had put them in danger. He said he had nothing to do with killing the cop or his friends, but someone was trying to frame him.

She needed to keep her mouth closed. She had no idea why every single time she was near Gideon, she felt compelled to share everything with him. "You don't need to ride the elevator with me, Gideon. You really have to go away."

"I'm not going to be able to stop reaching out to you." He made the revelation like he was confessing a sin.

She didn't answer him. She should have, but the image of that little boy with those sad, too-old eyes welled up and made her heart ache for him. She wasn't going to forgive or forget what he'd done. She couldn't ever trust him to put her first, but he came when he shouldn't have, when he knew she was in trouble. His doctor was probably having convulsions right about now.

The elevator door opened, and she started to step in. Gideon's palm wrapped around the nape of her neck, halting her. "It's hard to let you go."

Rory didn't turn around. She hadn't once looked up at him. She still didn't. She couldn't. She wasn't that strong. Her world had already begun to unravel. She wanted to cling to him, but he wasn't real. She wanted him to be, but he wasn't. She had to accept that what she wanted in a man, in a partner, wasn't the man she'd thought Gideon was. That wasn't his fault; it just was what it was.

"I understand, Gideon. I really do. It's difficult for me too. You need to go home. I have to get inside and try to sleep. I'm working again tonight and we're down a bartender."

"All right, Red." He leaned down and swept her hair from her neck.

Rory felt the brush of his lips against her skin, and it felt like a lash of flames. Then he was gone, and she was ice-cold all over again. She refused to turn around and look out of the glass door to watch him go. She felt his gaze on her and she couldn't face him. Gripping the brass guardrail with both hands, she took the ride to the main floor, where she knew the women waited in the lounge for her.

Exhaustion settled over her as she stepped off into the wide foyer. Her phone began to ding frantically, as if someone had repeatedly messaged her. She saw that her boss, Brad Fitzpatrick, had called, leaving her four voice mails, and he'd texted her numerous times. He clearly was panicky, trying to get ahold of her. Afraid someone had told him about her car and he was worried, she called him back.

Her boss hadn't heard about her problems. He had enough of his own, and now he dumped them on Rory, as if she could fix everything. She turned around to start down the hall and ran straight into Javier. He scared her because her warning system hadn't gone off, and he was so silent she hadn't heard him. Now her heart was pounding, and she wanted to resort to violence. He looked calm and in control, the way he always did.

"Go away. I'm not talking to you."

One of his eyebrows shot up. He didn't stand aside. "Why are you angry with me?"

Rory went around him, or tried to. He just paced along beside her as she stalked down the hall toward the smaller lounge. "Because you won't leave Gideon alone. You're driving him crazy, Javier. You can't do that to him. He knows his limitations. If you keep pushing him and reminding him he's hurt, he's going to explode. You need to stop. He's not a child." She yanked at the door to the lounge, but he slammed his palm against it, effectively keeping it from opening.

"You're telling me you're angry with me because I'm upsetting Gideon?"

"Yes. Now go away. I already have a major headache from a million other things, and you're just adding to it."

"I have an idea why someone might have trashed your car. You might want to hear it."

Rory wished she did want to know. She pressed her hands to her throbbing temples. "Right now, Javier, I want to put my feet up, drink a cup of coffee and pretend none of this is happening. I don't want to think about my car. Or Gideon. Or you. Or Harvey. Or Jarrod. Or dead men. Not the bar. Or bartenders leaving in droves. I just want coffee."

Javier studied her face for a long moment, and then he removed his hand, dropped it to the knob and pulled open the door. "I'll talk to you later." He sounded firm.

"Yeah, you do that. I'll be the one at the bar. Day and night. It'll be my new home."

"Maybe try getting some sleep."

"Not sure when that's supposed to happen."

"And use your nebulizer. You're wheezing."

As if she didn't know. She entered the lounge, and Javier pulled the door closed behind her. The women were waiting. Rory gave them a little wave and flung herself into her favorite chair. Lydia had set up her machine and had her medicine right beside it. Most importantly, her favorite to-go mug was sitting on the end table beside her machine.

"Hot coffee. Who do I ask to marry me?" She took a cautious sip and found it hot and reviving. "I'm in love. But maybe with the coffee."

The women laughed.

"My life has gone to hell," Rory announced. "It isn't a laughing matter. The only good thing aside from all of you is this delicious and lifesaving coffee. Every sign pointed to me leaving San Francisco as soon as possible. I make up my mind to go, I turn in my two-weeks' notice, and my boss is practically in tears begging me to stay. That makes me feel guilty, but I hold on to my resolve and decide to stick to my guns and refuse to retract it, even though we are down a bartender."

"It was Gideon," Cindy said. "I don't know why you two broke up, but you wanted to leave because of him. It wasn't about the crazy things happening here at the apartments. The break-ins or dead bodies. You would have stayed. It was him. You're in love with him."

Rory was grateful she didn't have a mouthful of coffee or she would have spewed it across the room. "Love?" She choked out the word. "That's a pretty scary word to throw around. I don't know what that even means."

"Really?" Lydia challenged her. "I've seen the look on your face when you say his name."

Rory waved their comments away. "I was going somewhere important with this commentary about fate and destiny directing my life." She took another sip of revitalizing coffee. She was coming back to life.

"Now, someone has destroyed my vehicle, my one means of transportation out of San Francisco. I can buy another car, but it will take a little time. I'll need to get the insurance money first." She tipped her head back to stare at the ceiling. "I just received another call from Brad, my boss at the bar. He didn't seem to care about my car. He was in a complete state of panic. It seems Barry, his most experienced bartender, has to leave unexpectedly."

She looked around at her friends, hoping for sympathy. There was none to be seen on their faces. In fact, they looked elated.

"Barry the bartender had to leave unexpectedly?" Lydia echoed.

"Yes. His mother had a heart attack." Rory tried not to sound glum. That was just plain mean, and she wasn't a mean person, or at least she tried not to be. But she was feeling sorry for herself. She hadn't been able to stop thinking about Gideon. She had become one of *those* women. Mopey. Thinking about him all the time and worrying about his health. An idiot. She could still feel his kiss on the back of her neck. It burned, as if he'd left behind a brand.

"Barry's going to have to take care of his mother. That means if I leave too, Brad will be down too many bartenders. Even if he hires someone else, he won't have anyone experienced enough." She looked at Lydia. "This is your chance. I can get you on and train you if you really want to try the job. I don't think I'll be going anywhere for the next few weeks."

Lydia's face lit up. "Do you think I could really do it? I haven't had any formal training."

"I've taught you the skills, Lydia. You've studied online. You know the glassware, the equipment, how to clean it; you can change out a keg, at least in theory; you know the lingo. You have knowledge of beer, wine and cocktails. How to mix the drinks. You just need to believe in yourself and sell it."

Lydia glanced at the others and then back to Rory. "The idea is scary."

"You can start as a barback, but you won't make near the money. Brad's going to have to bring up our best barback as it is, so we're going to be down one. He'd hire you for that position, but honestly, it would be better if you just come on board and start making drinks right away. I know you can do it. We've spent hours now practicing, and you've gotten fast. You can make them in your sleep."

"I can do it. I know I can. But then there's Ellen. I'll worry."

Cindy cleared her throat. "I'm staying. I'll put a bed in my room, and she can sleep in my apartment when you're working. You can come and get her when you get off. She'll just be asleep, Lydia, and she probably won't even know."

Lydia looked around at all of them, took a deep breath, looking determined, and nodded.

Rory measured her medication into the machine and turned it on. At least Lydia was going to get something good out of all the mess going on.

15

The bar was noisy and packed as usual. Rory thought it was becoming even more popular. She was happy for Brad. He was a good man, paid his employees well, treated them even better and was fair if things took a bad turn. As a rule, he was in a good mood. He worked hard and expected his employees to do the same. For that reason, she had been up front about Lydia.

Rory had asked Brad for a private meeting. She wanted to be as transparent with him as possible because she thought he was fair. She'd explained that Lydia was a good friend who needed the work. She also told him that she'd spent weeks teaching her and that Lydia had also gone online to learn as much as possible. She was hardworking and would give her all at the job, but she had no practical experience. Rory was still asking for the favor. Brad had agreed to try Lydia out, more, Rory thought, because he needed extra hands at the bar than for any other reason. He also knew he owed Rory, and this was the first time she'd asked for anything.

Lydia was doing great. She worked hard and didn't slow down

even if she accidentally stepped in the barback's path. She hadn't yet picked up the natural flow of traffic behind the bar, but she was getting there. Rory was proud of her.

Rory worked on autopilot, keeping one eye on Lydia just in case she needed help, which she did occasionally. She scanned the bar for trouble whenever she felt a possible shadow. She tried to stay alert for trouble, but being the only experienced bartender in a crowded bar made it difficult to do much besides keep her mind on what was happening around her.

There were two women seated at a table at the back of the bar, not in her section, who she had originally considered might be part of Gideon's family. There was just something about them that seemed different, but she couldn't put her finger on what it was. Neither paid the least attention to her. They shared an animated conversation that flowed naturally between them.

Both were beautiful, but one of the women was absolutely gorgeous. That could be trouble if the crowd turned rowdy, or any of the groups of men drinking quite a bit turned ugly. She tried to keep an eye out for them, but after Rory was slammed with so many customers, she couldn't watch over the two women sitting close to the front door. That was the bouncer's job.

Halfway through the night, she began to get a nagging feeling in her gut that told her something was wrong. No matter how many times she scanned the bar, she couldn't find the source of the lengthening shadow. It seemed distant.

The last thing she wanted to do was reach out to Gideon, especially since she'd already opened herself up to him. Each time they connected telepathically, the bond between them only strengthened. Her declaration to have him stay away from her hadn't lasted very long. But what if he had ripped open that wound again, and he was bleeding internally? He had come close to death the last time.

Torn, she made several drinks, hoping the feeling would go away. It didn't. She glanced at Lydia several times. She was laughing and talking with the customers, looking carefree, although Rory could see a little bit of strain on her face from trying to concentrate. The nagging feeling that something was wrong kept growing. Eventually, Rory felt she had no choice.

Reluctantly, she reached out to him. *Gideon?* She held her breath, waiting for him to answer. She should have tried to text Javier. She'd kept his phone number. Why hadn't she done that first?

Red.

Just his name for her. The relief was tremendous. *Are you feeling weak at all?*

No, not really. I'm feeling fine. Why?

She tried to analyze his denial. Not really. What did that mean? *Do me a favor and send for that doctor of yours. He's always driving you nuts. I know it's the middle of the night, but they have to earn their money somehow. Have him go to you right away and examine you. Make sure that wound didn't open back up.*

He was silent for a little while, but she felt him moving through her mind. She talked to several customers, answering them, giving them bright smiles, all the while focusing her attention on Gideon, willing him to do as she asked.

You're certain the danger isn't to you? It isn't there in the bar?

Gideon. She hissed his name, allowing her impatience to show.

Red, the moment you asked me to call the doctor, I texted him. He's on the way. I feel the foreshadowing you're feeling. The intensity is growing. I'm certain the repair the doc did on me is holding. I'll have him check, but I don't think your warning system is going off because of me. Who else? Can you judge the distance?

If not Gideon, who would it be? She did a quick rundown of her friends. Lydia was working with her. Janice and Pam were at work.

She sent them both a quick text, asking if everything was going okay. Cindy was watching Ellen, and she would have immediately gotten ahold of Lydia if anything had happened to the little girl. Sally had come to the bar to lend moral support to Lydia. That accounted for everyone she was close to. She waited a little anxiously until Pam and Janice checked in with her, affirming they were both fine.

She made drinks and talked to customers as she assessed the shadow spreading through her. It wasn't going away. *Distance.* She texted Cindy just to be on the safe side. Making sure.

Doc's here. He's checking me internally. Says repairs are holding and mending better than last time.

Not Gideon, then. Who? What? Was someone in danger? Could it be Harvey? She wasn't close to Harvey, but she knew him. She couldn't very well text him. She'd broken off contact with him and didn't want to start up with the police breathing down her neck. Still . . .

Why hadn't Cindy texted her back? She nearly dropped a glass as she spun it around to place it on the bar, and that brought her up short. She was really agitated. It was nearly closing time. Cindy was most likely asleep. There was no reason to be panicking. But she was.

Gideon, is Javier around? What if it was Javier? She hadn't even thought of him. He could be in trouble. He just seemed so invincible.

He was here with me when you called. He just left to look around.

Her phone vibrated, and she stepped back from the bar to take the time to look at the text from Cindy. It was long.

Called Larrsen and his partner. Lydia's apartment broken into. Same with Sally's. They destroyed furniture like in ours but didn't take anything. The noise was reported, and two men were seen running from Sally's apartment. They were both heavier set and wore those pullover beanie things with the eyes cut out. Two other men had been in Lydia's apartment. They were seen running down the stairs. One was slender, pretty fit, the other looked older and a bit heavier, both wore masks covering their faces.

Rory let her breath out slowly. Her lungs burned for air. This was another blow she hadn't been expecting, but she should have been. She and her friends were being targeted, but she couldn't figure out why. Whoever had done this was searching for something. What? And why?

Not the worst. Jarrod Flawson's body found. Stuffed in suitcase between machines in laundry room. The lady who found him was so hysterical they had to sedate her. He'd been there for some time. He'd been tortured and shot, the same as Dustin, except he was stuffed in the suitcase.

Rory had to work at keeping her body from panicking. All the signs were there. Numbness. Tingling. Dizziness. She signaled to Brad she needed to use her inhaler and would be right back. He nodded and stepped up to take her place.

Rory went to the break room and sank down into a chair, needing to get off her feet before she fell to the floor while she used her inhaler. No doubt Harvey was next if they could find him. Then her? Was Harvey right about framing him? Framing her?

Talk to me, Red. I can feel how upset you are.

She sent him the text from Cindy. She saw no reason not to share. He would know soon enough there had been another break-in. And another death.

Ask Cindy if this woman who found the body or the police confirmed who the suitcase belonged to.

Rory's breath caught in her lungs. She hadn't thought of that. It hadn't occurred to her to even ask that question. Panic began to grip her all over again.

Just take slow, steady breaths. It's my job to think of all the possibilities, sweetheart. What was the point of putting the body in the laundry room? Whoever killed him wanted him found. The suitcase was wedged between two machines. The killer knew that sooner or later someone was going to get curious and open it.

Rory forced her breathing to stay under control, but it took effort. Gideon made sense. She asked Cindy the question.

Black suitcase on rollers. Very expensive-looking, Cindy texted back. Shandra, the woman who found the suitcase, even has a photo of it.

Rory closed her eyes as relief poured through her. *Not mine, Gideon. If the intention was to frame me, they didn't use my suitcase. I have cheap but very adequate ones.*

Are Lydia and Sally aware their apartments have been broken into?

She was very grateful Gideon changed the subject. *I don't think so. Not yet. Even with a new job, Lydia will have a difficult time replacing the contents of her apartment. She has renter's insurance, but the money isn't going to come in overnight. I've got money I saved to move that I'll be able to help her with, but she's very independent, and she won't want to take it. She'll be embarrassed, and it could ruin our friendship.*

What if the money wasn't specifically coming from you? Or just to her? You said your friend Sally lost everything as well. You did. So did Janice and Pam and Cindy. That's all of you, right? We can set up something online to donate to, but also there in the apartment building and at the bar and in the harbor and at local restaurants. That would add up fast. We know a few people who are generous with contributions. Let me see what I can get started. If we have it in place immediately, all we need to do is figure out what to do for a couple of days for her and the others.

Gideon's instant response was the reason she had fallen so fast and hard for him. There was no doubt in her mind that he would have something in the works by morning to ensure that money would be flowing toward fixing Lydia's problem. Not just Lydia's but all their problems. For all she knew, he might have already been doing that. It would be just like him.

She wished things were different between them. She wanted, this once, to lean on his strength. It wasn't as if she felt weak, just tired, exhausted from all the body blows.

That's a good idea. Thank you for thinking of it.

I'll get that started now.

In the middle of the night?

Can't sleep. Haven't been sleeping since I screwed things up with you. I keep going over it and what I should have done differently. But then I'm not even sure the things I'm thinking I should have done would have been right either. Never had a mother or father to show me the way. I guess those lessons count for something.

She felt his genuine regret. Rory put her inhaler away and rubbed at her lower lip. She didn't know any more about relationships than he did. Who was she to judge? *Since you're going to be up anyway, and I am too after work, maybe you can fill me in on your childhood.*

She found herself holding her breath. This was his opportunity. She'd cracked open the door. A crack only. She hoped he recognized that was all it was. He could take it or leave it.

Like you, I never talk about it because mine was a shit childhood.

I don't remember my past. You do. She wasn't going to push him. If he didn't want that door to open any further, a part of her would be grateful. She wasn't even certain what she would do if he told her personal things he never talked about to anyone. She was terrified to think about letting him back in.

Our place?

She stood up. Break was over. She had to get back to work, but her treacherous heart skipped a beat at his question. They had a special place. It was rather silly when he had his cool rooftop and she had hers. The little patio in the Koi Garden where they spent those first early morning hours just talking and laughing together. She treasured that time. The San Francisco fog had enclosed them, making her feel as if they were the only two people in the world. They talked about everything and nothing, yet she had fallen hard for him.

She should go back to the apartments and help Lydia, but she knew Lydia would stay with Cindy. Sally would be fine with Janice and Pam. She had no idea where she would be staying, but it didn't matter, not if Gideon was really going to share something of himself with her. She wanted his childhood. Nothing else. Something of his that was private that he didn't share, didn't give to others. Something she could hold on to even if she never had him for herself.

See you there if you don't change your mind. She gave him an out and abruptly broke off all contact with him.

Rory knew by now that Brad would be feeling desperate. Once more behind the bar, the customers were lined up several rows deep. She immediately took over her station, spotting Detective Larrsen entering as she stepped up, glanced quickly through the tickets and then took several orders at once. She went on autopilot fast, keeping her eye on Larrsen, knowing he was about to break the news to Sally and Lydia.

This was Lydia's first day on the job, and the pressure on her was horrendous. If she blew her one chance with Brad, she could lose the high-paying job she needed. The tips alone were better than the money she made from her day job. She wasn't just good; she had every appearance of being one of the better bartenders, who would be sought after if she kept at it.

Rory was able to get drinks out at a fast rate, moving the lines quickly, making the waitresses happy. She took care of the beer drinkers, mixed the cocktails fast, especially the ones that were the same, and then the whiskey drinkers. Next were those in the blenders.

She loved Kevin, her barback. He kept up with her with the ice, bitters and syrups. Each time she needed citrus, ice or a fresh keg, he had it immediately. She never had to ask. Her glasses were clean and replaced. She was always generous sharing her tips and was elated that Brad was just as fair with all his employees. He treated his barbacks as valuable members of the family he was trying to create. He'd had setbacks, losing two of his experienced bartenders, but he wanted his business to succeed, and he paid as much as he could to waitresses and barbacks, more so than other bars.

Larrsen finally reached Lydia. She looked to Brad, asking for a break. He nodded and took her position. Lydia allowed Larrsen and Sally to step behind the bar and accompany her to the break room. Rory knew what a body blow it had been to see her apartment torn to shreds. It was such a violation to know that someone had been in your personal space, that you weren't safe.

Sally lived alone, just as Rory did. That really made a woman feel unsafe. Lydia had a child to protect. Ellen was only three. It must be devastating to think that you might not be able to keep your child safe. And then there was replacing your things. That was not an easy task.

Rory hadn't had much. She moved around. But the others had many items they treasured, some of monetary value, but most were sentimental. Rory's notebooks with her lyrics and her guitar were the most sentimental items she had. Fortunately, both had remained mostly intact.

She hustled even faster, trying to cover more customers so that if Lydia fell completely apart, Brad wouldn't get too upset if she left. Rory would be able to explain to him after she closed the bar. Brad glanced at his watch a few times, but he was clearly aware

Larrsen was a policeman, and he didn't demand Lydia return when her break was over.

Sally and Detective Larrsen emerged first. Sally had obviously been crying. They walked together out of the bar. Brad's gaze followed them out and then flicked to Rory before turning back to the customers. Rory's phone vibrated. She served more customers and then pulled it out to glance down.

They broke into my apartment and Sally's. Ellen's with Cindy. I'm not losing this job. Be out in a minute.

Rory continued to work for another five minutes before Lydia came out of the back room. She had obviously washed her face and applied fresh makeup before coming out. Lydia tapped Brad on the shoulder and indicated she was able to return to her position. He looked her over before stepping aside with a little nod.

Rory kept her eye on Lydia, but she didn't have to. Lydia did her job like a professional. She seemed more determined than ever to work with the customers and get every drink right. After closing, she helped clean. Brad came over to help as well.

"Tell me what's going on, you two."

Lydia took the cleaner out of Rory's hand. "You're allergic to this. Let me do it."

"What do you mean, she's allergic to the cleaner? She closes all the time and uses that cleaner. She's never said a word," Brad protested.

"She runs home and showers," Lydia explained. "Five of us have had our apartments broken into and everything destroyed. Rory's was broken into a few nights ago, and mine tonight. Fortunately, a friend was watching my daughter in her apartment, not mine."

"Your apartment was broken into and everything was destroyed, yet you stayed and finished your shift?" Brad said.

"There wasn't much I could do about what happened. I knew I couldn't get into my apartment because the police were photographing everything. I'm going to sleep at Cindy's." Lydia glanced up from where she was cleaning the bar. "Cindy has extra beds because the boys are still at her parents. She said you can sleep there too, Rory. Warren—" She stopped. "I mean, Detective Larrsen is coming back to walk us home."

Rory was tempted to tease her about the detective, but Lydia was doing her best to be very professional. She wanted Brad to think she could handle any crisis.

"We'll have to do a fundraiser," Brad said. "I'll get something put together fast, and we'll have your apartments put back together in no time. I'm not having two of my employees out on the street. Do you need money for hotel rooms for the next week?"

Lydia stopped working to look at him, blinking rapidly. Rory wasn't in the least surprised by Brad's generosity. She knew he couldn't really afford it, but he would do his best to help them out.

"I'm good, Brad," Rory said, giving Lydia time to recover. "And we do have a place to stay. That's so sweet of you. Thank you. That means a lot that you'd want to help us."

"Does that mean I have the job?" Lydia asked.

"Yeah, kid, you've got the job. Larrsen's here to walk you two home. Let the others finish closing tonight," Brad said. "He's outside the back door. He just texted me. Get out of here, both of you."

"Thanks, Brad," Rory said again. Lydia gave him a little tentative wave.

Instantly Rory spotted Gideon standing in the darker shadows. He stood several feet behind the detective. Her gaze slid past him to scan the parking lot. Gideon wasn't alone; she was certain Javier or one of the others was close, but she couldn't spot anyone.

"Lydia, Gideon is waiting for me, if you'll be okay," Rory said. Lydia hugged her. "You're certain?"

"It will give you a little time to be alone," Rory whispered in her ear. "You need that. Take your time walking back. Cry if you need to, before you get back to Ellen and everyone else. It's okay to lean on him. Larrsen's a good man."

Lydia clung to her for a brief minute. "He is, isn't he?"

Rory tightened her hold. "I was very proud of you tonight. You were awesome."

"I'm a good bartender."

"Yes, you are." Rory let her go to hand her over to the detective. "She got the job."

Larrsen smiled down at Lydia. "There wasn't a doubt in my mind that you would. Congratulations. We'll have to celebrate."

Lydia smiled up at him and took the hand he offered her. "I'll see you back at the apartment," Lydia said to Rory.

Rory watched her friend walk away, Lydia's body very close to the detective. Larrsen's posture was very protective, bringing an ache to Rory's heart. She pressed a fist to her chest. She wanted that for Lydia. She also wanted that for herself. She was probably making the biggest mistake of her life meeting Gideon. She'd reached out to him in a moment of weakness. The entire day had been one long moment of weakness.

Gideon's hand brushed lightly down the back of her hair and then settled on the small of her back. "How is she?"

"She's strong. She was absolutely magnificent tonight. I asked Brad to give her a chance when she had no experience. He did it for me, but he didn't want to. We both knew we'd get slammed tonight." She didn't look up at him. She couldn't. Not yet.

His hand felt like a hot brand on her back, urging her forward. She took that first step toward the path that was familiar, the one leading to the gardens on the other side of her apartments, where the secluded covered patio was. She thought of it as their place. She'd never once gone there during the day, and she knew she never would without him.

"She didn't let me down. She worked hard and she knew every-thing. She'd studied and practiced at home so much, it was like she'd been bartending for years. She didn't let anything throw her, not even when she was told about her apartment."

"You admire her."

"So do you." That was one of the things she'd noticed about him right away. He was obviously extremely intelligent and had money, yet he never seemed to look down on anyone. He paid attention to the waiters and waitresses, addressing them by name. He thanked them and tipped them well.

He didn't answer. He never did if she gave him a compliment. That was another thing she'd noticed about him. He was quiet whenever she said anything nice about him.

"Gideon, do you like who you are?" She didn't look up at him but kept walking along the little path, the shortcut between the buildings she hadn't known was there until Gideon had shown it to her.

He remained silent for several steps as they walked together. "Like who I am?" he finally echoed. "That's an interesting question. I guess I never really thought about it. I like what I do for our country. For others."

His answer bothered her. Really bothered her. There was a heaviness in him that she'd felt from the beginning. The more time she spent with him, connected mind to mind, the more she was able to sense that burden he bore.

"That's not the same thing, Gideon. I'm asking about you. The man you are. I like me as a person. Do you like you?"

She had the impression that the burden he carried made him feel unworthy of happiness. Of a good life. He had stepped in front of Javier and taken the bullets that would have ended Javier's life. Gideon had done so deliberately, knowing he would die. Javier had said it wasn't the first time. More than once now, she caught glimpses of darker shadows in Gideon that made her afraid for him. She'd lashed out at Javier for continually reminding Gideon of his wounds, but it wasn't only Javier. She was just as guilty. She knew Javier wasn't the only one. His team members were all concerned for him. Was that concern because, like her, they sensed Gideon just didn't care enough about his own life?

Rory found herself working to control the sudden rapid beating of her heart. Gideon was a good man whether he thought so or not. Why didn't he see that?

"I promised myself I'd be honest with you, Red." There was reluctance in his voice. "So, no, I don't think much of myself, especially after what I did to you."

"I've had time to think things through. If you believed I was a threat to a baby, you would have had to take steps to protect the child. Maybe you didn't protect me, but you did the child when you couldn't do both. You knowingly sacrificed your own happiness to ensure the baby's safety, and there's something beautiful and noble in that."

"I hurt you."

There was no denying that fact. No getting around it. "Yes, you did. That doesn't make you a bad person, Gideon. I don't think hurting me was where you started thinking you were a bad person."

They were coming up on the gardens. He opened the gates, and the large arbor with climbing vines seemed to welcome them as they passed under it and stepped onto the flat stones leading to the small patio where they'd enjoyed sitting together surrounded by the various flowers and grasses growing throughout the garden.

Gideon pulled out a chair and waited for her to settle in it. She liked facing the rose trees. Some of them were tall, with branches extending out and covered in small pink roses. Others were a little smaller, with larger yellow blossoms. The newer rose trees were much smaller but still blossoming and had various colors of flowers on them.

Gideon took the chair to her right, where he could see her and the entrance to the garden, but also keep an eye on either side of them. He waited for her to take out her travel nebulizer and put her medication in it before speaking.

"You have a great deal of compassion in you, Rory, but you know you haven't looked at me once since you walked out on me."

She hadn't. She couldn't. She nodded her head in acknowledgment. Understanding intellectually why he'd had to do what he did was one thing. Admiring him for it went along with that. Her heart didn't necessarily understand. That was a different situation altogether. She couldn't go through a betrayal again. He had his family. His loyalties. Whatever he did with them, that was a lifetime commitment.

She pressed her fingertips to her lips to keep him from seeing them tremble. She wasn't going to cry, although she felt burning behind her eyelids. She hadn't agreed to meet him to make him feel worse. She knew he suffered. She knew he was devastated. She hadn't wanted to give him false hope any more than she wanted to give herself false hope. The temptation to be with him had been too strong to resist. That was the truth, and she always made herself face the truth.

"I know, Gideon. I'm not being entirely fair, but I'm trying. I just want you to talk to me. Tell me about you. Your childhood. You've never given me anything of you. I need that to understand you." She just needed to know about him. She needed to hear his voice. To sit with him. To be with him. She just needed . . . *him.*

He sighed. Ran both hands through his hair to create more chaos. She watched him out of the corner of her eye, trying not to look at his face. She liked his hair unruly. Untamed. It went along with that man she'd first seen in the bar. By turns sweet and gentle and then predatory and dangerous. Sexy and tempting. He had so many looks.

"It isn't pretty, Red. In fact, most of the time, I can't sleep. You already have nightmares. You're sensitive and compassionate. Putting my childhood in your head might not be a good idea."

"There you go again, Gideon. Protecting everyone around you. I'm asking you to tell me. Do your friends know your childhood? What you went through?"

"Some of it." His voice was clipped. Abrupt. "But no, not the things I would be telling you."

He was saying he would understand if she retaliated and told her friends. Even his friends. She wasn't like that. If he told her the darkest moments in his life, she would never repeat them. She would hold them close to her, thankful he trusted her and wanted to repair the damage he'd done enough to give that to her. She wasn't going to say that to him. She wouldn't use the words "trust" or "safe." She would let him make up his mind.

She started the nebulizer and kept her gaze on the San Francisco sky. It was dark, and the fog had rolled in over the water. It looked ominous, but it hadn't reached the harbor or inland yet. There were clouds drifting, but she caught glimpses of stars.

The cold night air made her shiver a little, but she preferred cold to heat, and she was certain Gideon had brought a blanket with him to tuck around her. He carried it in the backpack he wore. He'd set the pack beside his chair, and she indicated it with a small gesture. He didn't need more than that sign, pulling the blanket out and folding it around her.

"I grew up in a neighborhood ruled by a mafia family. It wasn't a sleek, cool mafia family like you see in movies or read about. At least not from my perspective. My father was involved. Most of the families I knew were involved, none in a good way. It turns out my father probably was a sociopath, but as a little kid, I didn't know that. I just knew he was cruel, and everyone, including me, was afraid of him, for good reason."

A chill went down her spine. A premonition that whatever he was about to tell her was far worse than anything she might have conceived of. Rory wanted to know about Gideon's past. She'd thought what drove him to be so protective had happened to him when he'd been living on the street, not when he'd had a home and family.

"He ran a whorehouse, but his favorite job was to do what he called "keep people in line." That was his joy in life: to hurt others. To see their pain. He was very good at causing pain, and he knew a million ways, emotional and physical, to cause it. He expected me to follow in his footsteps, and he'd take me along with him to proudly show me his work."

She inhaled the medicine because she couldn't do anything else. Her heart hurt for that child. For Gideon. The stars above her blurred together. Beneath the blanket, she gripped her thigh hard with her free hand, wishing the world were a better place. Picturing Gideon as a child with his beautiful blue eyes and mop of curly black hair, his protective nature. The last thing he would ever want to do was to hurt someone. What was wrong with his father that he wouldn't know that?

Gideon was in her head. Reading her mind.

"Red. He did know I couldn't bear seeing him taking a hammer to a man or woman or child. Not to their pets. He wanted me to suffer. He enjoyed my pain and tears every bit as much as he enjoyed those of the ones he was torturing and killing. He was making a man out of me, he'd say. He'd try to force me to help him. He'd threaten to kill my sister if I didn't help him. I had a dog, and he'd threaten to kill my dog. He'd beat me nearly every day to help me get tougher. He did it in front of my mother."

Rory's hand crept from under the blanket to her throat. She

needed to feel the pulse of her heart beating there. Taking the nebulizer from her mouth, she lowered it to the table. "Didn't your mother try to stop him?"

"She laughed and cheered him on. She was a junkie and would do whatever he said. She whored for him when his friends came over when he told her to. More than once, he had her heat up knives and press them into me. She would do it and laugh as she did, all the while telling me to stop being a baby if I made a sound."

Rory wanted him to stop talking. He was peeling the layers away from those shadows inside him, the ones covering the part of him he was ashamed of. She no longer wanted him to share his horrific childhood traumas with her, but maybe he needed to.

"Inevitably, there came a time when he wouldn't take no for an answer, and he insisted I torture my dog or my sister. I tried to go after him, but even after he beat me, he dragged Marietta outside and lifted the machete. I told him I'd do it. I killed my dog for him so he'd leave Marietta alone." He whispered the confession, his face turned away from her.

"You didn't do it for him, Gideon," she contradicted gently. "You did it for your sister and you did it for your dog. You didn't let the animal suffer, did you?" At the shake of his head, she continued. "He would have."

"That still didn't spare Marietta. Or Jaimie." He whispered that as a confession as well.

Rory couldn't stop herself. His pain was tangible to her, his terrible grief, as if his loss had just occurred. She slipped from her chair to straddle his lap, sliding her arms around his neck and laying her head against his chest, covering both of them with the blanket. His arms surrounded her, and he dropped his chin on top of her head, just holding her close to him.

"Marietta was my twin sister. We were close. I don't think he liked me being close to anything or anyone. He didn't want me to have friends or pets or sisters. He always referred to Marietta as a whore. He said she had no brain and was useless, but then he thought all women were whores and useless but for one thing."

He fell silent. She felt the slight shake of his head, but she remained quiet. Waiting. He needed to get it out. Let it go. Tell someone. Her. He needed to tell her.

"I made a terrible mistake, Rory. I should have found a way to kill him. I knew I needed to do it. I knew I had to. I saw the way he looked at Marietta. I knew she was afraid of him. I wanted to think I could wait until I was older. It wasn't that I was afraid I couldn't do it. I knew I could. By that time, I'd been practicing a few psychic talents I accidentally discovered I had. With the birds. With concealing myself. A couple of other things. I worked at it all the time. I was smarter than he was. I knew I could kill him. I just wasn't ready. But I waited too long, and Marietta suffered because of me. That's on me. Then Jaimie."

Rory pressed closer to him, her ear over his heart. She could only offer comfort. The layers had peeled away. He was laid bare, and his shame was there, that dark burden lying heavy in his soul for her to see.

"I came home from school to find Marietta dead. She'd hung herself in her bedroom. She'd left me a note, telling me that he'd been forcing her to perform for him, to learn technique so she'd be a decent whore and earn him good money. Our mother would beat her if she didn't cooperate. She'd tell Marietta he had every right because he'd brought her into the world, so she was his to do whatever he wanted with her. Marietta didn't tell me. She was too ashamed, and she knew I would have killed him. I left that night. Even then, I didn't kill him. I just walked out and told the two of them never to look for me, that if they did, I would come looking for them. I think he saw it in my eyes that I would kill him. For the most part, he left me alone."

Rory knew it wasn't over. He'd mentioned Jaimie more than once. She waited. She didn't ask about Javier. She didn't need to know Javier's story. She needed to know Gideon's. Why the guilt? He couldn't have prevented what happened to his twin if he didn't know. He might not have been able to stop what she had done even had he known. More and more, she understood Gideon's deep need to protect others.

16

Red," Gideon whispered. All that dark cherry hair she had, thick and soft. Every time the sun or the moon or any light touched it, the color burst into flame. To him, she represented life. Being alive. His way back into the world again when he'd been dead inside for so long. "The story just gets uglier. Everything about me just gets uglier."

Rory lifted her head and framed his face, for the first time looking directly at him. He felt the impact of her vivid green eyes. There was no judgment there. Rory's gaze was filled with compassion. He wasn't certain telling her anything more about his childhood was a good idea. He didn't want the way she looked at him right at that moment to change, and he feared it would.

"Gideon, that's not true. Nothing about you is ugly. Not one single thing. Not at all. Believe me, honey, I can see inside you where no one sees, where maybe even you can't see, and there isn't anything ugly."

"You don't know what happened, because I didn't act when I

should have." That place inside him, dark and forever shadowed, stirred and spread, threatening to take him over.

"Then tell me." Her voice was very quiet, her gaze steady.

Gideon couldn't make the confession looking into her eyes. The back of her head fit into his palm, and he pressed her face against his chest and held her to him. Over his heart. He needed her there while he gave her this.

"Jaimie has one of those amazing brains you read about. She started high school at age eight. Physically, she was very small. Tiny. You can imagine what it could have been like for her being the brightest one in school and being a little kid. Mack and Kane took it on themselves to look out for her."

He paused. "I didn't go to school very often. Her mother was an elementary school teacher. Very sweet woman. She knew my circumstances, as did Mack's mom. They helped me out when they could. Jaimie's mom worked with me on schooling quite a bit when she had the time, although she was working two jobs."

He drew in a deep breath. Tightened his arms around her. "I should have known my father was watching, and he wouldn't leave things alone. He might not be able to get to me, but he got to Jaimie's mom. He killed her. Stabbed her sixteen times. He made sure she felt every single stab wound and took a long time to die. Jaimie found her. She was such a little thing, even then in her teens. It was heartbreaking and my fault. Had I killed him, Jaimie would still have her mother. I just—didn't."

Rory shook her head, but she didn't interrupt him. She waited for him to continue. Instinctively, she knew there was more.

"I told you I spent a lot of time studying the birds and connecting with them, learning about them. It wasn't just that it was a hobby, something to pass the time, but I felt an affinity with them, especially the raptors. I didn't want to think I'd inherited anything from my father, especially his ability to kill other human beings, but I always knew I was capable. When we were little kids, Marietta and I would talk about it, how we wanted him dead. She said she couldn't do it. I knew I could."

Rory stirred then. He didn't allow her to lift her head away from his chest. That didn't prevent her reaction. "Being able to kill another human being doesn't make you like him, Gideon. He obviously took joy in seeing others in pain. He liked to torture men, women and children. Even animals. That's not you. I can see inside of you. That was never you. You might kill when you need to, or when justice is involved, but you don't torture for the sake of gaining pleasure the way he did. You aren't anything like him."

"I have predatory instincts."

"Perhaps you do. I've sensed the hunter in you. That makes you good at your job. To do whatever it is you do, I would think you would need those instincts."

"I hunted him and I killed him. My own father, Rory. I didn't hesitate. He was celebrating with his buddies, and I killed them too. They were like him, torturing families because the rent wasn't paid on time or some other misdemeanor. I think I might have gone a little crazy, because I went to the house of their boss. I was covered in blood. I still slipped past the guards and found him in his garden having coffee looking smug. He didn't look so smug when I finished talking to him. I told him if he tried to come after me or any of the kids on the street with me, I'd take out his family and his men, that he'd never be able to find me. I made him believe me. I told him I just wanted to be left alone and then told him to clean up the mess so the cops wouldn't be looking for me. He did."

After a few moments, Rory stirred, and this time, he allowed her to tip her head back. Once again, her vivid green eyes collided with his.

"I imagine I would have done the same under the circumstances, Gideon." She narrowed her gaze. "How did you manage to slip past his guards?"

His Rory. He should have known she would ask for those details, not how he killed. "I told you, when I was little and I wanted to get away from him, I would hide, or try to. In my mind, I disappear. I practiced disappearing in the shadows. If I was against a wall, I would tell myself I was part of the wall. Whatever was there. I started noticing that Marietta couldn't always see me right away. Eventually, I got better and better at hiding myself from everyone. I knew it would be useful, and eventually, I practiced all the time. I still do, although I think it's automatic now."

Gideon had deliberately brought up his ability to cloak himself against walls, hoping to trigger Rory's memory of when she was young and she'd saved Rose and Ivy from being captured or killed by hiding their presence. He could hide himself from others, but he couldn't hide his team members. That talent was extraordinary. Whitney had something very special right in front of him when Rory was a child, and he hadn't recognized it. Whitney had enhanced Gideon's talent, but Gideon still wasn't able to shield his teammates from enemies.

Rory's lashes fluttered. Long and thick, each time Gideon looked at those lashes up close, where he could see the shade of red tipping the ends, his heart performed strange somersaults in his chest.

"Did he leave you alone?"

"He did. For a while." He'd promised her the truth, but he didn't want to look into her eyes any longer while he relayed any more of his sins to her. She saw too much of him. It was strange that she could see into those vulnerable places, when he was around his GhostWalker brothers and sisters, and had been most of his life, yet they hadn't seen inside him—not the way she did.

Once more, he palmed the back of her head and urged her to lay her face against his chest. She didn't fight his command. She laid her ear over his heart, but not before she pressed a kiss there first. His heart jumped. Clenched. He couldn't lose her. He had to find a way to win her back.

"His name was Elio Barone, and he kept claiming more and more territory, which meant there was always a bloody war with other rival families, who weren't nearly as brutal as he was. He ordered drive-by shootings in neighborhoods and would burn businesses to the ground to prove the other families couldn't take care of their people. His enforcers had been trained by my father, and they were vile men. They used machetes to hack up families. They rammed big trucks into cars coming home from work or school."

Deep inside him, that black shadow—which was so dense he sometimes thought it had taken over not just his soul but his entire being—darkened and spread again until he was choking on it. He felt his throat close, as it did so many times in his sleep when he awoke sweating and tangled in his sheets, unable to breathe.

He buried his face in Rory's neck and inhaled her fresh, clean scent. She should have smelled like the bar, but her skin gave off a subtle fragrance of lavender and citrus, soothing him.

"I believe just meeting you, Rory, saved my life. Just knowing you're in the world."

Her fist bunched in his hair and then stroked caresses into his scalp. "Don't say that, Gideon."

For the first time, there was a small tremor in her voice. A hint of fear, of trepidation, and more knots in his gut formed and tightened. He could face bullets and torture. He wasn't so certain he could face losing her again after the very real hope of having her back.

"I swore I'd give you the truth no matter what it cost me, Red."

"I don't know what I'm going to do about us."

She whispered her confession against his heart, her breath warm through the material of his shirt. He felt the heat of her breath on his skin, branding his muscles and bones as if she could brand him.

"I feel like such a coward after hearing what you've been through, but . . ." She trailed off.

"We'll talk about it," Gideon said. "I should have talked about everything with you. I should have given you these things about me before I even tried to hook you in close. I was afraid you wouldn't even take a chance with me. I've got so much violence inside. It comes easily to me, and you're soft inside. I thought if you knew the real me, you'd run away so fast, I'd never be able to find you and explain."

He kept her there on his lap, his arms tight, when he sensed she was thinking of pulling away from him. He needed her to stay when he told her what happened next. "Just settle for a couple more minutes, Rory. There's so much more, but this is the *more* that could have been prevented if I had just followed through and done what I should have. Sometimes I have an intuition or premonition, not even that exactly. It's more of a very strong gut feeling that I need to take action. When I was a kid, because that feeling involved violence, I refused to act on it. I didn't want to be anything like my father. I abhorred anything in me that had to do with violence, afraid it made me like him. That particular sensation was very strong and would trigger flashbacks of the horrific, brutal things I'd seen him do."

"That would be natural, Gideon."

He stroked her hair. He loved that mass of cherry-colored silk. The soft richness of it. The color. The wild, untamed riot of waves and curls that seemed to drive her crazy but made him want to slam her up against the nearest wall and claim her for his own.

"I suppose so, but back then, I rejected anything that in any way connected me to my father. I should have known Elio Barone would eventually come back into my life. He was a greedy man and lived for power. He had such a thirst to be the man everyone feared. Even as a kid, I knew that about him. I could read it when I spoke to him. He was evil. I saw it in his eyes. His soul was completely rotted through, just like my father's was. Even back then, when I was a kid, I came to the conclusion that evil men surrounded themselves with evil men. They find others they can corrupt."

As he'd been sent on missions to various places around the world, he'd found that premise to be true. Power seemed to corrupt and evil crept in. The need to control and gain more power became the ultimate goal, stamping out humanity in certain individuals until they seemed to have no moral compass.

"Barone sent his men to Mack's neighborhood, the one sanctuary left to us. His mother would allow us to sleep in her house. She'd feed us. It wasn't like she had money, but that never mattered to her. She found a way to get clothes for the younger ones. It was freezing in the winter months, and we'd huddle down in the basement with blankets and sleeping bags. She provided hot stew and bread. Her little car was one of the ones Barone's men rammed with their giant truck. She died instantly."

Rory's body jerked. "Oh, Gideon. I'm so sorry. How terrible for Mack. For you. For all of you."

"She'd taken in Jaimie after Jaimie's mother had been murdered. Now all of us were without a home—due to my negligence."

"No. That's not right. You can't possibly believe that, and I certainly hope Mack doesn't. Or Jaimie. You have nothing to do with what your father or Barone did."

This time there was no stopping Rory from pulling out of his arms and jumping to the patio floor. She was all pent-up energy. A hot, restless flame rejecting his conclusion completely—furious that he would even consider such a possibility. He was certain if the sun was out, her hair would crackle with outrage. For him. She was standing up for him. Not condemning him as he'd expected her to do.

Gideon's first feelings were of overwhelming relief that she was still right there with him. On the heels of that, he didn't know what to feel. His childhood memories were nearly all bad. He wanted to give her decent things about himself, but what could he find in his past that was good or funny that she would relate to?

Rory suddenly whirled around to face him, hands on her hips. "You feel you owe them. That's why you're always standing in front of them, Gideon. That's why you sacrifice not only your happiness but your life for them. It isn't just because you view them as family and you love them. It isn't just your intense loyalty to them. You feel you owe them because you didn't kill your father and this horrid man Barone when you were a child. A *child*, Gideon. And don't say 'teen,' because as far as I'm concerned, a teenager isn't grown."

He didn't know whether to laugh or cry. She was so fierce in his defense. He'd never had that before. He didn't know how to handle it.

"Red." It came out gentle.

She held up a hand, palm out to prevent him from speaking. "Did they blame you? Jaimie and Mack? Did they blame you?"

He shoved his fingers through his hair again. Had they? He could barely remember their reactions. He had been too busy blaming himself. They'd all been grief-stricken. Devastated. Over both deaths. Losing Mack's mother had made losing Jaimie's mother fresh all over again and tripled his guilt. His sister. Jaimie's mother. Mack's mother.

"Mack didn't. I don't think Jaimie did either. It was just me. I felt guilty because all along, I had known eventually something bad was going to happen."

"Feeling something isn't the same as knowing, Gideon, especially when you're a child. I get feelings all the time. I can't act on them."

He could now. Once he could pinpoint where the threat was coming from, he could and did act on it every time.

Gideon watched her pacing back and forth, every movement fluid. She seemed to flow over the patio, but the energy surrounding her was always low, contained, never spilling out in swamping waves as it would with a normal person when they were passionate about anything. He should have known she was a GhostWalker just by the way she moved. Every member of his team should have known.

All along, Javier had been suspicious. Gideon had questioned whether she was a GhostWalker multiple times. There were only a very few GhostWalkers able to hide from other GhostWalkers. Gideon was one of them. It stood to reason that the woman Whitney would have paired him with could do the same.

"I worked at developing that particular radar as well," he admitted. "Over the years, it's become stronger. I've learned to zero in on the threat, although in a large crowd and from a distance, doing so takes time and a tremendous amount of concentration. It doesn't always work."

She stopped pacing again and faced him, her expressive face lit up with interest. "You can do that?"

Gideon resisted the urge to go to her. He didn't want her to realize how much time she was spending with him. For the first time since he'd lost her, he was beginning to relax. He'd told her most of the worst of him, and she hadn't run. She might not ask for the rest of his sins. He'd confess if she did, but he hoped she'd just let it go.

When she looked at him, she had a way of doing so like no one else ever had. He wasn't a white knight, but she made him feel like one. It didn't seem to matter to her what his father had been or that he hadn't done what he should have to save two good women or his sister from monsters. She still viewed him as someone special.

"I've tried to pinpoint threats," she admitted. "Especially when I know the danger is to someone else, but I'm not good at finding the exact location. I knew something was wrong tonight, but I didn't know where or to whom."

"Neither did I," Gideon pointed out.

"But the break-ins at the apartments weren't a specific threat to anyone you knew."

That was true.

"Gideon, what did you do after Mack's mother died?"

His heart dropped. His eyes met hers. "Red. Baby. Do you really want me to go into detail? It wasn't pretty. In fact, it was downright ugly. I never wanted Barone's family, any member of it, to step into his shoes. Not one of his brothers or any of those working for him. I had failed the ones I considered my family, and I wasn't doing it again."

Rory didn't look away from him. Her vivid green eyes seemed to look right into his soul. More importantly, she moved in his mind. He let her. He didn't have much more to lose. He'd already lost her through his own stupidity. If she needed to see everything about him, he would let her in—at least as far as he could. Childhood memories he could give her.

He was classified now, and the things he did were classified. He couldn't give her that. He would share if he could, but he had sworn an oath, and until she was with him as a GhostWalker, he had no choice but to keep what he did now confidential.

"I went after Barone and his brothers. Systematically. One by one. Then their men. I killed them. Murdered them. They didn't stand a chance against me. I sent the birds into the air during the day to spy for me, to tell me where they were. I sent the owls at night to show me. I was small enough to get into spaces they never would think I could be in. They couldn't see me because I could blend into anything and be part of it. There was no way to keep me out of a fortress or a house. No lock was strong enough. I didn't blow up cars dramatically. I didn't do it with fanfare. I entered their bedrooms and cut their throats. If they were in a bathtub or shower, I ended their life there."

He refused to bow his head or turn away from her. He didn't feel remorse. He felt guilt for not having done it sooner.

"Didn't they try to find you?"

"Yes. But I always knew when they were coming for me because my birds let me know."

"Did they go after the others? Your street family? They must have been vulnerable."

"I had Mack and Kane hiding them. They knew what I was doing."

He'd wiped out the Barone family's reign of terror. It had taken time, but he'd done it, and he'd known his family was safe. Mack's street family had established a reputation, and no one was going to mess with them, no matter how tough a rival gang might be.

It always surprised him how the city had its music. He could hear the water lapping at the piers even though they were a few blocks away. There was little traffic on the street close to them. He heard the flutter of wings. Through it all, Gideon waited for her judgment.

"You did what you felt you had to do to keep everyone safe," she murmured softly.

He sighed and ran both hands through his hair. "I don't want there to be any misconceptions here, Red. I killed a lot of people. I don't feel any remorse over killing them. I feel guilty because I didn't kill them when I should have. My nightmares aren't because I killed them. I never dream about them. I dream about the things my father tried to make me do. I dream about my sister and how I didn't save her. I dream about Jaimie's mother and Mack's mother. How they should still be alive. Those are the people I feel guilt over."

Rory nodded her head. "I'm well aware what you're saying to me."

"I just don't want there to be a misunderstanding."

"There isn't. I understand you so much better, Gideon. You really had no childhood at all, did you?"

He wished he could say he understood her so much better. He did know more about her childhood. She didn't have one either. Whitney had robbed her of any chance of one, yet she was loving and compassionate. He knew he had been born with protective traits off the charts, and Whitney's enhancements had just added to those elements. No doubt Whitney had enhanced all of Rory's best qualities as well. He didn't see many of her negative traits.

Rory laughed. The sound played along his nerve endings, making them sing.

"We're connected, Gideon. I can catch parts of what you're thinking. I do have a bad temper. And I'm not at all trusting."

He inclined his head, trying not to smile, because he didn't consider Rory's temper atrocious. She had good reason for her trust issues. He hadn't helped in that area.

"Stop blaming yourself, Gideon. You take on everyone's problems. You don't need to fix everyone and everything."

He loved the way her eyes went dark green when she became passionate about anything—especially when it had to do with him.

"You're impossible. I don't think I can do anything wrong in your eyes. You'll be in for a shock one of these days."

Rory sank into her chair and tried glaring at him. She wasn't very good at it.

"Wrap the blanket around you, sweetheart. You're beginning to shiver. I'd like to move on to Harvey and the conversation you had with him."

She made a face as she pulled the blanket around her. "Harvey thinks he's being set up to take the fall for killing Detective Ramsey, and frankly, I agree with him. Sadly, I'm worried my friends and I might be somehow targeted for that as well. The more I've been thinking about the questions the police have asked us, the more it feels as if they seem to believe we knew the dead men and Harvey a lot better than we did."

"It's clear that someone believes one of you has something important and that you've hidden it."

"We all get that. The police have questioned us. They also seem to think that Detective Ramsey said something to us before he died. They've asked us over and over in a dozen different ways, but the only thing he said was to run, which we did. I felt guilty for leaving him facing a shooter when he was clearly wounded. I'm sure Westlake blames us for leaving him, and that's why he's so angry with us—especially me. I was the last one out the door."

Gideon didn't take his piercing gaze from her face. She was uncomfortable discussing the subject with him. She didn't want to talk to him about Harvey and was purposely deflecting, shifting the subject to what the police might be considering. She wanted to keep her own counsel when it came to matters she decided were private, because she believed he would share them with his team.

"Did Harvey threaten you in any way?"

"No."

Single word. Decisive. She was trying to shut down any further questioning.

"You passed on the message?"

She nodded. "And I deleted the message from my phone without telling him it was ever there. And told him no more messages through me."

"Yet Scott Tinsdale was in the garage. If you told Harvey no more being his go-between, and he was going to listen, what business would Tinsdale have there? And you told me the man he was talking to had been in your bar."

"I don't know why Tinsdale was in the garage, and I don't care. I told Harvey I wouldn't deliver any more messages regardless of threats. I believe he understood." She waved her hand as if the subject was closed.

"You do know Harvey is dangerous and can't be trusted?" He wanted to make that perfectly clear.

"You do know Javier is dangerous and can't be trusted? You're dangerous and can't be trusted. Most likely, everyone you know is dangerous and can't be trusted," she countered.

He'd walked into that one. There wasn't one thing she'd said that wasn't true from her perspective. He refused to take the bait and be offended.

"I see what you mean. You make a good point. The things I know about Harvey make me believe he isn't a good person and could possibly want to harm you, but I've never spoken to him, and you have. You're capable of hearing lies. He must have made you believe that he had no desire to hurt you."

"I don't altogether trust my ability to hear lies or truth."

Gideon's heart clenched hard. That was his fault. She'd believed him when he told her she was safe with him. He'd meant every single word. He'd believed it when he said it. It hadn't occurred to him that he would have to give her up to protect Sebastian and Rose. Or Mack and Jaimie. Or the rest of his GhostWalker family.

He pressed his fingers to his temples. Sometimes his headaches were killers, and he could feel the beginnings of one pushing hard right behind his eyes.

"Gideon."

That voice of hers. So soft and compassionate. He tried not to let it affect him. He tried not to hope. Maybe he should be the one to end their time together, but he knew he wouldn't.

"You weren't the one to make me distrust my abilities. I've been shaky for a little while now but have no idea why. The nightmares have been getting worse, and with them, my abilities to do certain things seem to come and go. Some gifts are sharper and other capabilities seem to be weaker."

She was moving the subject far away from Harvey Matters, and he didn't see how he was going to turn it back without getting her very upset. He would have to find a way to circle back around at another time.

"Are you still feeling that odd sensation with your skin?" He continued to press at his temples, reminiscent of the way she pressed against the spot above her left temple.

She moistened her lips and nodded slowly, as if she were reluctant to admit it to him. "Yes. I did think about what you'd told me. I even practiced saying that horrible man's name over and over until I could do it without getting sick."

Rory fell silent and Gideon didn't ask for anything else. The fact that she at least had considered what he'd told her about her past instead of dismissing everything he'd said because she was so hurt by him made him admire her all the more. That was the other thing about Rory that got to him. She was sitting here with him even though he'd hurt her. Not just hurt her but truly shattered her. He'd felt the true depth of her devastation. She'd meant it when she'd said she didn't want to see or hear from him again. Yet she'd been so worried about him, she'd reached out to ensure he wasn't bleeding internally again. That was Rory. He needed that sweetness to balance him out.

"I like that you can talk to the birds the way you do, Gideon. I think that's amazing. I loved hearing you talk about the places you've been to study the birds."

"The first night I ever heard you laugh, I'd gone up to my rooftop because I was hurting like hell. I hadn't been able to sleep in days. I thought I might be going a little insane. Every time I closed my eyes, I saw things I just couldn't take, and I needed to meditate to try to get the images out of my mind. The doc didn't want me to climb the stairs, but I did anyway. I had just about found a way to shut everything down, and Javier joined me. I knew he wanted to talk about what happened, and it was the last thing I wanted to do."

Gideon watched Rory pull her legs up onto the seat. They disappeared beneath the blanket. There were things about her he knew so well now, things he loved watching her do.

"When he left, I had to start all over again, trying to meditate and get above the pain. That's when I heard you laugh. My hearing is very acute. I knew you had to be a few blocks away. I could tell you were surrounded by a large group of people. I just had to wait for you to laugh again to pinpoint your exact location."

"My hearing is excellent, but yours has to be extremely good to hear me in those conditions, unless I was laughing like a hyena."

"I assure you, you were not." He sent her a faint grin. "I found myself straining to catch the smallest sound from you so I could send one of my spies. I wanted to know everything there was to know about you."

Her long lashes fluttered. He waited to see her reaction. She didn't disappoint him. He saw it in her eyes first. Recognition. Then amusement. Her smile was radiant. "That very naughty sparrow who came to visit me on my rooftop."

He nodded. "She found you at the bar first and then followed you home."

"It scared me when she flew into the cabinet door."

"That wasn't part of the plan."

"I can't do anything cool like use birds to spy. I love to study them and take pictures. I'm more of a gardener. I love to design gardens. I meant it when I told you that someday, I'm going to have my own vegetable and herb gardens. I want to stay home and cook.

I'd love to bake my own bread and pasta. I wouldn't work at the bar as many hours so I'd have time for all of that."

"What about your songwriting?"

"I do that in my head all the time."

"Wouldn't you want a little recording studio?"

She shook her head. "I'm not a singer."

"You have a good voice."

She shook her head even more adamantly this time. "I love to write songs, but I would never want to sing in front of a crowd. I really do want to design my gardens and cook. That's the dream. Someday, it'll happen. I've got so many recipes stored in my head. And I just look at empty spaces and see gardens planted in them everywhere I go."

She looked around her. "Gideon, it's almost morning. Lydia and the others are going to be worried. I'd better be getting back."

He stood immediately and reached out his hand to help her up. "Thank you for meeting me. And for being understanding about my past."

"I appreciate you telling me. I know it wasn't easy to share."

He took the blanket and shoved it into his backpack. She didn't object to holding his hand as they walked to the back entrance of her apartment building. He went in with her and escorted her to Cindy's apartment. He wasn't taking any chances with her, not after all that had happened. He waited until she was safely inside before he started back to his home. Javier joined him once he was out on the street. Neither spoke as the SUV picked them up.

17

Ladies," Detective Larrsen said, looking around the small room at the six women he'd asked to meet him here. "This is Detective Miles Abbott."

Rory covered her yawn with her hand as she observed the newcomer. He appeared to be about ten years older than Larrsen. He had sandy-colored hair and was clean-shaven and nearly as fit. He wore a dark suit. Pam and Janice exchanged quick looks, and both glanced at his left hand to see if he wore a ring. They'd met him before, but not in such an official capacity. He'd questioned them with Westlake and Carver, but he hadn't said much.

"Ladies," Abbott said. He had a deep voice.

"This is Detective Morgan Wilson."

Detective Morgan Wilson was closer to fifty. Married, wore his suit well, dark hair with threads of silver running through it. Nice smile that lit his very intelligent eyes. He had coffee-colored skin and chocolate eyes. If Rory had to guess, he was the boss.

She was suddenly very tense. Looking around at the other

women, she had the feeling they were as well. To cover her nerves, she sipped at her coffee. She had every excuse to appear tired. She was certain the cops had reviewed the security cameras and seen her drag in at the crack of dawn holding hands with Gideon.

"What's going on, Detectives?" Janice demanded. "If you know who broke into our apartments, it would be nice to let us in on it."

"I wish we had that information for you," Detective Abbott said. "We know you've been asked questions over and over, and you're most likely tired of answering, but sometimes, after you've had time to think about it, new details come into your mind."

Rory couldn't imagine what new details they were looking for.

"We'd like you to re-create the day Detective Ramsey was killed, where each of you were sitting when you first heard the gunshots and what you were doing. What you said and did and what you saw," Detective Larrsen added.

"We always meet in this room to sort our mail, visit and have coffee," Janice said. "It's always in the afternoon because Rory, Pam and I work at night and sleep in. Sally arranges her schedule around our times. Cindy and Lydia work from home, so they do as well."

"Do you always meet at the same time?" Detective Abbott asked.

"Yes, around three. That gives everyone time to work out if they want to before we meet here," Sally said. "And I can finish my dog grooming appointments."

"You've been meeting like this for how long?" Detective Wilson asked. "And how often?"

"Tuesdays and Thursdays are here for coffee," Lydia said. "Workouts are Monday, Wednesday and Friday. We started meeting regularly about six months ago. Rory and Sally moved in later and joined us a little over four months ago."

Rory could see that all three detectives were keeping separate notes. She studied their faces carefully under the veil of her lashes. None of them had the underlying anger that Westlake displayed or the accusatory glare Detective Carver sometimes seemed to have in his eyes when he looked at them. It didn't seem as if they believed the women were guilty of conspiring to withhold evidence from the police as Westlake and Carver did.

"These are the seats you commonly sit in? The same ones you were sitting in that day Detective Ramsey came into the room with you?" Detective Abbott asked.

Janice looked around and nodded. "We all got in the habit of sitting in the same spots, so we tend to always take the same seats."

"What were you doing?" Abbott asked.

"Drinking coffee. Sorting mail. We toss the junk mail," Lydia explained. "I had Ellen with me. Cindy didn't have the boys that day."

Cindy shook her head. "No, I didn't, and I'm so grateful. They were visiting my parents. We were laughing and talking, and then we heard a very distinctive popping sound. It was definitely gunfire in the apartments on the main floor. We all jumped up."

"A man came in through the side door. We'd never seen him before." Lydia took up the narrative. "He had blood on his chest and thigh and a gun in his hand. I scooped up Ellen and ran toward the back door of the lounge. It exits into the back hall. I was so scared for Ellen."

"I ran too," Pam said.

"He was staggering," Janice added. "And yelling for us to run, so I did. I followed Sally and Pam out."

Rory put her coffee on the end table and pressed her hand over her heart. "We were all on our feet running toward the door, but I felt terrible leaving him like that. He was clearly hurt. I turned back and saw the side door swing open." She pointed to it. "That's the door he came through. Someone was firing at him, and he was firing back. He yelled at me to run again, and Cindy pulled me to the back door. That was the last I saw of him. We ran down the hall to the back exit of the apartment building. Once we were in the gardens, we were all calling 911."

"You saw the door open, as if whoever had shot at him chased him into the lounge where you were?" Detective Abbott persisted.

Rory nodded. "Yes. The door was flung open so hard it hit the stop and then banged back. I could see the flash of a gun."

"Did you see who was firing? A man? A woman? Any impression?" Abbott persisted.

"I didn't. Whoever it was stood to the side of the door, because the detective was firing back at them."

"What about a hand around the gun? Were they wearing a glove?" Detective Larrsen persisted.

Rory pressed her fingers to her eyes. "I wish I had an answer for you. He yelled, 'Get out of here,' and I did." She looked at Cindy. "Did you see anything?"

Cindy shook her head. "I just grabbed your arm and yanked you as hard as I could."

"Did you go back into the room?" Abbott asked.

"No, there were officers everywhere," Sally said. "Later, one of them returned our mail to us, but we weren't allowed into the lounge for a couple of days."

Janice crossed her arms over her chest. "If someone would tell us what you're looking for or what you think we heard or saw, we'd be happy to help. No one wants to see a good man murdered like that. It happened practically right in front of us. We have no idea why someone is breaking into our apartments or Rory's car."

"Oh my God, what if they destroy my grooming van?" Sally said, sounding horrified. "Even with insurance, I could never replace it. Never. That's my livelihood. I'd be out on the streets." She looked at the detectives. "They might, right?"

Larrsen sighed. "Don't panic, Sally—Ms. Hudson," he corrected himself. "We're keeping a watch on your van."

"I wish we could help you," Lydia said. "Do you think the person who killed the detective dropped the gun he shot him with in the lounge? Does he think one of us picked it up or something?" Her voice rose just a little, as if she were fighting hysteria.

Rory got up and switched to the love seat so she could put her arm around Lydia. "I doubt he thinks that, Lydia. We're not exactly going to blackmail someone who shot a police detective. It's going to be all right. We're going to be all right."

Rory couldn't help thinking about the card Harvey had given her, the one that contained only a single phone number and nothing else. Harvey had said if they called that number, his men would get them to a safe house and no one would be able to follow them. Did she trust him enough to put her friends' lives in his hands? She didn't have that answer yet.

She wished Gideon hadn't broken faith with her. She might understand why he had done it. She might understand him. But now she didn't know who she could trust. If it was just her life, that would be one thing, but these women were the closest thing she had to a family. She wasn't willing to risk them until she was certain she knew they would be safe wherever they went.

Her heart said Gideon. He was protective, and if he took them on, he would one hundred percent fight for them. She had woken up that afternoon to a text from her boss telling her that many of the owners of the businesses along the wharf had put together a fundraiser for the women who had lost their belongings in the break-ins. Gideon and his team were already hard at work doing exactly as he had promised. Lydia had shown her the same text the moment she saw her.

Still, she did believe Harvey when he said he hadn't killed his business partners or Detective Ramsey. She also believed that not only was he being framed but that it was possible she was also being framed right along with him. Or all the women were.

"Have any of you seen Harvey Matters?" Detective Abbott asked.

Rory counted herself lucky that he was looking at Janice when he asked the question. Larrsen was staring at Lydia with concern in his eyes. Unfortunately, Detective Morgan Wilson had his gaze locked on Rory. Ellen chose that moment to wrap her arms around Rory's neck and transfer her little body to Rory's lap.

"Mommy's sad," she whispered into Rory's ear.

Rory couldn't help but be appreciative that the techniques she'd learned on the videos she'd watched and implemented on selective mutism had gained her Ellen's trust enough that the child talked to her. More, she spoke in front of others now. She exchanged a triumphant smile with Lydia.

"Very good talking in front of everyone, Ellen," she praised. "Sometimes mommies get sad just like you do, Ellie May Rider," Rory whispered back, ignoring Wilson's probing gaze. She concentrated on the little girl. Ellen had to be confused. She wasn't in her own bed, surrounded by her toys at night or when she woke in the morning.

"How would any of us see Harvey?" Janice demanded. "He's most likely dead. Everyone else is."

Ellen's arms tightened around Rory's neck, nearly choking her. Rory glared at Janice. "There's a child in the room, Janice." She rocked Ellen gently. "Janice is being silly, Ellie May. Are you a princess or a rider today?"

"I might be a princess." The whisper was so soft, Rory could barely hear it.

"You're so brave to talk in front of everyone. Princesses are very brave. It's good that you're a princess today, because I'm not so certain I'd be a good pony. I didn't sleep last night. I stayed up talking to a friend of mine, mostly about birds. Do you like birds?" She wanted to distract the little girl and, at the same time, hopefully not have to participate in the conversation about Harvey. "Yes or no, Princess Bo Peep."

"No one has seen Harvey since he left here." Pam echoed Janice.

Sally and Cindy nodded in agreement. Rory nodded as well without looking at the cops. She kept her eyes on Ellen. She wasn't about to look at them when she lied. She was certain they would see right through her.

Lydia caught her daughter's hand. "I saw him once."

All the women gasped, including Rory. Lydia hadn't said a word. Rory stared at her in utter astonishment.

"You didn't say anything. Not a single word," Rory said.

"Lydia." Detective Larrsen sounded both disappointed and worried. "Why didn't you tell me you'd seen him?"

"You didn't tell us you were looking for him. You didn't ask about him. You didn't say he was a suspect in Detective Ramsey's death. You still haven't said that he is. Is he? Or are you concerned that whoever murdered the other men—Dustin, Jarrod and Ret— might want to kill him? We aren't told anything at all. We're just asked a lot of questions."

"He's a person of interest," Detective Abbott explained. "When did you last see him?"

"Rory, it was the night you had a date with Gideon to go to his house. You were going to meet Gideon after work. You came home, showered, changed and then left. I was excited for you, so I walked out the front door with you and stood outside watching as you went down the block. Just as I started back inside, I saw him on the opposite side of the street. He was kind of hidden in the shadows, but he was walking the same way as Rory was. He was a good distance behind her and acting strange."

"Did he look like he was following her?" Detective Wilson asked.

Rory thought it was telling that he asked Lydia the question instead of asking her if she'd been aware of Harvey tailing her.

Lydia shook her head. "I didn't think he was. I didn't keep watching because there were police cars going up and down the street, and I thought she would be safe. Not only that, but Gideon's building is only a couple of blocks up from us."

"Did Harvey approach you?" Abbott asked Rory.

She shook her head. "No, he didn't. I went to Gideon's home and let myself in. He'd given me the code to get in. It was fairly foggy that night, and I was anxious to see him. I never saw Harvey, or for that matter any cops. I guess I should have been paying more attention to my surroundings."

Every single word she said was the absolute truth, and if the cops were adept at hearing truth, her tone rang with sincerity. She nuzzled Ellen's neck.

"I like birds," the child confided in a whisper. "'Specially blue ones."

"If any of you see Harvey again, don't approach him or talk to him. Consider him dangerous. Immediately contact the number we give you. Speak only to one of us," Larrsen cautioned. "If you think of anything else you remember about the day Detective Ramsey was shot, again, call the number we give you and speak only to one of us."

Rory took the card Larrsen handed to her. She glanced down at it. Unlike the card with only a single number on it that Harvey had given her, this one had several names under the number, each belonging to one of the detectives. She couldn't help but notice Westlake and Carver weren't listed, not that she would ask for either of them even if she did have to call the number.

The women waited until the detectives had filed out before they exchanged another long round of looks, this time with a hint of despair.

"I don't think this nightmare is ever going to end," Sally whispered. "Do you think they suspect we had something to do with killing that detective?"

"How could we?" Lydia asked. "We didn't know him. I barely saw him. The minute I heard gunfire, I picked up Ellen and ran out of here. And Warren wouldn't be able to talk to me the way he does on an active investigation, at least I don't think so."

"You haven't had a real date," Pam pointed out. "He's made it very clear he'd like to go out with you, but he hasn't taken you to dinner or anything like that. I don't think he can if you're considered a suspect."

"Or maybe even a witness," Janice speculated.

"Can't she just ask him?" Sally said. "That way, we'd all know if we're considered suspects. They did use that kit on our hands that first day to rule out any of us firing a gun. Wouldn't that have ruled us out altogether?"

"We wouldn't have to pull the trigger to be an accessory," Cindy said. "I should have taken the boys and moved."

"That might have made you look even guiltier," Pam pointed out.

They sat together in silence, looking glum.

"Men suck," Lydia announced.

Rory didn't want that for her, not when she was certain Larrsen was one of the good ones. "I don't believe Detective Larrsen believes you had anything to do with Ramsey's murder, Lydia. I think he's trying to protect you. Maybe all of us."

Lydia brightened. "That could be. I hope you're right. I want to think he's everything I think he is. He's so sweet with Ellen. Even she likes him." She dropped a kiss on Ellen's head.

The little girl smiled up at her mother and then slid to the floor, where she began playing with the toys her mother had brought for her. Lydia pointed to them. "He bought those for her. They've become her new favorites."

Rory looked at the castle-and-princess playset with ponies and stables. The detective had covered all the bases. Smart man. He was another Gideon. The moment the thought entered her mind, she tried to push it away. Gideon had been her fantasy man, and he hadn't lived up to the fantasy. Maybe no man could. Maybe no woman could.

She considered the things Gideon had told her about his family. No doubt he'd had fantasies about the perfect parents. His mother and father certainly hadn't lived up to his expectations. Did anyone? It was possible everyone put far too many expectations on relationships. Since she didn't know the first thing about them, she didn't know one way or the other.

"Do people even have good marriages anymore?" Lydia asked. "It seems to me no one lasts more than a few years, and then it's on to the next person."

"My parents may be elitist snobs," Cindy said. "And they do drive me crazy, but they love each other. They've been together for forty-seven years, and they still gaze at each other across the room like teenagers. When I was a kid, I remember being embarrassed that they were always holding hands, and Dad would grab Mom and dance with her across a room. Now I think it's incredibly sweet. I felt like I found that with Matthew, the boys' father. I adored him almost from the moment I set eyes on him. There was never anyone else for me."

She looked down at her hands, and Rory's heart lurched. She looked so alone, so destroyed. For the first time, Rory felt a kinship with her. Of all the women she'd become close with, she knew Cindy the least. Cindy came from money. She was always composed. It was difficult to tell at times whether she was hurting or not. She didn't let anything show on her face.

Instinctively, Rory knew she would never want another man after losing Gideon. He was the only man who would ever work for her. They fit. It was that simple. He would have been the love of her life. She just knew that when he was close to her, something deep inside opened up where she'd been so closed off. It sounded corny even to her, but her heart sang around him. Rory was all about music. Lyrics. Poetry. Gideon amplified those traits in her.

Was that how Cindy felt about her husband? They'd had two children together. She was struggling to bring them up in the way she believed he would want them raised.

"That's nice to hear," Lydia said. "I really like him. I want Warren to be real."

Rory closed her eyes and pressed her to-go mug to her forehead. How many times had she said that very thing to herself? She'd wanted Gideon to be real.

I am real, Red. I'm sorry I let you down.

To her dismay, she'd connected with him. She tended to do that when she was upset. More and more, that was happening, as if she couldn't stop herself. The spot just above her left temple gave off that strange sensation, as if her skin were so tight it wanted to peel away. She didn't fight the impression but rather sank into it, allowing the pain to wash over her.

I know you didn't mean to, Gideon. I understand you better now.

Just because she understood him didn't mean it didn't still hurt like hell. She needed to feel like she belonged somewhere. With someone. She wanted to be number one in his life the way he was in hers. That probably wasn't fair since she had no past and no family. If she had, she might put them in front of him just as he had done.

"If you want my honest opinion of Detective Larrsen, Lydia," Cindy said, "I believe he's as real as they get. My advice is to go slow. You have a child, so it makes sense to be cautious, but if you're attracted to him and he is to you, take the chance."

Janice sighed. "I'm not the best with men, you know that, but

I'm going to second Cindy on this one, Lydia. I like the man. He's a good cop. And he's totally into you."

Pam nodded her approval.

Sally beamed at her. "You know what I think of him. I spent a little time talking to him after the break-in at my apartment when he walked me back from the bar, and he was so nice. He didn't have to be. I don't think any of the other detectives would have taken the time with me when I was so distraught. I don't know why I thought I was going to be skipped over, but I did."

Rory could feel Lydia's gaze on her. She forced a smile. "I already told you, hon. Detective Larrsen is clearly a good man. You have good judgment. You don't need any of us to tell you what you should do." She put down the to-go mug. "We've both got to work tonight, and I still need to try to catch up on sleep."

~

The crowd seemed rowdier than usual, which was saying a lot. Rory leaned across the bar to better hear the orders being shouted to her from customers two rows deep.

"Utter chaos," Brad yelled, grinning from ear to ear. "This is what success sounds like."

"I suppose so," Rory called back as she lined up eight shot glasses and poured tequila for Dana's customers. She added two whiskey sours to her tray and handed four more to customers seated on barstools. As soon as they vacated their seats, four more people replaced them. Rory noted one of them was the man who had stood beside Scott Tinsdale in her parking garage.

She ignored him, made seven Bloody Marys and handed them to the row behind those on the barstools. Two groups of what appeared to be college boys were hollering for beer. That was an easy order to accomplish, and she did so quickly, getting the ten of them out of the way. A round of martinis for two tables was next, and then she made gin and tonics. Her barback was right there, ringing up drinks and keeping tabs for her.

She'd never seen her boss so happy. Lani was working a bartending station and so was Lydia. Brad filled in on breaks. Brad worked as a barback if necessary. He rang up tabs. Work was going smooth even with how chaotic it was.

Rory slapped napkins down in front of the customers on barstools, including the man who had been talking to Tinsdale. "What can I get for you?" He and three of the others were repeat customers. The other three were new. She didn't know the man's name, but he'd been in before and he'd ordered whiskey. No ice. No frills. The other three repeat customers had ordered whiskey sours.

"Ballard," he volunteered. "Theo Ballard. Whiskey. No ice."

The other three ordered their usual, and the new three wanted rum and Cokes. Rory made small talk while she made the drinks. To her surprise, Ballard vacated his seat to allow others to take it and order. He joined another man at a small table near the back exit.

Rory kept her eye on them as the night wore on, but neither man gave off the kind of energy that set off her radar. They weren't in her section, and Trudi was their waitress, not Dana. Had they been in her section, she might have thought Theo Ballard had been sent by Harvey to deliver another message, but he didn't seem to be paying attention to her. Other than watching him as she did everyone, Rory dismissed him to the background of the bar and concentrated on keeping up with her work.

Toward the end of the night, Brad bumped her with his hip. "Mandatory break, Rory. You need to use your inhaler. Seriously. You haven't slowed down for a minute. I've got this."

She'd been in the zone and hadn't noticed time passing. Brad was right. She was beginning to find it hard to breathe. "Thanks."

Switching places smoothly, she hurried to the employee bathroom, not realizing how long it had been since she'd been able to go.

As she unbolted the door to step back out, Theo Ballard blocked her way, pressing a hand to her belly to push her back inside. He followed her in and slid the bolt.

"I'm not going to hurt you. Harvey wanted you to know that a gun was supposedly found in his apartment. That weapon fired the bullets that killed Ramsey, Ret and Jarrod, and also the bullet that was fired into Dustin after he was tortured and hanged. Harvey didn't own a gun. He didn't touch that gun. Also, the suitcase Jarrod was found in did belong to him. It was taken out of his room." Ballard slid the bolt and ducked out of the bathroom before she could say a word.

Rory stared after him in shock. There were no cameras in the back. Brad couldn't afford them. She didn't know how to respond to what Ballard had just told her. How would Harvey know that kind of information? Was that why the detectives had shown up in force at the apartments to question her and her friends again? She guessed they couldn't tell them about the gun or the suitcase. They had said Harvey was a person of interest.

She went to the break room feeling slightly sick. Now she really couldn't breathe properly. If Harvey was telling the truth, someone was really framing Harvey for the death of the detective. Was she going to be next? Was Lydia? She doubted it. That wouldn't be a logical conclusion. Lydia had a child. If they took Harvey up on his offer of a safe house, would they be playing into his hands by being set up to take the fall?

Red? Tell me why you're so distressed. You were laughing and having a good time just minutes ago, and now you're extremely upset.

She took a breath and pulled out her inhaler, trying to think. It was always difficult when she wasn't getting enough oxygen. *Give me a minute.*

She felt Gideon's connection to her, but he didn't try to push his way into her mind, and she appreciated that. She needed to make her own decisions. She needed a little time to sort things out. Using her inhaler bought her time.

Gideon was patient. He didn't hurry her, and he didn't ask her again. His calm and belief in her were her deciding factors. When she felt she could breathe again, she relayed what had happened, from the visit from the detectives to Theo Ballard's revelations.

Harvey gave me a card with a number on it to call if I felt we were in trouble. It only has a number, nothing else. He said someone would answer and text us a route to a safe house. They would run interference so no one could follow us. The house would be set up for all of us, including the children, for however long we needed it. He said he didn't like that he'd dragged us into his mess. At that time, he told me he knew he was going to be framed and he didn't have a gun. He hadn't fired at the cop. None of them had. He certainly hadn't killed his partners. That's what he told me, and I believe him. I'm worried I'm being framed with him.

She was grateful Gideon didn't make a snap judgment. He turned the information over in his mind.

We can keep your crew safe here or at one of our places. We're a security company, and it would be nearly impossible to infiltrate.

The cops might use a search warrant.

They would have to know where you are. You would disappear. We would take only those who would want to come. You would have to persuade your friends to come with us.

It was tempting, but Janice would be afraid of losing contracts. Sally was afraid of losing customers. Pam might stay and work with Janice. Cindy would go to her parents. She'd be safe there. Lydia might be persuaded. Would Rory go? No. She'd be afraid of harming Gideon and his friends. He'd convinced her she was dangerous to them. She didn't think she was to others, but she was afraid she was to the GhostWalkers. She didn't know what the difference was, but she knew there was one.

That's a good offer. Thank you for that. If we need it, I'll see if I can persuade them.

But you won't come.

I've thought a lot about what you said. The ticking time bomb and everything in my head. I'm not taking chances with you or your friends. I still have to figure that out. I will. It's just that all of this is getting in the way.

She felt his hesitation, and her stomach tightened into knots. *Don't say anything about your friends helping me. I can't bear to think about them knowing my secrets. I just can't face them. I'm dealing with too much right now, Gideon. Let me take care of whatever this is with my friends at the apartments, then I'll think about whether to go or stay and face everyone.*

She didn't want to hurt him, and she knew she had. She hadn't meant it that way. She was being honest with him.

I'm not trying to persuade you one way or the other, Red. I just want you to know they don't judge. They want to help you. They consider you one of us. Family. Because you're mine. Because you're a GhostWalker.

You have to stop talking. He did have to stop. He couldn't say another word. Already, she felt sick all over again. Shattered. Despondent. Maybe she always would whenever she thought about being a GhostWalker. Or when she thought back on what he'd done—telling the others her darkest secret. She *never* would give him up to anyone. For any reason.

To save my life? To save Lydia's life? Or Ellen's?

Her heart clenched hard in her chest. Her stomach did another sickly spasm. She didn't want to think about that. Exchanging Gideon's secrets for Ellen and Lydia? Or his life? That wasn't a fair request. She wasn't going to put herself in that position. Was that being a coward? Yes, of course it was. She didn't care. She wasn't going there in her mind. Not now, maybe never.

I need to get back to work. It's crazy busy and my boss is covering for me.

She drank water and stretched before making her way slowly back to the bar.

Red. I want to see you tonight. After work.

She should shut that down before it was too late and she was pulled back in.

I'm not sure that's a good idea. I can't make snap decisions, Gideon. When I see you, it's too difficult to think straight. I had a fantasy of who you were. That's not your fault and I'm not blaming you. I'm really not. It's just that I let you in.

So far in when no one else had ever gotten there. She wanted him back, but then who was she wanting back? The Gideon she'd fantasized over? Or the one she knew him to be? Which was real? She had to know before she took another chance.

How can you know if you don't spend time with me?

He had a point. Protecting herself was a sure way to keep from ever having a relationship with him. On the other hand, if he was right about her, and she was a threat to him and his people, what would be the point of even trying again? That didn't make sense. She was just setting both of them up for more heartache.

Brad was clearly relieved to get her back, and she quickly caught up with her customers. The fierce rush didn't seem to slow down even as the end of the night approached and they were nearing last call. Although the crowd had thinned somewhat and the chaos wasn't nearly as bad and the bouncers had managed to shut down any arguments quickly before they'd turned into full-blown fights, Rory had begun to feel a dark shadowy threat looming close. She scanned the bar over and over but couldn't find it.

There was no one she could identify fitting with that malevolent shadow directed toward her. Customers exited as the closing hour drew near. Brad announced last call. Rory paid even closer attention, but no one left in the bar seemed to be a threat. Once everyone was gone, her radar continued to tell her she was in trouble, but she couldn't tell where the threat was coming from.

She helped close with Lydia, the two waitresses, the barbacks and Brad. They made short work of it.

Gideon, we're leaving the bar now. I think something is wrong. Lydia and I are going out the back way, and we'll take the shortcut home.

Lydia opened the back door leading into the parking lot as Rory pulled on her jacket.

Javier and I will come to escort you home. Wait for us.

That sounds like a good idea.

"Wait for me, Lydia," she called. "I need to use my inhaler before we go."

The moment she stepped outside the bar to call Lydia back in, she felt the terrible premonition of danger surrounding her. A car pulled up beside Lydia, and two men leapt out, masks covering their faces. One caught at Lydia, jerking her toward the vehicle.

Rory ripped Lydia away from him, kicking the man in his belly, driving him back. She spun Lydia around and thrust her back toward the open door of the bar.

"Run. Get inside now. Run." She pushed authority into her voice as well as compulsion. "Lock the door." *Gideon.* She ran after Lydia back toward the bar.

Something crashed down hard against the back of her head, and everything went black.

18

Red? Baby, you need to answer me. I know you can hear me. Open your eyes. You aren't breathing right.

Gideon had to find her fast. His entire team was waiting. They'd spread out looking for her, trying to track her, but they'd come up with nothing. Rory had shoved Lydia back into the bar before she'd been taken, and Lydia had only seen three men in masks. She couldn't even identify the car that Rory had been shoved into.

The men had attempted to take Lydia, but Rory had ripped her right out of her captor's hands, kicked one in the belly and thrust her toward the bar, putting her body between them. Lydia had done exactly what Rory had told her to do, although she hadn't slammed and locked the door until she saw Rory go down, blood all over the back of her head.

Gideon had been sharing Rory's mind, and he'd felt that crushing blow, blinding pain, and everything had gone black. He'd put birds in the air, but he had no idea what to look for. She was gone that fast. No direction. Javier and the others had spread out while Gideon had searched from the air, trying to find her.

Throughout the next few hours, he would feel faint stirrings as if she struggled to come to. Pain. Icy shivers. Moments when she was semilucid and someone was asking her questions. Repeating the same question over and over. There was something over her head, restricting her sight, her ability to breathe. She hadn't used her inhaler before leaving the bar, and now, with the covering over her head, it was nearly impossible for her to breathe. She struggled to follow what was being asked of her.

The voices were too muffled. He was certain she had a concussion. She couldn't understand what they were saying, so he couldn't understand. He forced himself to be patient. To be alert when she showed the slightest sign of consciousness.

Red, tell me where you are. Gideon spoke very firmly, making it a command, trying to get past the haze in her mind.

Don't know. Can't see.

Impressions.

Echoes. Pipes. Dripping water.

Her breathing was rough. She was gasping. Wheezing.

Baby, slow your breathing. Try to match mine. Deliberately, he drew air into his lungs, sending her the image. In. Out. Trying to get her to follow him.

Something hard smashed into her stomach, driving the air out of her. Out of him. Another blow landed on her left cheek. Then her right one. The blows rained down on her, one after another, until, once again, everything faded away.

Gideon swore, the dark shadows in him spreading until he felt as if he were being consumed. He stood on his rooftop, the sun pouring down, directing his spies to every part of the wharf. The car couldn't have gone far. He'd been too close. He should have been able to track her even after they'd knocked her out. They'd disappeared too fast. That meant they hadn't been on the street long enough for his birds to spot them.

The men had taken her somewhere close and concealed her. They were interrogating her. At one point, he'd felt the slice of a knife going into her skin over and over. They were torturing her. Was it Whitney's men? Was he angry because she hadn't done the job he'd sent her out to do? It would be like Whitney to keep her from breathing properly.

"Anything?" Javier demanded.

Gideon shook his head. He didn't speak. He knew he was in the same state he'd been in when he'd gone after Elio Barone's empire and taken it down. He just needed a direction. A hint of one. The brief, distorted glimpses Rory had given him were all over the place. He had to wait.

The GhostWalkers had swarmed all over the wharf, the parking garages, apartments and anywhere there might be places with pipes and dripping water. He continued to wait—counting the seconds, the minutes, the next hour—until he felt that faint stirring in his mind again.

Pain exploded in his head. His lungs felt raw. Burned. So did his throat. His body ached. He was afraid to move.

Red. Breathe. Take a breath.

Can't.

She had to.

Where are you? Give me a direction.

It could be him.

Gideon felt his heart stutter. Her breath came in shudders. She was struggling. Really struggling. *It doesn't matter.*

It does. A pause.

More struggling against the mask to draw in air. He thought she drew in strands of material, or maybe it was plastic. Now his heart was pounding. Could they have covered her mouth and nose with plastic?

Think it's him.

Rory, listen to me. It doesn't matter who it is. I just need a direction. Give that to me.

If she gave him more than a short burst of consciousness, without her brain being so confused and chaotic, he could track her. One tiny clue and he'd find her.

They're coming back.

The fear in her mind was overshadowed by her determination to keep him safe. To keep Sebastian safe. Whoever was questioning her would get nothing from her. She was willing to die to save Gideon and the little boy.

Rory, I want a direction from you now. He poured command into his voice. Few could resist his compulsion. So far, he'd never known anyone who could.

The problem with being paired with Rory—and he was certain Whitney had paired them—was that usually meant she would be the one person who could resist his voice. In order for them to be compatible, they had to be able to work together as partners.

He heard footsteps. His scalp hurt as someone caught at her hair where she'd been struck. They yanked her head back and started yelling something at her. He couldn't make out the words. The words were muffled by the covering over her head, roaring in her ears and the terrible wheezing.

"She's not going to make it."

He heard that voice much clearer.

"She dies and he's going to be pissed."

"This is bullshit. Torturing her isn't going to get answers. We never should have taken her in the first place. She can't breathe."

Gideon heard that very distinctly. The voice belonged to a man. He was in a mask, that much he could tell because there was a slight distortion, but the speaker was close to Rory. Suddenly, someone pulled the covering from her head. She didn't lift her head or look around.

Red. Open your eyes for me. Just open your eyes. Take a breath.

Was she that far gone that she couldn't?

Breathe for me. I need you to do this for me. He was pleading. He didn't give a damn if she heard the pleading in his voice. *Rory, I'm asking you to do this for me. Open your eyes and look around you and take a deep breath.*

Who knew when she might get another one? All he needed was one look at her surroundings. That was it. One look. She just needed one good breath to sustain her, and they would come for her. She could be angry with him later. He'd sort it out, but he needed her to live.

Her lashes fluttered and then lifted. The lenses appeared blurry, but she slowly looked around her, uncaring of the two men staring back at her. Gideon ignored them as well. He filed their appearances away to take out to examine later. Right now, all that mattered was the place Rory was being held.

He could see he didn't have much time before she collapsed again. Already her eyes were closing. The two men cursed. One slammed the hood back over her head.

"Let's get out of here. I'm hungry. If he wants to talk to her later, if she's still alive, he can deal with her."

"You going to bandage those cuts?"

"Why bother?"

"The rats are going to get her."

Gideon cursed under his breath, but he was already on the move, sending his people texts, certain he knew the vicinity. She was going to need Paul—and not just to find out whether she was a risk to the rest of his teammates.

"Let 'em. She's not going to make it anyway."

The voices were fading. Gideon heard the sound of a metal door clanging. He was certain now of the direction. He slid down the staircase using only the rails and hit the first floor running. The front door opened automatically for him. Javier joined him on the sidewalk, and they swerved around three people walking toward them as they raced around the corner and cut behind the building to the back alley.

"Ethan's bringing a car. Paul's got the equipment for everything he thinks we'll need for her," Javier said. "You want her back at your place or Mack's?"

"Mine," Gideon said decisively, without hesitation. He wasn't going to take chances with Rory again. She was his. He was going to sort them out one way or another, even if that meant leaving his team for a while and living apart from them. Mack wouldn't like it and neither would any of the others, but he wasn't losing her.

They came up on the high chain-link fence blocking the way to where rows and rows of containers coming in from the sea were stored. Neither man slowed. They simply leapt over the fence and landed, still running without breaking stride. Behind them, Mack and Kane were at the fence, engaging with the guards, while Ethan, driving the car containing Paul and the medical equipment, waited for their commander to get them inside with official approval.

Running at the same pace as Gideon and Javier but on the opposite side of the guard gate were Rhianna and Brian Hutton. They also leapt over the fence and were running through the rows of containers to provide backup for Gideon and Javier. On the rooftop of the building across from them was Lucas Atherton, a member of their team considered an excellent marksman. Rose was on another rooftop with a sniper rifle covering the team from a different angle. Marc Lands, an experienced field medic, set up everything they might need to treat Rory at Gideon's home.

Unerringly, Gideon blew past the tall rows of shipping containers and down several metal steps to a platform below another metal deck closer to the water, where containers were off-loaded from ships. Large pipes led into a building that housed huge tanks. The pipes ran in a network throughout the building, along the floor up toward the ceiling and in and out of the tanks. The warehouse was unbearably hot. Water dripped steadily from condensation that formed on a few of the pipes.

Rats scurried away as Javier and Gideon ran to the motionless woman tied to the metal chair in between two of the tanks. She was slumped over, arms strapped to the chair, open wounds sliced into them so that blood ran down the sides. Her thighs had open cuts as well. Her captors had used a knife blade to slice through her skin with thin cuts.

Gideon whipped the hood from her head. There was thick congealed blood on the back of her scalp. She didn't open her eyes. Her breathing was shallow—too shallow. Javier cut the ties binding her ankles and wrists, and Gideon scooped her into his arms. Gideon ran with her out into the fresh air. Ethan had the car waiting, the back door open, and Gideon slid inside beside Paul. Ethan slammed the door closed and rushed around to the driver's side, and they were away that fast.

Javier stayed with Rhianna and Brian to pick up any signs of who may have taken Rory. They left tiny cameras in several places to ensure that when someone came to check on Rory, they would know and be able to track them.

~

"Share with me everything you see, Paul," Gideon ordered. "Everything. I don't care how bad it is. I had everyone, apart from Mack, leave for a reason. If it comes down to it, I'll take Rory, and we'll go as soon as she's able to travel."

He didn't look at Mack when he spoke to Paul, but he made it clear to both that he meant what he said. "I'm not willing to give her up again. It's going to take a lot of persuasion on my part to get her to take me back after betraying her the way I did. So, you tell me everything you see and what she's facing."

Paul nodded. "Don't talk, Gideon. This type of work isn't the easiest. First, before anything, she needs oxygen. Let me deal with her lungs. I mean it. Don't talk." He poured authority into his voice.

Gideon had heard Paul speak in that tone when he was saving lives, and his heart dropped. He exchanged a quick look with Mack, who would know just how bad things were with Rory. Gideon hadn't been able to reach her, but that was because she was unconscious. Not because she was near death. Not breathing right. Not hit too hard. The cuts Marc had been working on weren't that bad. They were shallow. He tried not to panic. He wasn't a man who ever panicked.

He watched Paul carefully, not once taking his sharp gaze from the man. He was a raptor, and he didn't miss details, especially not this close. Paul's eyes had gone nearly opaque. Crystalline. His eyes had gone to a strange silvery blue, almost like ice with a bluish cast, as if he had gone inward. He held his hands palms outward, hovering them just an inch or so over Rory's lungs. There were no colorful lights. No flashes of healing or anything at all to give away the fact that Paul was one of the rarest of healing powers possibly on earth. He simply breathed normally and held himself still, not moving, with no expression on his face.

Gideon became even more alarmed when Paul stayed in the same position for what seemed far too long. He had been with Paul when he worked on patients. Even when he did psychic surgery on patients, complicated surgeries on patients, it hadn't taken that long in one spot. As a rule, Paul looked very young. Now, despite his expressionless mask, Gideon could detect a strain.

Time passed. It seemed far too long before Paul's palms slowly moved up Rory's bronchial airways. In truth, that didn't make Gideon feel any better. Paul spent another inordinate amount of time there as well before he took a step back, staggered and clearly wheezed when he tried to draw in air. Gideon caught him and eased him into the chair behind him. Mack handed him a bottle of water with the cap already off. Paul didn't try to talk until he drank half of it.

"Her lungs are bad. Airways nearly closed completely. You got to her just in time, Gideon. She wouldn't have lasted much longer. There's an obstruction in her lungs, and her bronchial tubes are far too narrow. I'll come back to that after I examine her thoroughly."

"One of Whitney's experiments, or do you think she was born that way?" Mack asked.

Paul frowned. "He enhanced her, and by doing so, he increased problems she was born with, but he was well aware of them prior to operating on her. He deliberately made her physical difficulties worse."

Paul drank more water and, after screwing on the cap, pressed the cold bottle to his forehead. "I'll start again."

"Don't wear yourself out," Mack cautioned. "But check for anything that could harm her or one of us. Then for programming."

Gideon didn't comment on what Mack was asking for. It had to be done, not just for the sake of the team but also because when Rory woke, she would never stay if she thought she was a threat to them. No matter what she really wanted, there would be no persuading her.

She had an IV in her, giving her necessary fluid, and an oxygen mask, so there was a continual flow of air going to her while Paul examined her. They wouldn't have too much time before she became aware of what was going on around her. Gideon did have his own request though.

"She reacts every time Whitney's name is mentioned by pressing her finger against this spot right here." He touched the exact place above her left temple. "She says there's a strange sensation, like her skin is cracking and wants to shed. Like a lizard or snake. I looked very closely at her skin and couldn't see anything different."

Paul nodded and lifted his palms, again placing them an inch from Rory. He started with her brain, hands steady, his eyes once more turning that strange silvery blue. He took his time examining each quadrant meticulously. Where she'd been struck, he spent time clearly healing the wound before moving around to the spot Gideon had pointed out. Again, he spent a very long time there before he stepped back, staggering a little, shaking his head.

Mack helped him to the chair this time. Paul sank into it gratefully, pressing his fingers to his temples as if to relieve a terrible headache. Gideon knew that at times the psychic surgeon briefly took on whatever his patient had wrong in his efforts to heal them. They waited until Paul was able to drink enough water to recover his ability to speak.

"That is one strong woman, Gideon. She's in pain. That strange sensation is no small thing. It's part of a cloaking device that's coming undone. It's been in place for years and has become part of her physical makeup."

"I don't understand," Gideon said. "I'm in her mind. How could she hide her ability to shield from me?"

"I don't believe she's aware she's doing it." Paul indicated the bar, and Mack immediately got him another bottle of icy water. Paul didn't drink it but pressed the bottle to the spot above his temple.

"Then Whitney did program and send her here for a reason." Mack sounded tired.

Paul sighed. "I saw absolutely no evidence of that. There's no bomb. No programming that I could discern. She's been experimented on multiple times, just as Rose has been. Her bronchial tubes have to be opened. And whatever obstruction he put in her lungs needs to be dealt with. She may have been born with poor lungs, but he introduced something foreign to her lungs to make her breathing problems worse. When I'm stronger, I'll do my best to take care of that for her."

"Let's go back to the shield she has," Mack said. "You say you don't believe Whitney placed it in her, and it's been there so long it's become part of her physical makeup. That doesn't make sense."

Gideon was beginning to understand. "It does if she was a child when she ran, Mack. Whitney drove her to the brink of suicide. I caught glimpses of things he said and did to her. She was in an attic wearing a mask, and she pried open a board covering a window and stepped outside. She was a couple of stories up. If she could cloak herself—and I know she could, because she had just come back from a mission, and she'd saved Rose and Ivy by shielding them from the enemy—she would have been able to hide from the guards while she escaped."

"Then what?" Mack demanded.

"Then suppose something happened, and she didn't remember to take down the shield, or she didn't remember how. She was a kid."

Mack began to pace. "That's a big leap."

"Not really," Paul said. "It makes sense. If her nightmares have been increasing, it's because the shield has been thinning. Memories are surfacing. The hood over her face for so long, the threats and being unable to breathe properly will most likely trigger even more memories, and she'll be confused. The pain is excruciating, by the way. It does feel as if the skin is being ripped away. In a way, it is. Like I said, that shield has become part of her physical makeup."

"Is there a way to make it more bearable for her?" Gideon asked.

"I can try if she'll allow me to. I need to rest, Gideon. I'm going to use one of your spare bedrooms for an hour. If she wakes up, tell her she isn't a threat to anyone, least of all you, and I can help her with her breathing problems."

Paul pushed up from the chairs, his movements heavier than his usual easy gait. He left the room without a backward glance.

"That was an unexpected diagnosis," Mack said. "A kid building that dense of a shield that none of us could penetrate it. Not even Whitney. She hid from him right out in the open for years."

Gideon took Rory's hand and brought it to his chest. "I want a few minutes with these men before we kill them."

"Gideon, you know we're going to have to let Larrsen know she's alive and that we've got cameras set up to catch whoever took her. He's a decent cop. As much as I want to do a little revenge on them, they killed a detective. We need to let them handle it. If they manage to slip through the cracks, then it will be our turn."

"We can claim military jurisdiction, say it's classified and take it out of their hands," Gideon pointed out.

"I understand how you feel."

"Do you? If this was Jaimie lying here, Mack, would you turn it over to the detective and just walk away? Because I don't believe you would. I know you. You'd hunt them down and slit their throats."

Mack was silent for a long time, and then he began to pace. "Yeah. That's exactly what I would do, but it wouldn't be right, Gideon. I'm trying to think what your woman would want you to do. I know Jaimie wouldn't want me to do it. Would Rory? Because she doesn't seem like a woman who would tell you to go find them and cut off their balls for her. I think she'd ask you to call Larrsen. I could be wrong." He turned back to face Gideon. "You know her a hell of a lot better than I do."

Gideon swore under his breath. He'd been sidelined for far too long. He needed action, and he desperately wanted to go after the men who had hurt his woman. He felt every ache. Every single cut, no matter how shallow. The punches they'd inflicted.

"Javier says the word, and I can have one of my birds follow them home. I can take them out with my rifle."

"Your call, Gideon. She's yours."

The stirring in his mind was gentle. Barely a whisper of a touch. A stroke of love. *I need to look after you, Gideon. Someone does.*

His heart felt as if it had melted in his chest. His gut clenched hard and did a slow roll. How was he ever going to let her out of his sight again? This could never happen again. Not ever.

Stay with me. He brought her fingers to his mouth and bit down on the tips. *I can never go through this again. I wanted to set the world on fire.*

He felt the beginnings of alarm, and her lashes fluttered as more awareness settled in. *Where am I? It isn't safe. You have to be safe.*

He turned his head. "Mack, I need a little privacy, please."

"I'll be in the other room until you make your decision, but it has to be soon."

Gideon nodded. "I am safe. I knew that would be your first concern, Rory, so I asked the doc to check you thoroughly. Whitney didn't plant a bomb or a program. He did, however, make your lungs worse. Doc thinks he can help with that if you want him to."

He nibbled at her fingers again and waited to see what she would do. She hadn't wanted any member of his team to help her.

"Doc saved your life. You were nearly dead when we got to you. Without him, there was no chance. I didn't hesitate to use every member of my team to find you. They helped me bring you home." He bit down gently on her fingertips again. "I'm just going to come clean here, Rory, and be honest with you. I was all for waiting as patiently as possible and persuading you to be with me, but I'm no longer going in that direction."

Her long lashes fluttered, and for one heart-stopping moment, her lips seemed to quirk as if she might be amused.

You aren't?

She sounded exhausted, as if she were going under again, and he was probably going to lose his moment with her. He had to tell her while he had her to himself.

"No, Red. I'm not letting you walk away from me. I screwed up bad. I know I did, but you're not better off without me, and I'm sure as hell not better off without you. So, bottom line, we're going to do this relationship thing. We're going to make it work. Getting your trust back will take work, and I'll put the time in, but you're staying."

Her lips did that little quirk again, and this time he did feel a hint of amusement in his mind. *Then call Larrsen.*

He bit down on her fingertips a little harder. "Rory, you have to know what I am. I told you. I'm not a choirboy. I'm a predator."

You're mine, choirboy or predator, but call Larrsen.

She sounded as if she was slipping away from him. He glanced toward the room where Paul was sleeping. He knew the toll that healing took on a psychic surgeon. Gideon had come so close to losing her.

"You're tying my hands, Red." He leaned over her and brushed kisses on her forehead. "They'll want your clothes. Photographs. Are you prepared for that? For a trial?"

Will it get that far?

She knew him so well. He'd never allow her to relive the trauma of what those men had put her through. "What's the point of letting Larrsen arrest them?"

My friends. Harvey. Clearing our names.

Of course she would worry about that.

"I'll make the call, Rory, but they'll want to ask you questions. Are you going to be up for that?"

Don't know, but I'll do my best. So tired.

"Sleep, Red. I'll have Doc with you when the police get here."

She didn't respond. Gideon called in Mack and told him his decision to call Larrsen. They discussed how they would handle the various questions that would naturally arise as to how Rory had been found and why the police hadn't been informed immediately.

Mack, as the commanding officer, made the call to Larrsen.

Larrsen informed Mack that he would be bringing two others with him—one his commander—and to expect them immediately. He also told Mack it was imperative not to tell anyone, not even her friends or boss, that she had been located, even before Mack had conveyed the same to Larrsen.

"I had my men set up cameras, and we're expecting the men who kidnapped her to return. When they do, we want to detain, identify and question them," Mack said.

"I presume you mean turn them over to the police," Larrsen said.

"That as well," Mack murmured.

"Is Rory able to talk?"

"Not so far, although the doctor said she should be coming round soon. We were careful with her clothing. It's bagged according to protocol. Photos of the damage to her body were taken. The doctor will have a full report for you. She was tortured. When we recovered her, she had a hood over her head, and her wrists and ankles were secured to a metal chair."

Gideon glanced at his watch. Too much time had gone by. The men who had left Rory in the warehouse had deliberately left open wounds that would attract rats to feed on the blood. They'd left a hood covering her face, knowing she could barely breathe. They had to believe she would die. What did they want?

"They expected her to die when they left her there, Mack," Gideon said.

"I got that." Mack's voice was grim.

"When I thought it was Whitney's men, it made sense. She didn't do her job. She was disposable to him. But what could these men want from her? I'm concerned that her friends might be in danger. They were shouting questions, but I couldn't understand what they were asking her. I think the hood and her lack of oxygen muffled everything for her, as it did for me."

"I'll call Larrsen back and tell him to round them up and get them into a safe house. He can bring them to one of ours."

Gideon nodded. "That might be a good idea."

"It might tip off our kidnappers."

"Better that than another one of these women gets taken. Two of them have children, Mack. Javier is an elite tracker. He's been in that warehouse for some time now. Jacob is with him. You know what he's like. Nothing gets past his nose. Whoever these men are, they aren't GhostWalkers. They're going to leave something for our boys, even if it's sweat. That will be enough for them to follow. We'll find them one way or another. Better the women are safe."

Mack agreed and made a second call.

Larrsen was hesitant. He had to talk to his boss and didn't seem to think the man would agree. There was too much at stake.

Mack argued: What was more important, protecting the women from kidnap and torture, or finding a cop killer? He ended up hanging up on the detective.

Gideon sent Mack a brief grin. "You still have that edge, Mack. Flares up every now and then."

"Total bullshit to say they can't round up those women quietly and bring them to us. We offered our safe house. They wouldn't be paying for it."

"It's possible they are suspects," Gideon pointed out. "All along,

Rory's been worried that someone has been trying to frame her or one of the other women. Or trying to implicate them in Ramsey's death. Rory looked as if she could be working in Harvey's organization because she moved around so much. Working in a bar, she would have a lot of contacts."

"I could see that." Mack was already texting his people, setting up at one of the buildings they owned to house the women. They just needed someone to persuade them to come to the apartments.

"Who are you sending?"

"Jaimie and Rhianna. I'll have Lucas back them up. We own the building across from our home. It's high-end, secure, and we have several apartments we can rent out. Rhianna and Jaimie can easily persuade them to come look at them. They're leaving now."

Gideon had total faith that the women could get the job done. From what Rory had told him, Cindy wanted to move. Janice and Pam had no reason to stay, and if Cindy could persuade Lydia, they could get Sally to move as well. Rhianna and Jaimie would keep the rents comparable to what the women had been paying. Once they were at the apartment building, Rhianna and Jaimie would convince them to stay until it was safe for them to leave. In other words, until they found whoever was responsible for murdering Detective Ramsey and kidnapping and torturing Rory.

19

Gideon knew the predator in him was showing. The three detectives were clearly uncomfortable in his presence, but he
didn't care. He wasn't about to back off. Rory looked fragile, with
her face swollen and bruised, her eyes dark and hollow. She still
seemed to struggle for air, and Gideon didn't want the cops questioning her; he wanted Paul working to undo whatever Whitney
had done to make her lungs worse than what she'd been born with.

Rory was nervous with the detectives close to her. The moment
Gideon sensed that, he moved to protect her, his killer instincts
taking over. He didn't bother to tone down the piercing stare or the
fact that he had warned them to keep a distance from her bed.

"This is Dr. Mangan. If he stops the interview, it's done,"
Gideon said. "No arguments. We found her barely alive. She insisted on trying to help you, or I would have forbidden this interview until she was better."

"Who are you to her?" Detective Morgan Wilson asked. He
had been introduced by Larrsen as the man in charge.

"Her fiancé," Gideon said without a qualm.

Rory's fingers curled in his hand, but she didn't otherwise react to his blatant statement.

Wilson nodded. "I'm so sorry this happened to you, Ms. Chappel. We're very thankful that your fiancé found you when he did."

"How exactly were you able to do that?" Detective Abbott asked.

Gideon was prepared for the question. Mack and he had discussed how best that would be answered. "Often, when she got off work, we would walk together to the Koi Garden and sit on the patio and talk. I knew she was going to walk Lydia home first, but I didn't like the idea of them walking alone, so I was on my way with one of my teammates to meet up with her. We got there just as she was being pulled into a vehicle, and the car took off. There was no license plate that either of us could see—"

"You called in the description of the car?" Larrsen interrupted.

"No," Mack said, his voice calm. "At the time, we were too busy running down every lead we could to find her. We were afraid if it got out that we even had that much, they might kill her."

"We're fast runners. Very fast," Gideon continued his explanation, "but the car was able to disappear. That meant it didn't get to the freeway or any of the main streets. She had to be somewhere in the harbor. We hunted every place they could have taken her."

Larrsen inched a little closer to the bed. "Rory, honey, are you up for a few questions?"

Her gaze jumped to his face. Her fingers clenched tighter inside Gideon's hand, but she nodded.

"Did you see their faces?"

She shook her head. Her lips trembled just for a moment, and it was all Gideon could do not to order the detectives out.

Red, you don't have to do this yet. In a couple of days, you'll be stronger.

Her gaze drifted over his face lovingly. It would have been impossible not to feel that emotion, let alone see it.

"Did you recognize their voices?"

She shook her head and then frowned. She held up four fingers. "One stayed silent. Angry. Felt his energy before. Knew him." She began coughing and turned her face away from the detectives.

Paul pushed between them, palms hovering above her lungs. *She needs to remain quiet. I need to work on her again, Gideon.*

They'll have to come back, Rory, Gideon decreed.

She shook her head, tears forming. "Have to tell them."

"Doc says it's dangerous for you to keep going. It's not worth your life."

"Book." She gasped the word. It came out a wheeze.

Larrsen hitched forward. "Rory, what do you mean by that?"

Gideon lifted his head and gave him the piercing stare of a raptor before it attacked its prey. That was all the warning he was giving the man.

"Back off now," Mack interpreted, just in case the detective didn't get it.

Have to tell them, Gideon. She coughed again. There were flecks of blood on her lips.

"We have to terminate this interview now, gentlemen," Paul said. "Rory. You cannot say another word."

"Tell me then, Red," Gideon ordered. "Don't speak."

He didn't give a damn what he was giving away to civilians. She wasn't going to kill herself to give them information.

"Gideon," Mack cautioned. *Classified.*

"She has to tell them something she thinks is important, Mack," Gideon said.

"What you're asking me to allow you to do is out of the question."

"Then we're at an impasse, because she can't talk."

"Give us a few minutes, gentlemen," Mack said. "This has become a military matter."

Detective Wilson started to follow Marc Lands out, but he turned back to them. "Detective Ramsey was not only a colleague but a good friend. He was an outstanding policeman who served in the military with distinction and then in the department. I will disclose to those of you in this room, as we're obviously putting you in a bad position, that he was investigating other policemen. We're walking a very fine line here, unable to trust too many of our own. It is very possible he was killed by someone he knew."

Gideon could see and hear that it was extremely difficult—even painful—for Wilson to admit that truth to them. He did so because he was aware that Rory might have valuable information for them and that Gideon might be able to convey it to them through a method that was unacceptable to his commanding officer. He was giving them something huge in return.

Mack's phone vibrated, and he pulled it out and glanced down. "The ladies are secure, just in case any of you were worried."

Wilson's head went up. "What does that mean?"

"It means you wouldn't do it, so we made certain no one could get to them. They came voluntarily," Mack added.

"Where are they?" There was demand in Wilson's tone.

Mack arched an eyebrow. "Safe. I need the room, gentlemen, while I speak with Gideon and the doctor. Marc can show you the report, Rory's clothes and the photographs we took of her body when we first were trying to save her life." He waved them away dismissively.

Gideon could see that just the reminder that the police had denied the women a safe house and guards had upset Mack all over again. The moment they were out of the room, Paul began to work on Rory again. Her cough seemed to have become worse. The more she coughed, the more it seemed her lungs and bronchial tubes spasmed. More little flecks of blood appeared on her lips. Gideon tried breathing evenly, using a support method, pushing the images into her mind, hoping to ease the panic building in her. He didn't dare ask Paul questions or seek reassurance. She needed the doctor's full concentration on her alone.

Red, you can breathe. Do it with me. He placed her palm over his left lung and inhaled deeply. *Think about breathing. Nothing else. Only that. We've done this together many times. Merge with me. Stay with me.*

He wouldn't allow himself to feel anything but how they belonged together. How they fit. She seemed so far from him. Then Mack was there. Breathing. Deep breath in. Let it out slowly. Jaimie joined them.

That's it, baby, stay with me. We're just breathing. You know how. You can do this with me.

Hard. She gasped the reply.

Gideon felt how difficult the struggle was, as if air couldn't get into her lungs. Her tubes were too restricted. He felt Paul's presence as he worked, but he didn't acknowledge it. His full concentration had to be on getting her to stay with the mechanics of just breathing. She was exhausted already. He was certain the beatings she'd taken had contributed to the difficulties of weakening her lungs even more.

Javier, Ethan and Lucas suddenly joined in. He felt the strength of their combined breathing, pushing the air through Rory's narrowed tubes with him. Then Jacob Princeton. He was their underwater specialist and had lungs that were amazing. His added breathing aided tremendously.

That's it, Red. Gideon pressed her palm tighter against his lung. *Feel that.*

Can't find air. Burns.

You're finding it. It just feels that way.

Rhianna and Rose joined them, synchronizing with all of them effortlessly. Kane and Brian and lastly Marc joined the breathing circle from the other room. Through Gideon, his entire team had surrounded his woman, helping her to breathe while Paul worked to widen her airways.

That's it, Rory. You're breathing again. The air is getting to your lungs. You feel that, baby? That burn is easing up.

Panic was beginning to subside. Just a little. Just enough that Rory was more aware of Gideon. That's what he needed from her. That awareness that he was with her. That he hadn't left her side and she wasn't alone. The more she was able to see around her, or feel, she would be cognizant of the others aiding her. He wanted her to see that they had rushed to her aid not only to look for her when she had been kidnapped but also now, when she'd been unable to breathe. She was a fellow GhostWalker. Not only would she always have him, but she would have a family.

Rory had to see for herself that his family could be hers. If she never did accept his team for herself, Gideon would have to be okay with it. She was going to be his wife. The center of his universe. He wanted her to love his family, but time took care of a lot of issues. She would have her other friends when he ran his missions, even if she didn't accept his people.

Mack might persuade her to join them as a GhostWalker on the team. If that happened, Gideon would need to come to terms with how he felt about it. He was protective, and having Rory in the danger zone would divide his attention when he needed his concentration wholly on his work. That was something to be discussed between them before it would ever go on the table with Mack.

Air slid smoothly through Rory's bronchial tubes to her lungs, and Gideon felt Paul pull back. Paul had managed to open the tubes so her lungs could bring in enough air for her to breathe adequately. The team continued to breathe with her for a few more minutes, ensuring she was able to quiet the spasming and coughing.

When the burning sensation had disappeared and the panic had ceased entirely, one by one his team members slipped away.

"She'll need her asthma medication. I'm going to rest again before I work on the blockage in her lungs. This isn't going to take away the asthma, Gideon, but it will make things much easier on her," Paul said. He sounded tired, but not at all the way he'd been before. "Don't let her talk. Get the information from her and just give it to them. She can tell them tomorrow or the next day. Keep in mind her internal organs have taken a beating. She had internal bleeding as well as other injuries. They meant to kill her, Gideon."

Gideon was certain they had planned to kill her from the moment they'd taken her. "Thanks, Paul. I appreciate everything you've done for her. I know it isn't easy on you."

Please tell him thank you from me.

"Rory wants me to thank you as well, Paul. Get some rest." Gideon leaned over Rory after Paul left the room. "You need to go back to sleep. Paul says Whitney did place some kind of an obstruction in your lungs, and he'd like to see if he can remove it. It won't take away your asthma, but it will certainly improve your ability to breathe. You'll have to be in much better shape than you are now for him to do that, Red. And under no circumstances are you to speak aloud."

I need to tell Larrsen what those men believe I have. And I think I might have it.

Gideon brushed back her hair. They hadn't washed the congealed blood out of it. They hadn't had time. That was for another day. "Tell me, sweetheart."

They kept asking about a notebook. Over and over. At first, I thought they had something to do with Whitney, so it didn't make any sense. They kept hitting me over and over. The man that felt angry and kept silent began cutting me with a knife. That only confused me more, because I realized it was a cop. It was Detective Ramsey.

Rory fell silent. Just that little bit of effort to speak to him tele-pathically had exhausted her, as Paul had predicted.

Gideon continued to stroke back the hair from her face, his fingertips lingering in the mass of cherry-colored strands. Her eyes had been closed, but she struggled to open them, lashes going up for just a brief moment so she could look straight at him.

You shouldn't touch my hair, Gideon. I'm a mess. It's disgusting.

Her lashes drifted down again. He couldn't help smiling at her reaction right in the middle of telling him something important she wanted to convey to the detectives.

Nothing about you is disgusting, Red. When the doc gives me the go-ahead, I'll wash your hair for you. Tell me what you think you have that these men want from you so you can sleep. Paul wants you to rest as much as possible.

She didn't answer him right away. He could feel her drifting. At least she was breathing easier. Paul insisted she still have the oxy-gen flowing to her. The mask, not just a simple nosepiece, and Gideon made certain it was securely in place. He sat beside the bed, not prompting her to say anything more, just waiting. If the detectives needed the information, they could wait as well.

A half an hour later, Mack returned to the room with the three detectives. "Anything?"

"She fell asleep, but she definitely has information she wants to relay. She said they kept asking her about a book. Over and over. At first that confused her. She didn't understand who they were or what kind of book or what they were talking about. One was very angry, and he beat her and cut her with a knife when she couldn't answer. But then she said she began to associate the question with Detective Ramsey. She said they kept asking the question over and over in various ways. Three of the four men questioned her."

"About a book?" Wilson exchanged a look with the other two detectives. "Peter Ramsey preferred to write everything by hand in a notebook rather than use a tablet. He was old-school when it came to that. Afterward, he typed up his reports, but when he was working, he liked to arrange his notes a certain way. He always used a brown notebook that resembled a diary."

"Did she say anything else?" Abbott prompted.

"She thought she might know where it was, but she didn't tell them that. She drifted off before she could tell me," Gideon said.

Wilson looked frustrated. "What did the doctor say about her condition? I read his report, and she's very lucky to be alive."

"He said to let her rest as much as possible. He still has more work to do on her," Gideon said. "Rory was very insistent she tell you what she thinks, but she drifted off before she could let me know. I'll call when I've got something for you."

"I can stay, if you don't mind," Larrsen said. "We've been working on this night and day for a couple of months. The four of us. Losing Ramsey was a terrible blow. The three men murdered felt like that was on us, and then the women being terrorized and now this happening to Rory. I'd rather stay and hopefully be here when she wakes. If you prefer, I can wait in my car just outside."

"I don't think that's necessary," Mack said before Gideon could answer him.

Thought this was my house.

Mack grinned at him. *You've got four floors and too many rooms to count. You're being an ass on purpose. Do you have a grudge against that man?*

At the moment, all of them. I'm still upset that they didn't figure out a way to protect the other women, especially Larrsen. Lydia, one of Rory's friends—who, by the way, has a three-year-old daughter—likes the man, and I thought he was all about her.

"In case the three of you haven't figured it out yet, instead of Rory lying here, this could be Lydia or Sally or one of the others," Gideon reminded them. "But I suppose, even with our offer of a safe house and guarding the women, it was too big of a risk to one of you quietly talking to them and asking them to come with our people."

Larrsen and Abbott both shifted their gazes to Wilson. Clearly, as the lead detective, he'd had to make the judgment call.

Wilson nodded. "We only had a short time to make the decision. We didn't have a safe house or anyone we could trust to watch over them. We couldn't take a chance that the information would get out over police channels. I didn't understand that your people were intending to keep them safe for us, and even if I had, I would have had to check with resources in Washington to ensure you were reliable."

Gideon could understand the man's dilemma to some extent, but he still felt the women should have been watched. There were three men. Someone should have been on them all the time. Larrsen should have warned them to stay together. Maybe he had. He'd remained suspiciously silent, not attempting to defend himself.

"Stay," Gideon capitulated gruffly. "There's plenty of room."

"If the kidnappers were going to return, wouldn't they have done so by now?" Abbott asked, looking at his watch. "According to the doctor's report, if you hadn't shown up when you did, she wouldn't have lasted even another twenty minutes."

"It's possible they don't intend to return," Mack said. "That doesn't mean we can't track them. My team is very specialized in what they do. We're going to give it another couple of hours. If nothing else, they may come back for her body to remove any physical evidence."

"I would understand that you might want to claim this as a military operation, but we need jurisdiction here," Wilson said. "This investigation has been ongoing for nearly two years and cost the life of a very good man. If you pick up a prisoner, or more than one, you can't interrogate them. You must turn them over immediately or risk blowing everything we've done."

Mack nodded abruptly. "I understand. As long as Rory's alive, we'll play ball with you. Anything changes on that score, all bets are off." He jerked his chin toward the door, and he and Marc immediately led the two detectives out before Wilson could protest.

There was a small silence as Larrsen waited for the front door to close, although the bedroom where Rory was located was a distance away.

"I asked the women to stick together and not go to work," Larrsen admitted. "And I did tell them if they were uncomfortable in any way, to go to your house, but to do it with all of them together. That could have gotten me fired, but Lydia, Ellen and the others were more important than my job. I trusted you to take care of them without a government report. Fortunately, the women trusted me enough to do as I asked, and they didn't leave the apartment building or one another's company until you sent someone for them."

"How did you know someone from my team came for them?" Gideon asked.

"Lydia texted me. She said a woman by the name of Jaimie said she was Mack's wife and that she knew Gideon. She said Gideon and Mack wanted all of them to look at some safer apartments, and in the meantime, they could stay there, where it was safer. I told her Mack was one of the good guys."

He refused to be intimidated by Gideon's piercing gaze and stepped closer to the bed. "Yeah, you didn't need to remind me this could have been Lydia. Now I can't raise her. She isn't answering my calls or my texts. Where is she?"

Gideon respected him even more for the ice in his voice and the steel in his gaze. "We had to shut down all communication. That's standard procedure in a safe house for their security. They were told the rules before they agreed. Lydia was made aware that you would know she wouldn't be able to contact you."

"I'm a detective."

"And you're most likely under observation."

Larrsen couldn't argue with him, and Gideon knew he wouldn't have a comeback. On the other hand, Gideon knew when he'd lost contact with Rory he'd nearly gone out of his mind.

"I'll do my best to get word to have one of my people get something to us so you can see she's fine."

"I'd appreciate it," Larrsen said, his voice gruff. Once more, his gaze was on the bruising on Rory's face. "I never thought anyone I knew would go this wrong."

"I learned that lesson when I was very young," Gideon said.

There was no expression on his features or in his voice, but there must have been in his head, because immediately Rory reacted. Her hand crept across the bed, seeking his, and he covered it to reassure her, stilling the movement.

A frown flitted across her face, her lashes fluttered but didn't lift, and he felt the faint stirring in his mind. *Why are you so sad?*

I'm not, Red. You're supposed to be asleep.

I am asleep. But you're frowning and you're sad. Now you're lying, and you're not a very good liar, Gideon.

She made him smile. He leaned down, bringing her knuckles to his mouth. Her hand felt very small in his.

I'm a very good liar, just apparently not to you. That's a good thing. But sleeping means you're not supposed to be aware of your surroundings. I'm looking out for you so you can sleep in peace.

Her lips curved into a smile and his breath caught in his throat. Then she seemed to be drifting again, but just as quickly, her breathing came too fast, and images poured in. Voices, dark and disturbing. Her free hand reached up to try to remove the oxygen mask. He stopped her very gently.

"Rory, open your eyes for me. You aren't there with them. You're here with me."

She continued to try to take the mask from her face, shaking her head. He had to use a little bit of force to keep her from taking it off.

You need to leave that on, sweetheart.

She shook her head, her frown back. *I can't stand it. Take it off me, Gideon. I feel like I have that hood on me.*

Inwardly he cursed. *Let me ask the doc if you'll be able to breathe.*

I can breathe. Take it off. Hurry.

He knew panic was setting in fast. He reached for it. *We aren't alone. Larrsen is here. I'm taking it off. Just breathe in and out. I'm talking to the doc now.*

Gideon turned his head to observe Larrsen even as he reached out to Paul telepathically. The detective was watching him, too much speculation in his gaze. Larrsen was extremely observant and very intelligent.

Rory's having a difficult time with the oxygen mask. Panicking. It feels like the hood to her. I took it off. Should I replace it with the nose-piece?

Gideon didn't like waking Paul when he knew the man needed rest, but he wasn't sure how removing the flow of oxygen would affect Rory.

I'll be right in to assess the situation. In the meantime, give her a break from the mask.

"The doctor will be in soon, sweetheart. Just keep breathing."
Rory nodded.

Larrsen moved away from the bed to take one of the two chairs close to the door. "You're able to speak to her telepathically. That's how you tracked her."

Gideon glanced at him but didn't reply. That was getting into classified information. The higher-ups would probably find someone who could remove memories from Larrsen's brain if they ever knew about the conversation.

"If she can tell you where she thinks Peter Ramsey's notebook is, I'd greatly appreciate the information. Or at least a starting point where to look."

Did you hear that? Larrsen stayed behind because the detective who was killed was in the middle of an investigation. The evidence he collected had been written in a notebook that looked like a diary with a brown cover. Does that sound familiar? Gideon asked her.

A little frown flitted over her face again. *We were in the lounge sorting our mail when he came into the room, and we ran. Later, an officer gave us our mail. I always kept my junk mail in a bag in the trunk of my car. When the bag was full, I'd take it to the bar and shred it. It always took a long time to get full.*

Gideon couldn't help himself. He rubbed at the frown with the pad of his thumb, seeking to erase it. *Red, if this is too hard for you, we can wait a little longer. Larrsen isn't going anywhere. He's patient.*

She coughed and hastily tried to stop. Gideon brushed her forehead with his lips, resisting the urge to put the oxygen mask back on her. Her hand turned in his and caught at him, clutching tightly.

"You're just having a bad moment, Rory. A spasm. This is going to pass. Keep breathing. In and out. You know how," Gideon coaxed.

Her gaze clung to his as if he were her lifeline, and she nodded. Once she was breathing properly, he brought her hand back to his mouth. *That's my girl.*

Her vivid green eyes moved around the room for the first time and found Larrsen in the chair by the door. Gideon felt her forming her thoughts and trying to put them into words.

"Don't talk. Paul said absolutely not. You'll destroy all his work, Rory."

Her gaze jumped back to his. *I'm sorry. I'm not used to this.*

You were telling me about the junk mail.

Yes, after the officer gave me the bag, I put it in the trunk of my car and forgot all about it until someone destroyed my car. The trunk was popped open, and the mail was thrown all over the parking garage floor. Janice picked it up and stuffed it back in the torn bag, and she put it in the closet in the lounge. I didn't look in the bag. It was junk mail. But I do recall someone mentioning a notebook. I use notebooks for my song-writing, but as a rule, I don't keep them in my trunk. I was so upset I didn't think to question it.

You never actually saw the notebook they talked about.

No. She shook her head.

Gideon leaned closer to her and caught her head between his hands to keep her still. Her gaze clung to his. *Red, we can't give any clues to Larrsen that we're speaking telepathically. He already suspects, and it's classified information. I don't want there to be any problems.*

She looked puzzled. He groaned and pressed a kiss to the corner of her mouth. Rory was never going to be one of the Ghost-Walkers who could look completely expressionless—at least he'd always be able to read her.

How are you going to relay whatever I tell you to him?

I'm just going to tell him, and later you can write it out for them. Or we'll write it out, and you can sign the statement. We'll make it work for their investigation.

The tote should be in the lounge. If he can't locate it, Janice will know exactly where it is. I don't want him to get his hopes up, Gideon, because I don't know for sure, but Detective Ramsey could have dropped the notebook into my tote as he was running out the door. Or it could be one of my notebooks, and I had it in the trunk and forgot about it.

It's a long shot, Gideon agreed. *But worth a try.*

On the other hand, if Ramsey knew his wounds were fatal and whoever had shot him was still coming at him, he would want to find a place to get rid of the notebook. He'd know that if he was dealing with a policeman, no one would think twice about a cop examining his body. He wouldn't want to keep the notebook on him. It would appear as if the cop was trying to help him. Forensics would go over the lounge, but the mail? No one would be looking at junk mail.

I'll get the word to Larrsen. I want you to cooperate with Paul. When he works on you, there's always an exchange.

Her little frown was back. *A risk, you mean. I told you how I felt about anyone taking risks for me.*

"Rory, Paul's a doctor. You have no idea how many doctorates he has. The kid can do any kind of surgery you need, and doctors are always consulting with him. He knows what he's doing. If he says something, you just do it."

She glared at him, her frown deepening, brows drawing together. *You're deliberately misunderstanding me. Go away. Take Larrsen into the other room and give him the information. But before you do, redeem yourself and tell me Lydia and the others are safe.*

That's all it will take to redeem myself? He flashed a grin at her. *Red, you're going to have to be a little tougher than that.*

He knew she never would be. His woman was all about compassion and kindness. He'd need her to balance his predatory traits.

They're safe, aren't they?

We've got them in our apartments across from Mack and Jaimie's warehouse. Very secure, under guard. Very nice apartments. They can rent them for the same as they were paying in the other place, each of them. We're making it easy for them to relocate once this is over.

You didn't offer me that deal.

Because you don't get the same deal. You're going to move in with me. You can visit them. He made it a decree, and he didn't plan on backing down from it. He might have gotten an eye roll, but he couldn't be sure.

Go away.

Not until Paul comes. He's on his way.

I feel him. He's moving slow, Gideon. She looked up at him, concern in her eyes.

Gideon took it as a good sign that she was becoming aware of her surroundings and also the people aiding her. She knew Larrsen was in the room and Paul was near. She was breathing on her own far better than she had been. Her mind seemed clearer.

I'm aware, Red. He won't work on you until he knows he's one hundred percent. He still needs to remove whatever Whitney did to your lungs. That's a huge undertaking. After that, when you're up to it, you and I will discuss it, and then you're going to decide if you want help with your skin issues.

Her eyes searched his. He felt her moving through his mind. He didn't attempt to keep anything Paul had seen from her. He wouldn't keep anything from her again. If she wanted to look, he would let her. She even saw the moment when he'd declared to Mack that he would leave the team and go away with her.

I did this to myself? I took my memories from me?

He nodded. *It makes sense. Think about your nightmares. It all fits. You protected yourself, Rory. Even as a child, you outsmarted Whitney. He thinks you're dead because you disappeared and he couldn't track you. That shield is beginning to fall apart, but if you want help, once we really talk about it, we have ways that will ensure he can't find you.*

Paul leaned over the bed. "How are you doing, Rory?"

"I'll leave you to it," Gideon said. "Come with me, Larrsen. I'll fill you in on a few things."

20

Wings folded, the red-tailed hawk sat very still on the narrow branch of the flowering dogwood tree, piercing brown eyes fixed on the two men across the street from her. She had been there for some time, watching dispassionately as the conversation became more and more agitated. One man waved his arms in the air and shook his head repeatedly. He was the older of the two and clearly disagreed with the younger man. At one point, he shoved his finger in the younger man's chest, poking him belligerently.

The younger man stepped back, spit on the ground and walked to his car. The hawk unfolded her wings and took to the air, letting out a hoarse scream that lasted three seconds as it soared above the car. The raptor flew in the air for several minutes until the car made a left turn, and then she cried out a second time.

"Westlake is on the move," Gideon reported. "He's heading toward the harbor. Let me know when you've got him in your sights."

"Copy that," Abbott's voice responded.

No one had returned to the warehouse, not even to retrieve Rory's body. Forensics had stayed away from the building where she'd been held captive at the wharf, even when it became apparent no one was coming back for her. Mack's people guarded the site to ensure it stayed pristine until Wilson could have his people meticulously look for evidence to convict the men who had kidnapped and tortured Rory. They didn't want any word to get out over the police scanners to tip off their prey that they were coming after them.

"I couldn't get everything they were arguing about," Rhianna said. "Reading lips from that distance is difficult, and Carver kept turning his body, but he wanted to get Rory's body and take it out to sea. He thought there was too much risk leaving it. Westlake wanted the rats to dine for a while."

The shadow in Gideon grew darker and spread. It wasn't easy allowing the cops to handle the men he considered evil. He could tell himself they would never make it to trial, to let Wilson arrest them first, but it was still difficult. The detectives needed that satisfying end when they'd lost one of their own. A GhostWalker could easily get in and out of a jail cell. No one would be the wiser when the four men ended up dead. Gideon would have an alibi. The GhostWalker team wouldn't even be in San Francisco when the four turned up dead. Still, hearing the conversation Rhianna just reported made him want to hunt Westlake, not just be the eyes for everyone.

Stand down, Gideon. Stay in control, Mack cautioned.

Why would you think I'm not in control? he demanded. *My middle name is Zen.*

Rory's little giggle in his mind was the most calming sound there was. *The entire building is shivering, Mr. Zen.*

You have nightmares, Red. Even sleeping right next to him, his arms tight around her, she woke nearly every hour terrified.

I'll get over it.

You'll get over it a lot faster knowing they're gone from this world.

Her laughter sounded like soft musical chimes, breaking through the shadows threatening to consume him. *You're so blood-thirsty. I think you need to work on your meditation skills.*

I'm so in love with you. He was. He didn't care who knew. He wanted her to know. That was what was important.

Carver is on the move, Rhianna reported.

Come back to the fold, Mack ordered.

Gideon directed the male red-tailed hawk into the air to follow Carver's car. The male was younger than the female. His eye color hadn't yet gone all the way from yellow to brown. Another year and he'd be there. He was very reliable and a strong flier. Smaller than the female, as males were, he was very fast and could maneuver through tree branches at a high rate of speed. In this case, he cut straight through the sky, while the car had to follow the road.

Gideon followed the car through the cries of the raptors and reported the road he was taking to Abbott. It appeared as if Carver was heading toward the wharf as well, but from a different direction than Westlake had come. Carver slowed his car and pulled over to the side of the road when he got near a junkyard. Jacob and Javier had tracked the car Rory had been pulled into by following the scent of her blood.

"Carver is parked across from the junkyard where they abandoned the car used to kidnap Rory. It was stolen and the license plate muddied so it was unreadable. Forensics isn't there yet, are they?" he asked Wilson.

"No, but the description of the car is out. We sent out the photograph that was captured on the camera across the street from the bar. It was blurry. We received a call from the worker at the junk-yard saying they think they have the car there. It's possible Carver got wind of the call. If he gets out of his car, let me know. I'll have officers there immediately to guard the car, and forensics will be all over it."

Gideon wasn't certain how Wilson thought he was supposed to keep Carver from getting to the vehicle in the junkyard while they waited for officers to show up to stop him from touching it.

The hawk screamed in three hoarse cries. "He's opening his door and starting across the street," Gideon warned. "I'd send the officers and forensic team now. Get it out over the radio. Let every-one know they're on the way."

Gideon sent a large flock of gulls into the air straight at Carver. They were big birds with dark heads and long snouts with hooks at the ends of their bills. The shrieking cries came first and then om-inous shadows blotting out light, casting patterns of moving wings, feathers and menacing macabre shapes darting down toward the street, blocking Carver from the junkyard.

The cop ducked down, covering his head with his hands, run-ning back toward his vehicle to take shelter. The gulls landed on the roof of his car. The hood. The trunk. They pecked at the win-dows, trying to break the glass to get at him.

Looks a bit like a scene from a horror movie, Gideon. You might want to tone it down, Rhianna recommended. She had followed Carver in her car but kept at a distance.

I got the idea from a movie—well, the trailer, Gideon admitted. *I never saw the movie. I didn't want to have nightmares.*

You're such a baby, Rhianna said. *Carver is starting up his car. Your gulls did the trick.*

"Carver is leaving, Wilson. Your forensic people can check the car."

"Thanks," Wilson said.

"Let me know when one of your people has Carver in sight." Not that Gideon's team would break off. They were going to make absolutely certain that every one of the monsters who had committed these crimes was arrested.

Rory's clothes and the hood had also been examined, all hair and fibers taken from them. The report she'd given about the notebook had been followed up on. Janice had shoved the tote bag in the lounge cupboard. The notebook had contained the damning evidence Detective Peter Ramsey had uncovered, including where he had hidden audiotapes he had recorded of Detectives Westlake and Carver and two retired detectives—Bill Morris and Jerome Michigan—conspiring to murder key members of a criminal organization and then murder Jarrod Flawson, Dustin Bartlet and Ret Barnes—three of the four heads of that organization. Next, they would frame Harvey Matters and kill him, then take over their organization.

Westlake had gone to the apartments with Ramsey that afternoon. Something must have made him suspicious, and he'd shot Ramsey. Once Westlake shot Ramsey, he knew he had to kill him and get any evidence he might have on him.

Gideon was certain it was Westlake who had been the one to really torture Rory. He was a sadistic man. He was certain Westlake had been the one to torture and kill Dustin Bartlet, as well as Ret Carnes and Jarrod Flawson. It was no wonder he'd been under investigation for so long. The other detectives had been careful, trying to find a way to make the charges stick.

Westlake was intelligent. What no one had realized at first was that he had partners. After they began to suspect Leo Carver might be in league with him, it hadn't occurred to them that anyone else from the department might be involved. There was nothing to point in that direction. There was no way of knowing that

Westlake had managed to recruit two retired and disillusioned cops until they had Ramsey's notebook.

～

The small flock of sparrows sat in the apple tree in the backyard of Bill Morris's home, watching him with their beady eyes. Judging. Morris wanted to throw something at them. Take out his gun and shoot them, one by one, right out of the tree. He had the feeling they knew what he'd done. He hadn't been able to sleep, and for the last two nights, he'd sat at the kitchen table with his service revolver in his lap.

The grill was hot, and he opened the lid. His wife, Deana, sat in a chair by the pool, talking to Jerome Michigan's wife, Nikki.

Deana looked up and smiled at him. "Babe, you want a beer?"

She never failed to ask him if he wanted something. She'd always been that way throughout their marriage. The way she looked at him—that never failed to move him. He never wanted her to look at him any differently.

"I'm good, Deana."

He could never give her children. He could never give her anything that she deserved. She'd always wanted to travel, but he'd always been working, and they really didn't have the money. She didn't shop or buy things. She gardened. She wasn't someone who wanted jewels or fancy clothes. She didn't care about cars. She didn't complain. He'd told her when he retired that they could travel, but that hadn't worked out the way he wanted. His investments had done poorly, and her multiple sclerosis had gotten a firm foothold. She didn't say one word about how he'd invested their money. She just told him she loved their home and was happy being in it with him.

His phone vibrated over and over. He took it out and glanced down. Westlake. Always Westlake and his demands. Each request was worse than the last. It was bad enough that Westlake had insisted on kidnapping the Chappel woman, but he had tortured her. He wanted them all to torture her. When Morris had refused to participate in hitting her, Westlake had become so incensed, he took out a knife and began slicing her up. Morris had been sick after that. He knew once he left, he wouldn't go back.

"You get the message from Westlake? He wants us to meet him at the apartments. We have to snatch another one of those women. One of them has the notebook." Jerome came up behind him. "We don't have any other choice. Ramsey had to have given it to one of them."

Gideon was able to pick up the conversation through the number of birds facing the two men.

"That's what he said about Chappel. He was positive she had it, and she had no idea what he was talking about. Did you see what he did to her? I couldn't get him to stop. He went insane, Jerome. Was that okay with you? Is that who you are?"

"Better her dead than us."

Morris shook his head. "I can't even look Deana in the eye. You want to help him, you go, but I'm not going near him."

"He'll kill you."

"Let him. I was dead the minute he started torturing that poor woman."

Jerome swore at him. "We've been friends a hell of a long time, Bill. You'd better not throw me under the bus." He turned toward the two women. "Nikki, I have to go into town. You stay right here with Deana and Bill until I get back." He didn't wait for his wife to reply; he just hurried around the house to his truck.

How the hell did they miss the notebook in the trunk of Rory's car? Mack asked.

When Larrsen questioned her, Janice said the tote had been thrown into a corner of the parking garage after someone ripped it with a knife.

They must have seen the junk mail and then thrown it. The mail fell everywhere when the tote was thrown, and the notebook landed in the corner in the dark, Gideon told Mack.

"Wilson, I think if you go visit Bill Morris personally right now, he'll either turn witness for you or commit suicide before you get a chance to talk to him," Gideon advised. "He didn't want to go along with what they did to Rory. They're apparently setting up to try to get one of the other women right now."

I'll volunteer to be Lydia or Sally, Rose said. *You know I can change my image.*

I can be one of the other women, Jaimie added.

I'll be one, Rhianna said. *It shouldn't take me long to get there.*

"Three of my team have volunteered to disguise themselves as the women these men will try to kidnap, Wilson," Mack said into the radio. "They are highly trained."

"Too big a risk," Wilson said.

"To your suspects?" Mack countered.

Wilson didn't reply, but Gideon heard the three women share laughter with the team members. It was a risk to the suspects. Rose and Rhianna were every bit as lethal as the men, and Jaimie was as well, given the right circumstances. They weren't very happy that Westlake, Carver and Michigan had tortured Rory and left her to die.

Half the flock of sparrows lifted from the apple tree, taking to the air, following Michigan as he made his way toward the apartments. Like Carver, he took a circular route, twice changing directions, clearly checking to see if anyone was following him. He never once thought to look to the sky.

"We've got Westlake in sight. He's pulling into the garage," Larrsen said. "Visitor parking. Used his police ID to get right in the front. He's sitting in his car, but he's nervous. He's looking around and spending lots of time on his phone."

"Stay back, Larrsen," Wilson cautioned. "I don't want him to spot you."

"He won't." There was complete confidence in Larrsen's voice.

Gideon didn't blame him. Javier had shown him a couple of places to conceal himself that gave him a good view of the front of the building and visitor parking.

Gideon felt movement behind him and knew immediately his woman had joined him on the rooftop. "What are you doing? You had strict orders to stay put."

Rory moved slowly, but she came up beside him. *I'm feeling better. I'm getting stiff just being in bed. I'd rather be up here with you.*

"Did you ask Paul first?"

She made a face at him. *I'm not three, Gideon. I wouldn't take a chance on messing up anything he worked so hard to repair, especially once I knew there was a risk to him. He told me to not speak aloud yet, but I can be up here with you. Just not to overdo it.*

"Climbing stairs might be overdoing it, Red. Sit right here next to me." Gideon patted the wide bench next to where he stood. "Are you warm enough?"

The truth was, he preferred having her close to him. He'd been with her nearly every moment since they'd found her in the warehouse, and he was uncomfortable leaving her alone, even though he could reach out to touch her telepathically.

Rory sank onto the bench and leaned against his hip. She had a new inhaler, one Paul had prescribed for her. It seemed to work better, but Gideon wanted Rory to be strong enough for Paul to be able to do the psychic surgery on her lungs. Paul didn't think she was ready yet.

"Leo Carver just pulled into the parking lot," Larrsen reported. "He appears to be very agitated. He's gotten out of his vehicle and into Westlake's."

What does Detective Larrsen plan to do once all of them show up

there at the apartments? The women aren't there. Won't that tip West-
lake off that they've been placed in a safe house? He'll know Lydia and
I aren't working. By now, he must know I'm not dead, right? Hasn't the
word gotten out?

"Not yet, but it's going to very soon."

Gideon felt Rory's frown in his mind, and he used the pad of
his thumb to rub at her lips. "Sweetheart, part of the plan is to keep
them off-balance. They need to find out you're alive. They'll know
forensics has the car, the place you were tortured, your clothes and
the hood they covered your face with. And the notebook. The
noose is closing around their necks."

Which will make them desperate. Desperate men do crazy things.
There was worry in her voice.

"We're going to be watching over Larrsen, Red." He read her
concern.

Larrsen is Lydia's choice. And he's a good man. You said so yourself.
I think Westlake will do everything he can to kill him.

"I think you're right. Wilson thinks he's going to make an arrest. I doubt if Westlake is going to go quietly," Gideon agreed.

Larrsen's voice interrupted. "Jerome Michigan just pulled up.
Carver and Westlake are checking their weapons. They mean business. Wait until they come back out before we confront them. We
don't want them taking hostages."

Can one of your team disable their vehicles while they're inside?
Would Wilson agree to let you do that? She sent the question to Mack
on the common team pathway.

"Wilson, I can have a member of my team get in there fast and
disable the cars. Need your okay. We're already working with you,"
Mack reminded him.

Wilson didn't hesitate. "That's a go."

"Sending you in, Rhianna. You're good with cars. Get it done.
You're already there, right behind Carver."

The cameras up inside? Mack asked. *I want to see and hear the reaction when they realize the women are gone.*

In place. Javier installed them. Take a look at your screens, Mack. You can see the three of them walking in like they own the place, Gideon said.

Rory pulled out her phone and Gideon took it from her to Air-Drop the program onto it so she could see what the other team members could. Westlake, Michigan and Carver strode straight to the lounge as if expecting to find the women there. They halted abruptly when they found it empty.

"Where's Morris?" Westlake demanded, glaring at Michigan.

"He couldn't leave. Deana's sick. You know she has MS. Nikki's with them. I told her to stay there until I get back."

"Nikki could have stayed alone with Deana," Westlake snapped. "She doesn't need Bill there." He stabbed at his phone ferociously, punching in numbers. Evidently, no one answered, which only added to his ire. He jammed the phone into his pocket. "Let's visit Lydia and her little brat. One of them has that notebook. We'll get it one way or another. We should have grabbed her first."

Rory circled Gideon's thigh with her arm. *Thank you for making sure my friends are safe, Gideon. That man is a monster.*

Gideon was well aware Westlake was evil. He'd been the one to carry Rory out of the warehouse to the car and pray to the universe that she stayed alive long enough to get her back to the house, where Paul could do surgery on her. If Paul hadn't been in the car, Gideon doubted if Rory would have lived.

He would hurt Ellen to get Lydia to tell him what he wanted to know, but she doesn't know anything. In the end, he would have killed them both.

Gideon rested his hand on top of her head, fingers automatically burrowing in the thick mass of hair. He'd indulged himself, washing and conditioning her hair the moment Paul had given him the go-ahead. Her dark cherry–colored hair fascinated him, and he knew she didn't like the feel of it being dirty. He didn't like the blood and dirt in it, reminding him he'd come so close to losing her.

"He won't have the chance to get them," Gideon said, indicating the screen on her phone.

They watched as the detectives went to Cindy's door and knocked. No one answered. They called Lydia first, then Cindy. Neither woman answered. Janice's and Pam's phones went to voice mail. For the first time, Westlake looked uneasy.

"I don't like this. Michigan, are you sure about Morris? He hasn't been talking to anyone, has he? He was acting strange," Westlake said.

Michigan hesitated. "He didn't like the way you treated Chappel. He objected several times. He told you, John. You know how he is."

"Would he sell us out?"

Wilson should send out the call to forensics to go to the warehouse, Gideon suggested to Mack.

Apparently, Wilson had the same idea, but he went a step further. He sent a forensic team to the warehouse but announced that Laurel Chappel had been found alive a couple of days earlier and was being held safe at an undisclosed location.

Westlake and the other two detectives froze as they received the news. Westlake burst into swearing. The three men hurried through the hall toward the front entrance.

"Morris had to have called in Chappel's location," he snapped as he yanked open the door leading outside. "No one could have found her. I'm going to kill him myself. But first I'll do his wife right in front of him."

"At least find out if he betrayed us first," Michigan cautioned. "You snapped when Chappel didn't answer and nearly beat her to death, but the rest of us thought she couldn't breathe. If you'd just given her air, we might have gotten answers."

Westlake stopped abruptly, swinging around to confront Michigan. "Maybe it was you, Michigan. As I recall, you didn't think it was a good idea to take her in the first place."

"I think maybe you're putting too much cocaine up your nose," Michigan fired back.

"We have to get out of here," Carver said. "Not fight amongst ourselves. Let's go. We can meet up somewhere else and discuss what to do."

Westlake spat on the ground in front of Michigan's shoes and burst into an unexpected sprint toward his vehicle. The others looked up to see the police emerging from every direction.

Wilson and Abbott stepped onto the asphalt from either side of the building. A ring of uniformed officers surrounded the lot. Larrsen walked straight toward Westlake.

Carver and Michigan both halted instantly. Westlake continued forward in a full run, his revolver out. Rhianna had finished disabling the vehicles and was sauntering out of the lot, looking as if she were a resident leaving the area, exiting via the sidewalk. At the last moment, Westlake switched directions, putting the front columns between him and the police. As he did, he fired his weapon and shot Rhianna in the calf to bring her down, clearly wanting a hostage.

A collective gasp went through the GhostWalker team. Before Gideon could stop her, Rory was up and leaning over the balcony. He didn't know why, because she couldn't see anything from there; at least he didn't think she could, and everything was happening so fast.

Rhianna, get up against the wall. Press tight against it. There was hard authority in Rory's voice.

Westlake ran straight at Rhianna. She'd dropped to the sidewalk, the bullet in the calf taking her down, but strangely there was no blood, not a single drop. Gideon viewed her from overhead, his vision usually sharp, but he seemed to look through a gray veil when he tried to see the sidewalk.

Westlake appeared frantic as he cast around for his victim. He couldn't find her, and he had to keep going. He ran around the corner right into what appeared to be a teenage boy on a skateboard, who nearly clotheslined him. The kid swept on past Westlake as he went down, choking and coughing but still clutching his revolver.

Larrsen came around the corner, ignoring Javier, who had hopped off the skateboard and gone up onto the sidewalk and was kneeling. Westlake fired several shots at Larrsen as other officers raced to back up the detective who called out orders to Westlake to put his weapon down.

Westlake shouted obscenities at Larrsen and fired again.

"What did you do, Rory?" Gideon asked. "Javier's with her now. Whatever it was, you can undo it."

She shrugged and sank down again on the bench. She was breathing heavily. *Don't let anything happen to Larrsen.*

Gideon was more worried that Rory had overtaxed herself. Rhianna had been a distance away. They were all waiting for a report on her condition from Javier. He'd shown restraint in not killing Westlake when he could have. He'd followed Mack's orders, which wasn't always the case.

"I think Larrsen and the police have it under control." He was watching the scene closely, although a big part of him was keeping an eye on Rory's physical condition. Another part was waiting to hear how Rhianna was doing.

"John, throw the gun down. Hands behind your head. You know there isn't any way out of here," Larrsen said patiently. "You know the drill."

"You're not arresting me. I'm a detective. You don't have the authority to arrest me."

"Put the gun down."

Westlake fired at him repeatedly. When his gun was empty, he drew a second one, put his head around the pillar and took careful aim. Several shots were fired at the same time, and his head snapped back, bright red blood blossoming from his temple, the top of his scalp and his eye.

Larrsen sighed and hung his head for a moment, watching the body topple.

Does Rhianna need Paul, Javier? Mack asked.

No. There was relief in Javier's voice. *Rhianna could have taken that bastard if he'd gotten near her. Rory gave her an out, so she took it. It's a flesh wound, nothing serious.*

Thanks, Rory, Rhianna added. *I have to say, that was very cool that he couldn't see me. He looked right at me too. He couldn't see the blood on the ground either.*

Gideon flashed her a small grin. "Red, I can shield myself, but I've never been able to shield my team or any other member of it. And certainly not from a distance. You just did it without even thinking. How can you know how to do that when you don't remember your past?"

To his consternation, her finger pressed hard into the spot above her left temple. This time, Gideon felt the sensation she'd told him about. He had stayed connected to her mind ever since he'd brought her out of the warehouse, unable to make himself completely let go. Paul was correct when he said the sensation had become agonizing. His woman had a very high pain tolerance.

"Don't answer that. Don't even think about it, Rory."

I need to think about it, Gideon. She was back to leaning her head against him. *I went back through the images in your head of what Paul went through to save me. He transfers whatever the injury is to his body in an exchange. That's why it's so dangerous and he's so weak afterward.*

"Yes, that's how it works. He performs surgery using his mind, not physically. In doing so, there's a huge risk to him. There are only a very limited number of people in the world who can do such a thing. We guard them carefully. No one, not even those above us, knows of their skills. It would be too dangerous if word ever got out."

He's talking to me about undoing what Whitney did to my lungs. Or attempting to. He isn't sure what it is yet. But that could be fatal to him. I've lived with my lungs this way for as long as I can remember. In my nightmares, I was the same way, so apparently, Whitney must have planted whatever he did when I was a child. Risking Paul's life seems unnecessary when I've been doing this for so long.

"He's a doctor, Rory," Gideon said as gently as possible.

She was trying to make him understand she really didn't mind. It wasn't about being a martyr. She didn't believe Paul should risk himself.

Put aside the fact that he's needed, Gideon, and just look at what a good person he is. He's kind and considerate. He's a good man. He looks out for everyone. There isn't a good enough reason to risk his life. I'm not in danger.

"That isn't true, Rory. You are. At times, you can barely breathe."

He opened my airways and gave me better medicine.

"Every time I think I couldn't love you more, you say and do things that make me know why I fall harder every moment I'm with you."

Rory glanced up at him from under the long dark reddish lashes with a look that made him feel like her white knight when he was anything but. Still, he'd take it.

"We'll put that aside for now and let Paul talk to you about it."

He sank down on the bench beside her. "Do you want to discuss removing the shield you cloaked yourself with as a child? Paul can help you with that. At the same time he does, the rest of the team can prevent Whitney from finding you in a permanent way. You will remember your past, including the horrors of his experiments. You would have the memories of girls you grew up with. Rose remembers you. She'd like to become reacquainted with you. There isn't any pressure, Red. If you never want to be part of the Ghost-Walker family with me, I'll be fine as long as I have you in my life."

The shield is already coming apart, Gideon. I'm remembering more and more. The nightmares are more persistent. The sensation of my skin peeling away has become worse, and now instead of just this odd crackling and tingling feeling, there's real pain, as if the skin is ripping apart.

"Paul said you put the shield in place so long ago and you were so young that it became part of your physical makeup. That would explain the ripping and tearing sensation you're feeling now. He would clarify it better than me, but it sounds as if the shield is pulling away from your skin."

A visible shudder went through Rory, so Gideon put his arm around her and pulled her beneath his shoulder.

It sounds as if it will be very painful to shed it all the way.

"I'll be with you, Rory."

I'm not sure I want you to be. I don't like you hurt. You do enough for everyone. I told you before, someone needs to look after you, and I want to be that someone.

His heart turned over. She could seriously melt it that easily. She made him feel things he hadn't ever thought possible. He brushed a kiss on top of the thick pile of hair. "I'll be with you regardless. I can't seem to be away from you, Red. In any case, if you think you want to do it, we can ask Paul to talk with us about how best it can happen."

Gideon hesitated. Rory seemed more comfortable with his

teammates. During the time she was in bed recovering, they had done breathing sessions together. She hadn't objected. Rhianna and Ethan had dropped by casually just to see if she needed them to sneak into her apartment building and bring her anything. Javier came every day. She hadn't met all the team members, but she knew all of them had rushed out to look for her.

"How do you feel about the others helping us through Paul removing the shield?" Gideon did his best to sound casual.

I've been giving it a lot of thought. They've really done their best to help me. I thought it would be good to meet them. Maybe a couple at a time to see if I want to run for the next state.

"That's not going to happen, Rory, not without me." Gideon made it a decree.

21

Two days later, Gideon remained quiet while Paul talked to Rory about shedding the shield that had been with her since she'd escaped Whitney. He believed it would be better for her if she allowed the team to surround her. They would help with breathing and lock out any chance that when the shield fell completely, Whitney might get a glimpse she was alive.

There would be pain, and while Gideon would help control it, if there were others there, they could ease the discomfort as well. Rory didn't want anyone else to suffer on her behalf. Gideon had known all along that would be her objection, but he stayed out of the discussion. Paul was patient and very gentle in the way he worded his facts. He didn't come at Rory from the emotional place Gideon would have.

Mack, as team commander, was also present for the discussion. "Rory, we work better as a group. We fit seamlessly together."

"But not me. I'm not part of you."

Gideon nearly blew it by objecting. He just managed to keep his mouth closed.

Mack gave Rory a small smile. "You might have a legitimate argument, honey, if you hadn't cloaked Rhianna so quickly and from a distance. You couldn't see her. You didn't really know her, and yet you took control and *seamlessly* fit with her. If you aren't part of us, how did you manage to do that?"

Rory's long lashes fluttered, and she turned her green gaze a little helplessly to Gideon as if asking him for the answer. He took her hand. "No one is hurrying your decision."

Talk to me, Red. What are you thinking?

I've been giving this a lot of thought since you first brought it up to me. Why would I have such a reaction to meeting your friends when they've been helping me? You know I have nightmares and deliberately made a point of remembering every one of them. In all of them, Whitney berated me and told me I endangered the other girls. That I shouldn't be near them. He said it over and over. Drilled it into me.

Gideon had shared a few of those nightmares with her. He knew Whitney reveled in repeating himself to Rory that she was useless and a danger to the others.

Intellectually, I know Whitney is still influencing me. I still have his voice in my head telling me I'll endanger my fellow GhostWalkers if I'm around them, even if it's subconscious.

Gideon groaned. *Subconscious is worse than having him yelling in your face. And then I made it worse by adding to that worry, playing right into his hands by fearing you were programmed by him to kidnap Sebastian.*

He had. He should have realized all along that he had reinforced Whitney's assessment of Rory's worth. He had made her feel that she would endanger the other GhostWalkers, that she was inferior to them, just as Whitney had.

I'm sorry, Red. I played right into his hands.

No, I did. I'm an adult. I've been stuck in my childhood.

We all carry the scars of our childhoods, thinking we aren't worthy. He still did. He probably always would.

Rory's green eyes moved over his face. *I don't want Whitney to have any influence on me.*

Gideon smiled at her. "Let's get it done, sweetheart."

Rory took a deep breath, turned to Paul, and nodded. She'd already made up her mind to take down the shield. She knew she was going to spend the rest of her life with Gideon. She could barely bring herself to be away from him.

"You said one thing at a time. All right, let's get it done," Rory said.

Paul was an intelligent man, and he didn't give Rory time to get nervous and back out. His palms moved up to the left side of her head, right over the spot where the sensation was always the worst for Rory.

Gideon merged with Rory, staying connected in her mind. He opened a telepathic circle to his teammates so they could join and begin a deep meditative breathing. As Paul carefully began separating the layers of skin, Gideon and the others felt the same sensations with Rory, the sickening horror of her skin cracking and splitting all over her body. The illusion was so real that Gideon twice looked down at his own skin to make certain he wasn't becoming a lizard. That earned him a little giggle from Rory. How she could manage to be amused when it hurt like hell, he didn't know, but he appreciated her sense of humor.

Blood began to trickle down the side of Rory's head. Sweat beaded on Paul's forehead. Gideon's teammates breathed without stopping in that same rhythm. Rory twice began coughing, her lungs spasming. Gideon pressed her palm to his lungs with one hand to lead the way for her while he handed her the inhaler with his other. He'd made certain it was close. He knew pain could bring on breathing problems, and this operation was very painful.

As the skin separated from the shield, images tumbled into her mind. Gideon swept them to the side, keeping her memories away from the others, blocking them for her. Those were private—her past. If she ever wanted to share, that was for her to do. He would protect her until she decided what she wanted to tell others about herself. He'd broken trust with her once; it wouldn't happen again. Rory was vulnerable right now, and while she was, he would guard her, stand in front of her and protect her even from the family he loved.

She used her inhaler, taking in the medicine while the Ghost-Walkers breathed for her. Once the first few thinning layers of skin were peeled away, Gideon could see how embedded the rest of the shield was. In places, it was thicker, stubbornly holding. Paul was patient, gently loosening the skin until he could cut around it as if he held a laser in his hands.

The moment the entire device dropped, the GhostWalkers erected a barrier between Rory and the outside world, jamming the dust chips installed in the tattoo on her ankle. Mack scanned the tattoo, looking through the leaves and berries to find the hidden trackers so they could destroy them. Paul did the same throughout her body, meticulously searching for any other trackers Whitney may have secreted in her that he would have to remove. Once Mack had destroyed the ones woven into the tattoo and Paul declared her free of any internally, Gideon's teammates left the breathing circle one by one.

Mack helped Paul to one of the guest bedrooms, and Marc Lands attended to the bleeding laceration on Rory's head. After he left, Gideon simply lifted her into his arms and put her into their bed. She was so exhausted, she didn't do more than cuddle into him and close her eyes, drifting off immediately.

Rory woke twice, crying, clinging to Gideon as he pulled her over his body, holding her close, his hands framing her face both times.

"I remember him. I remember him."

"Look at me, Red." Gideon waited until her wild gaze settled on his steady, calm one. "I'm right here with you. Whitney can't get to you."

Another sob escaped. "What if he gets to you? What if he takes you away from me?"

"He can't take me away from you."

"He knows people high up in the government, people who will have you go out on missions. They can set you up, Gideon. I know he does that kind of thing when he wants soldiers to disappear."

She had too many memories rushing at her too fast. He wrapped his arms around her and rocked her gently. "Sweetheart, my team sticks together. You know how Javier is with me. Do you honestly think he's going to let anyone hurt me, especially now that I have you?"

Gideon brushed caresses down the side of her head until she fell into a fitful sleep, her body sprawled over his.

The second time she woke, she came awake fighting, trying to roll off the bed, calling for him, her voice strained. Choking. Coughing. In her mind, it was Gideon choking, not Rory, and she couldn't get to him. She tried breathing air into his lungs the way he'd done for her, but he was too far away.

Gideon easily subdued her, holding her to his chest with his arms, wrapping his legs around hers. Pushing his way into her frantic nightmare.

Red, open your eyes. Feel me with you. The real me. You know my voice. You know my touch. Whitney can't separate us. He doesn't have any idea you're alive or that we're together. Even if he did, he knows what I'm like. He thinks he's the smartest man in the room.

Because he does, he also has a very healthy fear of the kind of predators he created.

Rory stopped struggling and lay passively over his body, her heart pounding against his. Very slowly, she lifted her long lashes, as if afraid that when she did, she would see something besides his blue eyes.

"That's right, sweetheart," he coaxed aloud. "Look at me. See me. I think we should have had Paul peel back the shield a little at a time rather than the entire thing at once so you wouldn't get swamped with so many childhood memories."

Her eyes searched his for a long time before she laid her head on his chest again. *It's like reliving my childhood all over again. Whitney is a horrible man. He really hated me. I tried not to think about him or the things he said and did to me before I fell asleep so I wouldn't have dreams, but I couldn't help it.*

"I can make you chocolate, Rory. We can go up to the roof and sit outside. Paul won't be happy, but if it stops your nightmares, I'll risk his wrath."

She pressed a kiss over his heart. *I think it's good to get it over with. I'd rather sift through all the memories with you right here to help me sort through them. You keep me from losing my mind.*

Gideon was grateful she trusted him enough to rely on him. "Go back to sleep, then, sweetheart. Whitney can't get near you here. He can't get to either one of us."

～

Two weeks later, Paul was back sitting on the rooftop with Gideon and Rory. Marc Lands and Javier were with him, and Gideon had a sinking feeling he knew why Paul had come. Gideon had installed a long lounger so he could stretch out with Rory, and they could be comfortable in the evenings. He'd built a cabinet so her nebulizer and several warm blankets could be stored as well.

They had agreed not to entertain friends on the rooftop, but he was renovating one of the floors so that Cindy's boys would have a large area to play in and the women would be comfortable visiting Rory. Ellen liked to be in the same room playing right next to them while they talked.

Rory looked up at Paul with a welcoming smile. She was recovering fast and was able to speak aloud, although Gideon noticed her voice was huskier than before. She spent time playing music and writing songs, but she didn't sing, even though he told her he found the lower register sexy. She just laughed at him.

"How are you feeling, Rory?" Paul greeted.

"Much better. So much so that you could just come in and say hello. How are you feeling?" she countered.

"I'm one hundred percent. I want to examine you again."

Gideon knew Paul wasn't going to leave it alone. Rory didn't look happy. She'd made it clear she wasn't going to risk Paul's life to find out what Whitney had done to her lungs.

"You're obsessed. Seriously, Paul, we talked about this. I thought we agreed we don't need to know what Whitney did. I'm so much better thanks to you." Rory's chin lifted, and she narrowed her eyes, trying to give Paul the stare-down, going for intimidation.

Red, you aren't going to win. I'm on your side, but first, you aren't intimidating. You're cute beyond all get-out, and Paul adores you. So does Javier, and he dislikes nearly everyone. Secondly, Paul may look young and accommodating, but he's the most stubborn man I know. He won't stop until he gets his way.

"I'm a healer. It's a gift and a curse, Rory. I have no choice. I can't sleep or eat. It's all I think about. I need to know what he did to you and whether I can fix it. If I can't"—Paul shrugged—"then I can't. I'll have to accept it. But in the meantime, I won't be able to live with myself unless I know."

Is he making that up to get his way?

370

You can hear truth the same as I can. Gideon tried not to wince as he said it to her. He needed to be able to treat her the way he would any GhostWalker, give her that respect. He'd messed up, but he'd always been giving her truth. He hadn't known the things she told him hadn't been safe with him.

Gideon, that's over. We're done with it. We're not going back and revisiting it over and over. We're moving forward.

She was the one who said to him that once a commitment was made, they couldn't go backward, they couldn't throw mistakes in each other's faces. He had been all for that, but he couldn't help the occasional pang of guilt.

Then you heard he was telling you the truth.

Rory reached for Gideon's hand. She did that often when she found herself facing anything uncomfortable. "What do you want me to do, Paul?"

"Just say yes. Let me do this now."

Rory's long lashes fluttered over and over, and she pressed against Gideon. "I'm sorry, I don't quite understand. You mean let you examine me again? Examine my lungs?"

"I would like you to come downstairs with me now. Marc is here. He can put you under. You're in good enough shape to go under. Javier and Gideon are both here."

Gideon felt her instant rejection of the plan. She even gave a short shake of her head.

"Why would you have to put me out?"

"I can examine you without any fear of compromising your ability to breathe," Paul said. "You won't worry about me, and I won't worry about you. Gideon will look after you, Rory."

"What if Whitney set a trap for a doctor? All of you were worried about that before. You have no idea what's in my lungs, Paul. It could be something he devised to hurt a doctor. He's malicious and vindictive. He wouldn't want anyone helping me."

"I'm not going in blind, honey," Paul said, his tone gentle. "I've had plenty of time to think about this. I'll know what I'm facing before I ever go in to attempt to remove or fix it. If it isn't possible, I wouldn't risk you."

"Or you, Paul," she objected. "You and Gideon have to get it through your thick skulls that neither of you are expendable."

Rory was so distressed that Gideon pulled her into his arms. "I've got too much to live for to think I'm expendable. Paul knows he isn't either. He's careful. I am too. Ultimately, Red, this is your call." He pushed his fingers through the silk of her hair, trying to comfort her.

"I can't eat or sleep, Rory," Paul reiterated.

She gave a groan of despair. "Fine, but if anything happens to you, I'll haunt you, Paul. You think I'm nice, but I'm not. I can be very mean when I need to be."

Gideon hid a smile, knowing that would get him in trouble. "Let's do this, then." He stood up, indicating the trapdoor.

The room was already set up for an operating procedure, and Rory scowled at Paul and Marc, not happy that they were so prepared. She flicked the gown they wanted her to put on with contempt. "Clearly you were certain you could persuade me."

"We hoped," Paul corrected, unfazed by her bad attitude.

Gideon jerked his chin toward the door, and the others went out, leaving him alone with his woman. "Red, you don't have to do this. You can take more time to think about it. I'll tell them they can't railroad you."

She lifted her arms up, and he pulled the mint green blouse over her head. She preferred to wear clingy blouses and swirling skirts to jeans and tees, and Gideon had to admit he was fond of her way of dressing. She always looked classy and feminine to him, although when she did wear jeans and a tee, she managed to look just as elegant.

Her little laugh escaped. "I think you just like the way I look."

He bent his head down to nuzzle the valley between her full breasts. "I know you're right about that. I love the way you look, but I meant what I said, Rory. I want you to allow Paul to look at your lungs because he thinks he can remove the obstruction, but I want you to get to a place of feeling confident in Paul's judgment."

Rory froze, her hands on the zipper of her skirt. "Did I sound like I wasn't confident in him?" She looked and sounded horrified. "I must have hurt his feelings. I don't feel that way at all, Gideon." Tears shimmered in her eyes. "I haven't been around people other than my friends from the apartments for so long, I don't think I know how to act properly. You should have stopped me."

"You didn't do anything wrong, Rory. You expressed your concern for someone you care about. That came through." Gideon unzipped her skirt and helped her step out of it. "I'm sure you made Paul feel good."

"You won't leave the room, will you? If anything goes wrong, if Whitney did set a trap for a doctor, you'll get Paul out." Rory made it a statement, as if she had every confidence in him.

Gideon covered his wince by moving around her to unhook her bra. He would be saving Rory before anyone else. He wasn't making promises unless he knew he could keep them.

"I forgot to tell you, your boss called again," he said, deliberately changing the subject. "Lydia is working full-time and holding her own. He said whenever you're ready to go back, the job's waiting. He loves Lydia and thanks you a thousand times for recommending her. She's a major asset to him."

Rory's eyes lit up. "I'm so glad. They all love the new apartment building. Cindy raves about it. Thank you for giving them such a deal on the rent. I know those apartments can't possibly go for the same we were paying at the other building. They're so much nicer and roomier. The security is better."

"You haven't been there."

"They send me pictures all the time. The fundraisers brought in enough money for new furniture as well for them. And they all had renter's insurance. So when they get a payout on that, they're going to be fine," Rory said. "I know you had a huge hand in that, Gideon."

"The team played a big part, Rory. It wasn't all me."

He helped her into the gown. The moment she had it on, the look of apprehension returned. To distract her, he caught her around the waist and lifted her onto the bed. The moment she was up on the edge of the bed, he gripped the back of her hair in his fist and tipped her head to take her mouth.

Sparks flew. Rockets went off. Not little sparklers. The full-blown sending-rockets-to-the-moon space-age powerful streams of white-hot energy. Lightning streaked through his bloodstream, aiming straight at his groin. Thunder roared, drowning out the sound of his heart pounding in his ears. She took him to another place with just her kisses, setting him on fire.

Abruptly he pulled back, knowing what they were doing was dangerous. He had slept beside her night after night, waiting for her to gain strength. Waiting for her body to heal. It was getting to the point where he could barely stay in control. Now wasn't the time, and tempting fate was pure stupidity.

Her arms remained around his neck, her green eyes moving over his face with that look she reserved for him alone. Her expression got to him every time.

"Thank you for finding me, Gideon. When they kidnapped me, I was afraid Whitney had caught up with me and was trying to hurt you, or he wanted Rose's little boy. I was never going to give you up. I would have died first."

His heart squeezed down hard like a vise in his chest. He'd felt that absolute resolve in her. When Rory made up her mind, she could be like Paul, or like Gideon; she had a will of iron. She wouldn't have given him up. Or Rose's son. That was his woman—soft, compassionate and kind, yet with a core of absolute steel.

"I was never going to give you up, Red," he admitted. "I wanted to be that man, stepping aside for my sins and giving you what you wanted and deserved, but all along, I knew I would follow you to the ends of the earth and try to win you back. The moment I knew you were in trouble, all bets were off."

"I couldn't help but feel bad that Bill Morris committed suicide when they came to arrest him," Rory said. "I know he was as guilty as the others, but he did try to stop Westlake. I knew there was one of them protesting what was going on."

Gideon wished he was as compassionate. He did feel bad for the man's wife. She didn't deserve to face the backlash alone, especially as ill as she was. She wasn't in any way to blame for what her husband had chosen to do. Deana had sent a note to Rory telling her she was sorry for what had happened to her. That had been unexpected and just made the circumstances seem even more tragic to Gideon. Rory had cried for the woman. That made Gideon even less compassionate toward Bill Morris. He hadn't been thinking of his wife when he'd left her alone to face his crimes.

"They have evidence to convict Leo Carver, but do you think they have enough to convict Jerome Michigan?" Rory asked.

Gideon ran his palm down the back of her head over all that thick dark cherry–colored hair he loved so much. She no longer winced when he touched the back of her scalp, where the men had hit her so hard and given her a concussion.

"Red." He kept his voice gentle, his gaze on hers. "You know it isn't going to matter one way or the other. They're never going to go to trial. We can't allow that. Wilson, Larrsen and Abbott deserved to follow through with the arrests, but you're not going to sit on a stand and relive a nightmare. Those men were dead the moment they put their hands on you. You have to know that."

He'd given her that truth and she'd even acknowledged it. At the time, she'd still been mostly swinging in and out of consciousness.

"Gideon, are you positive this is the life you want? Do you ever consider getting out?"

He kept his expression blank, but his gut knotted. He'd promised honesty no matter the cost. He didn't know what she was thinking. She had that faint little frown, her brows slightly drawn together, full lips turned down just enough to be a temptation for him to coax them upward. He always found her frown irresistible.

"Never. Not once," he admitted. "Even before Whitney enhanced me, I had a darkness in me when those around me were threatened. I had already developed several of my psychic talents and continued to strengthen them in order to use them to hunt when I needed to. I have that in me, Rory, and it isn't going to go away. As a GhostWalker, I can use those skills for my country. I can guard my team. If I were a civilian, what would I do? I'm not the kind of man to be idle."

GhostWalkers couldn't just walk away from the service. He would explain that later. For now, it was important to him to understand what she was thinking.

"I just want you to be happy." Her finger traced the line of his jaw, her touch featherlight. "I don't want to sit in a courtroom and face those men or have to think about what they did to me, but I'd rather that than have you do something that would haunt you for the rest of your days. You don't have to look after me, Gideon. Let me be the one person in your life who looks after you."

She might just be capable of ripping out his soul. He brushed his lips over hers, recognizing the emotion he was feeling was tenderness. He hadn't known he was capable. "You're looking after me, Red. Have no worries on that score."

"Call Paul in, Gideon. I'm as ready as I'll ever be."

~

Gideon had to admit he was more nervous than he'd first thought, watching Paul perform an actual exploratory surgery on Rory. Paul had taken his time examining Rory's lungs, looking much like one would do with an X-ray to see what Whitney had done to make it more difficult for her to breathe.

When Paul stepped back, he shook his head, looking puzzled. "The mass, which is in both lungs, appears to be calcification. It has stayed the same size, or seems to have, since she was a child. I can't see signs of growth. I would have to biopsy it to be certain if I was treating this as a regular doctor. What that calcification originated from is anyone's guess."

"Is there a possibility the blockage developed naturally?" Gideon asked.

"In both lungs? I doubt it, but I'll wait to see what exactly it is. If I can clear it, I will."

Paul, as usual, didn't waste time speaking. He lifted his palms and placed them an inch from Rory's left lung, his features serene but still a mask of concentration. Watching Paul work was fascinating. Watching him work on Rory was nerve-wracking.

Gideon fixed his gaze on Rory's face. She looked like an angel to him, with her dusting of golden freckles and the dark cherry–colored hair spread across the pillow. He wrapped his fingers around her much smaller hand and held her palm against his heart. After what seemed liked hours, Paul finally stepped away from the bed and staggered backward until he found the chair behind him.

Marc handed him a bottle of cold water, and Gideon waited, noting Paul struggled to breathe properly. It took a good half hour before Paul could talk to him, and then only in a whisper.

"Whitney introduced a bacterial infection. That created calcified granulomas—several—to block her airway. They aren't cancerous, which is the good news. I was able to remove them. Whitney made it as difficult as possible for Rory to breathe. I'm not certain why, when she was already having trouble with asthma." Paul sounded exhausted.

"I'll help you to bed, Paul," Marc said.

"She's going to need rest, Gideon. This was a surgery. Don't let her run around for a few days. I did my best to promote healing at the surgery sites, but she's going to need care." Paul stood up, swaying a little.

"She'll get it," Gideon assured him. "Thanks, Paul."

Paul lifted a hand but didn't reply as Marc helped him from the room.

THREE WEEKS LATER

Rain fell, the drops hitting the wide bank of windows that ran along one wall of the bedroom. The moan of the wind heralded the storm coming in from the sea. Clouds appeared in various shades of dark purples, deeper blues and blacks, rolling and tumbling low. Lightning forked in the lower edges of the clouds, leaping from one to the next.

Gideon felt the fierceness of the gathering storm in his body, matching the one moving in rapidly from over the sea. Rory lay in his bed beside him, staring up at him with her vivid green eyes filled with so much desire. She didn't try to hide it from him. She never did. She reached up to touch his jaw with the pads of her fingers. He treasured when she stroked those caresses along his stony features, painting his jaw and lips with her love. The way she touched him always felt like a potent mixture of love and sensuality. He found her sexy beyond measure.

He took his time, leaning over her, needing to see her eyes change color, grow even darker with the fusion of love and heated lust right before her dark cherry–colored lashes fluttered and lowered as he took possession of her soft, perfect lips. He loved everything about her mouth. He pulled her into him, holding her closer, kissing her over and over, his heart nearly exploding.

Gideon hadn't known he was capable of feeling this depth of emotion—the overwhelming kind of emotion that meant he knew if he lost Rory, it would utterly destroy him. He certainly hadn't been aware he could feel such a powerful passion for any woman, let alone such intense love.

A ferocious need clawed at his belly and groin, raging to claim her, to make her wholly his. It was a primitive need, and again, one he didn't recognize. Love kept his touch tender as he kissed his way from her lips to her chin, down her throat to her generous breasts. He kissed his way over the sweet curves. Her skin was like satin. Soft and smooth next to the roughness of him.

She gasped when he nuzzled her left nipple, her hips bucking. He pinned her beneath him with his body, fitting his hips into the cradle of hers as he drew the stiff peak into the hot cavern of his mouth. She cried out, her arms cradling his head to her, back arching to offer him better access. He pinched and tugged her right nipple gently. All the while, her body responded, hips jerking and body shivering or shuddering in answer.

He pulled back just enough to ensure desire was still foremost. She wore a dazed expression, her eyes dark with a combination of heat and lust. He ran his hand possessively from her throat to the slick cherry-red curls between her legs. All his. His need was once again taking a brutal grip on him as sparks of electricity crackled between them.

Murmuring reassurances to her, he kissed his way down her body, desperate to taste her. He felt like a man starving. Her scent had been wreaking havoc with him for weeks, threatening to drive him insane. Sometimes he woke at night, certain her taste was in his mouth. He dreamt of her and this moment, with her soft skin and hot body.

Settling his wide shoulders between her thighs, he cupped her bottom with his palms and lifted her to his waiting mouth. He felt as if he'd waited a lifetime for this moment.

Gideon.

She sounded breathless as he breathed warm air into her slick heat. His name. She made his name sound like love, passion, adoration. He ran his tongue up first one thigh and then the other, making himself wait. Making her wait. Very gently, he circled her clit, feeling her nerve endings burst into fiery life, sizzling and sparking. Her body jerked, and she whispered his name again, this time in a plea.

You need to be ready for us, Rory.

He dipped his head and ran his tongue through her slick folds, sending shock waves of white-hot fire through her entire bloodstream. He stayed connected with her to ensure he was giving her pleasure, not realizing until that moment that by sharing with her, it would amplify his passion too. He craved her taste, was completely addicted. Desperate for more. He lapped greedily at her, devouring as much of the liquid spilling from her as he could.

The primitive predator in him fought for control. His mind, her mind, ceased all coherent thought. They both needed, and that need was all-consuming. The fire burned like the storm outside, out of control, flames so hot it threatened to consume them both. His tongue was rough and then gentle, stabbed deep and then lapped at her clit, and circled and flicked. There was no rhythm to catch, only the continuous sensations that took her closer and closer to the edge.

Let go for me, Rory.

He was desperate to have her, his cock nearly bursting. He fit his mouth over her hot little clit and suckled. Instantly, he saw the bright hot flashes behind her eyes, the sparkling colors, and felt the intense sensations pouring through her in waves as she cried out her pleasure.

Gideon didn't wait. He knelt between her spread legs and lodged the thick head of his cock into her scorching entrance. Outside, thunder rolled as lightning cracked across the sky. The roaring in his ears accompanied the hot, bright lightning streaking through his entire body. His heavy cock was thick in his fist, raging with a brutal, merciless demand. He clenched his teeth, fighting for control when her body was scorching hot and doing everything to drag him inside where he belonged.

"Red, you have to let me do this gently," he tried to warn her. She was looking at him with those eyes of hers, desperate for him. Hot for him. Too hot. Red flames seemed to burn in her hair. Over her skin.

He entered her slowly, or tried to. She was a silken sheath of sheer fire, surrounding his cock with a tight fist of scorching muscles.

"More. Hurry. Don't stop." Her nails dug into his forearms.

Gideon took her at her word, surging forward as he needed to do, past her thin barrier, to bury himself deep in her body, connecting them until he was completely surrounded by all that scorching fire. She gasped, her eyes going wide. She nodded at him.

He lost himself in her, dragging his heavy cock deliberately over her most sensitive spot again and again to give her the most pleasure. Her silken muscles stroked and squeezed his shaft like a fist and then would create the sensation of tongues rubbing and lapping at him ruthlessly. She was blazing hot and tight as hell.

Her hips rose to meet his as he shifted positions, angling his body over hers and catching her legs on his forearms for a different access. Her breath caught in her throat. She moaned his name. Gideon kept his mind firmly in hers and refused to let her gaze drop away from his. This was the two of them together. He was claiming her, and he wanted her to know who she was with. He belonged with her. She belonged with him.

He set a faster, harder pace, the friction nearly unbearable, it was so good. At times, he thought he might not survive the pleasure. She was that hot, that tight. He couldn't have stopped if he'd been so inclined. Nothing could have stopped him. The storm outside wasn't nearly as wild or turbulent as the one inside, the one raging between them. It just burned brighter and hotter and more out of control, until he felt that white-hot fist begin to clamp down on his cock like a vise. Power swept through him. Bright. Hot. Coiling deep.

"Let go, Red. Fly with me."

He refused to look away from her. His woman. Meant to be. Always meant to be. Her vivid green gaze clung to his. He could see love there. He knew she could see it there for her in his eyes. Tenderness. A promise.

And then they were soaring together. High. Paradise. In a storm of passion, of love, that Gideon had never thought possible for him. Somehow, he'd been granted that miracle when he wasn't certain he deserved it, but he was taking it and was grateful.